Praise for *Harvesting the Heart*

"In this breathless, startling novel, Jodi Picoult reveals the fragile threads that hold people together, or let them break apart. Her narrative, especially her sense of family, is reminiscent of a young Anne Tyler. Hers is a remarkable new voice, and it tells us a story that goes straight to the heart."
—Mary Morris, author of *A Mother's Love* and *Nothing to Declare*

"Picoult weaves a beautiful tale from threads of sympathetic characters into a pattern told from two points of view, then fringes it with suspense and drama."
—*The Charlotte Observer*

"A brilliant, moving examination of motherhood, brimming with detail and emotion."   —*Richmond Times-Dispatch*

"Picoult's depiction of families and their relationships over time is rich and accurate. . . . *Harvesting the Heart* [is] a moving portrayal of the difficulties of marriage and parenthood."
—*Orlando Sentinel*

"Picoult considers various forces that can unite or fracture families and examines the complexities of the human heart in both literal and figurative ways."
—*Library Journal*

"Picoult brings her considerable talents to this contemporary story of a young woman in search of her identity. . . . Told in flashbacks, this is a realistic story of childhood and adolescence, the demands of motherhood, the hard paths of personal growth and the generosity of spirit required by love. Picoult's imagery is startling and brilliant; her characters move credibly through this affecting drama."
—*Publishers Weekly*

PENGUIN BOOKS

HARVESTING THE HEART

Jodi Picoult grew up in Nesconset, New York. She received
her A.B. in Creative Writing from Princeton University and
her M.Ed. from Harvard University. *Harvesting the Heart*
was her second novel. Her others include *My Sister's Keeper,*
Second Glance, Perfect Match, and *Salem Falls.* She received the
2003 New England Book Award, given by the New England
Booksellers Association, for her body of work. Jodi Picoult
lives in New Hampshire with her husband and three children.
Visit her Web site at www.jodipicoult.com.

Jodi Picoult

Harvesting
the Heart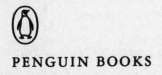

PENGUIN BOOKS

PENGUIN BOOKS

Published by the Penguin Group

Penguin Group (USA) Inc., 375 Hudson Street, New York, New York 10014, U.S.A.

Penguin Group (Canada), 90 Eglinton Avenue East, Suite 700, Toronto, Ontario,
Canada M4P 2Y3 (a division of Pearson Penguin Canada Inc.)

Penguin Books Ltd, 80 Strand, London WC2R 0RL, England

Penguin Ireland, 25 St Stephen's Green, Dublin 2, Ireland
(a division of Penguin Books Ltd)

Penguin Group (Australia), 250 Camberwell Road, Camberwell,
Victoria 3124, Australia (a division of Pearson Australia Group Pty Ltd)

Penguin Books India Pvt Ltd, 11 Community Centre,
Panchsheel Park, New Delhi – 110 017, India

Penguin Group (NZ), cnr Airborne and Rosedale Roads, Albany,
Auckland 1310, New Zealand (a division of Pearson New Zealand Ltd)

Penguin Books (South Africa) (Pty) Ltd, 24 Sturdee Avenue,
Rosebank, Johannesburg 2196, South Africa

Penguin Books Ltd, Registered Offices: 80 Strand, London WC2R 0RL, England

First published in the United States of America by Viking Penguin,
a division of Penguin Books USA Inc., 1993
Published in Penguin Books 1995

38 37

PUBLISHER'S NOTE

This is a work of fiction. Names, characters, places, and incidents either are the product of the
author's imagination or are used fictitiously, and any resemblance to actual persons,
living or dead, events, or locales is entirely coincidental.

THE LIBRARY OF CONGRESS HAS CATALOGUED THE HARDCOVER AS FOLLOWS:
Picoult, Jodi.
Harvesting the heart/Jodi Picoult.
p. cm.
ISBN 978-0-670-85099-0 (hc.)
ISBN 978-0-14-023027-7 (pbk.)
1. Women—United States—Fiction. I. Title.
PS3566.1372H37 1993
813'.54—dc20 93-7190

Printed in the United States of America
Set in Garamond No. 3
Designed by Cheryl L Cipriani

For Kyle Cameron van Leer,
through whose eyes I get a chance to rediscover the world

Acknowledgments

I am grateful to all the professionals who willingly shared their time and their expertise: Dr. James Umlas, Dr. Richard Stone, Andrea Greene, Frank Perla, Eddie LaPlume, Troy Dunn, Jack Gaylord, and Eliza Saunders. For their help with fact checking, baby-sitting, and brainstorming, thanks also to Christopher van Leer, Rebecca Piland, Kathleen Desmond, Jane Picoult, Jonathan Picoult, and Timothy van Leer. Special thanks to Mary Morris and Laura Gross, and a standing ovation to Caroline White—who is as wonderful an editor as she is a friend.

Harvesting
the Heart

prologue

Paige

N icholas won't let me into my own house, but I have been
watching my family from a distance. So even though I've
been camping out on the front lawn, I know exactly when
Nicholas takes Max into the nursery to change his diaper. The light
switches on—it's a little dinosaur lamp that has a shade printed with
prehistoric bones—and I see the silhouette of my husband's hands
stripping away the Pampers.

When I left three months ago, I could have counted on one hand
the number of times Nicholas had changed a diaper. But after all,
what did I expect? He had no choice. Nicholas has always been a
master at emergency situations.

Max is babbling, strings of syllables that run together like bright
beads. Curious, I stand up and climb the low branches of the oak that
stands closest to the house. With a little bit of effort, I can pull myself
up so that my chin is level with the sill of the nursery. I have been

in the dark for so long that when the yellow light of the room washes over me, I keep blinking.

Nicholas is zipping up Max's blanket sleeper. When he leans close, Max reaches up, grabs his tie, and stuffs it in his mouth. It is when Nicholas pulls the tie away from our son that he sees me at the window. He picks up the baby and deliberately turns Max's face away. He strides over to the window, the only one close enough to look into, and stares at me. Nicholas does not smile, he does not speak. Then he pulls the curtains closed, so that all I can see is a line of balloons and ponies and elephants playing trombones—all the smiling images I painted and prayed to when I was pregnant, hoping fairy tales could calm my fears and guarantee my son a happy childhood.

≈≈≈

On this night when the moon is so white and heavy that I cannot sleep without fearing I will be crushed, I remember the dream that led me to my missing mother. Of course I know now that it was not a dream at all, that it was true, for whatever that is worth. It is a memory that started coming after Max was born—the first night after his delivery, then the week we brought him home—sometimes several times a night. More often than not, I would be picturing this memory when Max awakened, demanding to be fed or changed or taken care of, and I am embarrassed to say that for many weeks I did not see the connection.

The watermarks on the ceiling of my mother's kitchen were pale and pink and shaped like purebred horses. *There,* my mother would say, pointing over our heads as she held me on her lap, *can you see the nose? the braided tail?* We called each other's attention to our horses daily. At breakfast, while my mother unloaded the dishwasher, I'd sit on the Formica countertop and pretend the fine china chime of bowl against mug was a series of magical hoofbeats. After dinner, when we sat in the dark, listening to the bump and grind of the laundry in the double-stacked washer and dryer, my mother would kiss the crown of my head and murmur the names of places our horses would take us: Telluride, Scarborough, Jasper. My father, who at that time was an inventor moonlighting as a computer programmer, would come home late and find us asleep, just like that, in my mother's kitchen. I asked him several times to look, but he could never see the horses.

When I told this to my mother, she said that we'd just have to help him. She held me high on her shoulders one day as she balanced on a low stool. She handed me a black marker with the powerful scent of licorice and told me to trace what I saw. Then I colored the horses with the crayons from my Wal-Mart 64-pack—one brown with a white star, one a strawberry roan, two bright orange-dappled Appaloosas. My mother added the muscular forelegs, the strain of the backs, the flying jet manes. Then she pulled the butcher-block table to the center of her kitchen and lifted me onto it. Outside, summer hummed, the way it does in Chicago. My mother and I lay beside each other, my small shoulder pressed to hers, and we stared up at these stallions as they ran across the ceiling. "Oh, Paige"—my mother sighed peacefully—"look at what we've accomplished."

At five, I did not know what "accomplished" meant, nor did I understand why my father was furious and why my mother laughed at him. I just knew that the nights after my mother had left us I would lie on my back on the kitchen table and try to feel her shoulder against mine. I would try to hear the hills and valleys of her voice. And when it had been three full months, my father took whitewash and rolled it across the ceiling, erasing those purebreds inch by lovely inch, until it looked as if the horses, and even my mother, had never been there.

≈≈≈

The light in the bedroom flashes on at 2:30 A.M., and I have a little surge of hope, but it goes off as quickly as it was turned on. Max is quiet, no longer waking three or four times a night. I shimmy out of the sleeping bag and open the trunk of my car, fish through jumper cables and empty diet Coke cans until I find my sketch pad and my conté sticks.

I had to buy these on the road; I couldn't even begin to tell you where in my house I buried the originals when it became clear to me that I could not attend art school and also take care of Max. But I started sketching again when I was running away. I drew stupid things: the Big Mac wrappers from my lunch; a Yield sign; pennies. Then, although I was rusty, I tried people—the checkout girl at the minimart, two kids playing stickball. I drew images of Irish heroes and gods I'd been told of my whole life. And little by little, the second sight I've always had in my fingers began to come back.

I have never been an ordinary artist. For as long as I can remember, I've made sense of things on paper. I like to fill in the spaces and give color to the dark spots. I sketch images that run so close to the edges of the page, they are in danger of falling off. And sometimes things are revealed in my drawings that I do not understand. Occasionally I will finish a portrait and find something I never meant to draw hidden in the hollow of a neck or the dark curve of an ear. I am always surprised when I see the finished products. I have sketched things I should not know, secrets that haven't been revealed, loves that weren't meant to be. When people see my pictures, they seem fascinated. They ask me if I know what these things mean, but I never do. I can draw the image, but people have to face their own demons.

I do not know why I have this gift. It doesn't come with every picture I draw. The first time was in the seventh grade, when I drew a simple Chicago skyline in art class. But I had covered the pale clouds with visions of deep, empty halls and gaping doors. And in the corner, nearly invisible, was a castle and a tower and a woman in the window with her hands pressed to her heart. The sisters, disturbed, called my father, and when he saw the drawing he turned white. "I didn't know," he said, "that you remembered your mother so well."

When I came home and Nicholas would not let me in, I did the next best thing—I surrounded myself with pictures of my husband and my son. I sketched the look on Nicholas's face when he opened the door and saw me; I sketched Max where he sat in Nicholas's arms. I taped these two on the dashboard of my car. They are not technically good, but I have captured the feeling, and that is something.

Today, while I was waiting for Nicholas to come home from the hospital, I drew from memory. I did sketch after sketch, using both sides of the paper. I now have more than sixty pictures of Nicholas and Max.

I am working on a sketch I began earlier this night, and I am so wrapped up in it that I don't see Nicholas until he steps onto the front porch. He is haloed in soft white light. "Paige?" he calls. "Paige?"

I move in front of the porch, to a spot where he can see me. "Oh," Nicholas says. He rubs his temples. "I just wanted to see if you were still here."

"I'm still here," I say. "I'm not going anywhere."

Nicholas crosses his arms. "Well," he says, "it's a little late for that." I think for a moment he is going to storm inside, but he pulls his robe tighter around himself and sits down on the porch step. "What are you doing?" he says, pointing to my sketch pad.

"I've been working on you. And Max," I say. I show him one of the sketches I did earlier.

"That's good," he says. "You always were good at that."

I cannot remember the last time I heard Nicholas giving me credit for something, anything, a job well done. He looks at me for a second, and he almost lets his guard down. His eyes are tired and pale. They are the same color blue as mine.

In just that second, looking at Nicholas, I can see a younger man who dreamed of getting to the top, who used to come home and heal in my arms when one of his patients died. I can see, reflected, the eyes of a girl who used to believe in romance. "I'd like to hold him," I whisper, and at that Nicholas's stare turns dark and shuttered.

"You had your chance," he says. He stands and goes into our house.

By moonlight, I work on my sketch. The whole time, I am wondering whether Nicholas is having trouble sleeping, too, and how angry he'll be tomorrow when he's not one hundred percent. Maybe because my attention is divided, my picture turns out the way it does. It's all wrong. I have captured the likeness of Max—his sticky fists, his spiky velvet hair—but something is completely off. It takes me a few minutes to figure it out. This time, instead of drawing Max with Nicholas, I have drawn him with me. He sits in the curve of my arm, grabbing for my hair. To an outsider, the picture would be fine. But hidden in the purple hollow of Max's outstretched palm is a faint woven circle of leaves and latticework. And in its center I've drawn the image of my running mother, who holds, like an accusation, the child I did not have.

Part I:
Conception

1985–1993

chapter 1
Paige

When I least expected to, I found Mercy. It was a diner on a seedy side street in Cambridge, and its clients were mostly students and professors who wanted to go slumming. I was down to my last twenty. The previous night I had realized that no one in their right mind would hire me as a nanny without references and that I wasn't going to get into art school on a smile and a song and my meager portfolio. So at five-thirty in the morning I squared up my shoulders and walked into Mercy, praying to a God I had wondered about my entire life that indeed this place would be my deliverance.

The diner was deceptively small and smelled of tuna fish and detergent. I moved to the counter and pretended to look at the menu. A large black man came out of the kitchen. "We ain't open," he said, and then he turned and went back inside.

I did not look up from the menu. Cheeseburgers, clam patties,

Greek antipasto. "If you aren't open," I said, "how come you unlocked the door?"

It took several seconds for the man to answer, and when he did, he came right up to the spot where I was sitting and placed one beefy arm on the counter on either side of me. "Shouldn't you be going to school?" he said.

"I'm eighteen." I tipped up my chin the way I had seen Katharine Hepburn do it in old black-and-white movies. "I was wondering if there might be a position available."

"A position," the man said slowly, as if he'd never heard of the word. "Position." His eyes narrowed, and for the first time I noticed a scar that reminded me of barbed wire, all snaked and spiky, which ran along the length of his face and curled into the folds of his neck. "You want a job."

"Well, yes," I said. I could tell from his eyes that he did not need a waitress, much less an inexperienced one. I could tell that at the present time he did not need a hostess or a dishwasher, either.

The man shook his head. "It's too damn early for this." He turned and looked at me, seeing, I knew, how thin I was, how disheveled. "We open at six-thirty," he said.

I could have left then. I could have gone back to the cool T station, the subway where I'd been sleeping these past few nights, listening to the soft violins of street musicians and the crazy screams of the homeless. But instead I took the grease-spattered paper that was clipped to the inside of the menu, listing yesterday's specials. The back was blank. I pulled a black marker from my knapsack and began to do the only thing I knew with confidence I could do well: I drew the man who had just dismissed me. I drew him from observation, peeking into a small pass-through that led to the kitchen. I saw his biceps curl and stretch as he pulled huge jars of mayonnaise and sacks of flour from shelves. I drew the motion, the hurry, and then when I drew his face I sketched it quickly.

I pulled back to see the picture. Spread over the broad forehead of this man I had drawn the outline of a strong old woman, her shoulders stooped from work and from denial. She had skin the shade of bootleg coffee, and crossing her back were the memories of lashed scars, which turned and blended into the distinctive twisted scar of the man's own face. I did not know this woman, and I didn't understand why she had come out on the page. It wasn't my best drawing, I knew that, but it was something to leave behind. I placed the paper on the counter and went just outside the door to wait.

Even before I had the power to sketch people's secrets, I had always believed I could draw well. I knew this the way some kids know they can catch pop flies and others can use felt and glitter to make the most creative covers for book reports. I always used to scribble. My father told me that when I was a toddler, I had taken a red crayon and drawn one continuous line around the walls of the house, at my eye level, skipping over the doorways and the bureaus and the stove. He said I did it just for the hell of it.

When I was five, I found one of those contests in the *TV Guide,* the one where you sketch a cartoon turtle and send it in and they give you a scholarship to art school. I had just been doodling, but my mother saw my picture and said there was no time like the present for securing a college education. She was the one who mailed it in. When the letter came back congratulating me on my talent and offering me enrollment in the National Art School in a place called Vicksburg, my mother swept me off my feet and told me this was our lucky day. She said my talent was hereditary, obviously, and she made a big deal of showing off the letter to my dad at dinner. My father had smiled gently and said they sent a letter like that to anyone who they thought would put up the money for some phony school, and my mother had left the table and locked herself in the bathroom. Still, she hung the letter on the refrigerator, next to my damp finger painting and my noodle-glued collage. The letter disappeared the day she left, and I always wondered if it was something she'd taken because she knew she couldn't take me.

I had been thinking a lot about my mother, much more than I had for several years. Part of it was because of what I had done before I left home; part of it was because I *had* left home. I wondered what my father thought. I wondered if the God he had so much faith in could tell him why the women in his life were always running away.

When, at six-ten, the black man appeared in the doorframe, filling it, really, I knew already what the outcome would be. He stared at me, openmouthed and bothered. He held my portrait in one hand and stretched his other hand out to help me up from the sidewalk. "The breakfast crowd starts coming in twenty minutes," he told me. "And I expect you ain't got no idea about waiting tables."

Lionel—that was the man's name—took me into the kitchen and offered me a stack of French toast while he introduced me to the dishwashing machine, the grill, and his brother Leroy, the head cook. He did not ask me where I was from, and he did not discuss salary, as if we had had a previous arrangement. Out of the blue, he told me that Mercy was the name of his great-grandmother and that she had been a slave in Georgia before the Civil War. She was the woman I'd drawn across his mind. "But you must be a prophet," he said, " 'cause I don't tell people about her." He said that most of those Harvard types thought the diner's name was some kind of philosophical statement, and anyway, that kept them coming in. He wandered off, leaving me to wonder why white people named girl babies things like Hope and Faith and Patience—names they could never live up to— and black mothers called their daughters Mercy, Deliverance, Salvation—crosses they'd always have to bear.

When Lionel came back he handed me a clean, pressed pink uniform. He gave a once-over to my navy sweater, my knee socks, and my pleated skirt—which, after all this time, hadn't lost its industrial-strength folds. "I ain't gonna fight you if you say you're eighteen, but you sure as hell look like some prep-school kid," he said. He turned his back and let me change behind the stainless-steel freezer, and then he showed me how to work the cash register and he let me practice balancing plates up and down my arms. "I don't know why I'm doin' this," he muttered, and then my first customer came in.

When I look back on it, I realize now that of course Nicholas had to have been my first customer. That's the way Fate works. At any rate, he was the first person in the diner that morning, arriving even before the two regular waitresses did. He folded himself—he was that tall—into the booth farthest from the door and opened his

copy of the *Globe.* It made a nice noise, like the rustle of leaves, and
it smelled of fresh ink. He did not speak to me the entire time I was
serving him his complimentary coffee, not even when I splashed some
onto the Filene's ad splayed across page three. When I came for his
order, he said, "Lionel knows." He did not look up at me as he said
this. When I brought his plate, he nodded. When he wanted more
coffee, he just lifted his cup, holding it suspended like a peace offering
until I came over to fill it. He did not turn toward the door when
the sleigh bells on its knob announced the arrival of Marvela and
Doris, the two regular waitresses, or any of the seven people who
came for breakfast while he was there.

When he finished, he lined his fork and his knife neatly across
the edge of the plate, the mark of someone with manners. He folded
his paper and left it in his booth for others to read. It was then that
he looked at me for the first time. He had the palest blue eyes I had
ever seen, and maybe it was only because of the contrast with his
dark hair, but it seemed I was just looking through this man and
seeing, behind him, the sky. "Why, Lionel," he said, "there are laws
that say you shouldn't hire kids until they're out of diapers." He
smiled at me, enough to let me know I shouldn't take it personally,
and then he left.

Maybe it was the strain of my first half hour as a waitress; maybe
it was the lack of sleep. I had no real reason. But I felt tears burning
behind my eyes, and determined not to cry in front of Doris and
Marvela, I went to bus his table. For a tip, he'd left ten cents. Ten
lousy cents. It was not a promising beginning. I sank down onto the
cracked banquette and rubbed my temples. I *would* not, I told myself,
start to cry. And then I looked up and saw that Lionel had taped my
portrait of him over the cash register. I stood, which took all my
strength, and pocketed my tip. I remembered the rolling brogue of
my father's voice telling me over and over again, *Life can turn on a
dime.*

≈≈≈

A week after the worst day of my life, I had left home. I suppose
I had known all along that I was going to leave; I was just waiting

until I finished out the school term. I don't know why I bothered, since I wasn't doing well anyway—I'd been too sick for the past three months to really concentrate, and then all the absences started to affect my grades. I suppose I needed to know that I could graduate if I wanted to. I did just that, even with two D's, in physics and in religion. I stood up with the rest of my class at Pope Pius High School when Father Draher asked us to, I moved my tassel from right to left, I kissed Sister Mary Margareta and Sister Althea and told them that yes, I was planning to attend art school.

I wasn't that far off the mark, since the Rhode Island School of Design had accepted me on my grades as a junior, which of course were recorded before my life had started falling apart. I was certain that my father had already paid part of the tuition for the fall, and even as I was writing him the note that told him I was leaving, I wondered if he'd be able to get it back.

My father is an inventor. He has come up with many things over the years, but it has been his misfortune usually to be a step behind. Like the time when he invented that tie clip with a roll-down plastic screen, to protect the fabric during business lunches. He called it the Tidy-Tie and was sure it would be his key to success, but then he learned that something remarkably similar already had a patent pending. The same things happened with the fogless bathroom mirror, the floating key chain, the pacifier that unscrewed to hold liquid medicine. When I think of my father, I think of Alice, and the White Rabbit, and of always being one step behind.

My father was born in Ireland and spent most of his life trying to escape the stigmas attached. He wasn't embarrassed to be Irish—in fact, it was the crowning glory of his life; he was just embarrassed to be an Irish *immigrant*. When he was eighteen he'd moved from Bridgeport, the Irish section of Chicago, to a small neighborhood off Taylor Street made up mostly of Italians. He never drank. For a time, he tried, unsuccessfully, to cultivate a midwestern twang. But religion for my father was not something you had a choice about. He believed with the zealousness of an evangelist, as if spirituality were something that ran through your veins and not through your mind. I have wondered if, had it not been for my mother, he would have chosen to be a priest.

My father always believed that America was just a temporary stop on his way back to Ireland, although he never let us know how long he planned on staying. His parents had brought him over to Chicago when he was just five, and although he was really city bred, he had never put the farm country of County Donegal out of his mind. I always questioned how much was memory and how much was imagination, but I was swept away anyway by my father's stories. The year my mother left, he taught me how to read, using simple primers based on Irish mythology. While other little kids knew of Bert and Ernie and Dick and Jane, I learned about Cuchulainn, the famous Irish hero, and his adventures. I read about Saint Patrick, who rid the island of snakes; Donn, the God of the Dead, who gave souls their directions to the underworld; the Basilisk, whose stale, killing breath I hid from at night beneath my covers.

My father's favorite story was about Oisin, the son of Finn Mac Cool. He was a legendary warrior and poet who fell in love with Niamh, a daughter of the sea god. They lived happily for several years on a jewel of an ocean island, but Oisin could not get thoughts of his homeland out of his mind. *Ireland,* my father used to say, *keeps runnin' through your blood.* When Oisin told his wife he wanted to return, she loaned him a magic horse, warning him not to dismount because three hundred years had passed. But Oisin fell from the horse and turned into a very old man. And still, Saint Patrick was there to welcome him, just like, my father said, he would one day welcome the three—and then the two—of us.

For the balance of my life after my mother left, my father tried to raise me in the best way he knew. That meant parochial school, and confession every Saturday, and a picture of Jesus on the Cross, which hung over my bed like a talisman. He did not see the contradictions in Catholicism. Father Draher had told us to love thy neighbor but not to trust the Jews. Sister Evangeline preached to us about having impure thoughts, and yet we all knew that she'd been a married man's mistress for fifteen years before entering the convent. And

of course there was confession, which said you could do whatever you
wanted but always come away clean after a few Hail Marys and Our
Fathers. I had believed this for quite some time, but I came to know,
firsthand, that there were certain marks on your soul that no one could
ever erase.

My favorite place in all Chicago was my father's workshop. It was
dusty and smelled of wood shavings and airplane glue, and in it were
treasures like old coffee grinders and rusted hinges and purple Hula
Hoops. In the evenings and on rainy Saturday afternoons, Daddy
would disappear into the basement and work until it was dark. Sometimes I felt as if I were the parent, hauling him upstairs and telling
him he really had to eat something. He would work on his latest
inventions while I sat off to the side on a musty green sofa and did
my homework.

My father turned into a different person in his workshop. He
moved with the grace of a cat; he pulled parts and wheels and cogs
out of the air like a magician, to make gadgets and knickknacks where
minutes before there was nothing. When he spoke of my mother,
which was not often, it was always down in the workshop. Sometimes
I would catch him staring up at the nearest window, a small cracked
rectangle. The light would fall on his face in a way that made him
seem ages older than he was; and I'd have to stop myself and count
the years and wonder how much time really had gone by.

It wasn't as if my father actually ever said to me, *I know what you
did.* He just stopped speaking to me. And it was then that I knew.
He acted anxious and he wanted time to pass quickly so I could leave
for college. I thought about something a girl in my PE class had said
once about having sex: that once you did it, everyone could tell. Was
the same true of abortions? Could my father read it on my face?

I waited one week after the fact, hoping that graduation would
bring about some kind of understanding. But my father suffered
through the ceremony and never even said "Congratulations!" to me.
That day, he moved in and out of the shadows of our house like
someone uncomfortable in his own skin. At eleven o'clock, we
watched the nightly news. The headline story was about a woman

who had bludgeoned her three-month-old infant with a can of salmon. The woman was taken to a psychiatric hospital. Her husband kept telling reporters he should have seen it coming.

When the news was over, my father went to his old cherry desk and took a blue velvet box from the top drawer. I smiled. "I thought you'd forgotten," I said.

He shook his head and watched with guarded eyes as I ran my fingers over the smooth cover, hoping for pearls or emeralds. Inside were rosary beads, beautifully carved out of rosewood. "I thought," he said quietly, "you might be needing these."

I told myself that night as I packed that I was doing this because I loved him and I didn't want him to bear my sins for the rest of his life. I packed only my functional clothes, and I wore my school uniform because I figured it would help me blend in. Technically I was not running away. I was eighteen. I could come and go as I pleased.

I spent my last three hours at home downstairs in my father's workshop, trying out different wordings for the note I would leave behind. I ran my fingers over his newest project. It was a birthday card that sang a little ditty when you opened it and then, when you pressed the corner, automatically inflated itself into a balloon. He said there was really a market for this stuff. My father was having trouble with the music. He didn't know what would happen to the microchip once the thing became a balloon. "Seems to me," he'd said just the day before, "once you've got something, it shouldn't go changing into something else."

In the end, I simply wrote: *I love you. I'm sorry. I'll be fine.* When I looked at it again, I wondered if it made sense. Was I sorry for loving him? Or because I'd be fine? Finally, I threw down the pen. I believed I was being responsible, and I knew that eventually I would tell him where I'd wound up. The next morning I took the rosary beads to a pawnshop in the city. With half my money, I bought a bus ticket that would take me as far away from Chicago as it could. I tried very hard to make myself believe there was nothing for me to hold on to there.

On the bus I made up aliases for myself and told them to anyone who asked. I decided at a rest stop in Ohio that I would get off the bus in Cambridge, Massachusetts. It was close enough to Rhode Island; it sounded more anonymous than Boston; and also, the name just made me *feel* good—it reminded me of dark English sweaters and graduating scholars and other fine things. I would stay there long enough to make money that would pay my way to RISD. Just because Fate had thrown another obstacle in my way didn't mean I had to give up my dreams. I fell asleep and dreamed of the Virgin Mary and wondered how she knew to trust the Holy Spirit when he came to her, and when I woke up I heard a single violin, which seemed to me the voice of an angel.

≈≈≈

I called my father from the underground pay phone in the Brattle Square bus station. I called collect. I watched a bald old woman knitting on a squat bench and a cellist with tinsel braided into her cornrows. I tried to read the sausage-link graffiti on the far wall, and that's when the connection came through. "Listen," I said, before my father had the chance to draw a breath, "I'm never coming home."

I waited for him to fight me on that point, or even to break down and admit he'd been frantically searching the streets of Chicago for two days. But my father only let out a low whistle. "Never say never, lass," he said. "It comes back to haunt you."

I gripped the receiver until my knuckles turned white. My father, the one—the *only*—person in my life who cared what would happen to me, didn't seem very concerned. Sure, I'd disappointed him, but that couldn't erase eighteen years, could it? One of the reasons I'd had the courage to leave was that, deep down, I knew he would always be there waiting; I knew I would not really be alone.

I shivered, wondering how I had misjudged *him* too. I wondered what else there was to say.

"Maybe you could tell me where you've gone off to," my father said calmly. "I know you made it to the bus station, but after that I'm a bit fuzzy on details."

"How did you find that out?" I gasped.

My father laughed, a sound that wrapped all the way around me. His laugh, I think, was my very first memory. "I love you," he said. "What did you expect?"

"I'm in Massachusetts," I told him, feeling better by the minute. "But that's all I'm going to say." The cellist picked up her bow and drew it across her instrument's belly. "I don't know about college," I said.

My father sighed. "That's no reason to up an' leave," he murmured. "You could have come to me. There's always—" At that moment a bus whizzed by, drowning out the rest of his words. I could not hear, and I liked that. It was easier than admitting I did not want to know what my father was saying.

"Paige?" my father asked, a question I had missed.

"Dad," I said, "did you call the police? Does anybody know?"

"I didn't tell a soul," he said. "I thought of it, you know, but I believed you'd come through that door any minute. I *hoped*." His voice fell low, dull. "Truth is, I didn't believe that you'd go."

"This isn't about you," I pleaded. "You've got to know that it isn't about you."

"It is, Paige. Or you wouldn't ever ha' thought to leave."

No, I wanted to tell him, *that can't be true. That can't be true, because all these years you've been saying it wasn't my fault that* she *left. That can't be true, because you are the one thing that I hated leaving behind.* The words lodged in my throat, stuck somewhere behind the tears that started running down my face. I wiped my nose on my sleeve. "Maybe I will come home someday," I said.

My father tapped his finger against the end of the receiver, just as he used to do when I was very little and he went on overnight trips to peddle his inventions. He'd send a soft *whap* through the phone lines. *Did you hear that?* he'd whisper. *That's the sound of a kiss runnin' into your heart.*

A bus from I don't know where was coming through the dark tunnel of the station. "I've been out of my head with worryin'," my father admitted.

I watched the bus's wheels blot the herringbone-brick terminal drive. I thought of my father's Rube Goldberg contraptions, the inventions he'd made just to entertain me: a faucet that sent water down a gully, which released a spinning fan, which in turn blew a paddle that connected a pulley that opened the cereal box and poured out my serving of Cheerios. My father could make the best out of anything he was given. "Don't worry about me," I said confidently. "After all, I'm *your* daughter."

"Aye," my father said, "but it seems you've got a bit of your mother in you too."

≈≈≈

After I'd worked two weeks at Mercy, Lionel trusted me enough to lock up. During the down times, like three in the afternoon, he'd sit me down at the counter and ask me to draw pictures of people. Of course I did the workers on my shift—Marvela and Doris and Leroy—and then I did the President and the mayor and Marilyn Monroe. In some of these portraits were the things I didn't understand. For example, Marvela's eyes showed a man dark with passion, being swallowed by the living sea. In the curl of Doris's neck I'd drawn hundreds of cats, each looking more and more like a human, until the last one had Doris's own face. In the fleshy swell of Marilyn Monroe's peach arm were not the lovers you'd expect but rolling farmland, rippled wheat, and the sad, liquid eyes of a pet beagle. Sometimes people in the diner noticed these things, and sometimes they didn't—the images were always small and subtle. But I kept drawing, and each time I finished, Lionel would tape the portrait over the cash register. It got so that the pictures stretched halfway across the diner, and with each one I felt a little more as though I truly belonged.

I had been sleeping on Doris's couch, because she felt sorry for me. The story I had given was that my stepfather had been making moves on me and so the minute I turned eighteen I had taken my baby-sitting money and left. I liked that story, because it was nearly half true—the eighteen and the leaving part. And I didn't mind a little sympathy; at this point, I was taking whatever I could get.

It was Doris's idea that we do some kind of blue-plate special—tack two bucks onto the price of a turkey club, and you'd get a free portrait with it. "She's good enough," Doris said, watching me sketch the frizzy lines of Barbra Streisand's hair. "These Joe Shmoes would be Celebrity for a Day."

I felt a little weird about the whole thing, kind of like being a circus sideshow, but there was an overwhelming response to the notice we stuck in the menu, and I got bigger tips drawing than I did waiting tables. I drew most of the regulars on the first day, and it was Lionel's idea to make those original sketches free and hang them up with my others for publicity. Truth be told, I could have drawn most of the diner's patrons without their posing for me. I had been watching them carefully anyway, picking up the outlines of their lives, which I would fill in in my spare time with my imagination.

For example, there was Rose, the blond woman who came for lunch on Fridays after having her hair done. She wore expensive linen suits and classic shoes and a diamond wedding band. She carried a Gucci pocketbook and she kept her money in order: ones, fives, tens, twenties. Once, she brought in a balding man, who held her hand tight throughout the meal and spoke in Italian. I pretended this was her lover, because everything else in her life seemed so picture perfect.

Marco was a blind student at the Kennedy School of Government, who wore a long black overcoat even on the hottest days in July. He had shaved his head and wore a bandanna around it, and he'd play games with us. *What color is it?* he'd ask. *Give me a clue.* And I'd say something like "McCarthy," and he'd laugh and say *Red.* He came in late at night and smoked cigarette after cigarette, until a gray cloud hovered at the edge of the ceiling like an artificial sky.

But the one I watched most was Nicholas, whose name I knew only because of Lionel. He was a medical student, which explained, Lionel said, his odd hours and the fog he was always in. I would stare at him point-blank because he never seemed to notice, even when he wasn't reading, and I tried to figure out what was so confusing about him. I had been at Mercy exactly two weeks when I figured it out: he just didn't fit. He seemed to gleam against the cranberry cracked vinyl seats. He held court over all the waitresses, holding up his glass when he wanted a refill, waving the check when he wanted to pay, and yet none of us considered him to be condescending. I studied him with a scientist's fascination, and when I imagined things about him, it was at night on Doris's living room couch. I saw his steady hands, his clear eyes, and I wondered what it was that drew me to him.

I had been in love in Chicago, and I knew the consequences. After all that had happened with Jake, I was not planning to be in love again, maybe not ever. I didn't consider it strange that at eighteen some soft part of me seemed broken for good. Maybe this is why when I watched Nicholas I never thought to draw him. The artist in me did not immediately register the natural lines of him as a man: the symmetry of his square jaw or the sun shifting through his hair, throwing off different and subtler shades of black.

I watched him the night of the first Chicken Doodle Soup Special, as Lionel had insisted on calling it. Doris, who had been working with me since the lunch rush, had left early, so I was by myself, refilling salt shakers, when Nicholas came in. It was 11:00 P.M., just before closing, and he sat at one of my tables. And suddenly I knew what it was about this man. I remembered Sister Agnes at Pope Pius High School, rapping a ruler against a dusty blackboard as she waited for me to think up a sentence for a spelling word I did not know. The word was *grandeur, e* before *u*. I had stood and hopped from foot to foot and listened to the popular girls snicker as I remained silent. I could not come up with the sentence, and Sister accused me of scribbling in the margins of my notebook again, although that was not it at all. But looking at Nicholas, at the way he held his spoon and the tilt of his head, I understood that grandeur was not nobility or dignity, as I'd been taught. It was the ability to be comfortable in the world; to make it look as if it all came so easily. *Grandeur* was what Nicholas had, what I did not have, what I now knew I would never forget.

Inspired, I ran to the counter and began to draw Nicholas. I drew not just the perfect match of his features but also his ease and his flow. Just as Nicholas was digging in his pockets for a tip, I finished and stepped back to view the picture. What I saw was someone beautiful, perhaps someone more beautiful than I had ever seen in my life, someone whom others pointed to and whispered about. Plain as day, in the straight brows, the high forehead, and the strong chin, I could see that this was someone who was meant to lead others.

Lionel and Leroy came into the main area of the diner, carrying leftovers, which they brought home to their kids. "You know what to do," Lionel said to me, waving as he pushed his way out the door. "See you, Nick," he called.

Very quietly, under his breath, he said, "Nicholas."

I stepped up behind him, still holding my portrait. "Did you say something?" I asked.

"Nicholas," he repeated, clearing his throat. "I don't like 'Nick.' "

"Oh," I said. "Did you want anything else?"

Nicholas glanced around him, as if he was just noticing he was the only customer in the diner and that the sun had gone down hours before. "I guess you're trying to close up," he said. He stretched out one leg on the banquette and turned the corners of his mouth up in a smile. "Hey," he said, "how old are you anyway?"

"Old enough," I snapped, and I moved closer to clear his plate. I leaned forward, still clutching the menu with his picture, and that's when he grabbed my wrist.

"That's me," he said, surprised. "Hey, let me see."

I tried to pull away. I didn't really care if he looked at the portrait, but the feeling of his hand against my wrist was paralyzing me. I could feel the pulse of his thumb and the ridges of his fingertips.

I knew by the way he touched me that he had recognized something in what I'd drawn. I peered down at the paper to see what I had done this time. At one edge of the picture I'd sketched centuries of kings, with high jeweled crowns and endless ermine robes. At the other edge I had drawn a gnarled, blossoming tree. In its uppermost branches was a thin boy, and in his hand he held the sun.

"You're good," he said. Nicholas nodded to the seat across from him. "If you aren't keeping your other customers waiting," he said, smiling, "why don't you join me?"

I found out that he was in his third year of medical school and that he was at the top of his class and in the middle of his rotations. He was planning to be a cardiac surgeon. He slept only four hours a night; the rest of the time he was at the hospital or studying. He thought I didn't look a day over fifteen.

In turn, I told him the truth. I said I was from Chicago and that I had gone to parochial school and would have gone to RISD if I hadn't run away from home. That was all I said about that, and he didn't press me. I told him about the nights I had slept in the T station, waking in the mornings to the roar of the subway. I told him I could balance four coffee cups and saucers on one arm and that I could say *I love you* in ten languages. *Mimi notenka kudenko,* I said in Swahili, just to prove it. I told him I did not really know my own mother, something I had never admitted to my closest friends. But I did not tell him about my abortion.

It was well past one in the morning when Nicholas stood up to leave. He took the portrait I'd drawn and tossed it lightly on the Formica counter. "Are you going to hang it up?" he asked, pointing to the others.

"If you'd like," I said. I took my black marker out and looked at his image. For a moment, a thought came to me: *This is what you've been waiting for.* "Nicholas," I said softly, writing his name across the top.

"Nicholas," he echoed, and then he laughed. He put his arm around my shoulders, and we stood like that, touching at the sides, for a moment. Then he stepped away. He was still stroking the side of my neck. "Did you know," he said, pressing a spot with his thumb, "that if you push hard enough here, you can knock someone unconscious?" And then he bent down and touched his lips to where his thumb had been, kissing the spot so lightly I might have imagined it. He walked out the door before I even noticed him moving, but I heard the sleigh bells tap against the steamed window glass. I stood there, swaying, and I wondered how I could be letting this happen again.

chapter 2

Nicholas

Nicholas Prescott was born a miracle. After ten years of trying to conceive a child, his parents were finally given a son. And if his parents were a little older than the parents of most of the boys he went to school with, well, he never noticed. As if to make up for all the other children they'd never had, Robert and Astrid Prescott indulged Nicholas's every whim. After a while he didn't even need to verbalize his wishes; his parents began to guess what it was that a boy of six or twelve or twenty should have, and it was provided. So he had grown up with season tickets to the Celtics, with a purebred chocolate Lab named Scout, with virtually guaranteed admission to Exeter and Harvard. In fact, it wasn't until Nicholas was a freshman at Harvard that he began to notice that the way he had been brought up was not the norm. Another young man might have taken the opportunity then to see the third world, or to volunteer for the Peace Corps, but that wouldn't have been Nicholas. It wasn't that he was disinterested or callous; he was just used to being a certain type of person. Nicholas Prescott had always received the world on a silver platter from his parents, and in return he gave them what was expected: the very model of a son.

Nicholas had been ranked first in his class forever. He had dated a stream of beautiful, blue-blooded Wellesley girls from the time he was sixteen and realized they found him attractive. He knew how to be charming and how to be influential. He had been telling people he was going to be a doctor like his father since he was seven, so medical school was a sort of self-fulfilling prophecy. He graduated from Harvard in 1979 and deferred his admission to the medical school. First he traveled around Europe, enjoying liaisons with light-boned Parisian women who smoked cigarettes laced with mint. Then he returned home and, at the urging of his old college crew coach, trained for the Olympic rowing trials with other hopefuls on Princeton's Lake Carnegie. He rowed seventh seat in the eight-man shell that represented the United States. His parents had a brunch for their friends one Sunday morning, drinking Bloody Marys and watching, on television, their son stroke his way to a silver medal.

It was a combination of things, then, that made Nicholas Prescott, age twenty-eight, wake up repeatedly in the middle of the night, sweating and shaking. He'd disentangle himself from Rachel, his girlfriend—also a medical student and possibly the smartest woman he'd ever known—and walk naked to the window that overlooked a courtyard below his apartment. Glowing in the blue shadow of the full moon, he'd listen to the fading sprint of traffic in Harvard Square and hold his hands suspended in front of him until the trembling stopped. And he knew, even if he didn't care to admit it, what lay behind his nightmares: Nicholas had spent nearly three decades evading failure, and he realized he was living on borrowed time.

Nicholas did not believe in God—he was too much a man of science—but he did think there was someone or something keeping track of his successes, and he knew that good fortune couldn't last forever. He found himself thinking more and more of his freshman roommate in college, a thin boy named Raj, who had got a C+ on a literature paper and jumped from the roof of Widener, breaking his neck. What was it Nicholas's father used to say? *Life turns on a dime.*

Several times a week he drove across the river to Mercy, the diner off JFK Street, because he liked the anonymity. There were always other students there, but they tended to be in less exacting disciplines: philosophy, art history, English. Until tonight, he didn't realize anyone even knew his name. But the black guy, the owner, did, and so did that slip of a waitress who had been stuck in the corner of his mind for the past two weeks.

She thought he hadn't noticed her, but you couldn't survive at Harvard Med for three years without honing your powers of observation. She thought she was being discreet, but Nicholas could feel the heat of her stare at the collar of his shirt; the way she lingered over the water pitcher when she refilled his glass. And he was used to women staring at him, so this should not have rattled him. But this one was just a kid. She'd said eighteen, but he couldn't believe it. Even if she looked young for her age, she couldn't be a day over fifteen.

She wasn't his type. She was small and she had skinny knees and, for God's sake, she had red hair. But she didn't wear makeup, and even without it her eyes were huge and blue. Bedroom eyes, that's what women said about him, and he realized it applied to this waitress too.

Nicholas knew he had a ton of work to do and shouldn't have gone to Mercy tonight, but he'd missed dinner at the hospital and had been thinking of his favorite apple turnover the whole ride back from Boston on the T. He'd also been thinking of the waitress. And he was wondering about Rosita Gonzalez and whether she'd got home all right. He was in Emergency this month, and a little after four o'clock, a Hispanic girl—Rosita—had been brought in, bleeding all over, a miscarriage. When he saw her history he had been shocked: thirteen years old. He had done a D&C and held her hand afterward as long as he could, listening to her murmur, over and over, *Mi hija, mi hija.*

And then this other girl, this waitress, had drawn a picture of him that was absolutely amazing. Anyone would be able to copy his features, but she had got something other than that. His patrician bearing, the tired lines of his mouth. Most important, there, shining back from his own eyes, was the fear. And in the corner, that kid— it had made a chill run down his spine. After all, she had no way of knowing that Nicholas, as a child, would climb the trees in his parents' backyard, hoping to rope in the sun and always believing that it was within his power to do so.

He had stared at the picture and caught the casual way she accepted his compliment, and suddenly he realized that even if he had not been Nicholas Prescott, even if he had worked the swing shift at the doughnut shop or hauled trash for a living, it was quite possible that this girl would still have drawn his portrait and still have known more about him than he cared to admit. It was the first time in his life that Nicholas had met someone who was surprised by what she saw in him; who did not know his reputation; who would have been happy with a dollar bill, or a smile, whatever he was able to spare.

He pictured, for the space of a heartbeat, what his life might have been like if he had been born someone else. His father knew, but it was not something they'd ever discuss, so Nicholas was left to speculate. What if he lived in the Deep South, say, and worked on a factory assembly line and watched the sun set every night over the muck of the bayou from a creaking porch swing? Without intending to be vain, he wondered what it would be like to walk down a street without attracting attention. He would have traded it all—the trust fund and the privilege and the connections—for five minutes out of the spotlight. Not with his parents, not even with Rachel, had he ever been given the luxury of forgetting himself. When he laughed it was never too loud. When he smiled he could measure the effect on the people around him. Even when he relaxed, kicking off his shoes and stretching out on the couch, he was always a little bit guarded, as if he might be required to justify his leisure time. He rationalized that people always wanted what they did not have, but he still would have liked to try it: a row house, a patched armchair, a girl who could hold the world in her eyes and who bought his white shirts at five-and-dimes and who loved him not because he was Nicholas Prescott but because he was himself.

He did not know what made him kiss the waitress before he left. He had breathed in the smell of her neck, still milky and powdered, like a child's. Hours later, when he let himself into his room and saw Rachel wrapped like a mummy in his sheets, he undressed and curled himself around her. As he cupped Rachel's breast and watched her fingers wrap around his wrist, he was still thinking of that other kiss and wondering why he never had asked for her name.

≈≈≈

"Hi," Nicholas said. She swung open the door to Mercy and propped it with a stone. She flipped over the Closed sign with a natural grace.

"You may not want to come in," she said. "The AC's broken." She lifted her hair off the back of her neck, fanning herself, as if to emphasize the point.

"I don't want to come in," Nicholas said. "I've got to get to the hospital. But I didn't know your name." He stood and stepped forward. "I wanted," he said, "to know your name."

"Paige," she said quietly. She twisted her fingers as if she did not know what to make of her hands. "Paige O'Toole."

"Paige," Nicholas repeated. "Well." He smiled and stepped off into the street. He tried to read the *Globe* at the T station but kept losing his place, because, it seemed, the wind in the underground tunnel was singing her name.

≈≈≈

While she was closing up that night, Paige told him about her name. It had originally been her father's idea, a good Irish name from the homeland. Her mother had been dead set against it. A daughter named Paige, she believed, would be cursed by her name, always having to do someone else's bidding. But her husband told her to sleep on it, and when she did she dreamed of the name's homonym. Maybe, after all, naming her daughter Paige would give her a beautiful blank slate: a starting point upon which she could write her own ticket. And so in the end she was christened.

Then Paige told Nicholas that the conversation about the history of her name was one of only seven conversations with her mother that she could remember in their entirety. And Nicholas, without thinking about it, pulled her onto his lap and held her. He listened to her heartbeats, between his own.

Early the year before, Nicholas had made the decision to specialize in cardiac surgery. He had watched a heart transplant from an observation lounge above, like God, as senior surgeons took a thick knotted muscle from a Playmate cooler and set it in the mopped raw cavity of the recipient's ribs. They connected arteries and veins and made tiny sutures, and all the while this heart was already healing itself. When it began to beat, pumping blood and oxygen and second chances into the shadow of a man, Nicholas realized he had tears in his eyes. That might have been enough to move him toward heart surgery, but he had also visited with the patient a week later, when the organ had been labeled a successful match. He had sat on the edge of the bed while Mr. Lomazzi, a sixty-year-old widower who now had the heart of a sixteen-year-old girl, talked baseball and thanked God. Before Nicholas left, Mr. Lomazzi had leaned forward and said, "I'm not the same, you know. I think like her. I look at flowers longer, and I know off the top of my head poems I never read, and sometimes I wonder if I'm ever going to fall in love." He had grasped Nicholas's hand, and Nicholas was shocked by the gentle strength and the warm rush of blood in the fingertips. "I ain't complaining," Lomazzi said. "I just ain't sure who's got control." And Nicholas had murmured a goodbye and decided right then that he'd specialize in cardiac surgery. Perhaps he'd always known that the truth of a person lies in the heart.

Which made him question, as he held Paige, what had prompted him to do so and what part of him, exactly, was in control.

≈≈≈

On his first free day for the month of July, Nicholas asked Paige out on a date. He told himself it wasn't really a date; it was more

like a big brother taking a little sister out to see the town. They had
spent time together the week before, going first to see Hurst pitch a
Red Sox game, then walking through the Common and riding on a
swan boat. It was the first time in the twenty-eight years Nicholas
had lived in Boston that he had been on a swan boat, but he did not
tell that to Paige. He watched the sun flame through her hair and
turn her cheeks pink and laughed when she ate the hot dog without
the roll, and he tried to convince himself that he was not falling in
love.

It didn't surprise Nicholas that Paige wanted to spend time with
him—at the risk of seeming arrogant, Nicholas was used to that kind
of thing; any doctor was a magnet for single women. The surprise
was that he wanted to spend time with *her*. It had come to the point
of obsession for Nicholas. He loved that she walked barefoot through
the streets of Cambridge at dusk, when the pavement cooled. He
loved that she chased ice cream trucks down the block and sang out
loud with their carnival jingles. He loved that she acted so much like
a kid, maybe because he'd forgotten the way it was done.

His day off happened to fall on the Fourth of July, and Nicholas
planned the outing carefully—dinner at a famous steakhouse north
of Boston, followed by fireworks on the banks of the Charles.

They left the restaurant at seven, plenty of time, Nicholas said,
to get to the Esplanade. But a car fire on the highway blocked traffic
for a good hour. He hated when things didn't go according to plan,
especially when they moved beyond the realm of his control. Nicholas
sat back and sighed. He switched on the radio, then he shut it off.
He honked his horn, even though they weren't moving at all. "I can't
believe this," Nicholas said. "We're never going to get there in time."

Paige was sitting cross-legged on the seat. "It doesn't matter,"
she said. "Fireworks are fireworks."

"Not these," Nicholas said. "You've never seen these." He told
her about the barges in the basin of the Charles and the way the
explosions were orchestrated to the "1812 Overture."

"The '1812 Overture'?" Paige said. "What's that?" And Nicholas
had looked at her and honked again at the immobile car ahead
of him.

After they'd played six games of Geography and three rounds of Twenty Questions, the traffic started to move. Nicholas drove like a madman toward Boston but couldn't get any closer to the Esplanade than Buckingham, Browne, and Nichols, a prep school that was miles away. He parked in the faculty lot and told Paige it would be worth the walk.

By the time they got to the Esplanade, it was a sea of people. Over the bobbing heads, in the distance, Nicholas could make out the Hatch Shell and the orchestra beneath it. A woman kicked him in the shin. "Hey, mister," she said, "I been camping out here since five in the morning. You ain't cutting in." Paige wrapped her arms around Nicholas's waist as a man pulled at the back of her shirt and told her to sit down. He felt her whisper against his chest. "Maybe," she said, "we should just go."

They didn't have a choice. They were pushed farther back by the heaving throng of people until they were standing underneath a highway tunnel. It was long and dark, and they could not see a thing. "I can't believe this," Nicholas said, and just as he was wondering how things could possibly get worse, a convoy of helmeted bikers cut him off, one ten-speed running over his left foot.

"Are you okay?" Paige asked, touching his shoulder as he hobbled around and winced at the pain. In the background, Nicholas heard the beginning bursts of fireworks. "Jesus Christ," he said.

Beside him, Paige leaned against the damp concrete wall of the tunnel. She crossed her arms. "Your problem, Nicholas," she said, "is that you always see the glass half empty instead of half full." She turned to stand in front of him, and even in the darkness he could see the bright glow of her eyes. From somewhere came the whistle of a Roman candle. "That's a red one," Paige said, "and it's climbing higher and higher, and now—there—it's shimmering across the sky and falling like a shower of hot sparks from a soldering iron."

"For God's sake," Nicholas muttered. "You can't see a thing. Don't be ridiculous, Paige."

He had snapped at her, but Paige only smiled. "Who's being ridiculous?" she said. She moved in front of him and placed her hands on his shoulders. "And who says I can't see a thing?" she said.

Two loud booms sounded. Paige turned so that her back was pressed against him and they were both staring at the same blank tunnel wall. "Two circles exploding," Paige said, "one inside the other. First blue streaks and then white streaks reaching over them, and now, just as they're fading, little silver spirals are showing up at the edges like dancing fireflies. And here's a fountain of gold spouting like a volcano, and this one is an umbrella, raining tiny blue spots like confetti."

Nicholas felt the silk of Paige's hair beneath his cheek; the tremble of her shoulders when she spoke. He wondered how one person's imagination could possibly hold so much color. "Oh, Nicholas," Paige said, "this is the finale.. Wow! Huge bursts of blue and red and yellow splashing over the sky, and just as they're fading, the biggest one yet is exploding—it covers *everything*—it's a huge silver fan, and its fingers are stretching and stretching, and they hiss and they sizzle and fill the sky with a million new glowing pink stars." Nicholas thought he could listen to Paige's voice forever. He pulled her tightly against him, closed his eyes, and saw her fireworks.

≈≈≈

"I won't embarrass you," Paige said. "I know which one is the salad fork."

Nicholas laughed. They were driving to his parents' home for dinner, and Paige's understanding of table etiquette had been the last thing on his mind. "Do you know," he said, "you are the only person in the world who can make me forget about atrial fibrillation?"

"I'm a girl of many talents," Paige said. She looked at him. "I know the butter knife too."

Nicholas grinned. "And who taught you all these grand things?"

"My dad," Paige said. "He taught me everything."

At a red light, Paige leaned out the open window to catch a better glimpse of herself in the side mirror. She stuck out her tongue. Nicholas looked appreciatively at the white curve of her neck and the tips of her bare feet, curled beneath her. "And what other things did your father teach you?"

Nicholas smiled as Paige's face lit up. She counted off on her fingers. "Never to leave the house without eating breakfast," she said, "to always walk with your back to a storm, to try to steer into a skid." She straightened her legs and slipped her shoes back on. "Oh, and to bring snacks to Mass, but not things that crunch." She began to tell Nicholas about her father's inventions—ones that had succeeded, like the automatic spinning carrot peeler, and ones that hadn't, like the canine toothbrush. In the middle of her reverie she cocked her head and looked at Nicholas. "He would like you," she said. "Yes." She nodded, convincing herself. "He'd like you very much."

"And why's that?"

"Because of what you have in common," Paige said. "Me."

Nicholas ran his hands around the edges of the steering wheel. "And your mother?" he said. "What did you learn from her?"

He remembered after he said it what Paige had told him about her mother at the diner. He remembered when it was too late, when the words, heavy and stupid, were hanging almost palpably in the space between them. For a moment Paige did not answer, did not move. He would have thought she hadn't even heard him, but then she leaned forward and switched on the radio, blasting the music so loudly she could only have been trying to crowd out the question.

Ten minutes later, Nicholas parked in the shade of an oak tree. He got out of the car and walked around to Paige's side to help her, but she was already standing and stretching.

"Which one is yours?" Paige asked, looking across the street at several pretty Victorians with white picket fences. Nicholas turned her by her elbow so that she would notice the house behind her, a tremendous brick colonial with ivy growing on its north side. "You've got to be kidding," she said, shrinking back a little. "Are you a Kennedy?" she murmured.

"Absolutely not," Nicholas said. "They're all Democrats." He walked her up the slate path to the front door, which, he thanked God, was opened not by the maid but by Astrid Prescott herself, wearing a wrinkled safari jacket, three cameras slung around her neck.

"*Nich*-olas," she breathed. She threw her arms around him. "I've

just gotten back. Nepal. *Amazing* culture; can't wait to see what I've
got." She patted her cameras, caressing the one on top as if it were
alive. She pulled Nicholas through the doorway with the force of a
hurricane, and then she took Paige's small, cold hands in her own.
"And you must be Paige." She pulled Paige into a breathtaking
mahogany-paneled hallway with a marble floor that reminded her of
the Newport mansions she had seen when visiting RISD as a junior.
"I've been back less than an hour, and all Robert's told me about is
this mysterious, magical Paige."

Paige took a step back. Robert Prescott was a well-known doctor,
but Astrid Prescott was a legend. Nicholas didn't like to tell acquain-
tances he was related to "*the* Astrid Prescott," which people said with
the same reverent tone they'd used a hundred years before to murmur
"*the* Mrs. Astor." Everyone knew her story: the rich society girl had
impetuously given up balls and garden parties to toy with photography, only to become one of the best in the field. And everyone knew
Astrid Prescott's photography, especially her graphic black-and-white
portraits of endangered species, which—Paige noticed—were placed
haphazardly throughout the hall. They were haunting photos, shadows and light, of giant sea turtles, bird-wing butterflies, mountain
gorillas. In flight, a spotted owl; the split of a blue whale's tail. Paige
remembered a *Newsweek* article she'd read some years ago on Astrid
Prescott, who was quoted as saying that she wished she'd been around
when the dinosaurs died, because that would have been quite a scoop.

Paige looked from one photograph to another. Everyone had an
Astrid Prescott calendar, or a small Astrid Prescott day diary, because
her pictures were remarkable. She caught the terror and the pride.
Next to this mythic woman, dwarfed by the monstrous house, Paige
felt herself slipping away.

But Nicholas was more affected by his father. When Robert Prescott entered the room, the atmosphere changed, as if the air had
become ionized. Nicholas stood straighter, put on his most winning
smile, and watched Paige from the corner of his eye, wondering for
the first time ever why he had to put on an act in front of his own
parents. He and his father never touched, unless you counted shaking

hands. It had something to do with showing affection, a forbidden thing among Prescotts, which left family members wondering at funerals why there were so many things that hadn't been said to the deceased but that should have been.

Over cold fruit soup and pheasant with new potatoes, Nicholas told his parents about his rotations, especially the emergency ward, downplaying the horrors for the dinner table. His mother kept bringing the conversation back to her trip. "Everest," she said. "You can't even take it with a wide-angle." She had removed her jacket for the dinner, revealing an old tank top and baggy khaki pants. "But damn if those Sherpas don't know the mountain like the back of their hand."

"Mother," Nicholas said, "not everyone is interested in Nepal."

"Well, not everyone is interested in orthopedic surgery, either, darling, but we all listened very politely." Astrid turned toward Paige, who was staring at the head of a tremendous buck poised above the door leading into the kitchen. "It's awful, isn't it?"

Paige swallowed. "It's just that I can't see you—"

"It's Dad's," Nicholas interrupted, winking at her. "Dad's a hunter. Don't get them started," he warned. "They don't always see eye to eye."

Astrid blew a kiss to the opposite end of the table, where Robert Prescott sat. "That awful thing got me my own darkroom in the house," she said.

"Fair trade," Robert called, saluting his wife with a fork-speared potato.

Paige turned her head from Nicholas's mother to Nicholas's father and then back again. She felt lost in the easy volley between them. She wondered how Nicholas had ever managed to get noticed while growing up. "Paige, dear," Astrid said, "where did you meet Nicholas?"

Paige toyed with her silverware, seizing her salad fork; something only Nicholas noticed. "We met at work," Paige said.

"So you're a . . ." Astrid left the sentence hanging, waiting for Paige to fill in *medical student,* or *registered nurse,* or even *lab technician.*

"Waitress," Paige said flatly.

"I see," said Robert.

Paige watched Astrid Prescott's warmth curl in around her, retreating like tentacles; she saw the hooded look Astrid passed to her husband: *She's not what we expected.* "Actually," Paige said, "I doubt you do."

Nicholas, whose stomach had been in knots since they sat down to dinner, did something else forbidden to Prescotts: he laughed out loud. His mother and father looked at him, but he only turned to Paige and gave her a smile. "Paige is a fabulous artist," he said.

"Oh?" Astrid said, leaning forward to offer Paige a second chance. "What an admirable hobby for a young lady. You know, that's how it all began for me." She snapped her fingers, and a maid appeared, whisking away her empty plate. Astrid leaned forward, placing her tanned elbows on the fine linen cloth. She smiled smoothly, but the light did not quite reach her eyes. "Where did you go to college, dear?"

"I didn't," Paige said evenly. "I was going to go to RISD, but something came up." She pronounced the name of the school as an acronym, as it was known.

"Riz-dee," Robert repeated coolly, staring at his wife. "Haven't heard much about that one."

"Nicholas," Astrid said sharply, "how is Rachel?"

Nicholas saw Paige's face fall at the mention of another woman, one whose name she'd never heard before. He crumpled his napkin into a ball and stood up. "Why do you care, Mother?" he said. "You never have before." He moved to Paige's chair and pulled it out, lifting her by her shoulders until she was standing. "I'm sorry," Nicholas said, "but I'm afraid we have to go."

In the car, they drove in circles. "What the hell was that all about?" Paige demanded when he'd finally reached a major highway. "Am I some kind of pawn or something?"

Nicholas did not answer her. She stared at him for a few minutes with her arms crossed, but finally sank back against the seat.

As soon as Nicholas reached the outskirts of Cambridge, she opened the door of the car. He came to a sudden stop. "What are you doing?" he asked, incredulous.

"I'm getting out. I can walk the rest of the way." She stood up, the moon looming behind her, soaking into the edge of the Charles River like a bloodstain. "You know, Nicholas," Paige said, "you sure aren't what I thought you were."

And as she walked away, a muscle throbbed along the edge of Nicholas's jaw. *She's just like the rest of them,* he thought, and just to prove her wrong, he sped past her on Route 2, screaming like a madman, shrieking until he thought his lungs would burst.

≈≈≈

The next day Nicholas was still seething. He met Rachel after her anatomy class and suggested they go for coffee. He knew a place, he said, where they do portraits of you while you eat. It was a bit of a hike, all the way across the river, but it was relatively close to his apartment, for afterward. And then he walked beside her to the car, counting the stares of other men as they took notice of Rachel's honey hair, her soft curves. At the door of the diner, he pulled her into his arms and kissed her hard.

"Well," Rachel said, smiling. "Welcome back."

He led her to the booth he always took, and she almost immediately disappeared to the bathroom. He couldn't see Paige, which made him angry. After all, why else had he come? He was still questioning himself when she came up behind him. She was as quiet as a breeze, and he would not have sensed her if not for the clean scent of pears and willows he had come to know her by. When she stood in front of him, her eyes were wide and tired. "I'm sorry," she said. "I didn't mean to piss you off."

"Who's pissed?" Nicholas said, grinning, but he distinctly felt the pinching of his heart, and he began to wonder if this was what cardiac patients always tried to describe.

At that point Rachel came out and slid into the booth across from Nicholas. "I'm sorry," Paige said, "but this booth is taken."

"Yes, I know," Rachel said coolly. She looked at Nicholas and then glared at Paige. She reached across the table and took Nicholas's hand, weaving her fingers through his with the quiet power of possession.

Nicholas couldn't have planned it better, but he didn't expect it to hurt quite so much. It wasn't that Paige stood rooted before him, her lips parted, as if she hadn't heard correctly. It was that when she turned, Nicholas did not see disappointment or betrayal. Instead, he realized she was looking at him, still, as if he were mythic. "What did you come here for?" she asked.

Nicholas cleared his throat, and Rachel kicked him under the table. "Rachel heard about the pictures and would like to have one done."

Paige nodded and left to get a pad. She sat at the front of the booth on a little stool, holding the pad tilted up the way she always did so the picture would be a surprise when she was finished. She drew clean, quick strokes and blended with her thumb, and as she drew, other diners peeked over her shoulder and laughed and whispered. When she finished, she threw the pad in front of Nicholas and walked into the kitchen. Rachel turned it over. There was her hair, her glittering eyes, and even the gist of her lovely features, but quite clearly the picture was that of a lizard.

≈≈≈

Although he was scheduled to be on call that night at the hospital, Nicholas did something he had never done before: he phoned in sick. Then he grabbed a bite at McDonald's and walked through Harvard Square after the sun went down. He sat on a brick wall on the corner of Brattle and watched a juggler with flaming torches, wondering if the guy worried about what might happen. Nicholas put a faded dollar bill in the case of a jazz guitarist, and he stood at the window of a toy store, where stuffed alligators wearing rain slickers tumbled in tinfoil puddles. When it was five to eleven, he walked to Mercy, wondering what he would do if Doris or Marvela or anyone other than Paige was locking up that night. He realized that he would just keep walking, then, until he found her.

Paige was emptying the ketchup bottles when he came in. Over her head, taped to the wall, was the picture of Rachel as a lizard. "I like it," he said, making her jump.

In spite of herself, Paige smiled a little. "I'm sure I've lost us one customer," she said.

"So what," Nicholas said. "You made *me* come back."

"And just what do I get?" Paige said.

Nicholas smiled. "Whatever you want."

Many years later, when Nicholas thought of that exchange, he realized he shouldn't have made promises he couldn't have kept. But he did believe that no matter what Paige wanted, he could be it. He had a feeling about this, a feeling that all Paige really needed was him, not his trappings and not his success, and that was so new to Nicholas that he felt as if the weight of the world had been lifted from his shoulders. He pulled Paige closer and saw her stiffen and then relax. He kissed her ear, her temple, the corner of her mouth. In her hair he smelled bacon and waffles, but also sunshine and September, and he wondered how he could be thinking the things he was.

When she put her arms around him, as if she was testing the water, he put his hands on her waist and felt the hint of her hips below. "Is Lionel still here?" he whispered, and when she shook her head he took the keys from her pocket and locked the front door, turned off the light. He sat on one of the counter stools and pulled Paige to stand between his legs, and he kissed her, letting his hands run from her neck to her breasts to her belly. Softly he kissed her, this child-woman, and when he stroked her thighs and she tensed, he had to smile. *She must be a virgin,* he realized, and he was overwhelmed by a sudden thought: *I want to be her first. I want to be the only one.* "Marry me," he said, as surprised as she was by the words. He wondered if this was the way his luck would run out; if his career would start its disintegration, if this would be the first downslide to the avalanche. But he held Paige and decided that the hollow in his heart was just the fanning of love. Nicholas marveled at the luck of finding someone who so needed his security, never considering that although the dangers could be different, maybe he needed to be protected too.

chapter 3
Nicholas

When Nicholas was four years old, his mother taught him about trusting strangers. She sat him down and told him twenty times in a row not to speak to someone on the street unless it was a friend of the family; not to take the hand of just anyone to cross the street; never, under any circumstances, to get into someone's car. Nicholas remembered fidgeting on the chair and wishing he could be outside; he'd wanted to check the tin of beer he'd left overnight on the porch to catch slugs. But his mother would not let him leave, would not let him even take a break for the bathroom—not until Nicholas could repeat, verbatim, her lesson. And by that time, Nicholas had conjured images of dark, stinking phantoms wearing ratty black capes, hiding in cars and in the creases of the sidewalk and in the alleys between stores, waiting to pounce on him. When his mother finally told him he could go outside to play, he'd chosen to remain indoors. For weeks after that, when the postman rang the doorbell, he had hidden beneath the couch.

Although he had got over his fear of strangers, he had never forgotten the consequences, which made Nicholas the one person in a group to stand off to the side. He could be charming if the situation called for it, but he was more likely to feign interest in a frieze on the ceiling than to be drawn into a conversation with people he didn't know. In some individuals this was passed off as shyness; but in someone of Nicholas's background and stature and classic features, it seemed more like aloof conceit. Nicholas found he didn't mind the label. It gave him time to size up a situation and to respond more intelligently than those who spoke too quickly.

None of which explained why he impulsively asked Paige O'Toole to marry him, or why he gave her the spare key to his apartment even before hearing her answer.

They walked from Mercy to his apartment in total silence, and Nicholas was starting to hate himself. Paige wasn't acting like Paige. He'd ruined it, whatever it was that he had liked about her. Nicholas was so nervous he couldn't fit the key into the door, and he didn't know what he was nervous about. When she stepped into the apartment he held his breath until he heard her say quietly, "My room was never this neat." And then he relaxed and leaned against the wall. He answered, "I could learn to live messy."

Conversations like that in the first hours after he proposed to Paige made Nicholas realize that there was a great deal he still did not know about her. He knew the big things, the sort of things that make up the talk at dinner parties: the name of her high school; how she became interested in drawing; the street she had lived on in Chicago. But he did not know the little details, the things only a lover would know—What had she named the mutt her father made her give back to the animal shelter? Who taught her to throw a sliding curve ball? Which constellations could she pick out in the night sky? Nicholas wanted to know it all. He was filled with a greed that made him wish he could erase the past, oh, six years of his life and relive them with Paige, so he wouldn't feel he was starting in the middle.

"This is all I've got," Nicholas said to Paige, holding out a box of stale graham crackers. He had sat her down on the black leather

couch and turned on the halogen lights. She had not said whether or
not she would marry him, a detail that Nicholas had not overlooked.
To all intents and purposes, he should have wanted her to pass off
his proposal as a joke, since he still wasn't sure what had prompted
him to make such a rash statement. But he knew Paige hadn't taken
it lightly, and to tell the truth, he wanted to know her answer. God,
he was all knotted up inside over the prospect of her laughing in his
face, which told him more than he cared to admit.

Suddenly he wanted to get her talking. He figured if she would
just stop looking at him as though she'd never seen him before in
her life, if she would start telling him about Chicago or quote one of
Lionel's little epigrams or introduce any other favorite subject of conversation, then she might happen to mention that, yes, she wouldn't
mind being his wife.

"I'm not really hungry," Paige said. Her eyes roamed the walls
of the apartment, the dark shadows of the hallway, and Nicholas
began berating himself for scaring the hell out of her. She was only
eighteen. No wonder she was shying away. Sure, he wanted to be
near her; maybe he could even admit that he was falling for her; but
bringing up marriage? He didn't know *where* that idea had come from.
Christ, that was like using a sledgehammer to kill a fly.

But he still didn't want to take back the offer.

Paige was looking down at her shoes. "This is weird," she said.
"This just feels so weird." She twisted her hands in her lap. "I mean,
I didn't have to worry about this before. This feeling. I hadn't planned
this. You know, when I was just sort of hanging around with you, it
wasn't—it wasn't—" She looked up, groping for the right words.

"So momentous?" Nicholas filled in.

"Yes." Paige's face broke into a smile, and she exhaled in one
long breath. "You always know what to say," she said shyly. "That's
one of the reasons I like you."

Nicholas sat beside her on the couch. He stretched his arm around
her. "You like me," he said. "That's a start."

Paige looked up at him as if she was going to say something,
then shook her head.

"Hey," Nicholas said, tipping up her chin. "Nothing's different. Forget I said anything. I'm still the same guy you told off in the middle of Route 2 a day ago. I'm still the one you can beat the pants off when you play poker."

"You just happened to mention getting married."

Nicholas grinned at her. "I did, didn't I?" He tried to sound flip, unconcerned. "That's the way I end a third date."

Paige leaned her head against his arm. "We haven't even *had* three real dates," she said. "I can't stop thinking about you—"

"I know."

"—but I don't even know your middle name."

"Jamison." Nicholas laughed. "My mother's maiden name. Now, what else is standing in your way?"

Paige turned up her head to look at him. "And what's my middle name?" she challenged, trying to make her point.

"Marie." Nicholas took a stab in the dark, trying to buy time to figure out his next counterargument. Then he realized he'd got it right.

Paige was staring at him, her mouth dropped open. "My father used to tell me I'd know when someone was the perfect match for me," she murmured. "He said God worked it so that you'd always be in the right place at the right time." Nicholas waited for her to elaborate, but she wrinkled her forehead and stared at the carpet. Then she turned to him. "Why did you ask me?" she said.

There were a million questions wrapped into that one, and Nicholas didn't know how to answer them all. He was still reeling from the fact that, unbidden, her middle name had just materialized in his thoughts. So he said the one thing that popped into his mind. "Because you didn't ask *me*," he said.

Paige looked up at him. "I really *do* like you," she said.

He leaned his head back against the couch, determined to have an ordinary conversation, the kind people who've been together forever have all the time. He brought up the weather, and the local sports teams, and then Paige began to gossip about the waitresses at Mercy. Nicholas was soothed by the sound of her voice. He kept asking her questions just to keep her talking. She told him in detail about the angles of her father's face; she told him that she'd once tried to read the dictionary from cover to cover because a classmate told her it would make her smarter, but she'd only got to N. She described wading into Lake Michigan at the end of May, so vividly that Nicholas actually shivered and got goose bumps up his arms.

They were lying side by side on the narrow couch when Nicholas asked Paige about her mother. She'd mentioned her at the diner, and from what Nicholas could tell, the elusive Mrs. O'Toole drifted across Paige's consciousness like a shadow from time to time but Paige wasn't willing to share the details. He knew that the woman had left; he knew that Paige had been five; he knew that Paige didn't remember her very well. But she had to have feelings about it. At the very least, she had to have an impression.

"What was your mother like?" Nicholas asked gently, so close his lips were brushing Paige's cheek.

He felt her tense almost instantly. "Supposedly she was like me," Paige said. "My father said she looked like me."

"You mean you look like *her*," Nicholas said, correcting.

"No." Paige turned and sat up on the end of the couch. "I mean she looked like *me*. I'm the one that's still around, right? So I'm the one that you should be comparing her to."

Nicholas didn't argue with that logic, but he sat up and leaned against the opposite end of the couch. He ran his fingers over the smooth black leather. "Did your father ever tell you why she left?"

Nicholas watched the color drain from Paige's face. And almost as quickly, a flush of red worked its way up her neck and into her cheeks. Paige stood. "Do you want to marry me or my family?" she said. She stared at Nicholas, who was speechless, for several seconds, and then she smiled so openly that her dimples showed and the honesty of it reached all the way into her eyes. "I'm just tired," she said. "I didn't mean to yell at you. But I really have to go home."

Nicholas helped her into her coat and drove her to Doris's apartment. He parked at the curb and clenched his hands on the steering wheel while Paige fished in her bag for the key. He was so intent on silently reviewing Paige's comments about her mother that he almost did not hear her speaking. He had frightened her away by asking her to marry him, and then just when she was warming up to him again, he'd blown it by asking about her mother. She had been so flustered by that one stupid question. Was there something she wasn't telling him? A Lizzie Borden kind of story? Was her mother crazy, and was she unwilling to mention that just in case Nicholas thought it might be hereditary? Or was Nicholas crazy himself, for trying to convince his conscience that this gaping hole in Paige's past couldn't really matter in the long run?

"Well," Paige said, facing him. "It's been some night, hasn't it?" When Nicholas didn't look at her, she turned her gaze to her lap. "I won't hold you to it," she said softly. "I know you didn't mean it."

At that, Nicholas turned and pressed his own spare key into Paige's palm. "I want you to hold me to it," he said.

He pulled Paige into his arms. "When will you be home tomorrow?" she whispered against his neck. He could feel her trust opening like a flower and passing through her fingertips to the places where she touched him. She tilted her head up, expecting his kiss, but he only pressed his lips gently to her forehead.

Surprised, Paige drew back and looked at Nicholas as if she were studying him for a portrait. Then she smiled. "I'll think about your question," she said.

≈≈≈

Paige was waiting for him the next day when he got home from the hospital, and things between them were back to normal. He knew it before he even opened the door, because the smell of butter cookies was seeping over the threshold, into the hall. He also knew that when he'd left that morning, his refrigerator had held little more than a moldy banana loaf and a half jar of relish. Paige had obviously walked all the way here with groceries, and he was shocked at how his whole center seemed to soften at the thought.

She was sitting on the floor, with her hands spread over the pages of *Gray's Anatomy* as if she were modestly trying to cover the naked musculoskeletal image of a man. At first she did not see him. "Phalanges," she murmured, reading. She pronounced the clinical names for fingers and toes all wrong, as if it rhymed with *fangs,* and Nicholas smiled. Then, hearing his footsteps, she jumped to her feet, as though she'd been caught doing something she shouldn't have been doing. "I'm sorry," she blurted out.

Paige's cheeks were flushed; her shoulders were shaking. "What are you sorry for?" Nicholas said, tossing his bag onto the couch.

Paige looked around, and following her glance, Nicholas began to see that she'd been doing more than baking cookies. She had cleaned the entire apartment, even scrubbed the hardwood floors, from the looks of things. She had taken the extra quilt out of the linen closet and draped it over the couch, so bright colors like lime and violet and magenta washed over the Spartan room. She had moved the copies of *Smithsonian* and the *New England Journal of Medicine* off the coffee table to make room for a *Mademoiselle* magazine open to a feature on shaping your buttocks. On the kitchen counter was a spray of black-eyed Susans, arranged neatly in a clean-washed peanut butter jar.

These subtle changes took the focus away from the antiques and the sharp edges that had made the place look so formal. In one afternoon, Paige had made his apartment resemble any other lived-in apartment.

"When you took me here last night, I kept thinking that there was something missing. It—I don't know—it just looked sort of stiff, like you lived in the pages of an *Architectural Digest* article. I picked the flowers on the edge of the highway," Paige said nervously, "and since I couldn't find a vase, I sort of finished the peanut butter."

Nicholas nodded. "I didn't even know I had peanut butter," he said, still gazing around the room. In the entire course of his life, he'd never seen a copy of *Mademoiselle* in his home. His mother would have died rather than see highway wildflowers on a table instead of her hothouse tea roses. He'd been brought up to believe that quilts were acceptable for hunting lodges but not formal sitting rooms.

When he started medical school, Nicholas had left the decoration of the apartment in his mother's hands because he hadn't the time or the inclination, and to no one's surprise it came out looking very

much like the house he'd grown up in. Astrid had bequeathed him
an ormolu clock and an ancient cherry dining room table. She'd commissioned her usual decorator to take care of the drapes and the upholstery, specifying the rich hunter-green and navy and crimson
fabrics that she felt suited Nicholas. He hadn't wanted a formal sitting
room, but he had never mentioned that to his mother. After the fact,
he didn't know how to go about changing one into a simple living
room. Or maybe he didn't know how to go about living.

"What do you think?" Paige whispered, so quietly that Nicholas
thought he had imagined her voice.

Nicholas walked toward her, wrapped his arms around her. "I
think we're going to have to buy a vase," he said.

He could feel Paige's shoulders relax beneath his hands. Suddenly
she started talking, the words tumbling out of her mouth. "I didn't
know what to do," she said, "but I knew it needed *something*. And
then I figured—I'm baking cookies, did you know that?—well, I
didn't know if what *I* liked would be what *you* liked, and I started
to think about how *I'd* act if I came home and someone I barely even
knew had rearranged my whole house. We don't really know each
other, Nicholas, and I've been thinking about that all night too: just
when I've convinced myself that this is the most right thing in the
world, my common sense comes tramping in. What's your favorite
—butter or chocolate chip?"

"I don't know," Nicholas said. He was smiling. He liked trying
to follow her conversation. It reminded him of a pet rabbit he'd had
once that he tried to take for a walk on a leash.

"Don't tease me," Paige said, pulling away. She walked into the
kitchen and pulled a tray out of the oven. "You've never used these
cookie sheets," she said. "The stickers were still on them."

Nicholas picked up a spatula and lifted a cookie off the sheet,
then bounced it from palm to palm as it cooled. "I didn't know I
had them," he said. "I don't cook much."

Paige watched him taste the cookie. "Neither do I. I guess you
should know that, shouldn't you? We'll probably starve within a
month."

Nicholas looked up. "But we'll die happy," he said. He took a second bite. "These are good, Paige. You're underestimating yourself."

Paige shook her head. "I once set the oven on fire cooking a TV dinner. I didn't take it out of the box. Cookies are my whole repertoire. But I can do *those* from scratch. You seemed like a butter cookie kind of guy. I tried to remember if you ever ordered chocolate at the diner, and you didn't, I don't think, so you have to be a vanilla person." When Nicholas stared at her, Paige grinned at him. "The world is divided into chocolate people and vanilla people. Don't you know that, Nicholas?"

"It's that simple?"

Paige nodded. "Think about it. No one ever likes the two halves of a Dixie ice cream cup equally. You either save the chocolate because you like it best, or you save the vanilla. If you're really lucky, you can swap with someone so you get a whole cup of the flavor you like best. My dad used to do that for me."

Nicholas thought about the kind of day he had just come from. He was still on rotation in Emergency. This morning there had been a six-car pileup on Route 93, and the wounded were brought to Mass General. One had died, one had been in neurosurgery for eight hours, one had gone into cardiac arrest. During lunch a six-year-old girl was brought in, shot through the stomach in a playground when she was caught in the crossfire of two youth gangs. And then, in his apartment, there was Paige. To come home to Paige every day would be a relief. To come home to her would be a blessing.

"I take it you're a chocolate person," Nicholas said.

"Of course."

Nicholas stepped forward and put his arms on either side of her, bracing her against the sink. "You can have my half of a Dixie cup anytime," he said. "You can have anything you want."

≈≈≈

Nicholas had read once of a five-foot-three-inch woman who had lifted an overturned school bus off her seven-year-old daughter. He had watched a *60 Minutes* segment about an unmarried soldier who threw himself on top of a grenade to protect the life of a fellow soldier who had a family waiting back home. Medically, Nicholas could credit this to the sudden adrenaline rush caused by crisis situations. Practically, he knew that some measure of emotional commitment was involved. And he realized, to his surprise, that he would have done such things for Paige. He would swim a channel, take a bullet, trade his life. The idea shook Nicholas, chilled his blood. Maybe it was only fierce protectiveness, but he was beginning to believe it was love.

In spite of himself, in spite of his hasty proposal, Nicholas did not believe in romantic love. He did not believe in being swept off your feet, or in love at first sight—either of which would have accounted for his near-immediate obsession with Paige. When he had lain awake in bed last night, he wondered if the attraction could be based on pity—the boy who had grown up with everything thinking he could light up the life of the girl who had not—but Nicholas had met women of less pedigreed backgrounds before, and none of them had ever affected him so strongly he forgot how to use his voice, how to breathe involuntarily. Those women, the ones Nicholas could win over with a bottle of house Chianti and a disarming smile, usually graced his bed for a week before he felt like moving on. He *could* have done that with Paige; he knew he could have if he'd wanted to. But whenever he looked at her, he wanted to stand beside her, to shield her from the world with the simple, strong heat of his body. She was so much more fragile than she let on.

Paige was sprawled in what was now his *living* room, thanks to her, reading *Gray's Anatomy* as if it were a murder mystery. "I don't know how you memorize all this stuff, Nicholas," she said. "I couldn't even do the bones." She looked up at him. "I tried, you know. I thought if I remembered them all without peeking, I'd impress you."

"You already impress me," he said. "I don't care about the bones."

Paige shrugged. "I'm not impressive," she said.

Nicholas, lying on the couch, rolled onto his side to look at her.

"Are you kidding?" he said. "You left home and got yourself a job and survived in a city you knew nothing about. Christ, I couldn't have done that at eighteen." He paused. "I don't know if I could do that now."

"You've never had to," Paige said quietly.

Nicholas opened his mouth to speak but didn't say anything. He never had to. But he had *wanted* to.

Both of Nicholas's parents had, in some way, changed their circumstances. Astrid, who could trace her lineage to Plymouth Rock, had tried to downplay her Boston Brahmin ties. "I don't see all the fuss about the *Mayflower*," she had said. "For God's sake, the Puritans were *outcasts* before they got here." She grew up surrounded by wealth that was so old it had always just been there. Her objections were not to a life of privilege, really, only to the restrictions that came with it. She had no intention of becoming the kind of wife who blended into the walls of a house that defined her, and so, on the day she graduated from Vassar, she flew to Rome without telling a soul. She got drunk and danced at midnight in Trevi fountain, and she slept with as many different dark-haired men as she could until her Visa ran out. Months later, when she was introduced to Robert Prescott at a tailgate party, she almost dismissed him as one of those rich, have-it-all boys with whom her parents were forever throwing her together. But when their eyes met over a cup of spiked cider, she realized that Robert wasn't what he appeared to be. He seethed below the surface with that hell-or-high-water pledge to escape that Astrid recognized running through her own blood. Here was her mirror image—someone trying to get *in* as badly as she was trying to get *out.*

Robert Prescott had been born without a dime and, apparently, without a father. He had sold magazines door to door to pay his way through Harvard. Now, thirty years later, he had honed his image to a point where he had such financial holdings no one dared remember if it was old money or new. He loved his acquired status; he liked the combination of his own glossy, crystalline tastes butted up against Astrid's cluttered seventh-generation antiques. Robert understood the part well—acting stuffy and bored at dinner parties, cultivating a taste for port, obliterating the facts of his life that could incriminate. Nicholas knew that even if his father couldn't convince himself he'd been to the manner born, he believed he rightfully belonged there, and that was just as good.

There had been a bitter argument once, when his father insisted Nicholas do something he had no inclination to do—the actual circumstances now forgotten: probably escorting someone's sister to a debutante ball or giving up a Saturday game of neighborhood baseball for formal dancing lessons. Nicholas had stood his ground, certain his father would strike him, but in the end Robert had sunk into a wing chair, defeated, pinching the bridge of his nose. "You would play the game, Nicholas," he had said, sighing, "if you knew there was something to lose."

Now that he was older, Nicholas understood. Truth be told, as much as he fantasized about living the simple life of a lobster fisherman in Maine, he enjoyed the perks of his station too much to turn his back and walk away. He liked being on a first-name basis with the governor, having debutantes leave their lace bras on the back seat of his car, getting admitted to college and medical school without even a half second of self-doubt or worry about his chances. Paige might not have grown up the same way, but still, she'd left *something* behind. She was a study in contrasts: as fragile as she seemed on the outside, she still had the kind of confidence it took to make a clean break. Nicholas realized that he had less courage in his whole body than Paige had in her little finger.

Paige looked up from the anatomy book. "If I quizzed you, would you know every little thing?"

Nicholas laughed. "No. Yes. Well, it depends on what you ask me." He leaned forward. "But don't tell anyone, or I'll never get my degree."

Paige sat up, cross-legged. "Take my medical history," she said. "Isn't that good practice? Wouldn't that help you?"

Nicholas groaned. "I do it about a hundred times a day," he said. "I could do it in my sleep." He rolled onto his back. "Name? Age?

Date of birth? Place of birth? Do you smoke? Exercise? Do you or does anyone in your family have a history of heart disease . . . diabetes . . . breast cancer. Do you or does anyone in your family . . ." He let his words trail off, and then he slid off the couch to sit next to Paige. She was looking into her lap. "I'd have a little problem with a medical history, I guess," she said. "If it's *my* medical history, why do you focus on everyone else in my family?"

Nicholas reached for her hand. "Tell me about your mother," he said.

Paige jumped to her feet and picked up her purse. "I've got to go," she said, but Nicholas grabbed her wrist before she could move away.

"How come every time I mention your mother you run away?"

"How come every time I'm with you you bring it up?" Paige stared down at him and then tugged her wrist free. Her fingers slipped over Nicholas's until their hands rested tip to tip. "It's no big mystery, Nicholas," she said. "Did it ever occur to you that I have nothing to tell?"

The dim light of Nicholas's green-shaded banker's lamp cast shadows of him and of Paige on the opposite wall, images that were nothing more than black and white and were magnified, ten feet tall. In the shadow, where you couldn't see the faces, it almost looked as if Paige had reached out her hand to help Nicholas up. It almost looked as if she were the one supporting him.

He pulled her down to sit next to him, and she didn't really resist. Then he cupped his hands together and fashioned a shadow alligator, which began to eat its way across the wall. "Nicholas!" Paige whispered, a smile running across her face. "Show me how you do it!" Nicholas folded his hands over hers, twisting her fingers gently and cupping her palms just so until a rabbit was silhouetted across the room. "I've seen it done before," she said, "but no one ever showed me how."

Nicholas made a serpent, a dove, an Indian, a Labrador. With each new image, Paige clapped, begged to be shown the position of the hands. Nicholas couldn't remember the last time someone had got so excited about shadow animals. He couldn't remember the last time he'd made them.

She couldn't get the beak right on the bald eagle. She had the head down pat, and the little open knot for the eye, but Nicholas couldn't mold her fingers just so for the hook in the beak. "I think your hands are too small," he said.

Paige turned his hands over, tracing the life lines of his palms. "I think yours are just right," she said.

Nicholas bent his head to her hands and kissed them, and Paige watched their silhouette, mesmerized by the movement of his head and the sleek outline of his nape and the spot where his shadow melted into hers. Nicholas looked up at her, his eyes dark. "We never finished your medical history," he said, and he slid his palms up her rib cage.

Paige leaned her head into his shoulder and closed her eyes. "That's because I don't have a history," she said.

"We'll skip that part," Nicholas murmured. He pressed his lips against her throat. "Have you ever been hospitalized for major surgery?" he said. "Say, a tonsillectomy?" He kissed her neck, her shoulders, her abdomen. "An appendectomy?"

"No," Paige breathed. "Nothing." She lifted her head as Nicholas grazed her breasts with his knuckles.

Nicholas swallowed, feeling as though he were seventeen all over again. He wasn't going to do something he'd regret. After all, it wasn't as if she'd done this before. "Intact," he whispered. "Perfect." He lowered his hands, still shaking, to Paige's hips and pushed her back several inches. He brushed her hair away from her eyes.

Paige made a sound that started low in her throat. "No," she said, "you don't understand."

Nicholas sat on the couch, curling Paige close beside him. "Yes I do," he said. He stretched out lengthwise, pulling Paige down so that their bodies were pressed together from shoulder to ankle. He could feel her breath, a warm circle on the front of his shirt.

Paige stared over Nicholas's shoulder to the blank wall, haloed in pale light, empty of shadows. She tried to picture their hands, knotted

together, fingers indistinguishable in the far reflection. Nothing she
could conjure in her mind was quite right; she knew she'd miscal-
culated the length of the fingers, the curve of the wrist. She wanted
to get that eagle right. She wanted to try it again, and again, and
again, until she could commit it, faultless, to memory. "Nicholas,"
she said. "Yes. I'll marry you."

chapter 4
Paige

I should have known better than to begin my marriage with a
lie. But it seemed so easy at the time. That someone like Nicholas could want me was still overwhelming. He held me the
way a child holds a snowflake, lightly, as if he knew in the back of
his mind I might disappear in the blink of an eye. He wore his self-
assurance like a soft overcoat. I was not just in love with him; I
worshiped him. I had never met anyone like him, and, amazed that
it was *me* he had chosen, I made up my mind: I would be whatever
he wanted; I would follow him to the ends of the earth.

He thought I was a virgin, that I'd been saving myself for someone like him. In a way he was right—in eighteen years I'd never met
anyone like Nicholas. But what I *hadn't* told him grated against me
every day leading up to our wedding. It was a nagging noise inside
my head, and outside too, in the hot hum of traffic. I kept remembering Father Draher speaking of lies of omission. So each morning

I woke up resolving that this would be the day I told Nicholas the truth, but in the end there was one thing more terrifying than telling him I was a liar, and that was facing the chance I'd lose him.

≈≈≈

Nicholas came out of the bathroom in the little apartment, a towel wrapped around his waist. The towel was blue and had pictures of primary-colored hot-air balloons. He walked to the window, shameless, and pulled down the shades. "Let's pretend," he said, "that it isn't the middle of the day."

He sat on the edge of the mattress. I was tucked under the covers. Although it was over ninety degrees outside, I had been shivering the whole day. I also wished it were nighttime, but not out of modesty. This had been such a tense, awful day that I wanted it to be tomorrow already. I wanted to wake up and find Nicholas and get on with the rest of my life. Our life.

Nicholas leaned over me, bringing the familiar scent of soap and baby shampoo and fresh-cut grass. I loved the way he smelled, because it wasn't what I had expected. He kissed my forehead, the way you would a sick child. "Are you scared?" he asked.

I wanted to tell him, No; in fact, you'd be surprised to know that when it comes to sex I can hold my own. *Instead I felt myself nodding, my chin bobbing up and down. I waited for him to reassure me, to tell me he wasn't going to hurt me, at least not any more than he needed to this first time. But Nicholas stretched out beside me, linked his hands behind his head, and admitted, "So am I."*

≈≈≈

I didn't tell Nicholas right away that I would marry him. I gave him time to back out. He asked that night in the diner after he'd brought his witch of a girlfriend in for coffee. I was terrified at first, because I thought I'd have to face all the secrets I had been running from. For a day or so, I even fought against the idea, but how could I stand in the way of something that was meant to be?

I knew all along he was the one. I could fall into step walking beside him, even though his legs were much longer. I could sense when he came into the diner by the way the sleigh bells on the door rang. I could think of him and smile in just a heartbeat. Although I would have loved Nicholas if he never had proposed, I surprised myself by thinking of tree-lined residential streets and soccer car pools and *Good Housekeeping* recipes curled into handmade sanded boxes. I envisioned a normal life, the kind I'd never had, and even if I would be living it as a wife now, I figured it was better late than never.

The dean of students at Harvard gave Nicholas a one-week hiatus from classes and hospital rotations, during which we would move into married student housing and set a date with a justice of the peace. There would be no honeymoon, because there wasn't any money anymore.

≈≈≈

Nicholas pulled the sheet away from me. "Where did you get that?" he asked, running his hands over the white satin. He slipped his fingers beneath the thin straps. His breath brushed the hollow of my neck, and I could feel us touching at so many points—our shoulders, our stomachs, our thighs. He moved his head lower and circled my nipple with his tongue. I ran my hands through his hair, watching a shaft of sun bring out the blue base under thick black.

≈≈≈

Marvela and Doris, the only two friends I had in Cambridge, took me shopping at a small discount-clothing store in Brighton called The Price of Dreams. They seemed to carry everything there for a woman's wardrobe: underwear, accessories, suits, pants, blouses, sweats. I had one hundred dollars. Twenty-five came from Lionel, a wedding bonus, and the rest was from Nicholas himself. We had moved into married student housing the day before, and when Nicholas realized that I had more art supplies in my knapsack than clothes, and that I had only four pairs of underpants, which I kept washing out, he said I needed to get myself some things. Although we couldn't afford it, he gave me money. "You can't get married in a pink uniform from Mercy," he had said, and I had laughed and answered, "Just watch me."

Doris and Marvela flew around the store like seasoned shoppers. "Girl," Marvela called to me, "you lookin' for something formal like, or you gonna go with funky?"

Doris pulled several pairs of panty hose off a rack. "Whaddya mean, funky," she muttered. "You don't do funky at weddings."

Neither Doris nor Marvela was married. Marvela had been, but her husband was killed in a meat-packing incident that she did not like to talk about. Doris, who was somewhere between forty and sixty and guarded her age as if it were the crown of Windsor, said she didn't like men, but I wondered if it was just that men didn't like her.

They made me try on leather-trimmed day dresses and two-piece outfits with polka-dotted lapels and even one slinky sequined cat suit that made me look like a banana. In the end, I got a simple white satin nightgown for the wedding night and a pale-pink cotton suit for the wedding. It had a straight skirt and a peplum on the jacket and, truly, it seemed to have been made for me. When I tried it on, Doris gasped. Marvela said, shaking her head, "And they say redheads ain't supposed to wear pink." I stood in front of the three-way mirror, holding my hands in front of me as if I were carrying a spilling bouquet. I wondered what it might have been like to have a heavy beaded dress hanging from my shoulders, to feel a train tug behind me down a cathedral aisle, to know the shiver of my breath beneath the veil when I heard the march from *Lohengrin*. But it wasn't going to happen, and anyway it didn't matter. Who cared about the trappings of one stupid day when you had the rest of your life to make perfect? And just in case I needed reassurance, when I turned again to look at my friends, I could see my future shining in their eyes.

≈≈≈

Nicholas's mouth traced its way down my body, leaving behind a hot line that made me think of Lionel's scar. I moved beneath him. He had never touched me like this. In fact, once the decision was made to be married, Nicholas had done little more than kiss me and caress my breasts. I tried to concentrate on what Nicholas must be thinking: if it stuck in his mind that my body—which had a will of its own—was not behaving in the shy, frightened manner of a virgin. But Nicholas said nothing, and maybe he was used to this kind of response.

He had been touching me for so long and so well that when he stopped, it took me a moment to notice, and then it was because of the terrifying rush of cold air that came instead in his absence. I pulled him closer, a hot human blanket. I was willing to do anything to keep myself from shaking all over again. I clung to him as if I were drowning, which I suppose I was.

When his hands skittered over my thighs, I stiffened. I didn't mean for it to happen, and of course Nicholas read it the wrong way, but the last time I'd been touched there, there had been a doctor, and a clinic, and a terrible tightening in my chest that I know now was emptiness. Nicholas murmured something that I did not hear but that I felt against my legs, and then he began to kiss the spaces in between his fingers, and finally his mouth came over me like a whisper.

≈≈≈

"They said congratulations," Nicholas told me when he'd hung up the phone after telling his parents about us. "They want us to come out tomorrow night."

It was clear to me after our first visit that Astrid Prescott liked me about as much as she'd like a Hessian army overrunning her darkroom. "They did not say that," I answered. "Tell me the truth."

"That *is* the truth," Nicholas admitted, "and that's what bothers me."

We drove to Brookline in near silence, and when we rang the doorbell Astrid and Robert Prescott answered together. They were dressed fashionably in shades of gray, and they had dimmed the lights in the house. If I had not known better, I would have assumed I'd arrived at a wake.

During dinner, I kept waiting for something to happen. When Nicholas dropped his fork, I jumped out of my seat. But there was no screaming, no earth-shattering announcement. A maid served roast duck and fiddleheads; Nicholas and his father talked about bluefishing off the Cape. Astrid toasted our future, and we all lifted our glasses so that the sun, still coming through the windows, splintered through

the twisted stems and littered the walls with rainbows. I spent the
main course being choked by the fear of the unknown, which lurked
in the corners of the dining room with the stale breath and slitted
eyes of a wolf. I spent dessert staring at the massive crystal chandelier
balanced above the lily centerpiece. It was suspended by a thin gold
chain, light as the hair of a fairy-tale princess, and I wondered just
what it could take before it broke.

Robert led us into the parlor for coffee and brandy. Astrid made
sure we all had a glass. Nicholas sat beside me on a love seat and put
his arm over my shoulders. He leaned over and whispered to me that
dinner had gone so well he wouldn't be surprised if his parents now
offered us a huge, extravagant wedding. I knotted my hands in my
lap, noticing the small framed photos tucked in every spare inch of
space in the parlor—in the bookshelves, on the piano, even beneath
the chairs. All were photos of Nicholas, at different ages: Nicholas on
a tricycle, Nicholas's face turned up to the sky, Nicholas sitting on
the front steps with a ratty black puppy. I was trying so hard to see
these pieces of his life, the things I had missed, that I almost did not
hear Robert Prescott's question. "Just how old," he said, "are you
really."

I was caught off guard. I had been examining the ice-blue satin
paper on the walls, the overstuffed white wing chairs, and the Queen
Anne side tables, tastefully highlighted with antique vases and
painted copper boxes. Nicholas had told me that the portrait over the
fireplace, a Sargent which had held my interest, was not anyone he
knew. It wasn't the subject that had led his father to purchase it, he
said; it was the investment. I wondered how Astrid Prescott had found
the time to create a name for herself and a house that could put a
museum to shame. I wondered how a boy could possibly grow up in
a home where sliding down the banister or walking the dog on a yo-
yo could unintentionally destroy hundreds of years of history.

"I'm eighteen," I said evenly, thinking that in my house—*our*
house—furniture would be soft, with curved edges, colored bright to
remind you you were alive, and everything, *everything,* would be
replaceable.

"You know, Paige," Astrid said, "eighteen is *such* an age. Why, I didn't know what I really wanted to do with my life until I was at least thirty-two."

Robert stood and paced in front of the fireplace. He stopped directly in the middle, blocking the face of the Sargent so that from where I sat it seemed he was the painting's center, hideously larger than life. "What my wife is trying to say is that of course you two have the right to decide what you'd like—"

"We already have," Nicholas pointed out.

"If you please," Robert said, "just hear me out. You certainly have the right to decide what you'd like out of life. But I wonder if perhaps your thoughts have been clouded by faulty judgment. Now, Paige, you've barely even lived. And Nicholas, you're still in school. You can't support yourself yet, much less a family, and that's to say nothing of the hours you'll spend doing your residency." He came to stand in front of me and placed his hand, cold, on my shoulder. "Surely Paige would prefer more than the shadow of a husband."

"Paige needs time to discover herself," Astrid said, as if I were not in the room. "I know, believe me, that it's virtually impossible to sustain a marriage when—"

"Mother," Nicholas interrupted. His lips were pressed together in a thin white gash. "Cut to the chase," he said.

"Your mother and I think you ought to wait," Robert Prescott said. "If you still feel the same way in a few years, well, of course you'll have our blessing."

Nicholas stood up. He was two inches taller than his father, and when I saw him like that my breath caught in my throat. "We're getting married now," he said.

Astrid cleared her throat and hit her diamond wedding band against the rim of her glass. "This is so difficult to bring up," she said. She looked away from us, this woman who had journeyed into the Australian bush, who, armed only with a camera, had faced Bengal tigers, who had slept in the desert beneath saguaros, searching out the perfect sunrise. She looked away, and all of a sudden she changed from the mythic photographer to the shadow of an aging debutante.

She looked away, and that was when I knew what she was going to say.

Nicholas stared past his mother. "Paige is not pregnant," he said, and when Astrid sighed and sank back in the chair, Nicholas flinched as if he had fielded a blow.

Robert turned his back on his son and put his brandy snifter on the mantel of the fireplace. "If you marry Paige," he said quietly, "I will withdraw financial support for your education."

Nicholas took a step backward, and I did the only thing I could: I stood up beside him and gave him my weight to lean on. Across the room, Astrid was looking blindly out the window into the night, as though she would do anything in her power to avoid watching this scene. Robert Prescott turned around. His eyes were tired, and in the corners were the beginnings of tears. "I'm trying to keep you from ruining your life," he said.

"Don't do me any favors," Nicholas said, and he pulled me across the room. He led me out of the house, leaving the door wide open behind us.

When we were outside, Nicholas started to run. He ran around the side of the house into the backyard, past the white marble birdbath, past the trellised grape arbor, deep into the cool woods that edged his parents' property. I found him sitting on a bed of dying pine needles. His knees were drawn up, and his head was bent, as if the air around him was too heavy to keep it upright. "Listen," I said. "Maybe you need to think this through."

It killed me to say those words, to think that Nicholas Prescott might disappear into his parents' million-dollar house and wave goodbye and leave my life what it used to be. I had come to the point where I truly did not think I could exist without Nicholas. When he was not around, I spent my time imagining him with me. I depended on him to tell me the dates of upcoming holidays, to make sure I got home from work safely, to fill my free time till I felt I would burst. It seemed so easy to blend into his life that at times I wondered if I had been anyone at all before I met him.

"I don't need to think this through," Nicholas said. "We're getting married."

"And I suppose Harvard is going to keep you on because you're God's gift to medicine?"

I realized after I said it that it was not phrased the way it should have been. Nicholas looked up as if I had slapped him. "I could drop out," he said, turning the words over like he was speaking a foreign language.

But I would not spend the rest of my life married to a man who, at least a little, hated me because he never got to be what he had wanted. I didn't love Nicholas because he was going to be a doctor, but I did love him because he was, unquestionably, the best. And Nicholas wouldn't have been Nicholas if he had to compromise. "Maybe there's a dean you can talk to," I said softly. "Not everyone at Harvard is made of money. They've got to have scholarships and student aid. And next year, between your salary as a resident and mine at Mercy, we could make ends meet. I could get a second job. We could take out a loan based on your future income."

Nicholas pulled me down beside him on the pine needles and held me. In the distance I heard a blue jay trill. Nicholas had taught me, a city girl, these things: the differences between the songs of blue jays and starlings, the way to start a fire with birch bark, the humming sound of a faraway flock of geese. I felt Nicholas's chest shake with every breath. I made a mental list of the people we would have to contact tomorrow to figure out our finances, but I felt confident. I could put off my own future for a while; after all, art school would always be there, and you could very well be an artist without ever having attended one. Besides, some part of me believed that I was getting something just as good. Nicholas loved me; Nicholas had chosen to stay with me. "I will work for you," I whispered to him, and even as I said it I had the dark thought of the Old Testament, of Jacob, who labored seven years for Rachel and still did not get what he wanted.

≈≈≈

I was going to lose control. Nicholas's hands and heat and voice were everywhere. My fingers traveled up his arms, across his back, willing him to

come to me. He moved my legs apart and set himself in the middle of them,
and I remembered how I was supposed to act. Nicholas kissed me, and then
he was moving inside me, and my eyes flew open. He was all that I could
see, Nicholas spread across this space and filling, completely, my sky.

≈≈≈

"I'd like to make a collect call," I told the operator. I was whispering although Nicholas was nowhere nearby. We were supposed to
meet at the office of the justice of the peace in twenty minutes, but
I told him I had to run an errand for Lionel. I was trying not to
touch the grimy glass of the booth with my good pink suit. I tapped
the edge of the pay phone with my finger. "Say it's Paige."

It took ten rings, and the operator was just suggesting I try again
later, when my father picked up. "Hello," he said, and his voice
reminded me of his cigarettes, True, and their cool gray package.

"Collect call from Paige. Do you accept?"

"Yes," my father said. "Oh, sure, yes." He waited a second, I
suppose to be certain the operator got off the line, and then he called
my name.

"Dad," I told him, "I'm still in Massachusetts."

"I knew you'd be callin' me, lass," my father said. "I've been
thinkin' about you today."

My hope jumped at that. If I didn't listen too closely, I could
almost ignore the thickness wrapped around his words. Maybe Nicholas and I would visit him. Maybe one day he would visit me.

"I found a photo of you this mornin', stuck behind my router.
D'you remember the time I took you to that pettin' zoo?" I did, but
I wanted to hear him talk. I hadn't realized until then how much I
missed my father's voice. "You were so lookin' forward to seein' the
sheep," he said, "the wee lambs, because I'd told you about the farm
in County Donegal. You couldn'a been more than six, I figure."

"Oh, I know the photo," I exclaimed, suddenly remembering the
image of myself hugging the fleece of a dun-colored lamb.

"I'd be surprised if you didn't," my father said. "The way you
got the wind knocked out of you that day! You went into that pen

as brave as Cuchulainn himself with a palm full of feed, and every llama and goat and sheep in the place came runnin' over to you. Knocked you flat on your back, they did."

I frowned, remembering it as though it were yesterday. They had come from all sides like nightmares, with their hollow, dead eyes and their curved yellow teeth. There had been no way out; the world had closed in around me. Now, under my wedding suit, I broke out in a light sweat; I thought how much I felt like that, again, today.

My father was grinning; I could hear it. "What did you do?" I asked.

"What I always did," he said, and I listened to his smile fade. "I picked you up. I came and got you."

I listened to all the things I wanted and needed to say to him racing through my mind. In the silence I could feel him wondering why he hadn't come to get me in Massachusetts; why he hadn't picked up the pieces and smoothed it over and made it better. I could sense him running through everything we had said to each other and everything we hadn't, trying to find the thread that made this time different.

I knew, even if he didn't. My father's God preached forgiveness, but did he?

Suddenly all I wanted to do was take away the pain. It was *my* sin; it was one thing for *me* to feel the guilt, but my father shouldn't have to. I wanted to let him know that he wasn't responsible, not for what I had done and not for me. And since he wouldn't believe I could take care of myself—*never* would, not now—I told him there was someone else to take care of me. "Dad," I said, "I'm getting married."

I heard a strange sound, as if I had knocked the wind out of him. "Dad," I repeated.

"Yes." He drew in his breath. "Do you love him?" he asked.

"Yes," I admitted. "Actually, I do."

"That makes it harder," he said.

I wondered about that for a moment, and then when I felt I was going to cry, I covered the mouthpiece with my hand and closed my eyes and counted to ten. "I didn't want to leave you," I said, the same words I spoke every time I called. "It wasn't the way I thought things would happen."

Miles away, my father sighed. "It never is," he said.

I thought about the easy days, when he would bathe me as a child and wrap me in my long-john pajamas and comb the tangles from my hair. I thought about sitting on his lap and watching the bluest flames in the fireplace and wondering if there was any finer thing in the world.

"Paige?" he said into the silence. "Paige?"

I did not answer all the questions he was trying to ask. "I'm getting married, and I wanted you to know," I said, but I was certain he could hear the fear in my voice as loudly as I could hear it in his.

≈≈≈

It built up in my stomach and my chest, the feeling, as if I were spiraling into myself. I could feel Nicholas holding back, tensed like a puma, until I was ready. I wrapped my arms and my legs around Nicholas, and, together, we came. I loved the way he arched his neck and exhaled and then opened his eyes as though he wasn't quite sure where he was and how he had got there. I loved knowing I had done that to him.

Nicholas cupped my face in his hands and told me he loved me. He kissed me, but instead of passion I felt protection. He pulled us onto our sides, and I curled myself in the hollow of his chest and tasted his skin and his sweat. I tried to burrow closer. I did not close my eyes to sleep, because I was waiting, as I had the last time I'd been with a man, for God to strike me down.

≈≈≈

Nicholas brought me violets, two huge bunches, still misted and swollen with the spray of a florist. "Violets," I said, smiling. "For faithfulness."

"Now, how do you know that?" Nicholas said.

"That's what Ophelia says, anyway, in *Hamlet*," I told him, taking the bunches and holding them in my left hand. I had a quick vision of the famous painting of Ophelia, where she floats faceup in a stream, dead, her hair swirled around her and tangled with flowers. Daisies, in fact. And violets.

The justice of the peace and a woman whom he introduced only as a witness were standing in the center of a plain room when we walked in. I think Nicholas had told me the man was a retired judge. He asked us to spell and pronounce our names, and then he said "Dearly beloved." The entire thing took less than ten minutes.

I did not have a ring for Nicholas and I started to panic, but Nicholas pulled from his suit pocket two bright gold bands and handed the larger one to me. He looked at me, and I could clearly read his eyes: *I didn't forget. I won't forget anything.*

≈≈≈

Within a few minutes I began to cry. It was not that I was hurt, which Nicholas thought, or that I was happy or disillusioned. It was because I had spent the past eight weeks with a hole in my heart. I had even started to hate myself a little. But in making love with Nicholas, I discovered that what had been missing was replaced. Patchwork, but still, it was better. Nicholas had the ability to fill me.

Nicholas kissed the tears off my cheeks and stroked my hair. He was so close that we were breathing the same square of air. And as he stirred beside me again, I began to erase my past until almost all I could remember was whatever I had told Nicholas, whatever he wanted to believe. "Paige," he said, "the second time is even better." And reading into this, I moved astride him and eased him inside me and started to heal.

≈≈≈

chapter 5
Paige

The best of the several memories I have of my mother involved the betrayal of my father. It was a Sunday, which had meant for as long as I'd been alive that we would be going to Mass. Every Sunday, my mother and my father and I would put on our best outfits and walk down the street to Saint Christopher's, where I would listen to the rhythmic hum of prayers and watch my mother and my father receive Communion. Afterward we'd stand in the sun on the worn stone steps of the church, and my father's hand would rest warm on my head while he talked to the Morenos and the Salvuccis about the fine Chicago weather. But this particular Sunday, my father had left for O'Hare before the sun came up. He was flying to Westchester, New York, to meet with an eccentric old millionaire in hopes of promoting his latest invention, a polypropylene pool float that hung suspended by wires in the middle of the two-car garages that were part of the new suburban tract houses. He called it the Sedan Saver, and it kept car doors from scratching each other's paint when they were opened.

I was supposed to be asleep, but I had been awakened by the dreams I'd been having. At four, almost five, I didn't have many friends. Part of the problem was that I was shy; part was that other kids were steered clear of the O'Toole house by their parents. The bosomy Italian mothers in the neighborhood said my mother was too sassy for her own good; the dark, sweating men worried that my father's bad luck in inventing could ooze uninvited over the thresholds of their own homes. Consequently, I had begun to dream up play-mates. I wasn't the type of kid who saw someone beside me when I took out my Tinkertoys and my dominoes; I knew very well when I was alone that I was truly alone. But at night, I had the same dream over and over: another girl called to me, and together we rolled mud-burgers in our hands and pumped on swings until we both grazed the sun with our toes. The dream always ended the same way: I would get up the courage to ask the girl's name so that I'd be able to find her and play together again, and just before she answered I'd wake up.

And so it was that on that Sunday I opened my eyes already disappointed, to hear my father tugging his suitcase down the hall and my mother whispering goodbye and reminding him to call us later, after we got home from Saint Christopher's, to tell us how it went.

The morning started the way it always did. My mother made me breakfast—my favorite today, apple pancakes in the shape of my in-itials. She laid my pink lace last-year Easter dress on the foot of my bed. But when the time came to leave for Mass, my mother and I stepped into one of those perfect April days. The sun was as filling as a kiss, and the air held the promise of freshly mowed grass. My mother smiled and took my hand and headed up the street, away from Saint Christopher's. "On a day like this," she said, "God didn't mean for us to rot away indoors."

It was the first time that I realized my mother had a second life, one that had nothing at all to do with my father. What I had always assumed was spirituality was really just the side effect of the energy that hovered around her like a magnetic field. I discovered that when my mother wasn't bending to someone else's whims, she could be a completely different person.

We walked for blocks and blocks, coming closer to the lake, I knew, by the way the wind hung in the air. It became unseasonably warm as we walked, reaching into the high seventies, maybe even eighty. She let go of my hand as we came to the white walls of the Lincoln Park Zoo, which prided itself on its natural habitats. Instead of keeping the animals locked in, they cleverly kept the people out. There were few fences or concrete barriers. What kept the giraffes penned was a wide-holed grate that their legs would have slipped through; what kept the zebras in were gulleys too wide to leap. My mother smiled at me. "You'll love it here," she said, making me wonder if she came often, and if so, whom she brought instead of me.

We were drawn to the polar bear exhibit simply because of the water. The free-form rocks and ledges were painted the cool blue of the Arctic, and the bears stretched in the sun, too warm in their winter fur. They slapped their paws at the water, which, my mother said, was just thirty-three degrees. There were two females and a cub. I wondered what the relationship was.

My mother waited until the cub couldn't take the heat anymore, and then she pulled me down a few shadowed steps to the underwater viewing lounge, where you could see into the underwater tank through a window of thick plexiglass. The cub swam right toward us, sticking its nose against the plastic. "Look, Paige!" my mother said. "It's kissing you!" She held me up to the window so that I could get a closer look at the sad brown eyes and the slippery whiskers. "Don't you wish you could be in there?" my mother said, putting me down and dabbing at my forehead with the hem of her skirt. When I did not answer her, she began to walk back up into the heat, still talking quietly to herself. I followed her; what else could I do? "There are many places," I heard her whisper, "I'd like to be."

Then she got an inspiration. She found the nearest totem pole directional sign and dragged me toward the elephants. African and Indian, they were two different breeds but similar enough to live in the same zoo space. They had wide bald foreheads and paper-thin ears, and their skin was folded and soft and spread with wrinkles, like the saggy, mapped neck of the old black woman who came to clean Saint Christopher's. The elephants shook their heads and swatted at gnats with their trunks. They followed each other from one end of their habitat to the other, stopping at trees and examining them as if they'd never seen them before. I looked at them and wondered what it would be like to have one eye on each side of my body. I didn't know if I'd like not being able to see things head-on.

A moat separated us from the elephants. My mother sat down on the hot concrete and pulled off her high heels. She was not wearing stockings. She hiked up her dress and waded into the knee-high water. "It's lovely," she said, sighing. "But don't you come in, Paige. Really, I shouldn't be doing this. Really, I could get in trouble." She splashed me with the water, little bits of grass and dead flies sticking to the white lace collar of my dress. She sashayed and stomped and once almost lost her footing on the smooth bottom. She sang tunes from Broadway shows, but she made up her own lyrics, silly things about firm pachyderms and the wonder of Dumbo. When the zoo guard came up slowly, unsure of how to confront a grown woman in the elephant moat, my mother laughed and waved him away. She stepped out of the water with the grace of an angel and sat down on the concrete again. She pulled on her pumps, and when she stood, there was a dark oval on the ground where her damp bottom had been. She told me with the serious demeanor she'd used to tell me the Golden Rule that sometimes one had to take chances.

Several times that day I found myself looking at my mother with a strange tangle of feelings. I had no doubt that when my father called, she would tell him we'd been at Saint Christopher's and that it had been just as it always was. I loved being part of a conspiracy. At one point I even wondered if the girlfriend I'd been seeing night after night in my dreams was really just my own mother. I thought of how convenient and wonderful that might be.

We sat on a low bench beside a lady who was selling a cloud of banana balloons. My mother had been reading my thoughts. "Today," she said, "today let's say I'm not your mother. Today I'll just be May. Just your friend May." And of course I didn't argue, because this was what I had been *hoping* anyway, and besides, she wasn't *acting* like my mother, at least not the one I knew. We told the man cleaning out the ape cage our white lie, and although he did not look up from his work, one large, ruddy gorilla came forward and stared at us, a very human exhaustion in her eyes, which seemed to say, *Yes, I believe you.*

The last place we visited in the Lincoln Park Zoo was the penguin and seabird house. It was dark and smelled of herring and was fully enclosed. It sat partially under the ground to maintain its cool temperature. The viewing area was a twisty hallway with windows exposing penguins behind thick glass. They were striking in their formal wear, and they tap-danced like society men on floes of white ice. "Your father," May said, "looked no different than that at our wedding." She leaned in close to the glass. "In fact, I'd be hard-pressed to pick one groom from the next. They're all the same, you know." And I said I did, even though I had no idea what she was talking about.

I left her staring at a penguin that had slipped into the water belly-up to do rolling, slow-motion calisthenics. I disappeared around a bend, pulled toward the other half of the house, where the puffins were. I didn't know what a puffin was, but I liked the way the word sounded: soft and squashed and a little bit bruised, the way your lips looked after you'd eaten wild blackberries. It was a long, narrow walkway, and my eyes had not adjusted to the lack of light. I took very tiny steps, because I did not know where I was going, and I held my hands in front of me like a blind man. I walked for what felt like hours, but I could not find those puffins, or the sliver of silver daylight near the door, or even the places where I had already been. My heart swelled up into my throat. I knew the way you know these things that I was going to scream or to cry or to sink to my knees and become invisible forever. For some reason I was not surprised when, in total darkness, my fingers found the comforting shape of May, who turned back into my mother, and she wrapped her arms around me. I never understood how she wound up in front of me, since I'd left her with the penguins and I hadn't seen her pass. My mother's hair fell like a dark curtain over my eyes and tickled my nose. Her breath echoed against my cheek. Black shadows wrapped around us like an artificial night, but my mother's voice seemed solid, like something I could grab for support. "I thought I'd never find you," my mother said, words I held on to and breathed like a litany for the rest of my life.

chapter 6

Nicholas

Nicholas was having a hell of a week. One of his patients had died on the table during a gallbladder removal. He'd had to tell a thirty-six-year-old woman that the tumor in her breast was malignant. Today his surgical rotation had changed; he was back in cardiothoracic, which meant a whole new list of patients and treatments. He'd been at the hospital since five in the morning and had missed lunch because of afternoon conferences; he still hadn't written up notes on his rounds; and if all that wasn't enough of a bitch, he was the resident on call and would be for thirty-six hours.

He'd been summoned to the emergency room with one of his interns—a third-year Harvard student named Gary who was green around the gills and reminded Nicholas nothing of himself. Gary had cleaned and quickly prepped the patient, a forty-year-old woman with superficial head and face wounds that were bleeding profusely. She had been assaulted, most likely by her husband. Nicholas let Gary continue, supervising his actions, his touches. As Gary sewed up the lacerations on her face, the patient began to scream. "Fuck you," she yelled. "Don't you touch my face." Gary's hands began to shake, and finally Nicholas swore under his breath and told Gary to get the hell out. He finished the job himself, as the woman cursed him out from beneath the sterile drapes. "Goddamned fucking pig asshole," she shouted. "Get the fuck away from me."

Nicholas found Gary sitting on a stained cube sofa in one of Mass General's emergency room lounges. He'd drawn his knees up and was doubled over like a fetus. When he saw Nicholas coming toward him, he jumped to his feet, and Nicholas sighed. Gary was terrified of Nicholas; of doing anything wrong; of, really, being the surgeon he hoped to be. "I'm sorry," he murmured. "I shouldn't have let her get to me."

"No," Nicholas said evenly, "you shouldn't have." He thought of telling Gary everything that had gone wrong for himself today. See, he'd say, all *that,* and I'm still standing up, doing my job. Sometimes you just have to keep pushing, he'd say. But in the end he did not say anything to his intern. Gary would figure it out eventually, and Nicholas didn't really want to recount his own failures to a subordinate. He turned away from Gary, a dismissal, feeling every bit the arrogant son of a bitch that he was reputed to be.

For years now, Nicholas had not gauged time by its usual measures. Months and days meant little; hours were things you logged onto a patient's fact sheet. He saw his life passing in blocks, in places where he spent his days and in medical specialties where he filled his mind with details. At first, at Harvard, he'd counted off the semesters by their courses: histology, neurophysiology, anatomy, pathology. His last two years of rotations had run together, experiences blending at the edges. Sometimes he'd be remembering an orthopedic patient at the Brigham, but he'd picture the decor of the orthopedic floor at Massachusetts General. He'd started his rotations with internal medicine; then came a month of psychiatry, eight weeks of general surgery, a month of radiology, twelve weeks of obstetrics/gynecology and pediatrics, and so on. He had forgotten about seasons for a while, shuttling from discipline to discipline and hospital to hospital like a foster child.

He'd decided on cardiac surgery—a long haul. The match had placed him at his first-choice hospital, Mass General. It was a large place, impersonal and disorganized and unfriendly. In cardiothoracic surgery, the attendings were a brilliant group of men and women. They were opinionated and impulsive; they wore pristine white lab coats over their cool, efficient demeanors. Nicholas loved it. Even during his postgraduate year one, he'd observe the easy motions of general surgery, waiting to be rotated back to the cardiac unit, where he'd marvel at Alistair Fogerty performing open-heart operations. Nicholas would stand for six hours at a time, listening to the thin ring of metal instruments on trays and the rustle of his own breath against his blue mask, watching life being put on hold and then recalled.

"Nicholas." At the sound of his name, he turned to see Kim Westin, a pretty woman who'd been in his graduating class and was now in her third year of residency in internal medicine. "How's it going?" She came closer and squeezed his arm, propelling him down the hall in the direction he'd been walking.

"Hey," Nicholas said. "You don't have anything to eat, do you?"

Kim shook her head. "No, and I've got to run up to five, but I wanted to see you. Serena's back."

Serena was a patient they'd shared during their final year of rotations at Harvard. She was thirty-nine and she was black and she had AIDS—which, four years earlier, had still been rare. She'd come and gone in the hospital over the years, but Kim, in internal medicine, had more contact with her than Nicholas. Nicholas did not ask Kim what Serena's status was. "I'll go by," he said. "What's the room?"

After Kim had disappeared, Nicholas went upstairs to round his new cardiac patients. That was the hardest part about being a resident in general surgery—the constant changes from department to department. Nicholas had swung through urology, neurosurgery, emergency room, anesthesia. He'd done a stint in transplants, and one in orthopedics, and one in plastic surgery and burns. Still, coming back to cardiac was better than the others; cardiac surgery felt like home. And indeed Nicholas had been rotated through cardiothoracic more than was normal for a third-year, because he had made it clear to Alistair Fogerty that one day he was going to have his job.

Fogerty was exactly what Nicholas had pictured a cardiac surgeon to be like: tall, fit, in his late fifties, with piercing blue eyes and a handshake that could cripple. He was a hospital "untouchable," his reputation having evolved into a surgical gold standard. There had once been a scandal about him—something involving a candy striper—but the rumors were squelched and there had been no divorce and that was that.

Fogerty had been Nicholas's attending physician during his internship, and one day last year Nicholas had gone to him in his office and told him his plans. "Listen," he'd said, even though his throat had been dry and his palms had been quivering. "I want to cut through the bullshit, Alistair. You know and I know I'm the best surgical resident you've got here, and I want to specialize in cardiothoracic. I know what I can do for you and for the hospital. I want to know what you can do for *me*."

For a long moment, Alistair Fogerty had sat on the edge of his mahogany desk, riffling through a patient's file. When he finally lifted his head, his eyes were dark and angry, but in no way surprised. "You, *Doctor* Prescott," he said, "have got bigger balls than even me."

Alistair Fogerty had got to be director of cardiac surgery by sticking his neck out, taking chances, and courting Fate so that it seemed to stay on his side. When he'd begun doing transplants, the newspapers dubbed him "The Miracle Maker." He was calculating, stubborn, and usually right. He liked Nicholas Prescott a hell of a lot.

And so even when Nicholas was rounding his regular patients in general surgery, and working under other attendings in other disciplines, he still found time to meet with Fogerty. When he had the chance, he rounded Fogerty's patients, did the quick daily pre- and postoperative exams, moved patients in and out of surgical ICU—in short, acted like a cardiothoracic fellow, a seventh-year resident. And in return, Fogerty had him in cardiac surgery more often than not and was grooming him to be the best there was—after Fogerty himself.

Nicholas moved quietly into the recovery room, where Fogerty's latest patient was resting. He read the vitals: here was a sixty-two-year-old man who had had aortic stenosis—the valve leading from the end of his ventricle to the aorta had been scarred down. Nicholas could have easily diagnosed this case from the symptoms: congestive heart failure, syncope, angina. He surveyed the clean white gauze over the patient's chest, the gelatinous orange antiseptic that still coated the skin. Fogerty's work, as always, would be perfect: the native valve removed and a pig valve sewn into its place. Nicholas checked the patient's pulse, tugged the sheet up, and sat down beside him for a moment.

It was cold in recovery. Nicholas crossed his arms and rubbed his hands up and down, wondering how the patient, naked, could be faring. But there, the pink circles at his fingertips and his toes proved that the heart, marvelous muscle, was still working.

It was merely fortuitous that he saw it then, the heart breaking down. He had been watching the steady rise and fall, the classic heartbeat pattern of the monitor, when everything went wrong. The steady *blip-blip-blip* of the machines accelerated, and Nicholas checked to see a sinusoidal pattern, the heart racing at nearly one hundred beats per minute. For a quick second, Nicholas held his hands over the patient like a faith healer. It was an arrhythmia—ventricular fibrillation. Nicholas had seen cases of it before, when a heart was exposed in the chest: beating like a bag of worms, swollen and writhing, not pumping blood at all. "Code!" he yelled over his shoulder, seeing the nurses at the nearby station spring into motion. The patient's heart had been traumatized, operated on, but Nicholas had little choice. In a matter of minutes, the man would be dead. Where was Fogerty?

Almost immediately, recovery was filled with at least twenty people—anesthesiologists, surgeons, interns, and nurses. Nicholas applied wet gel pads to the patient's raw chest, then put the defibrillator paddles to the skin. The body jumped with the shock, but the heart did not correct itself. Nicholas nodded to a nurse, who adjusted the charge. He ran his hand across his forehead, pushing back his hair. His mind was filled with the god-awful sound of the monitor, irregular and screeching, and the rustle of the nurses' starched dresses as they moved around him. He was not certain, but he thought he could smell death.

Nicholas cleared the defibrillators and replaced the paddles on the patient's chest. This time the shock was so violent that Nicholas took a step away, artificial life kicking back like a rifle's recoil. *You will live,* he willed silently. He raised his eyes to the monitor screen, seeing the thin green line dip and peak and dip and peak, the craggy crests of a normal heartbeat. Alistair Fogerty entered the recovery room as Nicholas pushed past him, deafened by the muted touches and calls of congratulation, suddenly a hero.

≈≈≈

Late at night on the patient floors, Nicholas learned to listen. He could tell by the flat beat of soles on the tiles when the nurses were making the midnight rounds. He saw old men recovering from surgery meet in the patient kitchens at 3:00 A.M. to steal the red jello. He waited for the slosh and whistle of the heavy industrial rag mops, shuffled up and down the halls by half-blind old Hispanic janitors. He noticed every patient call sounded at the nurses' desk, the tear of sterile paper that revealed virgin gauze, the sucked-in breath of a syringe. When he was on call and things were quiet, Nicholas liked to wander around the floors, his hands deep in the pockets of his white lab coat. He did not stop into patient rooms, not even when he was on a general surgery rotation and the patients were more than just names and charts posted on the door. Instead he moved like an insomniac, roaming, interrupting the night with his own shrouded footsteps.

Nicholas did not wake Serena LeBeauf when he entered her room in the AIDS ward. It was well after two in the morning by the time he could spare a minute. He sat down in the stark black plastic chair beside her bed, amazed by her deterioration. Her vitals indicated that she weighed less than seventy pounds now; that she had pancreatitis, respiratory failure. An oxygen mask covered her face, and morphine dripped into her continuously.

Nicholas had done something very wrong the first time he met Serena—he let her get under his skin. It was something he had hardened himself to, seeing death every day the way he did. But Serena had a wide smile, with shocking white teeth; eyes light like a tiger's. She had come in with her three children, three boys, all of different fathers. The youngest, Joshua, was six back then, a skinny kid— Nicholas could see the bumps of his backbone under his thin green T-shirt. Serena did not tell them she had AIDS; she wanted to spare them the stigma. Nicholas remembered sitting in the consultation room with the attending physician when she learned she was HIV positive. She had straightened her spine and had gripped the chair so tight that her fingers whitened. "Well," she had said, her voice soft like a child's. "That's not what I expected." She did not cry, and she asked her doctor for all the information she could get, and then, almost shyly, she asked him not to mention this to her boys. She told them, and her neighbors and distant relatives, that it was leukemia.

Serena stirred, and Nicholas pulled the chair closer. He reached for her wrist, telling himself it was to check her pulse, but he knew it was just to hold her hand. Her skin was dry and hot. He waited for her to open her eyes or to say something, but in the end he held his palm soft against her cheek, wishing he could take away the gray haze of her pain.

≈≈≈

Nicholas began believing in miracles his fourth year of medical school. He had been married just months when he decided to do a rotation in Winslow, Arizona, for the Indian Health Service. It was only four weeks, he'd said to Paige. He was tired of doing the scut work of interns at Boston-based hospitals: patient histories and physical exams, clerking for residents and attendings and anyone ranked above you. He'd heard about the rotation on the reservation. They were so short-staffed that you did everything. *Everything.*

It was a three-hour drive from Phoenix. There was no town of Winslow. Black houses, abandoned shops and apartments, stood impassively around Nicholas, their empty windows blinking back at him like the eyes of the blind. As he waited for his ride, tumbleweed edged across the road, just like in the movies, skittering over his shoes.

Fine dust covered everything. The clinic was just a concrete building set into a cloud of earth. He'd taken a red-eye flight, and the doctor who'd met him in Winslow had been there by 6:00 A.M. The clinic wasn't open yet, not officially, but there were several parked pickup trucks, waiting in the cold, their exhaust hanging in the air like the breath of dragons.

The Navajo were quiet people, stoic and reserved. Even in December, the children had played outside. Nicholas remembered that —the brown-skinned babies in short sleeves, making snow angels in the frosted sand, and nobody bothering to dress them more warmly. He remembered the heavy silver jewelry of the women: headbands and belt buckles, brooches that glittered against purple and deep-turquoise calico dresses. Nicholas also could remember the things that had shocked him when he first arrived: the endless alcoholism; the toddler who bit her lip, determined not to cry as Nicholas probed a painful skin infection; the thirteen-year-old girls in the prenatal clinic, their bellies grotesquely swollen, like the neck of a snake that has swallowed an egg.

On Nicholas's first morning at the clinic, he was called into the emergency room. A severely diabetic elderly man had consulted a shaman, a tribal medicine man, who had poured hot tar on his legs as part of the treatment. Horrible sores blistered up, and two physicians were trying to hold down his legs while a third examined the extent of the damage. Nicholas had hung back, not certain what he was needed to do, and then the second patient was brought in. Another diabetic, a sixty-year-old woman with heart disease, who had gone into cardiopulmonary arrest. One of the staff doctors had been jamming a plastic tube down the woman's throat to manage the airway and to breathe for her. He did not look up as he shouted at Nicholas. "What the hell are you waiting for?" he said, and Nicholas stepped up to the patient and began CPR. Together they had tried to get the heart moving again, forty minutes of CPR, defibrillation, and drugs, but in the end the woman died.

During the month that Nicholas spent in Winslow, he had more autonomy than he'd ever had as a student at Harvard. He was given his own patients. He wrote up his own notes and plans and ran them by the eight staff physicians. He rode with public health nurses in four-wheel-drive vehicles to find those Navajos with no true addresses, who lived off the paths of roads, in huts with doors that faced the east. "I live eight miles west of Black Rock," they wrote on their face sheets, "just down the hill from the red tree whose trunk is cleaved in two."

At night Nicholas would write to Paige. He mentioned the dirty hands and feet of the toddlers, the cramped huts of the reservation, the glowing eyes of an elder who knew he was going to die. More often than not, the letters came out sounding like a list of his heroic medical feats, and when this happened Nicholas burned them. He kept seeing the unwritten line that ran through the back of his mind: *Thank God this isn't the kind of doctor that I'm going to be*—words never committed to paper that were still, he knew, indelible.

On his last day at the Indian Health Service, a young woman was brought in, writhing in the throes of labor. Her baby was breech. Nicholas had tried palpating the uterus, but it was clear a C-section was going to be necessary. He mentioned this to the Navajo nurse who was acting as translator, and the woman in labor shook her head, her hair spilling over the table like a sea. A Hand Trembler was called in, and Nicholas respectfully stepped back. The medicine woman put her hands over the swollen belly, singing incantations in the language of the People, massaging and circling the knotted womb. Nicholas told the story when he returned to Boston the next day, still thinking of the dark gnarled hands of the medicine woman, suspended above his patient, the red earth flurrying outside and hazing the window. "You can laugh," he said to his fellow interns, "but that baby was born headfirst."

≈≈≈

"Nicholas," Paige said, her voice thick with sleep. "Hi."

Nicholas curled the metal cord of the pay phone around his wrist. He should not have awakened Paige, but he hadn't spoken to her all day. Sometimes he did this, called at three or four in the morning. He knew she'd be asleep, and he could imagine her there with her hair sticking up funny on the side she'd been sleeping on, her nightgown tangled around her waist. He liked to picture the soft down comforter, sunken in spots where her body had been before she had reached to answer the phone. He liked to imagine that he was sleeping next to her, his arms crossed under her breasts and his face pressed into her neck, but this was unrealistic. They slept at opposite sides of the bed, both fitful sleepers, unwilling to be tied by someone else's movements or smothered by someone else's heated skin.

"Sorry I didn't call this afternoon," Nicholas said. "I was busy in ICU." He did not tell Paige about the patient he'd had to code. She always wanted details, playing him for a superstar, and he wasn't in the mood to go into it all over again.

"That's okay," Paige said, and then she said something muffled into the pillow.

Nicholas did not ask her to repeat herself. "Mmm," he said. "Well, I guess I don't have anything else to say." When Paige did not respond, he hit the # button on the phone.

"Oh," Paige said. "Okay."

Nicholas scanned the hall for signs of activity. A nurse stood at the far end, dropping little red pills into cups that were lined up on a table. "I'll see you tomorrow," Nicholas said.

Paige rolled onto her back; Nicholas knew by the crinkling of the pillows and the fluff of her hair when it settled. "I love you," Paige said.

Nicholas watched the nurse, counting the pills. Eighteen, nineteen, twenty. The nurse stopped, pressed her hands into the small of her back as if she was suddenly weary. "Yes," Nicholas said.

≈≈≈

The next morning Nicholas did prerounds at five-thirty and then began regular rounds with Fogerty and an intern. The patient Nicholas had coded yesterday was doing fine, comfortably settled in surgical ICU. By seven-thirty they were ready for their first surgery of the day, a simple bypass. As they scrubbed, Fogerty turned to Nicholas. "You did well with McLean," he said, "considering you'd just come onto the rotation minutes before."

Nicholas shrugged. "I did what anyone would have done," he said. He scrubbed at invisible germs under his nails, around his wrists.

Fogerty nodded to an OR nurse and shrugged into his sterile gown. "You make decisions well, Dr. Prescott. I'd like you to act as chief surgeon today."

Nicholas looked up but did not let the surprise he felt show in his eyes. Fogerty knew he'd been on call all night, knew he'd need a second wind to measure up. Fogerty also knew it was virtually unheard of for a third-year resident to lead a bypass operation. Nicholas nodded. "You got it," he said.

Nicholas spoke quietly to the patient as the anesthesiologist put him under. He stood beside Fogerty as the second assistant, a resident more senior than Nicholas who was obviously angry, shaved the legs, the groin, the belly, and covered the body with Betadine solution. The patient lay motionless, stark naked, stained orange, like a sacrifice for a pagan god.

Nicholas supervised the harvest of the leg vein, watching as blood vessels were clamped off and sewn, or were cauterized, filling the operating suite with the smell of burning human tissue. He waited until the vein was settled in solution for its later use. Then, stepping up to the patient, Nicholas took a deep breath. "Scalpel," he said, waiting for the nurse to pick the instrument off a tray. He made a clean incision in the patient's chest and then took the saw to cut through the sternum. He held the ribs spread apart with a rib spreader, and then he exhaled slowly, watching the heart beating inside the man's chest.

It never failed to amaze Nicholas how much power was in the human heart. It was phenomenal to watch, the dark-red muscle pumping quickly, turning hard and small with each contraction. Nicholas cut the pericardium and separated out the aorta and the vena cava, connected them to the bypass machine, which would oxygenate the blood for the patient once his heart was stopped by Nicholas.

The first assistant poured the cardioplegia liquid onto the heart, which stopped its beating, and Nicholas, along with everyone else in the room, turned his eyes to the bypass machine, to make sure it was doing its job. He bent closer toward the heart, snipping at the two coronary arteries that were blocked. Nicholas retrieved the leg vein, delicate, and turned it so that the valves did not hold blood back but let it through. With careful sutures he sewed the vein onto the first coronary artery before the point of blockage, and then attached the other end after the point of blockage. His hands moved with a will of their own, precise and steady, fingers blunt and strong beneath the translucent gloves. The next steps streamed through his mind, but the procedure and his role in it had become so natural to him, like breathing or batting right-handed, that Nicholas began to smile. *I can do this,* he thought. *I can really do this on my own.*

Nicholas finished the bypass five hours and ten minutes after he'd begun. He let the first assistant close for him, and it was only after he'd left the operating suite to scrub that he remembered Fogerty and the fact that he hadn't slept in twenty-four hours. "What did you think?" Nicholas said to Fogerty, who was coming up beside him.

Fogerty peeled off his own gloves and ran his hands under the hot water. "I think," he said, "you should go home and get some sleep now."

Nicholas had been untying his mask, and in his shock he let it drop to the floor. He had just done his first *bypass,* for God's sake. Even an asshole like Fogerty should have some constructive criticism, maybe a word of praise. He'd done a terrific job, not one glitch, and even if it took an hour longer than Fogerty's usually did, well, it was to be expected because it was his first.

"Nicholas," Fogerty said, "I'll see you at evening rounds."

≈≈≈

There were many things about Paige that Nicholas did not know when they had been married. He celebrated her birthday two weeks late because she had never told him when it was. He couldn't have guessed her favorite color until their first anniversary, when she picked emerald stud earrings over sapphires because of their sea-green glow. He certainly couldn't have predicted her disastrous cooking experiments, like Miracle Whip Stew and Turkey-Marshmallow Kabobs. He didn't know she'd sing car-commercial jingles when she dusted or that she'd have the skill of stretching a paycheck to cover the interest on a graduate student loan, groceries, condoms, and two tickets to the discount movie theater.

In Nicholas's defense, he did not have much time to discover his new wife. His rotations kept him at the hospital more often than he was at home, and after he graduated from Harvard, he was even more pressured for time. When he did stumble into the apartment, starved and blind with fatigue, Paige so seamlessly fed him, disrobed him, and loved him to sleep that he began to expect the treatment and sometimes forgot that Paige was connected to it.

When he came home from performing his first solo bypass, he did not turn the lights on in the apartment. Paige was at work. She was still waiting tables at Mercy, but only in the mornings. Afternoons, she worked at an OB/GYN office as a receptionist. She had taken on the second job after some night courses in architecture and literature at Harvard Extension didn't work out. She hadn't been able to keep up with the reading and the housework and told Nicholas that two incomes meant more money and that more money meant they'd move out of debt more quickly so she could go to college full time. Back then, Nicholas had wondered if it was just an excuse to drop out of her classes. He'd seen her attempts at writing papers, after all, which were really no more than high-school caliber; and he'd almost said something to Paige, until he remembered that it was just what they *would* be.

Nicholas never voiced his doubts to Paige. For one thing, he didn't want her to take it the wrong way. And also, Nicholas had hated seeing her surrounded by yellowed used textbooks, her hair springing free of its braid as she wound her fingers through it in concentration. Truthfully, Nicholas liked having Paige all to himself.

She was at the gynecologists' office, since it was well after two, but she'd left him a meal to heat up in the oven. He didn't eat it, although he was very hungry. He wanted Paige to be there, although he knew it wasn't possible. He wanted to close his eyes and, for once, become the patient, soothed by the cool ministrations of her tiny, fine hands.

Nicholas fell onto the bed, neatly made, amazed by the darkness and the cold of the late day. He fell asleep listening to the beat of his own heart, thinking of the directions patients gave at the Indian reservation. My home is west of Mass General, he would say, light-years beneath the brittle winter sun.

≈≈≈

Serena LeBeauf was dying. Her sons were heaped like huge puppies on the edges of the hospital bed, holding her hand, her arm, her ankle—whatever pieces of her they could hold. They had brought things they thought would comfort her. There on her frail chest was the cut-out travel-brochure picture of San Francisco, where she'd lived when she was younger. Tucked under her arm were the stubby remains of a threadbare stuffed monkey. Curled across the hollow of her belly was her diploma, the college degree she'd worked so damned hard for and received just a week before her AIDS was diagnosed. Nicholas stood in the doorway, not wanting to intrude. He watched the liquid brown eyes of Serena's sons as they stared at their mother, and he wondered where they would all go, especially the little one, when she died.

He was paged, and he raced down three flights of stairs to surgical ICU, where his bypass patient was lying. The room was a rush of activity, physicians and nurses jockeying into place as the heart went into failure. As if he were watching a replay of the day before, Nicholas stripped the gown from his patient and gave an external shock. And another. Sweat ran down his back and into his eyes, searing. "Goddammit," he muttered.

Fogerty was there. Within minutes he had moved the patient to an operating suite. Fogerty cracked the chest open again and slid his hands into the bloody cavity, massaging the heart. "Let's go," he said softly. His gloved fingers slipped over the tissue, the still-new sutures, rubbing and warming the muscle, kneading life. The heart did not pulse, did not beat. Blood welled around Fogerty's fingers. "Take over," he said.

Nicholas slipped his own hand around the muscle, forgetting for a second that there was a patient, that there was a past attached to this heart. All that mattered was getting the thing going again. He caressed the tissue, willing it to start. He pumped oxygen through his patient's system manually for forty-five minutes, until Fogerty told him to stop and signed the death certificate.

≈≈

Minutes before Nicholas left the hospital for the night, Fogerty called him to his office. He was sitting behind the mahogany desk, his face shadowed by the slatted vertical blinds. He did not motion for Nicholas to enter, did not even lift his head from the paper he was writing upon. "You couldn't have done a thing," he said.

Nicholas pulled on his jacket and wandered toward his car in the parking garage, wondering if he'd ever be given a bypass to do again. He searched his memory to find something he'd overlooked, a torn capillary or an additional blockage, something Fogerty smugly hadn't mentioned after the operation that day, something that might have saved the guy. He pictured the still amber eyes of Serena LeBeauf's youngest son, mirrors of what her own used to be like. He thought about the Navajo Hand Trembler and wondered what potions and blessings and magic decrees might fall between the cracks of common knowledge.

≈≈≈

When he turned the key in the apartment door, Paige was sitting on the floor of the living room, stringing cranberries on black thread. The television had been moved to make room for an enormous blue spruce, thick at the middle, which swelled across half of the little room. "We don't really have any ornaments," she said, and then she looked up and saw him.

Nicholas had not gone straight home. He'd headed into Cambridge, to a seedy bar, where he'd had six straight shots of Jack Daniel's and two Heinekens. He'd bought a bottle of J & B from the bartender and driven home with it by his side, swilling at the stoplights, almost hoping he'd get caught.

"Oh, Nicholas," Paige said. She came to stand in front of him, and she put her arms around him. Her hands were sticky with tar, and he wondered how she'd managed to get that enormous thing into the wobbly tree stand all by herself. Nicholas stared down at her white face, the thin brass hoops dangling from her earlobes. He hadn't even known it was near Christmas.

He seemed to fall forward at the same moment Paige put her arms around him. Staggering under his weight, she helped him sit on the floor, knocking over the bowl of cranberries. Nicholas crushed some as he sat, grinding them into the cheap yellow throw rug, a stain that looked suspiciously like blood. Paige knelt beside him, moving her fingers through his hair, telling him softly it was all right. "You can't save them all," she whispered.

Nicholas gazed up at her. He saw, swimming, the planes of an angel's face, the spirit of a lion. He wanted to make it all go away, everything else, to just cling to Paige until the days ran into each other. He dropped the bottle of J & B and watched it roll with a shudder under the fragrant skirt of Paige's naked Christmas tree. He pulled his wife toward him. "No," he said. He breathed in the quiet clean of her as though it were oxygen. "I can't."

chapter 7
Paige

W hen Nicholas was dressed in a tuxedo, I would have done anything he asked. It was not just the sleek line of his shoulders or the striking contrast of his hair against a snowy shirt; it was his presence. Nicholas should have been *born* wearing a tuxedo. He could carry it off—the status, the nobility. He commanded attention. If this were his everyday uniform, instead of the simple white coat or scrubs of a senior surgical fellow, he'd probably have been the head of Mass General by now.

Nicholas leaned over me and kissed my shoulder. "Hello," he said. "I think I knew you in a different life."

"You did," I said, smiling at him in the mirror. I slipped the clasp onto one of my earrings. "Before you were a doctor." I had not seen Nicholas—really *seen* him—in a long time. Hours of surgery and rounds, plus hospital committee meetings and politically necessary dinners with superiors, kept him away. He had slept on call at the hospital last night, and he'd had a triple bypass and an emergency surgery during the day, so he hadn't had time to phone. I hadn't been sure he'd remember the fund-raising dinner. I'd dressed and gone downstairs, watching the clock move closer to six, and as usual I waited in silence, impatient for Nicholas to get home.

I hated our house. It was a little place with a nice yard in a very prestigious pocket of Cambridge—one with an awful lot of lawyers and doctors. When we first saw the neighborhood, I had laughed and said the streets must be paved with old money, which Nicholas did not find very funny. Despite everything, I knew that in his heart Nicholas still *felt* rich. He'd been wealthy too long to change now. And according to Nicholas, if you were rich—or if you *wanted* to be—you lived a certain way.

Which meant that we'd taken out a large mortgage in spite of the fact that we had tremendous loans from medical school to repay. Nicholas's parents had never come back groveling, as I knew he'd hoped they would. Once, they had sent a polite Christmas card, but Nicholas never filled me in on the details and I didn't know if he was protecting my feelings or his own. But in spite of the Prescotts, we were working our way back into the black. With Nicholas's salary—a finally respectable $38,000—we had started to make a dent in the interest we owed. I wanted to save a little just in case, but Nicholas insisted that we were going to have more than we needed. All I had wanted was a little apartment, but Nicholas kept talking about building equity. And so we bought a house beyond our means, one that Nicholas believed would be his ticket toward becoming chief of cardiothoracic surgery.

Nicholas was never at the house, and he probably knew when we bought the place that he wouldn't be, but he insisted on having it decorated a certain way. We had almost no furniture, because we couldn't afford it, but Nicholas said it just made the place look Scandinavian. The entire house was the color of skin. Not beige and not pink, but that strange pale in-between. The wall-to-wall carpeting matched the wallpaper, which matched the shelving and the track of recessed lighting. The only exception was the kitchen, which was painted a color called Barely White. I don't know who the decorator thought she was kidding; it most certainly *was* white—white tiles, white Corian counters, white marble floor, white pickled wood. "White is in," Nicholas had told me. He'd seen white leather couches and white carpets like spilled foam all over the mansions of doctors he worked with. I gave in. After all, Nicholas knew about this kind of life; I didn't. I didn't mention how dirty I felt sitting in my own living room; or how I stuck out like a sore thumb. I didn't tell him how I thought the kitchen was just crying out to be colored in, and how sometimes, while chopping carrots and celery in that seamless room, I wished for an accident—some splash of blood or stripe of grime that would let me know I'd left my mark.

I was wearing red to the hospital benefit, and both Nicholas and I seemed starkly drawn against the fading beige lines of the bedroom. "You should wear red more often," he said, running his hand over the bare curve of my shoulder.

"The nuns used to tell us never to wear red," I said absentmindedly. "Red attracts boys."

Nicholas laughed. "Let's go," he said, pulling my hand. "Fogerty's going to be counting every minute I'm late."

I didn't care about Alistair Fogerty, Nicholas's attending physician and, according to Nicholas, the son of God himself. I didn't care about missing the sumptuous shrimp fountain at the cocktail hour. If the choice had been mine, I wouldn't have gone. I didn't like mingling with the surgeons and their wives. I had nothing to contribute, so I didn't see why I had to be there at all.

"Paige," Nicholas said, "come *on*. You look *fine*."

When I married Nicholas, I truly believed—like a fool—that I had him and he had me and it was plenty. Maybe it would have been if Nicholas didn't move in the circles he did. The better Nicholas became at his job, the more I was confronted with people and situations I didn't understand: jacket-and-tie dinners at someone's home; drunk divorcées leaving hotel keys in Nicholas's tuxedo pockets; prying questions about the background I'd worked so hard to forget. I was not nearly as smart as these people, not nearly as savvy; I never got their jokes. I went, I mingled, because of Nicholas, but he knew as well as I did that we had been kidding ourselves, that I would never fit in.

When we had been married for a couple of years, I tried to do something about it. I applied to Harvard's Extension School and signed up for two night courses. I picked architecture for me and intro to lit for Nicholas. I figured that if I knew Hemingway from Chaucer and Byron, I'd be able to follow the subtle artsy references that Nicholas's friends batted across dinner conversations like Ping-Pong balls. But I couldn't do it. I couldn't stay on my feet all day at Mercy and have dinner ready for Nicholas and still have time to read about rococo ceilings and J. Alfred Prufrock. I was scared of my professors, who spoke so quickly they might as well have been lecturing in Swedish.

Most of my classmates dabbled in schooling; nearly all had already graduated from somewhere. They didn't have a future at stake, like me. I realized that at the rate I could afford to take courses, it would take nine years for me to get a college degree. I never told Nicholas, but I got an F on the only paper I ever wrote for one of those courses. I can't remember if it was architecture or lit, but I will never forget the professor's comments: *Buried somewhere in this muck,* he had written, *you do have some qualified ideas. Find your voice, Ms. Prescott.* Find your voice.

I had made some excuse to Nicholas and dropped out. To punish myself for being a failure, I took on a second job, as if working twice as hard could make me forget just how different my life had turned out from what I had imagined as a child.

But I had Nicholas. And that meant more than all the college degrees, all the RISD courses in the world. I hadn't changed much in seven years—and I had no one to blame for that but myself—but Nicholas was very different. For a minute, I looked up at my husband and tried to picture what he'd been like back then. His hair had been thicker, and there wasn't the gray that was coming in now, and the lines around his mouth weren't as deep. But the biggest changes were in his eyes. There were shadows there. Once Nicholas had told me that when he watched a patient die, a little piece of him went as well, and that he'd have to work on that, or one day when he was close to retirement he'd have nothing left at all.

≈≈≈

Mass General had been having a Halloween ball at the Copley Plaza for ages, although about ten years earlier, costumes had been traded for formal wear. I was sorry about that. I would have given anything for a disguise. Once, when Nicholas was a general surgical resident, we had gone to a costume party at the medical school. I had wanted to be Antony and Cleopatra, or Cinderella and Prince Charming. "No tights," Nicholas had said. "I wouldn't be caught dead." In the end we had gone as a clothesline. Each of us wore a brown shirt and pants, and stretched between our necks was a long white cord, pinned with boxer shorts, stockings, bras. I loved that costume. We were literally tied together. Everywhere Nicholas went, I had followed.

On the drive into Boston, Nicholas quizzed me. "David Goldman's wife," he'd say, and I'd answer, *Arlene.* "Fritz van der Hoff?" *Bridget.* "Alan Masterson," Nicholas said, and I told him that was a trick question, since Alan had been divorced the previous year.

We pulled off the Mass Pike and stopped at the corner of Dartmouth. Copley Square danced around us, lit with the glitter and whirl of Halloween. Beside the car stood Charlie Chaplin, a gypsy, and Raggedy Andy. They held out their hands as we slowed, but Nicholas shook his head. I wondered what they had expected and what others had given. A sharp rap on my window surprised me. Standing inches away was a tall man dressed in britches and a waistcoat, whose neck ended in a bloody stump. He cradled the blushing oval of a face under his right arm. "Pardon me," he said, and I think the face smiled, "I seem to have lost my head." I was still staring at him, at his plumed green cape, as Nicholas sped away.

Although there were more than three hundred people in the Grand Ballroom of the Copley Plaza Hotel, Nicholas stood out. He was among the youngest, and he attracted attention for having come so far so fast. People knew he was being groomed; that he was the only resident Fogerty thought was good enough to do transplants. As we moved through the double doors, at least seven people came forward to talk to Nicholas. I gripped his arm until my fingers turned white. "Don't leave me," I said, knowing well that Nicholas would not make promises he couldn't keep.

I heard words in a familiar foreign language: infectious endocarditis, myocardial infarction, angioplasty. I watched Nicholas in his element, and my fingers itched to draw him: tall, half in shadow, steeped in his own confidence. But I had packed away my art supplies when we moved, and I still did not know where they were. I had not sketched in a year; I had been too busy working at Mercy in the morning, at Dr. Thayer's office in the afternoon. I had tried to get other jobs, in sales and management, but in Cambridge I was easily beat out by people with a college education. I had nothing to my name except Nicholas. I was riding on his coattails, which, ironically, I had paid for.

"Paige!" I turned to hear the very high voice of Arlene Goldman, a house cardiologist's wife. After my last experience with Arlene, I had told Nicholas that I physically could not sit through a dinner party at their house, and so we'd declined invitations. But suddenly I was glad to see her. She was someone to cling to, someone who knew me and could justify my presence there. "So good to see you," Arlene lied, kissing the air on both sides of my cheeks. "And there's Nicholas," she said, nodding in his general direction.

Arlene Goldman was so thin she seemed transparent, with wide gray eyes and sunny gold hair that came out of a bottle. She owned a personal shopping service, and her biggest claim to fame was being sent by Senator Edward Kennedy to choose his fiancée's engagement ring at Shreve, Crump and Low. She wore a long peach-colored sheath that made her look naked. "How are you, Arlene," I said quietly, shifting from foot to foot.

"Ducky," she said, and she waved over some of the other wives I knew. I smiled around at them and stepped back, listening to conversations about Wellesley reunions and six-figure book deals and the merits of low-E glass for houses on the ocean.

The wives of surgeons did it all. They were mothers and Nantucket real estate agents and caterers and authors all at once. Of course they had nannies and chefs and live-in maids, but they did not acknowledge these people. They spent galas dropping names of celebrities they'd worked with, places where they'd been, spectacles they'd happened to see. They chained themselves in diamonds and wore blush that threw off sparkles in the subtle light of the chandeliers. They had nothing in common with me.

Nicholas dipped his head into the circle of faces and asked if I was all right; he was going to ask Fogerty about a patient. The other women crowded around me. "Oh, Nick," they said, "it's been too long." They put their cold arms around me. "We'll take care of her, Nick," they said, leaving me to wonder when my husband had decided it was all right to be called something other than Nicholas.

We danced to a swing orchestra, and then the doors were opened for the banquet. As always, dinner was a learning experience. There were so many things I still did not know. I didn't realize that there was something called a fish knife. I didn't realize that you could eat snails. I blew on my leek soup before I figured out it was being served cold. I watched Nicholas move with the practiced ease of a professional, and I wondered how I had ever stumbled into this kind of life.

One of the other doctors at the table turned to me during dinner. "I've forgotten," he said. "What is it you do, again?"

I stared down at my plate and waited for Nicholas to come to my rescue, but he was speaking to someone else. We had discussed it, and I wasn't supposed to let people know where I worked. It wasn't that he was embarrassed, he'd assured me, but in the political scheme of things, he had to present a certain image. Surgeons' wives were supposed to present Rotary plaques, not blue-plate specials. I put on the brightest smile that I could and affected the flip voice of the other women. "Oh," I said, "I go around town breaking hearts so my husband has something to do at work."

It seemed like years before anyone said a word, and I could feel my hands shaking under the fine linen tablecloth, sweat breaking out in the hollow of my back. Then I heard laughter, like shattering crystal. "Wherever did you find her, Prescott?"

Nicholas turned from the conversation he'd been having. A lazy grin slipped across his face to hide the line of his eyes. "Waiting tables," he said.

I didn't move. Everyone at the table laughed and assumed Nicholas was making a joke. But he'd done exactly what we weren't supposed to do. I stared at him, but he was laughing too. I pictured the other doctors' wives, driving home with their husbands, saying, *Well, this explains a lot.* "Excuse me," I said, pushing my chair from the table. My knees shook, but I walked slowly to the bathroom.

There were several people inside, but nobody I recognized. I slipped into a stall and sat on the edge of the toilet. I balled up some tissue in my palm, expecting tears, but they didn't come. I wondered what the hell had convinced me to live at the end of someone else's life rather than live my own, and then I realized I was going to throw up.

When I finished I was hollow inside. I could hear the echo of blood running through my veins. Women stared at me as I stepped out of the stall, but nobody asked if I was all right. I rinsed my mouth with water and then I stepped into the hallway, where Nicholas was waiting. To his credit, he looked worried. "Take me home," I said. "Now."

We did not speak during the ride, and when we reached the house I pushed past him at the door and ran to the bathroom and got sick again. When I looked up, Nicholas was standing in the doorway. "What did you have to eat?" he said.

I wiped my face on a towel. The back of my throat was raw and burning. "This is the second time tonight," I told him, and those were the last words I planned to say.

Nicholas left me alone while I undressed. He'd draped his bow tie and cummerbund over the footboard, and in the play of the moonlight they seemed to shift like snakes. He sat on the edge of the bed. "You're not mad, are you, Paige?"

I slid between the covers and turned my back to him. "You know I didn't mean anything by it," he said. He moved beside me and held my shoulders. "You know that, don't you?"

I straightened my back and crossed my arms. I would not speak, I told myself. When I heard Nicholas's even breathing I let the tears come, spilling across my face like hot mercury and burning their path to the pillow.

≈≈≈

I got up as usual at 4:30 A.M. and made Nicholas coffee to take on the road, and I packed a light lunch, as I did every day, because I knew he'd need it between his operations. Just because my husband was being an asshole, I told myself, was no reason for patients to suffer. He came downstairs with two ties. "Which one?" he said, holding them to his throat. I pushed past him and walked back upstairs. "Oh, for Christ's sake, Paige," he muttered, and then I heard the door slam behind him.

I ran to the bathroom and threw up. This time I was so dizzy I had to lie down, and I did, right on the fuzzy white bath mat. I fell asleep, and when I woke I called in sick to Mercy. I would not have gone to Dr. Thayer's, either, that afternoon, but I had a hunch. I waited until she had a lull between patients, and then I left the reception desk and stood beside her at the counter where we kept the jars for urine samples, the Pap smear glass slides, and the information sheets on breast self-examination. Dr. Thayer stared up at me as if she already knew. "I need you to do me a favor," I said.

≈≈≈

This was not the way it was supposed to happen. Nicholas and I had discussed it a million times: I would support us until Nicholas's salary began to pay off the loans; then it was my turn. I was going to go full time to art school, and then after I got my degree we would start a family.

It shouldn't have happened, because we were careful, but Dr. Thayer shrugged and said nothing was completely effective. "Be happy," she told me. "At least you're married."

That was what brought it all back. As I drove slowly through the traffic in Cambridge, I wondered how I could have missed the signals: the swollen breasts and spread nipples, the way I'd been so tired. After all, I had been through this before. I hadn't been ready then, and in spite of what Dr. Thayer said, I knew that I wasn't ready now.

The realization sent a shiver through my body: I was never going to art school. It would not be my turn for many years. It might never actually happen.

I had made my decision to attend art school after I had taken just one formal art course, connected with the Chicago Art Institute. I was only in ninth grade; I had won free tuition for a course through a city-wide student art contest. Figure Drawing was the only class offered after school hours, so I signed up. On the first night, the teacher, a wiry man with purple glasses, made us go around the room telling who we were and why we were there. I listened to the others say they were taking the class for college credit or for updating a portfolio. When it was my turn I said, "I'm Paige. I don't know what I'm doing here."

The model that night was a man, and he came in in a satin robe printed with theater ticket stubs. He had a steel bar he used as a prop. When the teacher nodded, he stepped onto a platform and shrugged off the robe as if it didn't bother him in the least. He bent and twisted and settled with his arms overhead, holding the bar like the Cross. He was the first man I'd seen completely naked.

When everyone began drawing, I sat still. I was certain I'd made a mistake in taking this course. I could feel the model's eyes on me, and that's when I touched the conté stick to the sketch pad. I looked away, and I drew from the heart: the knotted shoulders, the stretched chest, the flaccid penis. The teacher came over shortly before class ended. "You've got something," he said to me, and I wanted to believe him.

For the night of the last class, I bought a piece of fine gray marbled paper from an art supply store, hoping to draw something I'd want to keep. The model was a girl no older than I, but her eyes were weary and jaded. She was pregnant, and when she lay on her side, her belly swelled into the curve of a frown. I drew her furiously, using white conté for the shine of the studio lights on her hair and her forearms. I did not stop during the ten-minute coffee break, although the model got up to stretch and I had to draw from memory. When I was finished, the teacher took my drawing around to show the other students. He pointed out the quiet planes of her hips, the slow roll of her heavy breasts, the spill of shadow between her legs. The teacher brought the picture back to me and told me I should think about art school. I rolled the drawing into a cylinder and smiled shyly and left.

I never hung up the drawing, because my father would have killed me if he'd known I'd willingly sinned by taking a course that exposed the bodies of men and women. I kept the picture hidden in the back of my closet and looked at it from time to time. I did not notice the obvious thing about the drawing until several weeks afterward. The images that came out in my sketches were not even hidden in the background this time. I had drawn the model, yes, but the face— and the fear upon it—was mine.

≈≈≈

"Hey," Marvela said to me as I walked into Mercy. She had a pot of coffee in one hand and a bran muffin in the other. "I thought you was sick today." She pushed past me, shaking her head. "Girl, don't you know you makin' me look bad? When you play hooky you supposed to stay away, not get them Catholic guilt feelings and show up mid-shift."

I leaned against the cash register. "I am sick," I said. "I've never felt worse in my life."

Marvela frowned at me. "Seems if I was married to a doctor, I'd probably be ordered to bed."

"It's not that kind of sick," I told her, and Marvela's eyes widened. I knew what she was thinking; Marvela had a thing for *National Enquirer* gossip and larger-than-life stories. "No," I told her before she could ask, "Nicholas isn't having an affair. And my soul hasn't been stolen by aliens."

She poured me a cup of coffee and leaned her elbows against the counter. "I s'pose I'm gonna have to play Twenty Questions," she said.

I heard her, but I didn't answer. At that moment, a woman stumbled through the door holding a baby, a shopping bag, and a huge paisley satchel. As she crossed the threshold, she dropped the satchel and hoisted the baby higher on her hip. Marvela swore under her breath and stood up to help, but I touched her arm. "How old is that kid?" I asked, trying to sound casual. "You figure six months?"

Marvela snorted. "He's a year if he's a day," she said. "Ain't you never baby-sat?"

Impulsively, I stood up and pulled an apron from behind the counter. "Let me serve her," I said. Marvela was hesitating. "You get the tip."

The woman had left her satchel in the middle of the diner floor. I pulled it over to the booth she'd gone to—the one that had been Nicholas's. The woman had the baby on the tabletop and was taking off its diaper. Without bothering to thank me, she unzipped the satchel, withdrew a clean diaper and a chain of plastic rings, which she handed to the baby. "Dah," he said, pointing to the light.

"Yes," the woman said, not even looking up. "That's right. Light." She rolled up the dirty diaper and fastened the new one and caught the rings before the baby threw them on the floor. I was fascinated; she seemed to have a hundred hands. "Can I get some bread?" she said to me, like I hadn't been doing my job, and I ran into the kitchen.

I didn't stay long enough for Lionel to ask me what the hell I was doing at work. I grabbed a basket of rolls and strode to the woman's table. She was joggling the baby on her knee and trying to keep him from reaching the paper place mat. "Do you have a high chair?" she asked.

I nodded and dragged over the little half-seat. "No," she sighed, as if she had been through this before. "That's a *booster* seat. That's not a high chair."

I stared at it. "Won't it work?"

The woman laughed. "If the President of the United States was a woman," she said, "every damn restaurant would have a high chair, and mothers with infants would be allowed to park in handicapped zones." She had been balling up a roll into bite-size nuggets that the baby was stuffing into his mouth, but she sighed and rose to her feet, gathering her things. "I can't eat if there's no high chair for him," she said. "I'm sorry to have wasted your time."

"I can hold him," I said impulsively.

"Pardon?"

"I said I could hold him," I repeated. "While you eat."

The woman stared at me. I noticed how exhausted she seemed, trembling almost, as if she hadn't slept for a very long time. Her eyes, an unsettled shade of brown, were locked onto mine. "You would do that?" she murmured.

I brought her a spinach quiche and gingerly lifted the baby into my arms. I could feel Marvela watching me from the kitchen. The baby was stiff and didn't fit on my hip. He kept twisting to grab my hair. "Hey," I said, "no," but he just laughed.

He was heavy and sort of damp, and he squirmed until I put him on the counter to crawl. Then he overturned a mustard jar and wiped the serving spoon into his hair. I couldn't turn away for a minute, even, and I wondered how I—how *anyone*—could do this twenty-four hours a day. But he smelled of powder, and he liked me to cross my eyes at him, and when his mother came to take him back, he held on tight to my neck. I watched them leave, amazed that the woman could carry so much and that, though nothing had gone wrong, I felt so relieved to give the baby back to her. I saw her move down the street, bowed to the left—the side she carried the baby on—as if he was sapping her balance.

Marvela came to stand beside me. "You gonna tell me what that's about," she said, "or do I got to piss it out of you?"

I turned to her. "I'm pregnant."

Marvela's eyes opened so wide I could see white all the way around the jet irises. "No shit," she said, and then she screamed and hugged me.

When I didn't embrace her back, she released me. "Let me guess," she said. "You ain't jumpin' for joy."

I shook my head. "This isn't the way it was supposed to happen," I explained. I told her about my plan, about our loans and Nicholas's internship and then about college. I talked until the phrases in my native tongue were foreign and unfamiliar, until the words just fell out of my mouth like stones.

Marvela smiled gently. "Lord, girl," she said, "whatever *does* happen the way it's supposed to? You don't *plan* life, you just *do* it." She looped an arm over my shoulder. "If the past ten years had gone accordin' to plan for me, I'd be eatin' bonbons and growin' prize roses and livin' in a house as big as sin, with my handsome son-a-bitch husband sittin' next to me." She stopped, looking out the window and, I figured, into her past. Then she patted my arm and laughed. "Paige, honey," she said, "if I'd stuck to my grand plan, I'd be livin' *your* very life."

≈≈≈

For a long time I sat on the porch outside the house, ignoring neighbors who stared at me briefly from the sidewalk or from car windows. I didn't know how to be a good mother. I hadn't had one. I mostly saw them on TV. My mind brought up pictures of Marion Cunningham and Laura Petrie. What did those women *do* all day?

Nicholas's car came into the driveway hours later, when I was thinking of all the things I wouldn't have access to that I needed for having a child. I couldn't tell Dr. Thayer about my mother's family history. I didn't know the details of her labor. And I would not tell Nicholas that there had been a baby before this and that I was someone else's before I was his.

Nicholas swung out of his car when he saw me, his body unfolding and straightening for an attack. But as he came closer he realized the fight had gone out of me. I sagged against the pillar of the porch and waited until he stepped in front of me. He seemed impossibly tall. "I'm pregnant," I said, and I burst into tears.

He smiled, and then he bent down and lifted me up, carrying me into the house in his arms. He danced over the threshold. "Paige," he said, "this is great. Absolutely great." He set me down on the skin-colored couch, smoothing my hair away from my eyes. "Hey," he said, "don't worry about the money."

I didn't know how to tell him that I was not worried, just scared. I was scared about not knowing how to hold an infant. I was scared that I might not love my own child. More than anything, I was scared that I was doomed before I began, that the cycle my mother had started was hereditary and that one day I would just pack up and disappear off the face of the earth.

Nicholas put his arms around me. "Paige," he said, holding my thoughts in the palm of his hand, "you're going to be a terrific mother."

"How do you know?" I cried, and then I said it again, softly: "How do you know?" I stared at Nicholas, who had done everything he'd ever set out to do. I wondered when I had lost control of my own life.

Nicholas sat down beside me and slipped his hand underneath my sweater. He unzipped the waistband of my pants. He spread his fingers across my abdomen as if whatever was growing inside needed his protection. "My son," he said, his voice thick at the edges.

It was as if a window opened, showing me the rest of my life as it lay, dissected and piecemeal. I considered my future, stunted and squeezed into boundaries defined by two men. I imagined being in a house where I was always the odd one out. "I'm not making any promises," I said.

chapter 8
Paige

*T*he first person I fell in love with was Priscilla Divine.

She had come from Texas to Chicago and enrolled in Our Lady of the Cross, my grade school, when I was in sixth grade. She was a year older than the rest of us, though she'd never been left back. She had long blond hair the color of honey, and she never walked but glided. It was said by some of the other girls that she was the reason her family had to move.

There was such an aura of mystery surrounding Priscilla Divine that she probably could have picked just about anyone she wanted to be her friend, but she happened to choose me. One morning during religion class she raised her hand and told Sister Theresa that she thought she might throw up and she'd like it very much if Paige could help her down to the nurse's office. But once we were in the hall she didn't look sick at all, and in fact she pulled me by the hand into the girls' bathroom and took a pack of cigarettes out of the waistband of her skirt and matches from her left sock. She lit up, inhaled, and offered the cigarette to me like a peace pipe. With my reputation hanging in the balance, I drew in deeply, knowing enough not to let myself cough. Priscilla was impressed, and those were the beginnings of my bad years.

Priscilla and I did everything we weren't supposed to. We walked through Southside, the black neighborhood, on our way home from Our Lady. We stuffed our bras, and we cheated on algebra tests. We did not confess these things, because as Priscilla taught me, there are certain things you do not tell priests. It got to the point where we had each been suspended from school three times, and the sisters suggested we give up each other's friendship for Lent.

We discovered sex on a rainy Saturday when we were in seventh grade. I was at Priscilla's, lying on my back on her lollipop bedspread and watching lightning freeze the street outside into still-life photos. Priscilla was thumbing through a *Playboy* that we'd stolen from her brother's room. We had had the magazine for several months and had already memorized the pictures and read all the letters to the "Advisor," looking up the words we didn't understand. Even Priscilla was bored by the same old thing. She stood up and moved to the window. For a moment a trick of lightning darkened her eyes and created shadows that made her look drained and disillusioned, as if she had been staring at the street below for ages rather than seconds. When she turned to me, arms crossed, I barely recognized her. "Paige," she said casually, "have you ever kissed an actual boy?"

I hadn't, but I wasn't about to let her know that. "Sure," I said. "Haven't you?"

Priscilla tossed her hair and took a step forward. "Prove it," she said.

I couldn't; and this very topic, in fact, had been one of my biggest worries. I had spent entire nights awake, practicing kissing with my pillow, but I couldn't figure out the finer points, like where my nose should go and when I was supposed to take a breath. "How am I supposed to prove it?" I said. "Unless there's a guy in here that I can't see."

Priscilla walked toward me, thin and almost see-through in the purple afternoon. She leaned over me so that her hair made a quiet tent. "Pretend," she said, "*I'm* the guy."

I knew that Priscilla knew I had been lying; just as well as I knew that I wasn't going to admit it. So I leaned forward and put my hands on her shoulders and pressed my lips against hers. "You see," I said, dismissing her with a wave of my hand.

"No," she said, "it's like this." And she turned her head and kissed me back. Her lips moved as much as mine hadn't, molding me beneath her until my mouth was doing the same thing. My eyes were wide open, still watching the lightning. In that instant I knew that every rumor told about Priscilla Divine in school, every nun's warning and every altar boy's sideways glance, was justified. Her tongue slipped over my lips, and I jumped back. Priscilla's hair clung to my shoulders and my face like a web, that's the kind of electricity we had generated.

We spent time after that getting kissing down to a science. We'd borrow Priscilla's mother's red lipstick and make out with the bathroom mirror, watching our own faces fog up as we learned to love ourselves. We went to the public library and hid in the stacks with adult romance novels, skimming the pages until we came to the sex scenes, and then we'd whisper them out loud. Occasionally we kissed each other, taking turns playing the boy. Whoever was the girl got to swoon and to lower her eyelashes and to whisper breathlessly like the women in those forbidden books. Whoever was the boy had to stand still and straight, to accept.

One day after school Priscilla showed up at my front door, out of breath. "Paige," she said, "you've got to come *now.*" She knew I was supposed to stay at home alone until my father returned from the office where he worked as a computer programmer to supplement his income from inventions. She knew that I never broke promises to my father. "Paige," she insisted, "this is important."

I went to Priscilla's that day and hid with her inside the hot dark closet in her brother's room, which smelled of gym shorts and bologna and Canoe. We watched the room settle, split through the closet door's slats. "Don't move," Priscilla whispered. "Don't even breathe."

Priscilla's brother, Steven, was a junior in high school and was the source of most of her information about sex. We knew he had done it, because he kept condoms hidden in his nightstand, as many as twelve at a time. Once, we had stolen one and opened its silver wrapper. I had unrolled the pale tube over Priscilla's arm, marveling as it stretched and grew like a second skin. I had watched my fingers slip over and over as if I were stroking velvet.

Minutes after we had settled ourselves in the closet, Steven came into his room with a girl. She was not someone from Pope Pius but probably a public-school girl from downtown. She had short brown hair and wore pink nail polish, and her white jeans rode low on her hips. Steven pulled her onto his bed with a groan and began to unbutton her shirt. She kicked off her shoes and wiggled off her pants, and before I knew what had happened they were both naked. I could not see much of Steven, which was good, because how would I ever have faced him? But there were the smooth circles of his bottom and the pink heels of his feet, and tangled across his back were the legs of this girl. Steven squeezed the breast of the girl with one hand, revealing a nipple like a strawberry, while he rummaged in his nightstand drawer for a condom. And then he began to move on her, rocking her back and forth like those playground animals on thick wiry springs. Her legs climbed higher, her toes crossed on Steven's shoulders, and they both started to moan. The sound rose around them like yellow steam, punctuated by the scrape of the bed on the hardwood floor. I was not sure what I was seeing, sliced as it was by the closet into strips, but it seemed a machine, or a mythical beast that shrieked as it fed on itself.

≈≈≈

Priscilla's crazy aunt from Boise sent her a Ouija board for her fifteenth birthday, and the first question we asked it was who would be the May Queen. May was Mary's month, or so we'd been told at Our Lady, and every year there was a parade on the first Monday night in May. The students would march in a procession from the school to Saint Christopher's, preceded by the discord and oompahs of the school band. At the end of the parade came the May Queen, chosen by Father Draher himself, and her court of attendants. The prettiest girl in the eighth grade was always the May Queen, and everyone assumed that this year it would be Priscilla, so when we asked the Ouija board I gave a subtle push toward *P,* knowing it would have gone that way no matter what.

"*P* what?" Priscilla said, impatiently tapping her fingers on the cursor.

"Don't tap," I warned her. "It won't work. It's got to feel the heat."

Priscilla rubbed her nose with her shoulder and said that the board didn't want to answer that question, although I wondered if it was because she was afraid the next letter might not be *R.* "I know," she said. "Let's ask it who you're going to go out with."

Since spying on Steven, Priscilla had been dating a steady stream of boys. She had let them kiss her and touch her breasts, and she told me that the next time she might even go to third base. I had listened to her describe the way Joe Salvatore jammed his tongue in her mouth, and I wondered why she would keep going back for more. First base, second base, third base—it reminded me of the Stations of the Cross, the special services during Lent where you said a prayer for each of the twelve steps leading up to the Crucifixion. I'd been doing it for years every Friday during Lent, and it was the same hour-long ordeal week after week. First Station, Second Station, Third . . . I would flip ahead in the prayer book to see how much longer I'd have to suffer. It seemed to me that in a different way, Priscilla was doing the same thing.

"*S-E-T-H,*" Priscilla pronounced. "You're going to go out with Seth." She took her fingers off the Ouija cursor and frowned. "Who the hell is Seth?" she said.

There was no Seth in our school, no Seth related to Priscilla or to me, no Seth anywhere in the world that we knew of. "Who cares," I said, and I meant it.

The next day in school Father Draher announced that the May Queen that year would be Paige O'Toole, and I almost died. I turned bright red and wondered what on earth had made them pick me, when Priscilla was clearly more beautiful. In fact, I could feel her eyes searing into my neck from the desk behind me and the cruel jab of her pencil in my shoulder blade. I also wondered why, for a rite honoring the mother of God, they'd pick someone who had no mother at all.

Priscilla was one of the May Queen's attendants, which meant she got off easy. I had to spend every day after school being fitted for the white lace gown I would wear during the procession. I spent hours listening to Sister Felicite and Sister Anata Falla as they pinned up the hem and adjusted the bustline from last year's queen. As I watched the setting sun run into the gutters of the wet streets, I wondered if Priscilla had found another friend.

But Priscilla did not hold the May Queen appointment against me. She cut her trig class two days later and stood outside the door of my English class until I noticed her waving and smiling. I took the bathroom pass and met her in the hall. "Paige," she said, "how do you feel about getting violently ill?"

We planned a way for me to get away from May Queen practice that day: I would start shaking during lunch and then get severe abdominal cramps, and although I would be able to troupe it out till the end of the day, I would tell Sister Felicite that it was that time of the month, something the sisters seemed to be overly accommodating about. Then I'd meet Priscilla behind the bleachers and we'd take the bus uptown. Priscilla said there was something she had to show me, and it was a surprise.

It was nearly four o'clock when we arrived at the old car lot, a blacktop area enclosed with high mesh fencing that someone had rigged with two netless basketball hoops. A shock of multicolored, sweating men were running up and down the makeshift court, passing a dirty ball back and forth. Their muscles flexed, outlined and taut. They grunted and gasped and whistled, hoarding the air like gold. Of course I had seen basketball before, but never like this. It was primal, angry, and wholehearted, played as if the players' souls were at stake.

"Look at him, Paige," Priscilla whispered. Her fingers gripped

the chain links so tightly that the joints paled. "He's so beautiful."
She pointed to one of the men. He was tall and lean and could jump
with the grace of a mountain lion. His hands seemed to cover the
basketball. He was black.

"Priscilla," I said, "your mother will kill you."

Priscilla didn't even look at me. "Only if some Goody Two-shoes
virgin May Queen rats on me," she said.

The game ended, and Priscilla called him over. His name was
Calvin. From the inside of the fence, he pressed his hands against
hers and pushed his lips through one of the little open diamonds to
kiss her. He was not as old as I'd originally thought; probably eighteen or so, a public high school kid. He smiled at me. "So we goin'
out or what?" he said, talking so fast that I had to blink.

Priscilla turned to me. "Calvin here wants to double-date," she
said. I stared at her as if she was crazy. We were in the eighth grade.
We couldn't go out in guys' cars; we had weekend curfews. "Just for
dinner," Priscilla said, reading my mind. "Monday night."

"Monday night?" I said, incredulous. "Monday night's the—"
Priscilla kicked my shin before I said anything about the May parade.

"Paige is busy until about eight," she said. "But then we can get
away." She kissed Calvin again, hard, through the fence, so that when
she pulled away she had crosses pressed into her cheeks, red as scars.

≈≈≈

On Monday night, with my father and the neighbors watching,
I was the May Queen. I wore a bride's outfit of white lace and a white
veil, and I carried white silk flowers. Before me went a stream of
Catholic children, and then my attendants in their best dresses. I was
last, their icon, the image of the Blessed Virgin Mother.

My father was so proud of me that he'd taken two entire thirty-
six-picture rolls of film. He did not question me when I said I'd be
celebrating with Priscilla's family after the service and that I'd stay
over at her house. Priscilla had told her mother she'd be with me. I
moved across the cooling pavement like an angel. I thought, *Hail
Mary full of grace,* and I repeated this to myself over and over as if
that might knock sense into me.

When we got to the church, Father Draher was standing by the tall marble statue of the Blessed Mother, waiting. I took the wreath of flowers that Priscilla had been carrying, and I stepped forward to crown Mary. I expected a miracle, and I watched the statue's face the entire time, hoping to see the features of my own mother. But my fingers slipped over Mary as I offered the wreath, and her pale-blue cheek stayed as cold and forbidding as hate.

Priscilla and I were picked up by Calvin in a red Chevy convertible on the corner of Clinton and Madison. In the front seat with him was another person, a boy with thick straight hair the color of chestnuts and smiling island-green eyes. He jumped out of the car and held the door open, bowing to Priscilla and to me. "Your chariot," he said, and that might have been when I fell in love.

Dinner turned out to be Burger King, and what amazed me most was not that the guys offered to pay but that they ordered an enormous amount of food, much more than I could even think of consuming. Jake—that was the name of my date—had two chocolate shakes, three Whoppers, a chicken sandwich, large fries. Calvin had even more. We ate in the car at a drive-in theater, under a moon that seemed to rest on the top of the screen.

Priscilla and I went to the bathroom together. "What do you think?" she asked.

"I don't know," I told her, which was the truth. Jake seemed all right, but we'd barely said more than hello.

"Just goes to show you," Priscilla said. "That Ouija board knew a thing or two."

"It said I'd go out with a Seth," I pointed out.

"Jake, Seth," Priscilla said. "They're both four letters."

By the time we returned to the car it had become dark. Calvin waited until Priscilla and I sat down, and then he hit the button that raised the roof of the convertible. It sealed itself with a faint sucking sound, covering us like a mouth. Calvin turned around to Jake and me in the back seat, and all I could see was the white gleam of his teeth. "Don't you all do anything I wouldn't do," he said, and he settled his arm around Priscilla like a vise.

I could not tell you what the movie was that night. I clasped my hands between my knees and watched my legs tremble. I listened to the sounds of Calvin and Priscilla, skin slipping against skin in the front seat. Once I peeked and there she was, swooning and batting her lashes and whispering breathlessly just as we had practiced.

Jake kept three inches between us. "So, Paige," he said quietly, "what do you usually do?"

"Not that," I blurted out, which made him laugh. I pulled myself farther away, laying my cheek against the steamed glass of the window. "I shouldn't be here," I whispered.

Jake's hand moved across the seat, slowly, so I could watch it. I grasped it, and that was when I realized how much I had needed the support.

We began to talk then, our voices blocking out the moans and echoes coming from the front seat. I told him I was only fourteen. That we went to parochial school and that I had been the May Queen just hours before. "Come on, baby," Calvin said, and I heard the tug of a zipper.

"How did you ever get together with someone like Priscilla?" Jake asked, and I told him I didn't know. Calvin and Priscilla shifted, blocking my view of the screen. Jake inched closer to the window. "Move over here," he said, and he offered the shelter of his arm. He kept his eyes on me as I hung back, like prey at the brink of a neatly laid trap. "It's okay," he said.

I rested my head against the soft pillow of his shoulder and breathed in the heavy smell of gasoline, oil, and shampoo. Priscilla and Calvin were loud; their sweating arms and legs made fart noises on the vinyl. "Jesus," Jake said finally, crawling across me to lean into the front seat. I adjusted myself around him while he pulled the driver's-side door handle. At the moment the door sprang free, I saw them in the flash of the moon. White spliced with black, Priscilla and Calvin were knotted at the waist. Calvin balanced himself above her on his arms, his shoulders straining. Priscilla's breasts pointed at the night, pink and splotchy where they'd been roughened by stubble. She was looking directly at me, but she did not seem to see.

Jake pulled me out of the car and put his arm around my waist.

He steered me to the front of the drive-in, before the lines of cars. We sat down on the damp grass, and I started to cry. "I'm sorry," Jake said, although it hadn't been his fault. "I wish you hadn't seen that."

"It's okay," I said, even though it wasn't.

"You shouldn't be hanging around with a girl like Priscilla," he said. He wiped at my cheeks with his thumb. His nails were creased with tiny black lines where motor oil had seeped in.

"You don't know anything about me," I said, pulling back.

Jake held my wrists. "But I'd like to," he said. He kissed my cheeks first, then my eyelids, then my temples. By the time he reached my mouth I was shaking. His lips were soft as a flower and just rubbed back and forth, quiet and slow. After all Priscilla and I had practiced, after all we had done, I had never considered this. This wasn't even a kiss, but it made my chest and my thighs burn. I realized I had much to learn. As Jake's lips grazed mine, I said what had been going through my mind: "No pressure?"

It was a question, and it was directed at him, but Jake didn't take it the way I intended. He lifted his head and pulled me to his side, keeping me warm but not kissing me, not coming back to me. Over our heads, the actors were moving like dinosaurs, hollow and silent and thirty feet tall. "No pressure," Jake said lightly, leaving me bothered and pounding, ashamed, wanting more.

chapter 9
Nicholas

Nicholas was going to harvest the heart. It had belonged to a thirty-two-year-old woman from Cos Cob, Connecticut, who had died hours before in a twenty-car pileup on Route 95. By tonight it would belong to Paul Cruz Alamonto, Fogerty's patient, an eighteen-year-old kid who'd had the misfortune to be born with a bad heart. Nicholas looked out the window of the helicopter and pictured Paul Alamonto's face: hooded gray eyes and thick jet hair, pulse twitching at the side of his neck. Here was a kid who had never run a mile, played quarterback, ridden a seven-alarm roller coaster. Here was a kid who—thanks to Nicholas and Fogerty and a jackknifed tractor-trailer on Route 95—was going to be given a renewed lease on life.

It would be Nicholas's second heart transplant, although he was still just assisting Fogerty. The operation was complicated, and Fogerty was letting him do more than he let anyone else do, even if he thought Nicholas was still too green to be chief surgeon during the transplant. But Nicholas had been turning heads at Mass General for years now, moving swiftly under Fogerty's tutelage from peer to near equal. He was the only cardiothoracic resident who acted as senior surgeon during routine procedures. Fogerty didn't even stand around during his bypass operations anymore.

Other resident fellows passed Nicholas in the scrubbed white halls of the hospital and turned the other way, unwilling to be reminded of what they hadn't yet achieved. Nicholas did not have many friends his age. He socialized with the directors of other departments at Mass General, men twenty years his senior, whose wives ran the Junior League. At thirty-six, he was for all practical purposes the associate director of cardiothoracic surgery at one of the most prestigious hospitals in the country. To have no friends, Nicholas reasoned, was a small sacrifice.

As the helicopter hovered over the tarmac on the roof of Saint Cecilia's, Nicholas reached for the Playmate cooler. "Let's go," he said brusquely, turning to the two residents he'd brought with him. He stepped from the helicopter, checking his watch out of nervous habit. Shrugging into his leather bomber jacket, he shielded his face from the rain and ran into the hospital, where a nurse was waiting. "Hi," he said, smiling. "I hear you have a heart for me."

It took Nicholas and the assisting residents less than an hour to retrieve the organ. Nicholas set the Playmate between his ankles when the helicopter lifted into the muddy sky. He laid his head against the damp seat, listening to the residents sitting behind him. They were good surgeons, but their rotation in cardiothoracic wasn't their favorite. If Nicholas recalled correctly, one of the doctors was leaning toward orthopedic surgery, the other toward general surgery. "Your call," one said, shuffling a deck of playing cards.

"I don't give a shit," the other resident said, "just so long as we don't play hearts."

Nicholas clenched his fists instinctively. He turned his head to see out the window but found that the helicopter was wrapped in a thick gray cloud. "Goddamn," he said, for no reason at all. He closed his eyes, hoping he'd dream of Paige.

≈≈≈

He was seven, and his parents were thinking of divorce. That was the way they had put it when they sat Nicholas down in the library. *Nothing to be alarmed about,* they had said. But Nicholas knew of at least one kid in his school whose parents were divorced. His name was Eric, and he lived with his mother, and at Christmas, when the class had made papier-mâché giraffe ornaments, Eric had had to make two, for two different trees. Nicholas remembered that well, especially the way Eric stayed late at the arts and crafts table when everyone else had gone to the gym to play kickball. Nicholas had been the last one leaving the room, but when he saw Eric's eyes turned up to the door, he got permission to stay. Eric and Nicholas had painted both giraffes the same shade of blue and had talked about everything but Christmas.

"Then where," Nicholas said, "will Daddy be for Christmas?"

The Prescotts looked at each other. It was July. Finally, Nicholas's father spoke. "It's just something we're considering," he said. "And no one said that I will be the one to leave. In fact," Robert Prescott said, "no one may be leaving at all."

Nicholas's mother made a strange sound through her clamped lips and left the room. His father crouched down in front of him. "If we're going to catch the opening pitch," he said, "we'd better get going."

Nicholas's father had season tickets to the Red Sox—three seats —but the boy was rarely invited along. Usually his father took colleagues, from time to time even a long-standing patient. For years Nicholas had watched the games on Channel 38, waiting for the camera to span the crowd behind third base, hoping to catch a glimpse of his father. But so far that had never happened.

Nicholas was allowed to go to one or two games each season, and it was always the high point of his summer. He kept the dates marked on the calendar in his bedroom, and he'd cross off each day leading up to the game. The night before, he'd take out the wool Sox cap he'd been given two birthdays ago, and he'd tuck it neatly into his Little League glove. He was up at dawn, and although they wouldn't leave until noon, Nicholas was ready.

Nicholas and his father parked the car on a side street and got on the Green Line of the T. When the trolley swung to the left, Nicholas's shoulder grazed his father's arm. His father smelled faintly of laundry detergent and ammonia, smells Nicholas had come to associate with the hospital, just as he connected the pungent film-developing chemicals and the hazy red lights of the darkroom with his mother. He stared at his father's brow, the fine gray hair at his temple, the line of his jaw, and the swell of his Adam's apple. He let his eyes slide down to his father's jade polo shirt, the knot of blue veins in the hollow of his elbow, the hands that had healed so many. His father was not wearing his wedding ring.

"Dad," Nicholas said, "you're missing your ring."

Robert Prescott turned away from his son. "Yes," he said, "I am."

Hearing his father speak those words, Nicholas felt the swell of nausea at the base of his throat ease. His father knew he was missing the ring. It wasn't on purpose. Certainly it was a mistake.

They slid into their wide wooden seats minutes before the game began. "Let me sit on the other side," Nicholas said, his view blocked by a thick man with an Afro. "That's our seat too, isn't it?"

"It's taken," Robert Prescott said, and as if the words had conjured her, a woman appeared.

She was tall, and she had long yellow hair held back by a piece of red ribbon. She was wearing a sundress that gapped at the sides, so that as she sat down, Nicholas could see the swell of a breast. She leaned over and kissed his father on the cheek; he rested his arm across the back of her chair.

Nicholas tried to watch the game, tried to concentrate as the Sox came from behind to crush the Oakland A's. Yaz, his favorite player, hit a homer over the Green Monster, and he opened his mouth to cheer with the crowd, but nothing came out. Then a foul ball tipped off by one of the A's batters flew directly toward the section where Nicholas was sitting. He felt his fingers twitch in his glove, and he stood, balancing on the wooden chair, to catch it as it passed. He turned, stretched his arm overhead, and saw his father bent close to the woman, his lips grazing the edge of her ear.

Shocked, Nicholas remained standing on his chair even when the rest of the crowd sat down. He watched his father caress someone who was not his mother. Finally, Robert Prescott looked up and caught Nicholas's eye. "Good God," he said, straightening. He did not hold out his hand to help Nicholas down; he did not even introduce him to the woman. He turned to her and without saying a word seemed to communicate a million things at once, which to Nicholas seemed much worse than actually speaking.

Until that moment, Nicholas had believed that his father was the most amazing man in the world. He was famous, having been quoted in the *Globe* several times. He commanded respect—didn't his patients sometimes send things after operations, like candy or cards or even once those three goslings? His father had known the answers to all the questions Nicholas could come up with: why the sky was blue, what made Coke fizz, why crows perched on electrical wires didn't get electrocuted, how come people on the South Pole didn't just fall off. Every day of his life he had wanted to be exactly like his father, but now he found himself praying for a miracle. He wanted someone to get coshed in the head with a stray ball, knocked unconscious, so that the manager of Fenway would call over the loudspeaker, "Is there a doctor in the house?" and then his father could come to the rescue. He wanted to see his father bent over the still body, loosening the collar and running his hands over the places where there were pulses. He wanted to see his father be a hero.

They left at the top of the seventh, and Nicholas sat in the seat behind his father on the T. When they pulled into the driveway of the big brick house, Nicholas jumped out of the car and ran into the forest that bordered the backyard, climbing the nearest oak tree faster than he ever had in his life. He heard his mother say, "Where's Nicholas?" her voice carrying like bells on the wind. He heard her say, "You bastard."

His father did not come in to dinner that night, and in spite of his mother's warm hands and bright china smiles, Nicholas did not want to eat. "Nicholas," his mother said, "you wouldn't want to leave here, would you? You'd want to be here with me." She said it as a statement, not a question, and that made Nicholas angry until he looked at her face. His mother—the one who taught him that Prescotts don't cry—held her chin up, keeping back the tears that glazed her eyes like a porcelain doll's.

"I don't know," Nicholas said, and he went to bed still hungry. He huddled under the cool sheets of his bed, shaking. Hours later, in the background, came the muffled splits and growls that he knew were the makings of an argument. This time it was about him. He knew more than anything that he did not want to grow up to be like his father, but he was afraid of growing up without him. He swore that never again would he let anyone make him feel the way he felt right now—as if he was being forced to choose, as if his heart was being pulled in two. He stared out the window to see the white moon, but its face was the same as that of the baseball lady, her cheek smooth and white, her ear marked by the brush of his own father's lips.

≈≈≈

"Wake up, Sleeping Beauty," one of the residents whispered into Nicholas's ear. "You've got a heart to connect."

Nicholas jumped, hitting his head on the low roof of the helicopter, and reached for the Playmate cooler. He shook the image of his father from his mind and waited for a surgeon's reserve of energy to come from his gut, pulse into his arms and his legs, and spring to the balls of his feet.

Fogerty was waiting in the operating suite. As Nicholas came through the double doors, scrubbed and gowned, Fogerty began to open Alamonto's chest. Nicholas listened to the whir of the saw slicing through bone as he prepared the heart for its new placement. He turned to face the patient, and that was when he stopped.

Nicholas had done more than enough surgeries in his seven years as a resident to know the procedure cold. Incisions, opening the chest, dissecting and suturing arteries—all these had become second nature.

But Nicholas was used to seeing a patient with wrinkled skin, with age spots. Under the orange antiseptic, Paul Alamonto's chest was smooth, firm, and resilient. "Unnatural," Nicholas whispered.

Fogerty's eyes slid to him above the blue mask. "Did you say something, Dr. Prescott?"

Nicholas swallowed and shook his head. "No," he said. "Nothing." He clamped an artery and followed Fogerty's instructions.

When the heart had been dissected, Fogerty lifted it out and nodded to Nicholas, who placed the heart of the thirty-two-year-old woman in Paul Alamonto's chest. It was a good fit, a near match, according to the tissue analyses done by computer. It remained to be seen what Paul Alamonto's body would do with it. Nicholas felt the muscle, still cold, slipping from his fingers. He mopped as Fogerty attached the new heart just where the old one had been.

Nicholas held his breath when Fogerty took the new heart in his hand, kneading it warm and willing it to beat. And when it did, a four-chamber rhythm, Nicholas found himself blinking in time with the blood. In, up, over, out. In, up, over, out. He looked across the patient at Fogerty, who he knew was smiling beneath his mask. "Close, please, Doctor," Fogerty said, and he left the operating room.

Nicholas threaded the ribs with wire, sutured the skin with tiny stitches. He had a fleeting thought of Paige, who made him sew loose buttons on his own shirts, saying he was better at it by trade. He exhaled slowly and thanked the residents and the operating room nurses.

When he moved into the scrub room and peeled off his gloves, Fogerty was standing with his back to him at the far side of the room. He did not turn as Nicholas jerked off his paper cap and turned on the faucet. "You're right about cases like that, Nicholas," Fogerty said quietly. "We *are* playing God." He tossed a paper towel into a receptacle, still facing away from Nicholas. "At any rate, when they're that young, we're fixing what God did wrong."

Nicholas wanted to ask Alistair Fogerty many things: how he'd known what Nicholas was thinking, how come he'd sutured a certain artery when it would have been easier to cauterize it, why after so many years he still believed in God. But Fogerty turned around to face him, his eyes sharp and blue, as splintered as crystal. "Seven o'clock, then, at your place?"

Nicholas stared for a moment, dumbfounded, and then remembered that he was giving his first dinner party for his "associates"— Alistair Fogerty, as well as the heads of pediatrics, cardiology, and urology. "Seven," he said. He wondered what time it was now; how long it would take him to change gears. "Of course."

≈≈≈

Nicholas had been having nightmares again. They weren't the same ones he'd had when he was in medical school, but they were every bit as disturbing, and Nicholas believed they stemmed from the same source, that old fear of failure.

He was being chased through a heavy, wet rain forest whose ivy vines dripped blood. He could feel his lungs near bursting; he pulled his legs high from the spongy ground. He did not have time to look back, could only brush the branches from his face as they lacerated his forehead and his cheeks. In the background was the banshee howl of a jackal.

The dream always started with Nicholas running; he never knew what it was he was running from. But sometime during the sheer physical concentration of sprinting, of balancing and dodging thick trees, he'd realize that he was no longer being chased. All of a sudden he was running *toward* something, just as faceless and forbidding as his pursuer had been. He gasped; he grabbed at a stitch in his side, but he couldn't move quickly enough. Hot butterflies slapped against his neck and leaves striped his shoulders as he tried to move faster. Finally, he hurled himself against a sandstone altar, carved with the leers of naked pagan gods. Panting, Nicholas slid to his knees in front of the altar, and beneath his fingers it turned into a man, a person made of warm skin and twisted bone. He looked up and saw his own face, older and broken and blind.

He always woke up screaming; he always woke up in Paige's arms. Last night when he had become fully conscious of his surroundings, she had been hovering over him with a damp washcloth, wiping his sweaty neck and chest. "Sssh," she said. "It's me."

Nicholas let a choked sound escape from his throat and pulled Paige to him. "Was it the same?" she asked, her words muffled against his shoulder.

Nicholas nodded. "I couldn't see," he said. "I don't know what I was running from."

Paige ran her cool fingers up and down his arm. It was in these moments, when his defenses were down, that he would cling to her and think of her as the one constant in his life and let himself give in completely. Sometimes when he reached for her after the nightmares, he would grasp her arms so tightly he left bruises. But he never told her the end of the dream. He couldn't. Whenever he had tried, he'd started shaking so badly he couldn't finish.

Paige wrapped her arms around him, and he leaned into her, still warm and soft with sleep. "Tell me what I can do for you," she whispered.

"Hold me," Nicholas said, knowing she would; knowing, with the unswerving faith of a child at Christmastime, that she would never let go.

≈≈≈

Paige hadn't wanted to tell anyone she was pregnant. In fact, if Nicholas hadn't known better, he would have thought she was avoiding the inevitable. She didn't run out to buy maternity clothes; they really didn't have the extra money, she said. In spite of Nicholas's urging, when she called her father she did not tell him the news. "Nicholas," she had told him, "one out of every three pregnancies ends in miscarriage. Let's just wait and see."

"That's only true through the first trimester," Nicholas had said. "You're almost five months along."

And Paige had turned on him. "I know that," she said. "I'm not *stupid.*"

"I didn't say you were stupid," Nicholas said gently. "I said you were *pregnant.*"

He drove home quickly, hoping Paige had remembered this dinner party even if he hadn't. She'd have to, after the way they'd fought over it. Paige insisted the house was too small, that she couldn't cook anything worthy of a dinner party, that they didn't have fine china and crystal. "Who cares?" Nicholas had said. "Maybe they'll feel bad and give me more money."

He opened the back door and found his wife sitting on the kitchen floor. She wore an old shirt of his and a pair of his pants rolled to the knee. She held a bottle of Drano in one hand and a glass in the other, ringed brown. "Don't do it," Nicholas said, grinning. "Or if you do, wouldn't sleeping pills be more pleasant?"

Paige sighed and put the glass down on the floor. "Very funny," she said. "Do you know what this means?"

Nicholas pulled open his tie. "That you don't want to have a dinner party?"

Paige held up her hand and let Nicholas pull her to her feet. "That it's a boy."

Nicholas shrugged. The ultrasound had said the same thing; the waitresses at Mercy said she was carrying out in front, the way you carry a boy. Even the old wives' tale had confirmed it—the wedding ring dangling from a string had moved back and forth. "Drano probably isn't the definitive test," he said.

Paige went to the refrigerator and began pulling out trays of food covered by aluminum foil. "You pee into a cup, and then you add two tablespoons of Drano," she said. "It's like ninety percent foolproof. The Drano people have even written to OB/GYNS, asking them to tell their patients this is not a recommended use for their product." She closed the door and leaned against it, her hands pressed against her forehead. "I'm having a boy," she said.

Nicholas knew that Paige did not want a boy. Well, she wouldn't admit it, at least not to him, but it was as if she just assumed that being the kind of person she was, it was impossible for her to be carrying anything other than a tiny replica of herself. "Now, really," Nicholas said, putting his hands on her shoulders, "would a boy really be so awful?"

"Can I still name him after my mother?"

"It would be hard," Nicholas said, "to be the only boy in first grade named May."

Paige gave him a smug look and picked up two of her platters.

She stuffed one into the oven and took the other into the living room, which had been turned into a dining room for the night. The tiny kitchen table was bolstered on both sides by card tables, and every chair in the house had been dragged into service. Instead of their usual dishes and glassware, there were ten places set with bright dinner plates, each one different and each with a matching glass. Painted on the surfaces were simple, fluid line drawings of diving porpoises, glacial mountains, turbaned elephants, Eskimo women. Curled in the glasses were paper napkins, each fanned in a different shade of the rainbow. The table spilled with color: vermilion and mango, bright yellow and violet. Paige looked uneasily at Nicholas. "It's not quite Limoges, is it," she said. "I figured that since we only have service for eight, this would be better than two place settings that looked entirely wrong. I went to the secondhand stores in Allston and picked up the plates and glasses, and I painted them myself." Paige reached for a napkin and straightened its edge. "Maybe instead of saying we're poor, they'll say we're funky."

Nicholas thought of the dinner tables he'd grown up with: the cool white china from his mother's family rimmed in gold and blue; the crystal Baccarat goblets with their twisted stems. He thought of his colleagues. "Maybe," he said.

The Fogertys were the first to arrive. "Joan," Nicholas said, taking both of Alistair's wife's hands, "you look lovely." Actually, Joan looked as though she'd had a run-in at Quincy Market: her tailored suit was a silk print of larger-than-life cherries and bananas and kiwis; her shoes and her earrings sported clusters of purple clay grapes. "Alistair," Nicholas said, nodding. He looked over his shoulder, waiting for Paige to arrive and take over the role of hostess.

She stepped into the room then, his wife: a little pale, even swaying, but still beautiful. Her hair had become thick during pregnancy and covered her shoulders like a shining, dark shawl. Her blue silk blouse curved over her back and her breasts and then billowed, so that only Nicholas would know that beneath it, her black trousers were secured with a safety pin. Joan Fogerty flew to Paige's side and pressed her hand against her belly. "Why, you're not even showing!" Joan exclaimed, and Paige looked up at Nicholas, furious.

Nicholas smiled at her and shrugged: *What could I do?* He waited until Paige lowered her gaze, and then he led Alistair into the living room, apologizing for the lack of space.

Paige served dinner to the Fogertys, the Russos, the van Lindens, and the Walkers. She had prepared Lionel's secret recipes: split-pea soup, roast beef, new potatoes, and glazed carrots. Nicholas watched her move from guest to guest, talking softly as she replenished the plates with spinach salad. Nicholas knew his wife well. She hoped that if she kept the plates full, no one would remember that they weren't a matched set.

Paige was in the kitchen, getting together the main course, when Renee Russo and Gloria Walker ducked their heads together and began to whisper. Nicholas was in the middle of a discussion with Alistair about immunosuppressive drugs and their effect on transplanted tissue, but he was listening to the wives with half an ear. After all, this was his home. Whatever transpired at his first dinner party could make or break him in the political ranks of the hospital as much as a brilliant piece of research. "I bet," Renee said, "she paid a fortune for these."

Gloria nodded. "I saw almost the same thing in The Gifted Hand."

Nicholas did not see Paige enter the room behind him, frozen by the gossip. "It's the *in* thing," Gloria added, "crayon drawings that look like they were done by monkeys, and then someone has the gall to sell them as original art." Gloria saw Paige standing in the doorway and offered a tight smile. "Why, Paige," she said, "we were just admiring your dishes."

And just like that, Paige dropped the roast beef so that it rolled onto the pale beige carpet, steeped in a pool of its own blood.

≈≈≈

The year that Nicholas was seven, his parents did *not* split up. In fact, just a week after the Red Sox game, Nicholas's life—and that of his parents—miraculously moved back on track. For three days Nicholas ate by himself at the kitchen table while his father drank Dewar's in the library and his mother hid in the darkroom. He walked through the halls only to hear the echo of his own footsteps. The fourth day, he heard banging and sawing in the basement, and he knew his mother was making a frame. She had done it before when she mounted her originals, like the famous Endangered exhibit, which hung at odd intervals in the hallway and up the staircase. She said she wouldn't trust her prints to some crackpot frame store, and so she bought her own wood, nails, and matting. Nicholas sat at the foot of the main staircase for hours, rolling a basketball over his bare toes, knowing he wasn't allowed to have a basketball in the house and wishing someone were around to tell him that.

When his mother came up from the basement she carried her framed print below her right arm. She brushed past Nicholas as if he weren't there, and she hung the photograph at the head of the stairs, at eye level, a place you couldn't help but notice. Then she turned and went into her bedroom, closing the door behind her.

It was a photo of his father's hands, large and work-rough, with a surgeon's blunt nails and sharp knuckles. Superimposed on them were the hands of his mother: cool, smooth, curved. Both sets of hands were very dark, silhouettes traced in a line of white light. The only detailed things in the picture were the wedding bands, gleaming and sparkling, swimming in the black. The strange thing about the picture was the angle of his mother's hands. You looked at it one way, and his mother's hands were simply caressing his father's hands. But when you blinked, it was clear that her hands were neatly folded in prayer.

When Nicholas's father came home, he pulled himself up the stairs by the banister, ignoring the small form of his own son in the shadows. He stopped at the photo at the top of the stairs and sank to his knees.

Next to the spot where Astrid Prescott had signed her name, she had printed the title: "Don't."

Nicholas watched his father go into the room where he knew his mother was waiting. That was the night that he stopped hoping he'd grow up with his father's glory and started wishing, instead, that he'd have his mother's strength.

≈≈≈

Everyone laughed. Paige ran upstairs to the bedroom and slammed the door shut. Rose van Linden washed the beef in the sink, made some new gravy; and Alistair Fogerty carved, making scalpel jokes. Nicholas mopped up the mess on the carpet and laid a white dish towel over it when the stain would not come out. When he stood up, his guests seemed to have forgotten he was there. "Please excuse my wife," Nicholas said. "She's very young, and if that isn't enough, she's also pregnant." At this, the women brightened and began to tell stories of their own labors and deliveries; the men clapped Nicholas on the back.

Nicholas stood apart, watching these people in his chairs, eating at his own table, and wondered when he'd lost control of the situation. Alistair was now sitting in *his* spot at the head of the table. Gloria was pouring wine. The Bordeaux curled into a glass meant for Paige, a crimson wave behind the painted image of a conch shell.

Nicholas walked up the stairs to the bedroom, wondering what he could possibly do. He wouldn't yell, not with everyone in the living room, but he was going to let Paige know she couldn't get away with this. For God's sake, he had an image to present. He needed Paige to attend these things; it was expected. He knew she wasn't brought up this way, but that wasn't a reason to fall apart every time she faced his colleagues and their wives. She wasn't one of them, but Jesus, in many ways he wasn't, either. At least, like him, she could pretend.

For a fleeting moment he remembered the way Paige had softened the edges of his apartment—hell, the edges of his whole *life*—just hours after he'd asked her to marry him. He remembered his wedding day, when he'd stood beside Paige and realized, giddy, that she was going to take him away. He'd never have to sit through another stuffy six-course meal with brittle, false rumors about people who hadn't been invited. He'd promised to love her and honor her, for richer and for poorer, and at the time, he really had believed that as long as he had Paige, either outcome would be fine. What had happened in the past seven years to change his mind? He'd fallen in love with Paige because she was the kind of person he'd always wanted to be: simple and honest, blissfully ignorant of silly customs and obligations and kiss-ass rituals. Yet he was poised at the edge of the doorway, ready to drag her back to his colleagues and their politically correct jokes and their feigned interest in the origins of the draperies.

Nicholas sighed. It wasn't Paige's fault; it was his own. Somewhere along the way he'd been tricked into thinking, again, that the only life worth living was the one waiting for him downstairs. He wondered what Alistair Fogerty would say if he took Paige and crawled out the window and shimmied down the drainpipe and ran out to the Greek pizza place in Brighton. He wondered how he had wound up coming full circle.

When he pushed open the bedroom door, he couldn't find his wife. Then he saw her, blended into the blue bedspread, tucked into the upper right corner. She was lying on her side, with her knees drawn up. "They made fun of me," she said.

"They didn't know it was you," Nicholas pointed out. "You know, Paige," he said, "not everything is about *you*." He reached for her shoulder, pulling her roughly to face him, and saw the mapped silver lines tears had cut across her cheeks. "About these dinner parties," he said.

"What about them?" Paige whispered.

Nicholas swallowed. He imagined Paige as she might have looked earlier that day, painstakingly painting the dishes and the glassware. He saw himself at age ten, learning table etiquette and patterned waltzes on Saturday mornings at Miss Lillian's Finishing Sessions. Well, like it or not, he thought, it all was a game. And if you had any intention of winning, you had to at least *play*. "You're going to go to these stupid dinners, whether or not you like them, for a long time. You're going to go out there tonight and apologize and blame it on hormones. And when you say goodbye to those two bitches, you're going to smile and tell them you can't wait to see them again." He watched Paige's eyes fill with tears. "My life, and your life, doesn't only depend on what I do in an operating suite. If I'm going to get anywhere I have to kiss ass, and it's sure as hell not going to help if I have to spend half the time making excuses for you."

"I can't do it," Paige said. "I can't keep going to your stupid parties and fund-raisers and watch everyone pointing at me like I'm the freak at the sideshow."

"You can," Nicholas said, "and you will."

Paige raised her eyes to his, and for a long minute they stared at each other. Nicholas watched new tears well up and spill over, spiking her lashes. Finally, he pulled her into his arms, burying his face in her hair. "Come on, Paige," he whispered. "I'm only doing this for you."

Nicholas did not have to look to know that Paige was staring straight ahead, still sobbing. "Are you," she said quietly.

They sat on the edge of the bed, Nicholas curling his body around Paige's, and they listened to the laughter of their guests and the *ting* of glasses being raised in toasts. Nicholas brushed a tear off Paige's cheek. "Jesus, Paige," he said quietly. "You think I like making you upset? It's just that this is important." Nicholas sighed. "My father used to tell me that if you want to win, you have to play by the rules."

Paige grimaced. "Your father probably *wrote* the rules."

Against his will, Nicholas felt his shoulders stiffen. "As a matter of fact," he said, "my father didn't have any family money. He worked to get what he has now, but he was born flat broke."

Paige pulled away to stare at him. Her jaw dropped open as if she was about to say something, but she only shook her head.

Nicholas caught her chin with his fingers. Maybe he had been wrong about Paige. Maybe money and breeding were as important to her as they were to his old girlfriends. He shivered, wondering what this admission had cost him. "What?" he said. "Tell me."

"I don't believe it."

"You don't believe what? That my father had no money?"

"No," Paige said slowly. "That he *chose* to live the way he does now."

Nicholas smiled, relieved. "It has its advantages," he pointed out.

"You know where the next mortgage payment is coming from. You know who your friends are. You don't worry nearly as much about what everyone else thinks of you."

"And that's what you care about?" Paige shifted away from him. "Why didn't you tell me this before?"

Nicholas shrugged. "It never came up."

In the distance, someone shouted out a punch line. "I'm sorry," Paige said tightly, balling her hands into fists. "I didn't know you made such a sacrifice to marry me."

Nicholas pulled her into his arms and stroked her back until he felt her relax. "I *wanted* to marry you," he said. "And besides," he added, grinning, "I didn't give it all up. I put it on hold. A few more dinner parties, a few less roasts on the floor, and we'll be in the black." He helped her stand. "Would it really be so awful? I want our baby to have the things I did when I was growing up, Paige. I want you to live like a queen."

Nicholas started to lead her into the hall. "What about what I want?" Paige whispered, so soft that even she could not clearly hear herself.

≈≈≈

When they walked back into the living room, Paige held on to Nicholas's hand so tightly that when she stepped away, marks from her fingernails were pressed into his palm. He watched her lift her chin. "I'm so sorry," she said. "I'm not feeling too well these days." She stood with the grace of a madonna while the women took turns holding their hands up to her stomach, prodding and pressing and guessing the sex of their child. She saw each pair of guests out, and as Nicholas stood on the porch, talking to Alistair about tomorrow's schedule, she went to clean up the dirty dishes.

Nicholas found her in the living room, throwing the plates and the glasses into the fireplace. He stood very still as she hurled the ceramic and watched her smile when the shards, littered with fragments of clouds and flamingos, fell at her feet. He had never seen her destroy her own work; even the little doodles on the telephone pad were tucked into a folder somewhere for future ideas. But Paige shattered dish after dish, glass after glass, and then she lit a fire underneath the pieces. She stood in front of the hearth, flames dancing in shadow over her face, while the colors and friezes were ashed over in black. And then she turned to face Nicholas, as if she knew he had been standing there all along.

If Nicholas had been frightened by her actions before, he was shocked by what he saw in Paige's eyes. He had seen it once before, when he was fifteen, the one and only time he had gone hunting with his father. They had walked in the mist of a Vermont morning, stalking deer, and Nicholas had spotted a buck. He had tapped his father's shoulder, as he'd been taught to do, and watched Robert raise the barrel of his Weatherby. The buck had been a distance away, but Nicholas could clearly see the tremble of its rack, the rigidity of its stance, the way the life had gone out of its gaze.

Nicholas took a step back into the safety of his living room. His wife was framed by fire; her eyes were those of an animal trapped.

chapter 10
Paige

S pread around my kitchen were the travel brochures. I was
supposed to be planning my family, painting the nursery and
knitting pale-peach sacque sets, but instead I had become ob-
sessed with places where I had never been. The leaflets were spilled
like a rainbow across the counter, they covered the length of the
window seat in splashes of aqua, magenta, and gold. Progressive Trav-
els. Smuggler's Notch. Civilized Adventures.

Nicholas was starting to get annoyed. "What the hell *are* these,"
he'd said, sweeping them off the black glass stovetop.

"Oh, you know," I had hedged. "Junk mail."

But they weren't. I had sent away for them, a dollar here and fifty
cents there, knowing I would receive in the mail a new destination
every day. I read the brochures from cover to cover, rolling the names
of the cities in my mouth. Dordogne, Pouilly-sur-Loire. Verona and
Helmsley, Sedona and Banff. Bhutan, Manaslu, Ghorapani Pass. They

were tours that were impossible for someone who was pregnant; most involved intense hiking or bicycling, preventive inoculations. I think I read them because they were exactly what I couldn't do. I would lie on my back on the floor of my pristine kitchen, and I'd imagine valleys heavy with the scent of rhododendrons, the lush parks and canyons where guanacos, serows, and pandas made their homes. I imagined sleeping in the Kalahari bush, listening to the distant thunder of antelope, buffalo, elephants, cheetahs. I thought about this baby, weighing me down more and more each day, and I pretended that I was anywhere but here.

My baby was eight inches long. He could smile. He had eyebrows and eyelashes; he sucked his thumb. He had his own set of fingerprints and footprints. His eyes were still closed, heavy-lidded, waiting to see.

I knew everything I could about this baby. I read so many books on pregnancy and birth that I memorized certain sections. I knew what the signs of false labor were. I learned the terms "bloody show" and "effacement and dilatation." Sometimes I actually believed that studying every possible fact about pregnancy might make up for the shortcomings I would have as a mother.

My third month had been the hardest. After those first few episodes, I was never sick, but the things I learned cramped my gut and took my breath away. At twelve weeks, my baby had been one and a half inches long. He weighed one twenty-eighth of an ounce. He had five webbed fingers, hair follicles. He could kick and move. He had a tiny brain, one that could send and receive messages. I spent much of that month with my hands spread over my abdomen, as if I could hold him in. Because once, a long long time ago, I had had another baby twelve weeks old. I tried not to compare, but that was inevitable. I told myself to be happy I did not know the facts about it then, as I did now.

The reason I had had an abortion was that I wasn't ready to be a mother; I couldn't have given a child the kind of life it deserved to have. Adoption wasn't an alternative, either, since that would have meant I'd be pregnant full term—I couldn't bring that kind of shame to my father. Seven years later, I had almost convinced myself that these were good excuses. But sometimes I would sit in my Barely White kitchen, run my fingers over the cool, smooth travel photos, and I would wonder if things were so different. Yes, I now had the means to support a baby. I could afford to buy the beautiful blond Scandinavian nursery furniture, the bright googly-eyed fish mobile. But I had two strikes against me: I still had no mother of my own as a model. I had killed my first child.

I went to stand and ground my belly into the edge of the kitchen table, wincing at the pain. My stomach was round but rock hard, and it seemed to have a million nerve endings. My body, curved in places where it never had been, was a hazard. I found myself stuck in tight spots—backed against walls, caught between closely placed restaurant chairs, trapped in the aisles of buses. I couldn't judge the space I needed anymore, and I willed myself to believe that this would change in time.

Restless, I pulled on my boots and went to stand on the porch. It was raining, but I didn't particularly care. It was my only day off all week, Nicholas was at the hospital, and I had to go somewhere—anywhere—even if it wasn't to Borneo or Java. These days, I seemed always to want to be moving. I twitched all night in bed, never staying asleep for a full eight hours. I paced behind the receptionist's desk at work. When I sat down to read, my fingers fluttered at my sides.

I pulled on my coat without bothering to button it and headed down the street. I kept walking until I reached the heart of Cambridge. I stood under the plexiglass hood of the T station, beside a black woman with three children. She placed her hands on my stomach, the way everyone did these days. A pregnant woman, I had discovered, was public property. "You been sick?" the woman asked, and I shook my head. "Then it's a boy." She pulled her children out into the rain, and they walked toward Mass. Ave., jumping in puddles.

I wrapped my scarf around my head and moved into the rain again. I walked down Brattle, stopping at a tiny fenced-in play yard attached to a church. It was wet and empty, the slide still coated with last week's snow. I turned away and kept moving down the street until the storefronts and brick buildings faded into residential clapboard mansions with spotty naked trees. I walked until I realized I was going to the graveyard.

It was a famous one, full of Revolutionary soldiers and startling tombstones. My favorite was a thin slate, jagged and broken, that announced the body of Sarah Edwards, who died of a bullet wound given by a man not her husband. The graves, placed irregularly and close together, looked like crooked teeth. Some of the markers had fallen onto their sides and were strewn with vines and brambles. Here and there a footprint was pressed into the frozen ground, making me wonder who, other than me, came to a place like this.

As a child, I had gone to graveyards with my mother. "It's the only place I can think," she once told me. Sometimes she went just to sit. Sometimes she went to pay her respects to near strangers. Often we went together and sat on the smooth hot stones, worn down by praying hands, and we spread between us a picnic.

My mother wrote obituaries for the *Chicago Tribune.* Most of the time, she sat at a phone and took down the information for the cheapest obituaries, the ones that were published in tiny black print, like classifieds: PALERMO, of Arlington, July 13, 1970. Antonietta (Rizzo), beloved wife of the late Sebastian Palermo, devoted mother of Rita Fritzski and Anthony Palermo. Funeral from the Della Rosso Funeral Home, 356 South Main St., Chicago, Monday at 9 A.M., followed by a funeral Mass celebrated in Our Lady of the Immaculate Conception Church, Chicago. Friends and relatives are respectfully invited to attend. Interment Highland Memorial Cemetery, Riverdale.

My mother took dozens of these calls every day, and she told me over and over again how she never failed to be surprised by the number of deaths in Chicago. She would come home and reel off the names of the deceased to me, which she had a knack for remembering the way some people have a thing for telephone numbers. She never went to the cemetery to see these people—the "classifieds"—at least not intentionally. But from time to time her editor let her write one of the real obituaries, the ones for semifamous people, set in skinny columns like news articles. HERBERT R. QUASHNER, the headline would read. WAS ARMY LAB FOREMAN. My mother liked doing those best. "You get to tell a story," she'd say. "This guy used to be a member of the Destroyer Escort Sailors Association. He was in World War II, on a submarine chaser. He belonged to the Elks."

My mother wrote these obituaries at home, sitting at the kitchen table. She used to complain about deadlines, which she said was pretty funny, given her business. When the articles were printed, she clipped them neatly and stored them in a photo album. I used to wonder what would happen to that album if we all died in a fire; whether the police would think my mother had been a sick serial killer. But my mother insisted on keeping a record of her work, which she left behind, anyway, the day she disappeared.

My mother would make a weekly list of the important names she wrote about. Then on Saturday, her day off, we'd go to the closest cemeteries, looking for the freshly turned earth that marked the new-est interments. My mother would kneel in front of the graves of these people she hardly knew, still without headstones. She would sift the fine brown dirt through her fingers like a sieve. "Paige," she'd say, throwing back her shoulders, "take a deep breath. What can you smell?"

I would look around and see the lilac bushes and the forsythia, but I wouldn't take a deep breath. There was something about being in the cemetery that made me monitor my breathing, as if without warning I might find that I'd run out of air.

Once, my mother and I sat under the red shade of a Japanese maple, having visited the former Mary T. French, a public librarian. We had eaten barbecued chicken and potato salad and had wiped our fingers on our skirts, devil-may-care. Then my mother had stretched out across an old grassy grave, resting her head on a flat marker. She patted her thighs, encouraging me to lie down as well.

"You're going to crush him," I said, very serious, and my mother obligingly moved to the side. I sat down beside her and put my head in her lap and let the sun wash over my closed eyes and my smile.

My mother's skirt blew about, whipping the edge of my neck. "Mommy," I said, "where do you go when you're dead?"

My mother took a deep breath, one that made her body puff like a cushion. "I don't know, Paige," she said. "Where do you think you go?"

I ran my hand over the cool grass to my right. "Maybe they're all underground, looking up at us."

"Maybe they're in heaven, looking down," my mother said.

I opened my eyes and stared at the sun until bursts of color exploded, orange and yellow and red, like fireworks. "What's heaven like?" I said.

My mother had rolled to her side, sliding me off her lap. "After sticking out life," she had said, "I hope it's whatever you want it to be."

It struck me as I moved through this Cambridge graveyard that my own mother could be in heaven now. If there was a heaven; if she had died. I wondered if she was buried in a state where it never snowed, if she was in a different country. I wondered who came to lay lilies at her grave and who had commissioned the inscription. I wondered if her obituary would mention that she was the devoted mother of Paige O'Toole.

I used to ask my father why my mother left, and he told me over and over the same thing: "Because she wanted to." As the years went by he said it with less bitterness, but that didn't make the words any easier to believe. The mother I imagined over the years, the one with the shy smile and the full skirts, who had the power to heal scrapes and bruises with a kiss and who could tell bedtime stories like Scheherazade, would not have left. I liked to think my mother was pulled away by forces greater than herself. Maybe it was some international intrigue she was involved in, and the final chapter meant trading her own identity to protect her family. For a time I wondered if she was half of a pair of fated lovers, and I almost forgave her running from my father if it meant being with the man who held her heart. Maybe she was just restless. Maybe she was looking for someone she had lost.

I ran my hands over the smooth graves, trying to picture the face of my mother. Finally, I came to a flat marker, and I lay down with my head upon it, crossing my hands over the life in my belly, staring at the ice in the sky. I stretched out on the frozen ground until it seeped into my bones: the rain, the cold, these ghosts.

≈≈≈

More than anything else in the world, my mother had hated opening the refrigerator and finding the juice pitcher empty. It was always my father's fault; I was too little to pour for myself. It wasn't as though my father did it on purpose. His mind was usually on other things, and since it wasn't a priority, he never checked to see how low the lemonade was when he stuck it back inside the Frigidaire. Three times a week, at least, I would find my mother standing in the slice of cold air from the open refrigerator, waving the blue juice pitcher. "What is so damned difficult about mixing a can of frozen Minute Maid?" she would yell. She'd stare at me. "What am I supposed to do with a half inch of juice?"

It was a simple little mistake, which she fashioned into a crisis, and if I had been older I might have suspected the larger illness for the symptoms, but as it happened I was five, and I didn't know any better. I'd follow her as she tramped down the stairs to accost my father in his workshop, brandishing the pitcher and crying and asking nobody in particular what she had done to deserve a life like this.

The year that I was five was the first time I was truly conscious of Mother's Day. I had made cards before, sure, and I suppose I even had my name tacked onto a present that my dad had bought. But that year I wanted to do something that was straight from the heart. My father suggested making a painting, or a box of homemade fudge, but that wasn't the kind of gift I wanted to give. Those other things might have made my mother smile, but even at five I knew that what she really needed was something to take the ragged edge off the pain.

I also knew I had an ace up my sleeve—a father who could make anything my mind conjured up. I sat on the old couch in his workshop one night late in April, my knees folded up, my chin resting on them. "Daddy," I said, "I need your help." My father had been gluing rubber paddles onto a cogwheel for some contraption that measured chicken feed. He stopped immediately and faced me, giving me his complete attention. He nodded slowly while I explained my idea—an invention that would register when the lemonade in the pitcher needed to be refilled.

My father leaned forward and held both my hands. "Are you sure that's the kind of thing your mother would be wantin'?" he asked. "Not a handsome sweater, or some perfume?"

I shook my head. "I think she wants something . . ." My voice trailed off as I struggled to pick the right words. "She wants something to make her stop hurting."

My father looked at me so intently that I thought he was expecting me to say more. But he squeezed my hands and tipped his head closer, so our brows were touching. When he spoke, I could smell his sweet breath, laced with the flavor of Wrigley's gum. "So," he said, "you've been seein' it too."

Then he sat on the couch beside me and pulled me onto his lap. He smiled, and it was so contagious I could feel my legs already bouncing up and down. "I'm thinkin' of a sensor," he said, "with some kind of alarm."

"Oh, Daddy, yes!" I agreed. "One that keeps ringing and ringing and won't let you get away with just sticking the pitcher back."

My father laughed. "I've never invented something before that will mean *more* work for me." He cupped my face in his palms. "But it's worth it," he said. "Aye, well worth it."

My father and I worked for two weeks in a row, from right after dinner until my bedtime. We'd run to the workshop and try out buzzers and alarms, electronic sensors and microchips that reacted to degrees of wetness. My mother would knock from time to time on the door that led to the basement. "What are you two doing?" she'd call. "It's lonely up here."

"We're making a Frankenstein monster," I'd cry out, pronouncing the long, strange word the way my father had told me to. My father would start banging hammers and wrenches around on the workbench, making an awful racket. "It's an unsightly mess down here,

May," he'd yell, laughter threaded through his voice like a gold filament. "Brains and blood and gore. You wouldn't want to see this."

She must have known. After all, she never *did* come down, in spite of her gentle threats. My mother was like a child in that respect. She never peeked early for her Christmas presents or tried to eavesdrop on conversations that would give her a hint. She loved a surprise. She would never spoil a surprise.

We finished the juice sensor the night before Mother's Day. My father filled a water glass and dipped in the thin silver stick and then slowly suctioned away the liquid. When less than an inch was left in the bottom of the glass, the stick began to beep. It was a high, shrill note—downright annoying—since we figured you'd need that kind of prodding to force you to replace the juice. It didn't stop until the water was refilled. And just for desperate measure, the top of the stick glowed blood red the whole time it was beeping, casting shadows on my fingers and my father's as we clutched the rim of the glass.

"This is perfect," I whispered. "This will fix everything." I tried to remember a time when, every day at four o'clock, my mother had not been chased into the bedroom by her own shadow. I tried to remember weeks when I had not caught her staring at the closed front door as if she was expecting Saint Peter.

My father's voice startled me. "At the very least," he said, "this will be a beginning."

My mother went out after Mass that Sunday, but we barely noticed. The minute she was out the door, we were pulling the fine linen and the fancy china from the closets, setting a table that wept with celebration. By six o'clock, the roast my father had made was wading in its own gravy; the green beans were steaming; the juice pitcher was full.

At six-thirty, I was squirming in my chair. "I'm hungry, Daddy," I said. At seven, my father let me lie down in the living room to watch TV. As I left, I saw him rest his elbows on the table and bury his face in his hands. By eight, he had removed all traces of the meal, even the ribboned package we'd set on my mother's chair.

He brought me a plate of beef, but I was not hungry. The television was on, but I'd rolled over on the couch so that my head was buried in the pillows. "We had a present and everything," I said when my father touched my shoulder.

"She's at her friend's place," he said, and I turned to look up at him. My mother, to my knowledge, had no friends. "She just called to tell me she was sorry she couldn't make it, and she asked me to kiss the most beautiful lass in Chicago good night for her."

I stared at my father, who had never in my life lied to me. We both knew that the telephone had not rung all day.

My father bathed me and combed through my tangled hair and pulled a nightgown over my head. He tucked me in and sat with me until he thought I had fallen asleep.

But I stayed awake. I knew the exact moment when my mother walked through the door. I heard my father's voice asking where the hell she had been. "It's not like I disappeared," my mother argued, her words angrier and louder than my father's. "I just needed to be by myself for a little while."

I thought there might be yelling, but instead I heard the rustle of paper as my father gave my mother her present. I listened to the paper tear, and then to the sharp gasp of my mother drawing in her breath as she read the Mother's Day card I'd dictated to my father. *This is so we won't forget,* it read. *Love, Patrick. Love, Paige.*

I knew even before I heard her footsteps that she was coming to me. She threw open the door of my room, and in the silhouetted light of the hall I could see her trembling. "It's okay," I told her, although it was not what I had wanted or planned to say. She crouched down at the foot of the bed as if she were awaiting a sentence. Unsure what to do, I just watched her for a moment. Her head was bowed, as though she was praying. I stayed perfectly still until I couldn't do it anymore, and then I did what I wanted *her* to do: I put my arms around my mother and held her like I couldn't for the life of me let go.

My father came to stand at the door. He caught my eye as I looked up over my mother's dark, bent head. He tried to smile at me, but he couldn't quite do it. Instead he moved closer to where I held my mother. He rested his cool hand on the back of my neck, just as Jesus did in those pictures where He was healing the crippled and the blind. He kept his hold on me, as though he really thought that might make it hurt any less.

≈≈≈

When I was little, my father wanted me to call him Da, like every little girl in Ireland. But I had grown up American, calling him Daddy and then Dad when I got older. I wondered what my child would call Nicholas, would call me. This is what I was thinking about when I called my father—ironically, from the same underground pay phone I had first used when I got to Cambridge. The bus station was cold, deserted. "Da," I said, on purpose, "I miss you."

My father's voice changed, the way it always did when he realized it was me on the phone. "Paige, lass," he said. "Twice in one week! There must be some occasion."

I wondered why it was so hard to say. I wondered why I hadn't told him before. "I'm having a baby," I said.

"A baby?" My father's grin filled the spaces between his words. "A grandchild. Well, now, that *is* an occasion."

"I'm due in May," I said. "Right around Mother's Day."

My father barely skipped a beat. "That's fittin'," he said. He laughed, deep. "I take it you've known for a while," he said, "or else I did a poor job teachin' you the birds and the bees."

"I've known," I admitted. "I just figured—I don't know—I'd have more time." I had a crazy impulse to tell him everything I'd carefully hidden for years; the circumstances I sensed he knew about anyway. The words were right there at the back of my throat, so deceptively casual: *You remember that night I left your home?* I swallowed hard and forced my mind into the present. "I guess I'm still getting used to the idea myself," I said. "Nicholas and I didn't expect this, and, well, he's thrilled, but I . . . I just need a little more time."

Miles away, my father exhaled slowly, as if he were remembering, out of the blue, everything I hadn't had the courage to say. "Don't we all," he sighed.

≈≈≈

By the time I reached the neighborhood where Nicholas and I lived, the sun had set. I moved through the streets, quiet as a cat. I peeked into the lit windows of town houses and tried to catch the warmth and the dinnertime smell that they held. Because I misjudged my size, I slipped against a hedge and fell flush against a mailbox, which was lolling open like a blackened tongue. On the top of a pile of letters was a pink envelope with no return address. It was made out to Alexander LaRue, 20 Appleton Lane, Cambridge. The handwriting was sloped and gentle, somewhat European. Without a second thought, I looked up and down the street and tucked the letter into my coat.

I had committed a federal offense. I did not know Alexander LaRue, and I did not plan to give him back his letter. My heart pounded as I walked as quickly as possible down the block; my face flushed scarlet. What was I doing?

I flew up the porch steps and slammed the door behind me, locking both locks. I shrugged off my coat and pulled off my boots. My heart choked at the back of my throat. With trembling fingers, I slit the envelope open. There was the same sloped hand, the same spiked letters. The paper was a torn corner from a grocery bag. *Dear Alexander,* it read, *I have been dreaming of you. Trish.* That was all. I read the note over and over again, checking the edges and the back to make sure that I hadn't missed anything. Who was Alexander? And Trish? I ran up to the bedroom and stuffed the letter into a box of maxipads in the bottom of my closet. I thought about the kinds of dreams Trish might be having. Maybe she closed her eyes and saw Alexander's hands running over her hips, her thighs. Maybe she remembered their sitting on the edge of a riverbank, shoes and socks off, feet blurred in the water by a frigid rushing stream. Maybe Alexander had also been dreaming of her.

"There you are."

I jumped when Nicholas came in. I raised my hand, and he looped his tie around my wrist and knelt on the edge of the bed to kiss me. "Barefoot and pregnant," he said, "just the way I like 'em."

I struggled into a sitting position. "And how was your day?" I asked.

Nicholas's voice came to me from the bathroom, interrupted by the splash of the faucet. "Come and talk to me," he said, and I heard the shower being turned on.

I went to sit on the toilet lid, feeling the steam curl my hair over the back of my neck where it had fallen from my ponytail. My shirt, too tight at the bust, misted and clung to my stomach. I considered telling Nicholas what I had done that day, about the cemetery, about Trish and Alexander. But before I could even run through my thoughts, Nicholas turned off the water and pulled his towel into the stall. He knotted it around his hips and stepped out of the shower, leaving the bathroom in a cloud of fresh steam.

I followed Nicholas and watched him part his hair in the mirror over my dresser, using my brush and stooping so that he could see his face. "Come over here," he said, and he reached behind him for my hand, still holding my eyes with his reflection.

He sat me down on a corner of the bed, and he pulled the barrette from my hair. With the brush, he began to make slow, lazy strokes from my scalp to my shoulders, fanning my hair from the nape of my neck to spread like silk. I tilted my head back and closed my eyes, letting the brush catch through damp tangles and feeling Nicholas's quiet hand smoothing the static electricity away a moment later. "It feels good," I said, my voice thick and unfamiliar.

I was vaguely aware of my clothes being pulled away, of being pushed back on the cold quilted comforter. Nicholas kept running his hands through my hair. I felt light, I felt supple. Without those hands weighing me down, I was certain I could float away.

Nicholas moved over me and came inside in one quick stroke, and my eyes flashed open with a white streak of pain. "No," I screamed, and Nicholas tensed and pulled away from me.

"What?" he said, his eyes still hooded and wild. "Is it the baby?"

"I don't know," I murmured, and I didn't. I just knew there was a barrier where there hadn't been one days ago; that when Nicholas had entered me I felt resistance, as if something was willing him out just as strongly as he wanted himself in. I met his eyes shyly. "I don't think it's all right—that way—anymore."

Nicholas nodded, his jaw clenched. A pulse beat at the base of his neck, and I watched it for a moment while he regained control of himself. I pulled the comforter over the swell of my stomach, feeling guilty. I never meant to scream. "Of course," Nicholas said, his thoughts a million miles away. He turned and left the room.

I sat in the dark, wondering what I had done wrong. Groping across the bed, I found Nicholas's discarded button-down shirt, glowing almost silver. I pulled it over my head and rolled up the sleeves, and I slipped underneath the covers. From the nightstand I pulled a travel brochure, and I flicked on a reading light.

Downstairs, I heard the refrigerator being opened and slammed shut; a heavy footstep and a quiet curse. I read aloud, my voice swelling to fill the cold spaces of the colorless room. " 'The Land of the Masai,' " I said. " 'The Masai of Tanzania have one of the last cultures on earth unaffected by modern civilization. Imagine the life of a Masai woman living much as her ancestors did thousands of years ago, dwelling in the same mud-and-dung huts, drinking sour milk mixed with cow's blood. Initiation rites, such as the circumcision of adolescent boys and girls, continue today.' "

I closed my eyes; I knew the rest by memory. " 'The Masai exist in harmony with their peaceful environment, with daily and seasonal cycles of nature, with their reverence for God.' " The moon rose and spilled yellow into the bedroom window, and I could clearly see her —the Masai woman, kneeling at the foot of my bed, her skin dark and gleaming, her eyes like polished onyx, gold hoops ringing her ears and her neck. She stared at me and stole all my secrets; she opened her mouth and she sang of the world.

Her voice was low and rhythmic, a tune I had never heard. With each tremble of her music, my stomach seemed to quiver. Her call said over and over, in a clicking honey tongue, *Come with me. Come with me.* I held my hands to my belly, sensing that quick flutter of longing, like a firefly in a sealed glass jar. And then I realized these were the first felt movements of my baby, reminding me just why I couldn't go.

chapter 11
Paige

To my disappointment, Jake Flanagan became the brother I had never had. He did not kiss me again after that lost moment at the drive-in. Instead he took me under his wing. For three years he let me tag along right at his heels, but to me even that was too far away. I wanted to be closer to his heart.

I tried to make Jake fall in love with me. I prayed for this at least three times a day, and once in a while I was rewarded. Sometimes, after the final bell of classes rang, I'd come out onto the steps of Pope Pius and find him leaning against the stone wall, biting on a toothpick. I knew that to get to my school, he had to cut his last class and take an uptown bus. "Hello, Flea," he said, because that was his nickname for me. "And what did the good sisters teach you today?"

As if he did this all the time, he would take my books from my arms and lead me down the street, and together we'd walk to his father's garage. Terence Flanagan owned the Mobil station on North

Franklin, and Jake worked there for him afternoons and on weekends. I would squat on the cement floor, my pleated skirt blown open like a flower, while Jake showed me how to remove a tire or how to change the oil. All the while he spoke in the soft, cool voice that reminded me of the ocean I had never seen. "First you pop the hubcap," he'd say, as his hands slid down the tire iron. "Then you loosen up the lug nuts." I would nod and watch him carefully, wondering what I had to do to make him notice me.

I spent months walking a fine line, arranging for my path to cross Jake's a few times a week without my becoming a pain in the neck. Once, I had got too close. "I can't get rid of you," Jake had yelled. "You're like a rash." And I had gone home and cried and given Jake a week to realize how empty his life could be without me. When he didn't call, I did not blame him; I couldn't. I showed up at the Mobil station as if nothing had happened, and I doggedly followed him from car to car, learning about spark plugs and alternators and steering alignment.

By then I knew that this was my first trial of faith. I had grown up learning of the sacrifices and ordeals others had survived to prove their devotion—Abraham, Job, Jesus Himself. I understood that I was being tested, but I had no doubts about the outcome. I would pay my dues, and then one day Jake would be unable to live without me. I swore by this, and because I had given God no alternative, it gradually became true.

But being Jake's sidekick was a far cry from being the love of his life. In fact, Jake went out with a different girl every month. I helped him get ready for his dates. I'd lie on my stomach on the narrow bed as Jake picked out three shirts, two ties, worn jeans. "Wear the red one," I'd tell him, "and definitely *not* that tie." I covered my face with a pillow when he dropped the towel from his hips and shrugged into his boxer shorts, and I listened to the slip of cotton over his legs and wondered what he would look like. He let me part his hair with the comb and pat the aftershave on his burning cheeks, so that when he left I would still be surrounded by the strong scent of mint and of man that came from Jake's skin.

Jake was always late for his dates. He'd tunnel down the stairs of his house, grabbing the keys to his father's Ford from the pegged knot on the end of the banister. "See you, Flea," he'd call over his shoulder. His mother would come out of the kitchen with three or four of the younger kids hanging on her legs like monkeys, but she would only just catch the edge of his shadow. Molly Flanagan would turn to me with her heart in her eyes, because she knew the truth. "Oh, Paige," she'd say, sighing. "Why don't you stay for dinner?"

When Jake came home from his dates at two or three in the morning, I always knew. I would wake up, miles away from where he was, and see, like a nightmare, Jake pulling his shirt from his jeans and rubbing the back of his neck. We had this connection with each other. Sometimes, if I wanted to talk to him, all I had to do was picture his face, and within a half hour he'd be on my doorstep. "What?" he'd say. "You needed me?" Sometimes, because I felt him calling out, I would phone his house late at night. I'd huddle in the kitchen, curling my bare toes under the hem of my nightgown, dialing in the pencil-thin gleam of the streetlight. Jake answered at the end of the first ring. "Wait till you hear this one," he'd say, his voice bubbling over with the fading heat of sex. "We're at Burger King, and she reaches under the table and unzips my fly. Can you believe it?"

And I would swallow. "No," I'd tell him. "I can't."

I had no doubt that Jake loved me. He told me, when I asked him, that I was his best friend; he sat with me the whole summer I had mononucleosis and read me trivia questions from those *Yes & No* game books that come with magic pens. One night, over a campfire on the shores of the lake, he had even let me cut his thumb and press it close to mine, swapping blood, so that we'd always have each other.

But Jake shrank away from my touch. Even if I brushed his side, he flinched as if I'd hit him. He never put his arm around my shoulders; he never even held my hand. At sixteen, I was skinny and small, like the runt of a litter. Someone like Jake, I told myself, would never want someone like me.

The year I turned seventeen, things began to change. I was a junior at Pope Pius; Jake—out of high school for two years—worked full time with his father at the garage. I spent my afternoons and my weekends with Jake, but every time I saw him my head burned and my stomach roiled, as if I'd swallowed the sun. Sometimes Jake would turn my way and start to speak: "Flea," he'd say, but his eyes would cloud over, and the rest of the words wouldn't come.

It was the year of my junior prom. The sisters at Pope Pius decorated the gymnasium with hanging foil stars and crinkled red streamers. I was not planning to go. If I had asked Jake he would have taken me, but I hated the thought of spending a night I had dreamed of for years with him humoring me. Instead I watched the other girls in the neighborhood take pictures on their front lawns, whirling ghosts in white and pink tulle. When they had left, I walked the three miles to Jake's house.

Molly Flanagan saw me through the screen door. "Come in, Paige," she yelled. "Jake said you would be here." She was in the den, playing Twister with Moira and Petey, the two youngest Flanagans. Her rear end was lifted into the air, and her arms were crossed beneath her. Her heavy bosom grazed the colored dots of the game mat, and between her legs, Moira was precariously reaching for a green corner circle. Ever since I had met her three years before, I had wanted Molly as my own mother. I had told Jake and his family that my mother had died and that my father was still so upset by it, he couldn't bear to hear her name brought up. Molly Flanagan had patted my arm, and Terence had raised his beer to toast my mother, as was the custom of the Irish. Only Jake realized I was not telling the truth. I had never actually come out and said this, but he knew the corners of my mind so well that from time to time I caught him staring at me, as if he sensed I was holding something back.

"*Flea!*" Jake's voice cut through the romping music of the television, startling Moira, who fell and caught her mother's ankle, pulling her down as well.

"Jake thinks he's the king of England," Molly said, lifting her youngest daughter.

I smiled and ran up the stairs. Jake was bent over in his closet, looking for something in the mess of socks and sneakers and dirty underwear. "Hi," I said.

He did not turn around. "Where's my good belt?" he asked, the simple question you'd put to a wife or a longtime lover.

I reached under his arm, tugging the belt from the peg where he'd placed it days before. Jake began to thread the leather through his khaki slacks. "When you go to college," he said, "I'm going to be lost."

I knew as he said it that I would never go to college, never even draw another picture, if Jake asked me to stay. When he turned to me, my throat ached and my vision grew blurry. I shook my head and saw that he was dressed for a date; that his grease-spotted jeans and blue work shirt were puddled in a corner under the window. I turned away fast so that he wouldn't see my eyes. "I didn't know you were going out," I said.

Jake grinned. "Since when haven't I been able to get a Friday-night date?" he said.

He moved past me, and the air carried the familiar scent of his soap and his clothing. My head began to pound, surging like a tide, and I believed with all my heart that if I didn't leave that room I was going to die.

I turned and ran down the stairs. The door slammed behind me, and the wind picked up my feet for me. I heard the concern in Molly's voice reaching out, and the whole way home I felt Jake's eyes and their questions burning into my back.

At home, I pulled on my nightgown and fell into bed, drawing the covers over my head to change the fact that it was only dinnertime. I slept on and off, waking with a start just after two-thirty. Tiptoeing past my father's room, I closed the door, and then I went down to the kitchen. Feeling my way through the night, I unlocked the door and I opened the screen for Jake.

He held a dandelion in his hand. "This is for you," he said, and I stepped back, frustrated because I could not see his eyes.

"That's a weed," I told him.

He came closer and pressed the wilted stem into my hand. As

our palms touched, the fire in my stomach leaped higher to burn my throat and the dry backs of my eyes. This was like being on a roller coaster, like falling off the edge of a cliff. It took me a second to place the feeling—it was fear, overwhelming fear, like the moment you realize you've escaped a car accident by precious inches. Jake held my hand, and when I tried to pull away, he wouldn't let go.

"Tonight was your prom," he said.

"No kidding."

Jake stared at me. "I saw everyone coming home. I would have gone with you. You know I would have gone with you."

I lifted my chin. "It wouldn't have been the same."

Finally, Jake released me. I was shocked by how cold I became, just like that. "I came for a dance," he said.

I looked around the tiny kitchen, at the dishes still in the sink and the muted gleam of the white appliances. Jake pulled me toward him until we were touching at our palms, our shoulders, our hips, our chests. I could feel his breath on my cheek, and I wondered what was keeping me standing. "There isn't any music," I said.

"Then you aren't listening." Jake began to move with me, swaying back and forth. I closed my eyes and pressed my bare feet against the linoleum, craving the cold that came from the floor when the rest of me was being consumed by flames I could not see. I shook my head to clear my thoughts. This was what I wanted, wasn't it?

Jake let go of my hands and held my face in his palms. He stared at me and brushed his lips over mine, just as he had three years before at the drive-in, the kiss I had carried with me like a holy relic. I leaned against him, and he twisted his fingers into my hair, hurting me. He moved his tongue over my lips and into my mouth. I felt hungry. Something inside me was tearing apart, and at my core was something hot, hard and white. I wrapped my arms around Jake's neck, not knowing if I was doing this right, just understanding that if I did not have more, I would never forgive myself.

Jake was the one who pushed away. We stood inches apart, breathing hard. Then he picked up his jacket, which had fallen to the floor, and ran out of my house. He left me shivering, my arms wrapped tight around my chest, terrified of the power of myself.

≈≈≈

"My God," Jake said, when we were alone the next day. "I should have known it would be like this."

We were sitting on overturned milk crates behind his father's garage, listening to the hiss of flies sinking into puddles left from the rain. We were not even kissing. We were simply holding hands. But even that was a trial of faith. Jake's palm enveloped mine, and the pulse in his wrist adjusted to fit the rhythm of my own. I was afraid to move. If I even took too deep a breath, I would wind up as I had when I had run into his arms and kissed him hello—pressed too close for comfort, lips burning a trail down his neck, with that strange reaching feeling that started between my legs and shot into my belly. For the first time in three years I did not trust Jake. What was worse, I did not trust myself.

I had been brought up with stricter religious values than Jake, but we were both Catholic, and we both understood the consequences of sin. I had been taught that earthly pleasure was a sin. Sex was for making babies and was a sacrilege without the bond of marriage. I felt the swelling of my chest and my thighs, heavy with hot running blood, and I knew that these were the impure thoughts I had been warned of. I did not understand how something that felt so good could be so bad. I did not know who I could ask. But I could not help wanting to be closer to Jake, so close I might squeeze through him and come out on the other side.

Jake rubbed his thumb over mine and pointed to a rainbow coming up in the east. I was itching to draw this feeling: Jake, me, protected by the bleeding strands of violet and orange and indigo. I remembered my First Communion, when the priest had put the dry little wafer on my tongue. "The body of Christ," he had said, and I dutifully repeated, "Amen." Afterward I had asked Sister Elysia if the Host really *was* the body of Christ, and she had told me it would be if I believed hard enough. She said how lucky I was to take His body into my own, and for that precious sunny day I had walked with my arms outstretched, convinced that God was with me.

Jake put his arm around my shoulder——creating a whole new flood of sensations——and wrapped his fingers in my hair. "I can't work," he said. "I can't sleep. I can't eat." He rubbed his upper lip. "You're driving me crazy," he said.

I nodded; I couldn't find my voice. So I leaned into his neck and kissed the hollow under his ear. Jake groaned and pushed me off the milk crate so that I was lying in the wet crabgrass, and he brutally crushed his mouth against mine. His hand slipped from my neck to my cotton blouse, coming to rest under my breast. I could feel his knuckles against the curve of my flesh, his fingers flexing and clenching, as if he was trying to exercise control. "Let's get married," he said.

It was not his words that shocked me; it was the realization that I was in over my head. Jake was all I had ever wanted, but I could see now that this fever inside me was just going to grow stronger and stronger. The only way I'd be able to put it out would be to give myself completely away——unraveling my secrets and baring my pain ——and I did not think I could do that. If I kept seeing Jake I would be consumed by this fire; surely I would touch him and keep touching him until I couldn't go back.

"We can't get married," I said, pushing away from him. "I'm only seventeen." I turned my face up to his, but all I saw in his eyes was a distorted reflection of myself. "I don't think I can see you anymore," I said, my voice breaking over the syllables.

I stood up, but Jake still held my hand. I felt the panic building in me, bubbling up and threatening to spill. "Paige," he said, "we'll go slowly. I know you better than you know yourself. I know you want what I want."

"Really?" I whispered, angry that my self-control was slipping away and that he was probably right. "What, exactly, Jake, do you want?"

Jake stood up. "I want to know what you see when you look at me." His fingers dug into my shoulders. "I want to know your favorite

Stooge and the hour you were born and the thing that scares you more than anything else in the world. I want to know," he said, "what you look like when you fall asleep." He traced the line of my chin with his finger. "I want to be there when you wake up."

For a moment I saw the life I might have, wrapped in the laughter of his big family, writing my name beside his in the old family Bible, watching him leave in the morning. I saw all these things I had wished for my whole life, but the images made me tremble. It wasn't meant to be; I didn't know the first thing about fitting into such a normal, solid scene. "You aren't safe anymore," I whispered.

Jake looked at me as if he were seeing me for the first time. "Neither are you," he said.

≈≈≈

That night, I learned the truth about my parents' marriage. My father was working in the basement when I came home, still restless and thinking of Jake's hands. He was bent over his sawhorse worktable, screwing a plastic fitting onto the back of his Medicine Pacifier, which, when finished, would be able to dispense controlled amounts of baby Tylenol and Triaminic.

My father had been everything to me for so long that it did not seem unnatural to ask him questions about falling in love. I was less embarrassed than I was afraid, since I figured he'd think I was speaking up out of guilt and send me off to confession. For a few minutes I watched him, taking in his light-brown hair and the whiskey color of his eyes, his capable, shaping hands. I had always thought I'd fall in love with someone like my father, but he and Jake were very different. Unless you counted the little things—the way they both let me cheat at gin rummy so I could win; the way they carefully weighed my words as if I were the Secretary of State; the fact that when I was miserable, they were the only two people in the world who could make me forget. In my whole life, only when I was with my father or with Jake was I able to believe, as they did, that I was the finest girl in the world.

"How did you know," I asked my father without any preliminary conversation, "that you were going to marry my mother?"

My father did not look up at me, but he sighed. "I was engaged to somebody else at the time. Her name was Patty—Patty Connelly —and she was the daughter of my parents' best friends. We all came over to the United States from County Donegal when I was five. Patty and I grew up together—you know, all-American kids. We went swimming naked in those little summer pools, and we got the chicken pox at the same time, and I took her to all our high-school proms. It was expected, Patty and me, you see."

I came to stand beside him, pulling a length of black electrical tape when he gestured for it. "What about Mom?" I said.

"A month before the wedding, I woke up and asked what in the name of heaven I was doing, throwing my life away. I didn't love Patty, and I called her and told her the wedding was off. And three hours later she called me back to let me know she'd swallowed about thirty sleeping pills."

My father sat down on the dusty green sofa. "Quite a turn of the cards, eh, lass?" he said, slipping into the comfort of his brogue. "I had to drive her to the hospital. I waited around until they were done pumping her stomach, and then I turned her over to her parents." My father rested his head in his hands. "Anyway, I went to a diner across the street from the hospital, and there was your mother. Sitting on one of the counter stools she was, and she had cherry Danish all over her fingers. She had on this little red-checked halter top and white shorts. I don't know, Paige, I can't really explain it, but she turned around when I came in, and the second our eyes connected, it was like the world just disappeared."

I closed my eyes, trying to picture this. I did not believe it was one hundred percent true. After all, I had not heard my mother's side of the story. "And then what?" I said.

"And then we got married in three months. It wasn't the easiest thing for your mother. Some of my old deaf aunts called her Patty at the wedding. She got china and crystal and silver picked out by Patty, because people had already bought the gifts when the first wedding was called off."

My father stood and went back to the pacifier. I stared at his back and remembered that on holidays, when my mother served with the rose-wreathed dishes and the gold-leaf goblets, she would get tight-lipped and uncomfortable. I started to wonder what it might have felt like to live your life in a place someone else had carved. I wondered if, had our china been blue-rimmed or geometric, she might have never left.

"And what," I said, "ever happened to Patty?"

≈≈≈

Late that night, I felt my father's breath at my temple. He was leaning over me, watching me sleep. "This is only the beginning," he said to me. "I know it isn't what you want to hear, but he isn't the one you'll be with for the rest of your life."

I heard his words still twisting in the air long after he'd left my room, and I wondered how he had known. A stale wind blew through my open window; I could smell rain. I stood up quickly and dressed in yesterday's clothes; I moved soundlessly down the stairs and out of the house. I did not have to look back to know that my father was watching me from his bedroom window, his palms pressed to the glass, his head bowed.

The first drops fell, heavy and cold, as I turned the corner away from my home. By the time I was halfway to the Flanagans' Mobil station, the wind shrieked through my hair and knotted my jacket around me. Rain battered my cheeks and my bare legs, so violent that I might not have found my way if I hadn't been going there for years.

Jake pulled me in from the storm and kissed my forehead, my eyelids, my wrists. He peeled the soaked coat from my shoulders and wrapped my hair in an old chamois. He did not ask why I had come; I did not ask why he had been there. We fell against the dented side of a Chevy sedan, skimming our hands over each other's faces to learn the hollows, the curves, and the lines.

Jake led me to a car waiting to be serviced, a Jeep Cherokee 4 × 4 with a broad open compartment in the back. Through the fishbowl rear window of the Jeep, we watched the storm. Jake pulled my shirt over my head and unfastened my bra, moved his tongue from one nipple to the other. He traced his way over my ribs, my stomach, unzipping my skirt and tugging it over my hips. I could feel the rough rug of the car against my legs, and Jake's hand on my breast, and then I felt the pressure of his lips against the thin film of my underpants. I shivered, amazed that his breath could burn hotter than the ache between my thighs.

When I was naked he knelt beside me and ran his hands over me, units of measure, as if I were something he owned. "You are beautiful," he said, as quiet as a prayer, and he leaned close to kiss me. He did not stop, not even as he undressed himself or stroked my hair or moved between my legs. I felt as if there were a thousand threads of glass woven in me, a million different colors, and they were stretched so tight that I knew they would snap. When Jake came inside me, my world turned white, but then I remembered to breathe and to move. At the moment when everything shattered, I opened my eyes wide. I did not think about Jake or about that quick sting of pain; I did not think about the heady scent of Marlboros and pomade that clung to the Jeep's interior. Instead I squinted into the frenzied night sky and I waited for God to strike me down.

chapter 12

Nicholas

The women lay on the blue industrial carpet like a string of little islands, their bellies swelling toward the ceiling and trembling slightly as they panted and exhaled. Nicholas was late for Lamaze class. In fact, although it was the seventh class in a series of ten, it was the first he'd attended, because of his schedule. But Paige had insisted. "You may know how to deliver a baby," she had said, "but there's a difference between a doctor and a labor coach."

And a father, Nicholas had thought, but he didn't say anything. Paige was nervous enough, whether or not she chose to admit it. She didn't need to know that every night so far during the third trimester, Nicholas had awakened, sheets soaked in sweat, worrying about this baby. It wasn't the labor; he could deliver a baby with his eyes closed, for Christ's sake. It was what happened afterward. He had never held an infant, except for his routine swing through pediatrics as an intern. He didn't know what you did to make them stop crying. He didn't

have the first idea how to make them burp. And he was worried about
what kind of father he would be—certainly absent more than he was
home. Of course Paige would be there day and night, which he far
preferred to the idea of day care—at least he thought he did. Nicholas
sometimes wondered about Paige, doubtful about the kinds of things
she might be able to teach a child when she herself knew so little
about the world. He had considered buying a stack of colorful
books—*How to Make Baby Talk, 101 Things to Stimulate Your Baby's
Mind, The* PARENTS' *Guide to Educational Toys*—but he knew Paige
would have taken offense. And Paige seemed so distressed about having the baby that he had vowed to stick to safe topics until she had
given birth. Nicholas gripped the edge of the doorway, watching the
Lamaze class, and wondered whether he had actually become ashamed
of his wife.

She was lying in the farthest corner of the room, her hair spilled
around her head, her hands resting on the huge round mound of her
stomach. She was the only person there without a mate, and as Nicholas crossed the room to join her, he felt a quick stab of remorse. He
sat behind her quietly as the nurse teaching the class came over to
shake his hand and offer him a name tag. NICHOLAS! it said, and in
the corner was a chubby, smiling cartoon baby.

The nurse clapped her hands twice, and Nicholas watched Paige's
eyes blink open. He knew from the way she smiled at him, upside
down, that she had not really been relaxing at all. She was faking it;
she'd known the very second he'd entered the room. "Welcome," she
whispered, "to Husband Guilt Class."

Nicholas leaned back against pillows he recognized from his own
bedroom, listening to the nurse recount the three stages of labor, and
what to expect during each one. He suppressed a yawn. She held up
plastic-coated pictures of the fetus, arms and legs crossed, its head
squeezing through the birth canal. A pert blond woman on the other
side of the room raised her hand. "Isn't it true," she asked, "that your
labor will probably be a lot like your mother's?"

The nurse frowned. "Every baby's different," she mused, "but
there does seem to be a correlation."

Nicholas felt Paige tense at his side. "Oh, well," she whispered. He suddenly remembered Paige as he'd seen her the night before when he came home from the hospital. She'd been sitting on the couch, wearing a sleeveless nightgown although it had been cold outside. She was crying, not even bothering to wipe the tears from her cheeks. He'd rushed to her side and taken her into his arms, asking over and over, "What is it?" and Paige, still sobbing, had pointed at the television, some insipid Kodak commercial. "I can't help it," she had said, her nose bubbling, her eyes swollen. "Sometimes this just happens."

"Nicholas?" the nurse said for the second time.

The other fathers-to-be were staring at him, smirking, and Paige was patting his hand. "Go ahead," she said. "It won't be so bad."

The nurse was holding up a padded white bowl-like thing crossed with straps and ties. "In honor of your first class," she said, helping Nicholas up from the floor. "The Sympathy Belly."

"For God's sake," he said.

"Now, Paige has been toting this around for seven months," the nurse scolded. "Surely you can make do for thirty minutes."

Nicholas shrugged into the armholes, glaring at the nurse. It was a thirty-four-pound contraption, a soft false belly whose insides sloshed from side to side unpredictably. When Nicholas shifted, a large ball bearing dug into his bladder. The nurse fastened the straps around his waist and shoulders. "Why don't you take a walk," she said.

Nicholas knew she was waiting for him to fall. He carefully raised and lowered his feet, undaunted by the shifting weight and the strain in his back. He turned back to the crowd, to Paige, triumphant. The nurse's voice came from behind him. "Run," she said.

Nicholas spread his legs wide and tried to move faster, half jogging, half hopping. Some of the women began to laugh, but Paige's face remained still. The nurse tossed a pen onto the floor. "Nicholas," she said, "if you wouldn't mind?"

Nicholas tried to ease toward the ground by bending his knees, but the liquid in the Sympathy Belly swished to the left, knocking off his sense of balance. He fell to the floor on his hands and knees, and he bowed his head.

Around him, laughter swelled, vibrating against his knees and ringing in his ears. He lifted his chin and rolled his eyes. He scanned the other husbands and wives, who were clapping now in response to his performance, and then his gaze fell on his wife.

Paige was sitting very quietly, not smiling, not clapping. A thin silver streak ran the length of her face, and even as he watched, her palm came up to wipe away the tear. She rocked until she was on her knees, then she heaved herself up to a standing position and came to Nicholas's side. "Nicholas has had a very long day," she said. "I think we've got to go."

Nicholas watched Paige unfasten the Sympathy Belly and slide it over his shoulders. The nurse took it from her before she could support the full weight. Nicholas smiled at the others as he followed Paige out the door, and followed her to her car. She wedged herself behind the steering wheel and closed her eyes as if she was in pain. "I hate seeing you like that," she whispered, and when she opened her eyes, clear and cerulean blue, she was staring right through her husband.

chapter 13

Paige

I gave birth in the middle of a class four hurricane. I was just at the end of my eighth month. All day long I had sat on the couch, weary from the sluggish heat, and listened to news reports of the coming storm. It was a freak weather pattern, a string of odd monsoon rains across the Northeast, coming three months too early. The weatherman told me to tape my windows and store water in the bathtub. Ordinarily I might have, but I did not have the energy.

Nicholas did not come home until midnight. The wind had already picked up, howling through the streets like a child in pain. He undressed in the bathroom and slipped into bed quietly so he wouldn't wake me, but I had been sleeping fitfully. I had a low, moaning backache, and I'd gotten up to pee three times. "I'm sorry," Nicholas said, seeing me stir.

"Don't worry," I told him, rolling myself into a sitting position. "I might as well hit the bathroom again."

As I stood, I felt drops of water at my feet, and I stupidly assumed it was the rain, somehow come inside.

Two hours later, I knew something was not quite right. My water had not broken, not the way they'd said it would in Lamaze class, but a thin trickle of fluid ran down my legs every time I sat up. "Nicholas," I said, my voice trembling, "I'm leaking."

Nicholas rolled over and pulled his pillow over his head. "It's probably a tear in the amniotic sac," he murmured. "You're a whole month early. Go back to sleep, Paige."

I grabbed the pillow and threw it across the room, fear ripping through me like the violence of winter. "I am not a patient, goddammit," I said. "I am your wife." And I leaned forward, starting to cry.

As I padded toward the bathroom again, a slow burn crept from my back around my belly and settled deep under my skin. It didn't hurt, not really, not yet, but I knew this was the thing the nurse at Lamaze could not describe—a contraction. I held on to the Corian counter and stared into the bathroom mirror. Another gripping knot shook me, hands deep inside me that seemed to be clutching from the inside, as if they would surely pull me into myself. It made me think of a science trick Sister Bertrice had done when I was in eleventh grade—she'd blown smoke into a Pepsi can until none of the oxygen was left and then capped the top with a rubber stopper, and when she lightly touched the side of the can it crumpled, collapsing just like that. "Nicholas," I whispered, "I need help."

While Nicholas was on the phone with my doctor's answering service, I started to pack a bag. It *was* an entire month before my due date. But even if it had been May, I knew I wouldn't have had a bag packed. That would have been admitting the inevitable, and right up till the last minute I did not truly believe that I was destined to be a mother.

Lamaze class had taught me that early labor lasted for six to twelve hours; that contractions started irregularly and happened hours apart. Lamaze had taught me that if I breathed the right way, *in*-two-three-four, *out*-two-three-four, and pictured a clean white beach, I could surely control the pain. But my labor had come out of nowhere. My contractions were less than five minutes apart. And nothing, not even the previous contraction, could prepare me for the pain of the next one.

Nicholas stuffed my bathrobe, two T-shirts, my shampoo, and his toothbrush into a brown paper grocery bag. He knelt beside me on the bathroom floor. "Jesus Christ," he said, "you're only three minutes apart."

Oh, it hurt, and I couldn't get comfortable in the car, and I had started bleeding, and with every grasp of the fist inside me I gripped Nicholas's hand. The rain whipped around the car, screaming as loud as I did. Nicholas turned on the radio and sang to me, making up words to the songs he did not know. He leaned out the window at the empty intersections, yelling, "My wife's in labor!" and drove like a madman through the blinking red lights.

At Brigham and Women's Hospital, he parked in a fire zone and helped me out of the car. He was cursing about the weather, the condition of the roads, the fact that Mass General had no maternity ward. The rain was a sheet, soaking through my clothes and plastering them to me, so that I could clearly see every tightening of my belly. He pulled me into the emergency admitting area, where a fat black woman sat picking her teeth. "She's preregistered," he barked. "Prescott. Paige."

I could not see the woman. I twisted in a plastic seat, wrapping my arms around my abdomen. Suddenly a face loomed—hers—round and dark, with yellow tiger eyes. "Honey," she said, "do you have to push?"

I couldn't speak, so I nodded my head, and she jumped to attention, demanding a wheelchair and an orderly. Nicholas seemed to relax. I was brought into one of the older labor and delivery suites. "What about those modern rooms," Nicholas demanded. "The ones with nice drapes and bedspreads and all that?"

I could have given birth in a cave on a bed of pine needles; I did not care. "I'm sorry, Doctor," the orderly said, "we're full up. Something about the atmospheric pressure of a hurricane makes women's waters break."

Within minutes, Nicholas stood to the right of me, a labor nurse to my left. Her name was Noreen, and I trusted her more than my own husband, who had saved the lives of hundreds. She rustled the sheet between my legs. "You're ten centimeters," she said. "It's show time."

She stepped out of the room, leaving me alone with Nicholas. My eyes followed the door. "It's okay, Paige. She's going to get Dr. Thayer." Nicholas put his hand on my knee and gently massaged the muscles. I could hear the steady rasp of my breathing, the hot pulse of my blood. I turned to Nicholas, and with the clarity and clairvoyance that pain brings, I realized I did not know this man at all and that the worst was yet to come. "Don't you touch me," I whispered.

Nicholas jumped away, and I looked into his eyes. They were ringed gray, surprised and hurt. For the first time in my life, I found myself thinking, *Well, good.*

Dr. Thayer blustered into the room, her scrubs flying untied behind her. "So you couldn't wait another month, Paige, eh?"

She squatted down in front of me, and I was vaguely aware of her fingers probing and flattening and stretching. I wanted to tell her I *could* wait, that I had been willing to wait the rest of my life rather than actually face this child, but suddenly that was not the truth. Suddenly I just wanted to be free of the throbbing weight, the splitting pain.

Nicholas braced one of my legs and Noreen braced the other while I pushed. I felt for sure I would crack in two. Noreen held a mirror between my legs. "Here's the head, Paige," she said. "Do you want to feel it?"

She took my hand and stretched it downward, but I pulled away. "I want you to get it out of me," I cried.

I pushed and pushed, knowing all the blood in my body was flooding my face, burning behind my eyes and my cheeks. Finally, I sank back against the raised table. "I can't," I whimpered. "I really can't do this."

Nicholas leaned close to me to whisper something, but what I heard was the muffled conversation between Noreen and Dr. Thayer.

Something about a special care team, about the baby not coming fast enough now. Then I remembered the books I had read when I was first pregnant. The lungs. At the end of the eighth month, the lungs have just finished development.

Even if he ever got here, my baby might not be able to breathe.

"One more time," Dr. Thayer said, and I struggled up and bore down with all the energy I could summon. Quite clearly I could feel the nose, a tiny pointed nose, pressed against the tight seal of my own flesh. *Get out,* I thought, and Dr. Thayer smiled up at me. "We've got the head," she said.

After that it all came easily: the shoulders and the thick purple umbilical cord, the long skinny creature that lay, howling, between my legs. It was a boy. In spite of what I knew, I had hoped till this last moment that I would be having a girl. For some reason it still came as a shock. I stared at him, unfolded, wondering how he had ever fit inside. Doctors took him away from me, and Nicholas, who was one of them, followed.

It was at least a half hour before I got to touch my son. His lungs were pronounced perfect. He was thin but healthy. He had the familiar newborn features: flattened Indian face, dark rat hair, obsidian eyes. His toes curled under, plump like early peas. On his belly was a red birthmark that looked like a funky scribbling of the number twenty-two. "Must be the stamp of the guy who inspected him," Nicholas said.

Nicholas kissed my forehead, staring at me with his wide-sky eyes, making me regret what I'd said before. "Four hours," he said. "How considerate of you to finish all the hard work in time for me to do my morning rotations."

"Well, you know," I said, "we aim to please."

Nicholas touched the baby's open palm, and the fingers curled together like a daisy at sunset. "Four hours is damn fast for a first delivery," he said.

The question died on my lips: *Was this my first?* Staring into the demanding face of this son, I thought that maybe, right now, it didn't matter.

Nearby, Dr. Thayer was completing the medical record. "Last name, Prescott," she verified. "Have you picked a first name?"

I thought of my mother, May O'Toole, and wondered if she knew in her corner of the world that she had a grandchild. I wondered if the baby might have her eyes, her smile, or her sorrow.

I turned my face up to Nicholas. "Max," I said. "His name is Max."

≈≈≈

Nicholas went to Mass General to round his patients, and I was left alone with my baby. I held him awkwardly in my arms as he screamed and thrashed and kicked. I felt beaten from the inside; I couldn't move very well, and I wondered if I was the best person for Max right then.

When I turned on the TV above the bed, Max quieted down. Together we listened to the wind shake the walls of the hospital as the reporters described a world that was falling apart.

At one point I found Max looking up at me, as if he'd seen the face before but couldn't place it. I inspected him, his wrinkled neck and blotchy cheeks, the bruised color of his eyes. I did not know how this child could possibly have come out of me. I kept waiting to feel that surge of mother love that was supposed to come naturally, the bond that meant nothing could keep me from my baby. But I was looking at a stranger. My throat seemed to swell up with a pain more raw than childbirth, and I recognized it immediately: I just wasn't ready. I could love him, but I had expected another month to prepare. I needed time. And that was the one thing I would not have. "You should know," I whispered, "I don't think I'll be very good at this." He placed his fist against my heart. "You have the upper hand," I told him. "I'm more afraid of you than you are of me."

≈≈≈

At Brigham and Women's, one of the options for new mothers was partial rooming-in. The baby could stay with you all day, and at night when you were ready to go to sleep, a nurse would roll the plastic bassinet to the nursery. If you chose to breast-feed, a nurse would bring the baby back when he woke up. Noreen told me it was the best of both worlds. "You get your rest," she said, "but you don't miss that special time with the little guy."

I wanted to tell her to take Max all day, because I did not have the first idea what to do with a newborn. I put him on the edge of my bed and unwrapped his receiving blanket, marveling at the length of his legs and his pale blue feet. When I tried wrapping him back up again, I made a horrible mess of it, and Max kicked the blanket free. I pushed the call button, and Noreen came back to show me the tight papoose bind. Then I went to put him back into his bassinet on his side—not on his stomach, because it would irritate the umbilical cord, and not on his back, because he might die of SIDS— but the edges of the basket were too high, and I half placed, half dropped him onto the soft padding. Max started to wail. "Don't do that," I said, but Max's eyes slit into dashes, and his mouth formed an angry red O. I held him at arms' length, watching his tightly swaddled legs wiggle like a mermaid's tail as he thrashed about. From the corner of my eye I saw several nurses walk by, but no one came in to offer help. "Oh, please," I said, tears coming, and I shifted Max onto my shoulder. Immediately he became quiet and grabbed fistfuls of my hair.

Noreen came into the room. "He's hungry," she said. "Try feeding him."

I looked at her blankly, and she helped me settle on the bed. She lifted a pillow onto my lap and laid Max across it, untied one shoulder of my hospital gown. She showed me how to hold my nipple, brown and unfamiliar, so that Max could get it into his mouth. "He doesn't really know how to do this," she said, "so you're going to have to teach him."

"Oh," I said. "The blind leading the blind."

But Max's gums clamped down on my nipple so hard that pain shot through my arm and brought tears to my eyes. "That can't be right," I said, thinking of the women on the TV formula commercials, who gazed down at their suckling infants as if they were the baby Jesus. "That hurts too much to be right."

"It hurts?" Noreen asked. I nodded. "Then he's got the right idea." She stroked Max's cheek as if she already liked him. "Let him go at it for a few more minutes," she said. "He's only getting colostrum now. Your milk won't come in for a few days."

Noreen told me that as I got used to this, I'd toughen up. She said she'd bring me damp tea bags to lay on my nipples when Max was finished, since something in the blend took away the soreness and the sting. Noreen left me to stare at the rain, pelting against the thick glass window and blurring the edges of the outside world. I fought back tears and waited for my son to suck me dry.

≈≈≈

In the middle of the night, an unfamiliar nurse wheeled the bassinet into my room. "Guess who's hungry," she said cheerfully. Sleep was still wrapped around my head like a thick, stuffed cloud, but I reached for Max as I knew I was supposed to. I had been dreaming. I had been picturing my mother, but as Max's lips pulled at my breast, I began to lose the image.

I could not keep my eyes open, and every muscle in my body was lead heavy. I was sure I'd fall asleep and Max would roll out of my arms and strike his head on the floor and die. I blinked often, seeing nothing, until Max's mouth slackened and I could call for a nurse.

Even as the squeaky wheels of the bassinet bumped and ground their way out the door, I was sinking into my pillow. I began to see the face of my mother. I was two, maybe three, and it was her birthday, and my father had given her a plant. It was tall and green in its plastic pot, and it had orange balls at the junctures of its leaves. When he gave it to her, she read the card out loud, although I was the only other person in the kitchen. "Happy Birthday, May," it said. "I love you." It wasn't signed, I guess, because my mother didn't read anything else aloud, such as my father's name. She kissed him, and he smiled and went down to his workshop.

When he left, she tapped the card on the counter and then gave it to me to play with. "What am I going to do with a plant?" she said, talking to me the way she always did, as if I were an adult. "He knows all I do is kill these things." She reached into the uppermost cabinet over the fridge, into the never-used ice bucket that held her forbidden packs of cigarettes. My father did not know she smoked— I realized this even though I was a baby, since she went to great pains to hide the cigarettes and she acted guilty when she lit one and she sprayed the air with cinnamon freshener after she'd flushed the ashes and the butt down the toilet. I don't know why she hid her smoking from him; maybe, like most other things, it was a game for her to play.

She pulled one from the wrinkled pack and lit it, drawing in deeply. When she exhaled she stared at me, sitting on the linoleum with my blocks and my favorite doll. It was a cloth one, with practice snaps and zippers and buttons, strategically placed through ten wrappings of bright cotton clothes. I could do everything but the shoe-laces. Cigarette ashes dropped on my doll. I looked up and saw a perfect red ring left by my mother's lipstick, just above the V of her fingers. "Two weeks," she said, nodding at the orange tree. "That thing'll be dead in two weeks." She stubbed the cigarette out in the sink and sighed, and then she pulled me up by the hands. "See here, Paige-boy," she said, using her pet name for me. She settled me on her hip. "I'm no good at taking care of things," she whispered confidentially, and then she began to hum. "Supercalifragilisticexpiali-docious," she sang, whirling me around and around in a fast, stomping polka. I giggled as we flushed the evidence away. I wondered just how much I knew about my mother that my father never would have guessed.

The wheels of the bassinet throbbed in my head, and I knew Max was coming long before the night nurse arrived. He was screaming. "Hard to believe they were worried about his lungs," she said, holding him out to me. For a moment I did not reach for him. I stared angrily at this greedy thing, who had twice in one night taken me away from all I had left of my mother.

chapter 14
Paige

When God wanted to punish me, He granted my prayers. I spent a year in the circle of Jake's arms, long enough to believe it was where I really belonged. I spent many evenings at the Flanagans', clapping along as Jake's father sang old Gaelic songs and the littlest children hopped and jigged. I was accepted at RISD, and Jake took me out to dinner to celebrate. Later that night, when we wrapped the heat of our bodies around each other like a blanket, Jake told me he would wait for me through college, or grad school, or the rest of my life.

In May I came down with the flu. It was strange, because the bug had passed around the school in early January, but I had all the same symptoms. I was weak and chilled, and I could not keep anything down. Jake brought me heather he'd picked from the side of the road and sculptures he made with wire and old Coke cans at work. "You look like hell," he said, and he leaned down to kiss me.

"Don't," I warned him. "You'll catch it."

Jake had smiled. "Me?" he said. "I'm invincible."

On the fifth morning I had the flu, I stumbled into the bathroom to throw up, and I heard my father walking by the door. He paused, and then he went down the stairs. I looked into the mirror for the first time in days, and I saw the thin, drawn face of a ghost: pale cheeks, red eyes, cracks at the corners of my mouth. And that's when I knew I was pregnant.

Because I was not sick, I forced myself to get dressed in my school uniform, and I went down to the kitchen. My father was eating corn-flakes, staring at the bare wall as if there were something there he could see. "I'm better, Dad," I announced.

My father lifted his eyes, and I saw a flicker of something— relief?—as he gestured to the other chair. "Eat something," he said, "or you'll blow away."

I smiled and sat down, trying to block out the smell of the cereal. I concentrated on my father's voice, laced with the sounds of his homeland. *One day, Paige,* he used to say, *we'll be takin' you to Ireland. It's the only place on God's great earth where the air is pure as fine crystal and the hills are a green magic carpet, streaked with blue-jewel streams.* I reached for the cornflakes and ate several out of the box, knowing I had learned the lesson he hadn't: there was no going back.

The cornflakes tasted like cardboard, and I kept staring at my father, wondering exactly how much he knew. My eyes began to swim with tears. I had been his biggest hope. He would be so ashamed.

I went through the motions of school that day like rituals, numbly going to my classes and taking notes from teachers I did not hear. Then I walked slowly to Jake's garage. He was bent over the hood of a Toyota, changing spark plugs. When he saw me, he smiled and wiped his hands on his jeans. In his eyes I could see the rest of my life. "You're all better," he said.

"That," I told him, "isn't quite true."

≈≈≈

I did not need parental consent for an abortion, but I did not want my father to know what I had done, so I committed the greatest sin of my life one hundred miles away from my hometown. Jake had found the name of a clinic in Racine, Wisconsin—far enough from Chicago that no one would recognize us or pass along rushed whispers. We would drive there early on Thursday, June 3, the first available appointment. When Jake had told me of the wait, I had stared at him in disbelief. "How many people," I whispered, "could there possibly be?"

The hardest part was surviving the weeks between when I first knew and when we left for Racine. Jake and I did not make love, as if this was our punishment. We'd go outside every night, and I would sit in the valley of his legs, and Jake would cross his hands over my stomach as if there were something he could truly feel.

The first night, Jake and I had walked for miles. "Let's get married," he said to me, for the second time in my life.

But I did not want to enter a marriage because of a child. Even if Jake and I wanted to marry someday, a baby would have changed the entire reason behind it. After every argument and every petty disagreement in years to come, we would both blame the child that brought us into the mess. And besides, I was going to college. I was going to be an artist. This was the reason I gave Jake. "I'm only eighteen," I said. "I can't be a mother now." I did not add the other reason that ran through my mind: *I don't know if I ever can be one.*

Jake had swallowed hard and turned away. "We'll have others," he said, resigning himself. He lifted his face to the sky, and I knew that traced among the stars, he saw—as I did—the face of our unborn child.

On the morning of June 3 I got up before six o'clock and slipped out of the house. I walked down the street to Saint Christopher's, praying that I wouldn't see Father Draher, or an altar boy who went to Pope Pius. I knelt in the last pew and whispered to my twelve-week-old baby. "Sweetheart," I murmured, "Love. My darling." I said all the things I never would get to say.

I did not enter a confessional, remembering my old friend Priscilla Divine and her knowing voice: "There are certain things you just don't tell a priest." Instead I silently recited a string of Hail Marys,

until the words all ran together and I couldn't distinguish the syllables in my mind from the sound of my pain.

Jake and I did not touch on the way to Racine. We passed thick
rolling farmland and fat spotty Holsteins. Jake followed the directions
the woman on the phone had given him, sometimes pronouncing the
names of the highways out loud. I unrolled the window and closed
my eyes into the wind, still seeing the rush of green, black, and white;
the flat, level land and its ornaments, tassels of new corn.

The small gray building had very little to mark it for what it
was. The entrance was at the back, so Jake helped me out of the car
and led me around the corner. Surrounding the front door was an
angry, snaking cord of picketers. They wore black raincoats splashed
with red, and they carried looming signs that said MURDER. As they
saw Jake and me they thronged about us, crying out gibberish I could
not understand. Jake put his arm around me and pushed me through
the door. "Jesus Christ," he said.

The tired blond woman who served as a receptionist asked me to
fill out my personal information on a white card. "You pay up front,"
she said, and Jake removed his wallet and, from it, three hundred
dollars he'd taken from the cash register at his father's garage the
night before. An advance, he'd called it, and he'd told me not to
worry.

The woman disappeared for a moment. I looked around the white
walls of the room. They were free of posters; there was only a handful
of dated magazines for people to read. The waiting area held at least
twenty people—mostly women—all looking as if they'd stumbled in
by mistake. In the corner was a small paper carton filled with plastic
blocks and Sesame Street dolls, just in case, but there were no children
to play with them.

"We're a little backed up today," the blond woman said, returning with a pink information sheet for me. "If you want to take a walk
or something, it will be at least two hours."

Jake nodded, and because we'd been told to, we shuffled outside
again. This time the picketers cleared a path for us and started to
cheer, assuming we'd changed our minds. We hurried out of the

parking lot and walked three blocks before Jake turned to me. "I don't know anything about Racine," he said. "Do you?"

I shook my head. "We could walk in circles," I said, "or we could just go straight and keep track of the time."

But the clinic was in a strange area, and though Racine wasn't all that big a town, we walked for what seemed like miles and all we saw were sectioned farms and a waste-water treatment plant and fields empty of cows. Finally, I pointed to a small fenced-in area.

The little playground was oddly misplaced in the middle of this town; we hadn't seen any houses. It had a string of swings, the cloth kind that hugged your bottom when you sat down. There was a jungle gym and monkey bars and a hexagon of painted wood that you could spin like a merry-go-round. Jake looked at me and smiled for the first time that day. "Race you," he said, and he started to run toward the swings.

But I couldn't. I was so tired. I had been told not to eat anything that morning, and anyway, just being there made me feel as heavy as lead. I walked slowly, carefully, as if I had something to protect, and I picked a swing next to Jake's. He was pumping as high as he could; the entire metal frame seemed to shake and hump, threatening to come loose from the ground. Jake's feet grazed the low, flat clouds, and he kicked at them. Then, when he'd gone higher than I'd thought possible, he jumped from the swing in midair, arching his back and landing, scuffed, in the sand. He looked up at me. "Your turn," he said.

I shook my head. I wanted his energy; God, I wanted to put this behind me and do what he had just done. "Push me," I said, and Jake came to stand behind me, pressing his hands at the small of my back every time I returned to him. He pushed me so forcefully that for a moment I was suspended horizontally, grasping the chains of the swing, staring into the sun. And before I knew it, I was on my way back down.

Jake climbed on the monkey bars, hanging from his knees and scratching his armpits. Then he put me on the merry-go-round. "Hold on," he said. I pressed my face into the smooth green surface of the wood, feeling the sheen of warm paint against my cheek. Jake spun the merry-go-round, faster and faster. I lifted my head but felt my neck get whipped by the force, and I laughed, dizzy, trying to search out Jake's face. But I couldn't make sense of anything, so I tucked my head back down against the wood. My insides were spinning, and I did not know which way was up. I heard Jake's labored breathing, and I laughed so hard that I crossed the fine line and started to cry.

≈≈≈

I did not feel anything, except the hot lights of the clean white room and the cool hands of a nurse and the distant suck and tug of instruments. In recovery, they gave me pills and I drifted in and out of sleep. When I came to, a pretty young nurse was standing next to me. "Is there someone here with you?" she asked, and I thought, *Not anymore.*

Much later, Jake came to me. He did not say a word. He leaned down and kissed my forehead, the way he used to from time to time before we became lovers. "Are you okay?" he asked.

It was when he spoke that I saw it: the image of a child, hovering just over his shoulder. I saw it as clearly as I saw Jake's face. And I knew by the storm of his eyes that he saw the same thing near me. "I'm fine," I said, and I realized then that I would have to get away.

When we arrived at my house, my father was not yet home; we had planned it this way. Jake helped me up to bed and sat on the edge of the comforter and held my hand. "I'll see you tomorrow," he said, but he made no move to go.

Jake and I had always been able to say things without words. I knew he heard it in the silence too: We would not see each other tomorrow. We would not see each other ever again; and we would not get married and we would not have other children, because every time we looked at each other the memory of this would be staring back at us. "Tomorrow," I echoed, forcing the word past the lump in my throat.

I knew that somewhere God was laughing. He had taken the other half of my heart, the one person who knew me better than I knew myself, and He had done what nothing else could do. By bringing us together, He had set into motion the one thing that could tear us apart. That was the day I lost my religion. I knew that I could no longer pass away in a state of grace, no longer make it to heaven. If there was a Second Coming, Jesus would no longer die for my sins. But suddenly, compared to everything I had been through, it didn't matter much at all.

Even as Jake was stroking the skin of my arm, making me promises he knew he would not keep, I was forming a plan. I could not stay in Chicago and know that Jake was minutes away. I could not hide my shame from my father for very long. After graduation, I would disappear. "I won't be going to college after all." I spoke the words aloud. The sentence hung, visible, black printed letters stretched across the space before me. "I won't be going."

"What did you say?" Jake asked. He looked at me, and in his eyes I saw the pain of a hundred kisses and the healing power of his arms around me.

"Nothing," I told him. "Nothing at all."

A week later, after graduation, I packed my knapsack and left my father a note that told him I loved him. I boarded a bus and got off at Cambridge, Massachusetts—a place I chose because it sounded, like its namesake, an ocean away—and I left my childhood behind.

In Ohio I reached into my knapsack and rummaged for an orange, but I came up instead with an unfamiliar worn yellow envelope. My name was printed on the outside, and when I opened it I read an old Irish blessing I'd seen a million times, cross-stitched on a faded violet sampler that hung on the wall over Jake's bed:

> *May the road rise to meet you.*
> *May the wind be always at your back.*
> *May the sun shine warm upon your face.*
> *May the rains fall soft upon your fields.*
> *And 'til we meet again,*
> *May God hold you in the palm of His hand.*

As I read the careful, rolling script of Jake's handwriting, I started to cry. I had no idea when he had left this for me. I had been awake the entire time he was in my room that final evening, and I had not seen him since. He must have known I would leave Chicago, that I would leave him.

I stared out the clouded window of the bus, trying to picture Jake's face, but all I could see was the strip of granite lining an unfamiliar highway. He was already fading from me. I fingered the note gently and ran my hands over the letters and pressed the curling edges of the paper. With these words, Jake had let go of me, which proved that he knew more about why I was leaving than even I did. I had believed that I was running away from what had happened. I did not know—not until I met Nicholas days later—that the whole time I was really running toward what was yet to be.

chapter 15
Nicholas

Nicholas watched his wife turn into a wraith. She never really slept, since Max wanted to nurse every two hours. She was afraid to leave him alone for even a minute, so she showered only every other day. Her hair hung down her back like tangled yarn, her eyes were ringed with shadows. Her skin seemed frail and transparent, and sometimes Nicholas reached out to touch her just to see if she would vanish at the brush of his hand.

Max cried all the time. Nicholas wondered how Paige could stand it, the constant shrieking right in her ear. She didn't even seem to notice, but these days Paige wasn't noticing much of anything. Last night, Nicholas had found her standing in the dark of the nursery, staring at Max in his wicker bassinet. He watched from the doorway, feeling a knot come into his throat at the sight of his wife and his son. When he came forward, his footsteps hushed on the carpet, he touched Paige's shoulder. She turned to him, and he was shocked by the look in her eyes. There was no tenderness, no love, and no longing. Her gaze was riddled with questions, as if she simply didn't understand what Max was doing there at all.

Nicholas had been at the hospital for twenty consecutive hours, and he was exhausted. Driving home, he had pictured three things over and over in his mind: his Shower Massage, a steaming plate of fettuccine, his bed. He pulled into the driveway and stepped out of the car, already hearing through sealed doors and windows the high-pitched screams of his son. At that one sound, all the spring left his body. He moved sluggishly onto the porch, reluctant to enter his own house.

Paige stood in the center of the kitchen, balancing Max on her shoulder, a Nuk pacifier in her hand and the telephone tucked beneath one ear. "No," she was saying, "you don't understand. I don't want daily delivery of the *Globe*. No. We can't afford it." Nicholas slipped behind her and lifted the baby from her shoulder. She could not see Nicholas, but she did not instinctively resist him when he took her child. Max hiccuped and vomited over the back of Nicholas's shirt.

Paige set the telephone into its cradle. She stared up at Nicholas as if he were fashioned of gold. She was still wearing her nightgown. "Thank you," she whispered.

Nicholas understood the clinical explanations for postpartum blues, and he tried to remember the best course of treatment. It was all hormonal, he knew that, but surely a little praise would help speed it along and would bring back the Paige he used to know. "I don't know how you do it," he said, smiling at her.

Paige looked at her feet. "Well, I'm obviously not doing it right," she said. "He won't stop crying. He can't ever get enough to eat, and I'm so tired, I just don't know what to try next." On cue, Max began to wail. Paige straightened her spine, and a quick glimmer in her eyes told Nicholas how hard she was working simply to keep on her feet. She smiled stiffly and said, over Max's cries, "And how was your day?"

Nicholas looked around the kitchen. On the table were baby gifts from his colleagues, some unwrapped; paper and ribbons were strewn across the floor. A breast pump ringed with milk sat on the counter beside an open tub of yogurt. Three books on child care were propped up against dirty glasses, open to the sections on "Crying" and "The First Weeks." Stuffed into the unused playpen were the dress shirts he needed brought to the laundry. Nicholas glanced at Paige. There would be no fettuccine.

"Listen," he said. "How about you lie down for an hour or two and I'll take care of the baby?"

Paige sank back against the wall. "Oh," she said, "would you really?"

Nicholas nodded, pushing her toward the bedroom with his free hand. "What do I have to do with him?" he asked.

Paige turned around, poised on the edge of the doorway. She raised her eyebrows, then she threw back her head and laughed.

≈≈≈

Fogerty had called Nicholas into his office two days after Paige gave birth. He offered a gift that Joan had picked out—a baby monitor—which Nicholas thanked him for, in spite of the fact that it was a ridiculous present. But how could Fogerty have realized that in a house as small as his, Max's shattering cries could be heard anywhere? "Sit down," Fogerty said, an atypical courtesy. "If I'm not mistaken, it's more rest than you've had in a while."

Nicholas had fallen gratefully into the leather wing chair, running his hands over the smooth worn arms. Fogerty paced the length of his office and finally perched on a corner of his desk. "I wasn't much older than you when we had Alexander," Fogerty said. "But I didn't have quite so much responsibility riding on my shoulders. I can't do it all over again, but you have the chance to do it right the first time."

"Do what?" Nicholas asked, tired of Fogerty and his obtuse riddles.

"Separate yourself," Fogerty said. "Don't lose sight of the fact that people outside your home are also depending on you, on your stamina, on your ability. Don't let yourself be compromised."

Nicholas had left the office and gone directly to Brigham and Women's, to visit Paige and Max. He had held his son, and felt the gentle swell of the baby's chest with each breath, and marveled at the fact that he had helped create a living, thinking thing. He had believed Fogerty was a sanctimonious old fool, until the night when Paige and Max came home. Then he had slept with a pillow wrapped over his head, trying to block out Max's cries, his noisy suckling, even the rustle of Paige getting in and out of bed to tend to him. "Come *on*, Paige," he demanded after being awakened for the third time. "I've got a triple bypass at seven in the morning!"

But in spite of Fogerty's cautions, Nicholas knew his wife was falling apart. He had always seen her as such a model of strength—working two jobs to pay his way through Harvard, scrounging together money to make the endless interest payments, and, before that, leaving her life behind to start again in Cambridge. It was hard to believe that something as tiny as a newborn child could throw Paige for a loop.

≈≈≈

"Okay, buddy," Nicholas said, taking a howling Max to the couch. "Do you want to play?" He held up a rattle that protruded from between two cushions and shook it in front of his son. Max didn't seem to see it. He kicked his legs and waved his small red hands. Nicholas bounced the baby up and down on his knee. "Let's try something else," he said. He picked up the television remote and flipped through the channels. The whir of color seemed to calm Max down, and he settled like a sleeping puppy in the hollow of Nicholas's chest.

Nicholas smiled. This wasn't so hard after all.

He slipped his hand under Max's legs and scooped the baby up, carrying him upstairs to the nursery. Silently, Nicholas moved past the closed door of the master bedroom. If he put Max down now, he could probably take a shower before the baby woke again.

The minute Max's head touched the soft bassinet mattress, he began to scream. "Shit," Nicholas said, grabbing the baby roughly.

He rocked him against his chest, holding Max's ear against his heart. "There," he said. "You're okay."

Nicholas took Max to the changing table and surveyed the arrangement of Pampers and A&D and cornstarch powder. He unsnapped the terry-cloth sleeper and pulled the edges of the tape from the corners of the diaper with a loud rasp. Max started to scream again, his face turning round and tomato red, and Nicholas began to hurry. He lifted the diaper, but when he saw a stream of urine arch from the raw, newly circumcised penis, he slapped the pad back in place. He took deep breaths, plugging an ear with one hand and holding Max's squirming body with the other. Then he slipped the old diaper away and put the new one on, knowing it was too low in the back but not caring enough to fix it.

He had to snap and unsnap the terry-cloth sleeper three times before he got it right. His hands were too big to secure the little silver circles, and there always seemed to be one snap he'd missed. Finally, he picked Max up and hung him upside down from his shoulder, just grasping his feet. *If Paige could see me,* Nicholas thought, *she'd murder me.* But Max became quiet. Nicholas paraded around the nursery in a circle, holding his son upside down. He felt sorry for the kid. All of a sudden, without warning, he was thrown into a world where nothing seemed familiar. Not much different from his parents.

He carried Max down to the living room, settling him on the couch in a nest of stuffed pillows. The baby had Nicholas's eyes. After the first day, the dark black had given way to cool sky blue, startling against the red oval of his face. Other than that, Nicholas couldn't tell. It remained too early to see whom Max would take after.

Max's glazed eyes roamed blindly over Nicholas's face, seeming for a moment to come into focus. He started to cry again.

"Jesus fucking Christ," Nicholas muttered, picking the baby up and starting to walk. He bounced Max on his shoulder as he moved. He sang Motown. He twirled around and around, very fast, and he tried hanging the baby upside down again. But Max would not stop crying.

Nicholas couldn't get away from the sound. It pounded behind his eyes, over his ears. He wanted to put the baby down and run. He was just thinking about it when Paige came downstairs, groggy but resigned, like a prisoner on death row. "I think he's hungry," Nicholas said. "I couldn't make him stop."

"I know," Paige said. "I heard." She took the baby from Nicholas and rocked him back and forth. Nicholas's shoulders throbbed with relief, as if a huge weight had been removed. Max quieted a little, his crying now a soft, grating whine. "He just ate," Paige said. She went to sit on the couch and flipped the television on. "Nickelodeon," she said to nobody. "Max seems to like Nickelodeon."

Nicholas slipped into the bedroom and set off the test button on his beeper. The soft chirps vibrated against his hip. He opened the door, to find Paige waiting. "I've got to go back to the hospital," he lied. "Complications on a heart-lung transplant."

Paige nodded. He pushed past her, fighting the urge to take her into his arms and say, *Let's get away. Just you and I, let's go, and everything will be different.* Instead he went into the bathroom, showering quickly and then changing his shirt, his pants, his socks.

When he left, Paige was sitting in the rocking chair in the nursery. She had her nightgown opened to her belly, still soft and round. Max's mouth was clamped to her right breast. With every tug of his lips he seemed to be pulling in more and more of her. Nicholas's gaze strayed to Paige's face, which was turned to the window. Her eyes held the ragged edge of pain. "It hurts?" Nicholas asked.

"Yes." Paige did not look at him. "That's what they don't tell you."

Nicholas drove quickly to Mass General, weaving in and out of traffic. He opened all the windows in the car, and he turned on the radio, some rap station, as loud as possible. He tried to drown out the sound of Max's cries in his ears, the image of Paige when he walked out the door. At least he was able to leave.

When he passed the nurses' station in the ER, Phoebe, who had known him for years, raised her eyebrows. "You're not on call tonight, Dr. Prescott," she said. "Did you miss me again?"

Nicholas smiled at her. "I can't live without you, Phoebe," he said. "Run away with me to Mexico."

Phoebe laughed and opened a patient file. "Such words from a man with a new baby boy."

Nicholas moved through the halls with the confidence people expected of him. He ran his fingers over the smooth aqua tiles lining the walls of the corridors, heading for the small room kept for the residents on call overnight. It was no more than a closet, but Nicholas welcomed the familiar smell of formaldehyde and antiseptic and blue woven cotton as if he had entered a palatial estate. His eyes swept the neat cot that filled up the room, and then he pulled back the covers. He turned off his beeper and set it on the floor below his head. He drew into his memory the only Lamaze class he had attended, the nurse's low voice washing over the temples of the pregnant women: *Imagine a long, cool white beach.* Nicholas could see himself stretched out on the sand, under a feverish sun. He fell asleep to the music of an invented ocean, beating like a heart.

chapter 16
Paige

I woke up in a pool of my own milk. It had been thirty minutes since I put Max down, and in the other room he was already talking, those high little squeaks he made when he woke up happy. I heard the rattle and spin of the striped wheel on his Busy Box, the toy he didn't recognize yet but kicked from time to time with his feet. Max's gurgles began to get louder, insistent. "I'm coming," I yelled through the adjoining wall. "Give me a minute."

I stripped off Nicholas's polo shirt—my own shirts were too tight across my chest—and changed my bra. I wedged soft flannel handkerchiefs into the cups, a trick of the trade I'd discovered after those disposable nursing pads kept bunching up or sticking to my skin. I did not bother putting on a new shirt. Max fed so often that sometimes I would walk around the house topless for hours at a time, my breasts becoming heavier and heavier as they replenished what Max had taken.

Max's little bud mouth was already working on the air when I got to his crib. I lifted him out and unhooked the front of the bra, unsure whether it was the left or right side he'd fed on last, because the whole day just seemed to run together. As soon as I settled into the rocking chair, Max began drinking—long, strong draws of milk that sent vibrations from my breasts to my stomach to my groin. I counted off ten minutes on my watch and then switched him to the other side.

I was in a rush this morning because of my adventure. It was the first time I was going out with Max, just the two of us. Well, I had done it once before, but it had taken me an hour to get his diaper bag together and figure out how to strap his car seat into place, and by the time we got to the end of the block he was screaming so hard to be fed that I decided to just turn around and send Nicholas to the bank when he got home. So for six weeks I had been a prisoner in my own house, a slave to a twenty-one-inch tyrant who could not live without me.

For six weeks I had slept the hours Max dictated, kept him changed and dry as he demanded, let him drink from me. I gave Max so much of my time that I found myself praying for him to take a nap so that I would have those ten or fifteen minutes to myself, and then I'd just sit on the couch and take deep breaths and try to remember what I used to do to fill my days. I wondered how it could happen so quickly: once Max had been inside *me*, existing because of *me*, surviving from *my* bloodstream and *my* body; and now, by quick reversal, I had simply become part of him.

I put Max on his back in the playpen and watched him suck on the corner of a black-and-white geometric-print card. Yesterday a woman from La Leche had come to the house, sent by the hospital for a follow-up visit. I had let her in reluctantly, kicking toys and cloth burping diapers and old magazines under the furniture as I led the way. I wondered if she'd say something about the dust piled on the fireplace mantel, the overflowing trash bins, or the fact that we hadn't fitted our outlets with safety plugs yet.

She didn't comment on the house at all. She walked straight to

Max's playpen. "He's beautiful," she said, cooing at Max, but I wondered if she said that about all the babies she saw. I myself had once believed all babies were cute, but I knew that wasn't true. In the hospital nursery, Max was the best-looking baby by far. For one thing, he looked like a little boy; there was no question. He had ebony hair, tufted and fine, and eyes that were cool and demanding. He was so much like Nicholas that sometimes I found myself staring at him, amazed.

"I've just come to see how the nursing is going," she said. "I'm sure you're still nursing."

As if that was the only option, I thought. "Yes," I told her. "It's going just fine." I hesitated and then told her that I was considering giving him one bottle of formula a day—just one—so that if I had to run an errand or take Max out, I could do it without worrying about having to nurse him in public.

The woman had been horrified. "You wouldn't want to do that," she said. "Not yet, at least. It's only been six weeks, isn't that right? He's still getting used to the breast, and if you give him the bottle, well, who knows what might happen."

I hadn't answered, thinking, *What might happen, indeed?* Maybe Max would wean himself. Maybe my milk would dry up and I could fit back into my clothes and lose the twelve pounds that still was settled around my waist and hips. I didn't see what the big deal about formula was. After all, I had been brought up on formula. Everyone had, in the sixties. We all turned out okay.

I had offered the woman tea, hoping she wouldn't accept, because I didn't have any. "I have to go along," she told me, patting my hand. "Do you have any more questions?"

"Yes," I said without thinking. "When does my life go back to normal?"

And she had laughed and opened the front door. "What makes you think it ever does?" she said, and disappeared down the porch, her shantung suit whispering around her.

Today I had convinced myself otherwise. Today was the day that I started acting like a regular person. Max was only a baby, and there really wasn't any reason that *I* couldn't control the schedule. He didn't *need* to eat every two hours. We would stretch that to four. He didn't *have* to sleep in his crib or his playpen; he could just as easily nap in his car seat while I went grocery shopping or bought stamps at the post office. And if I got up and left the house, breathed some fresh air and gave myself a purpose, I wouldn't find myself exhausted all the time. Today, I told myself, was the day I'd begin all over again.

I was afraid to leave Max alone for even a minute, because I'd read all about crib deaths. I had fleeting visions of Max strangling himself with the Wiggle Worm toy or choking on the corner of the red-balloon quilt. So I tucked him under my arm and carried him into his nursery. I laid him on the carpet while I packed the diaper bag with seven diapers, a bib, a rattle, and, just in case, trial sizes of Johnson's shampoo and Ivory Snow.

"Okay," I said, turning to Max. "What would you like to wear?"

Max looked up at me and pursed his lips as if he were considering this. It was about sixty degrees outside, and I didn't think he needed a snowsuit, but then again, what did I know? He was already wearing an undershirt and a cotton playsuit embroidered with elephants, a gift from Leroy and Lionel. Max started to squirm on the floor, which meant he was going to cry. I scooped him into my arms and pulled from one of his near-empty dresser drawers a thin hooded sweatshirt and a bulky blue sweater. Layers, that's what Dr. Spock said, and surely with both of these on, Max couldn't catch a cold. I placed him on his changing table, and I had his sweatshirt half on when I realized I needed to change his diaper. I pulled him out of the sweatshirt, making him cry, and started to sing to him. Sometimes it made him quiet right down, no matter what the song. I let myself believe he just needed to hear my voice.

The sweater's arms were too long, and this really annoyed Max, because every time he stuffed his fist into his mouth, fuzz from the wool caught on his lips. I tried to roll the sleeves back, but they got chunky and knotted. Finally, I sighed. "Let's just go," I told Max. "You won't even notice after a while."

This was the day of my six-week checkup at Dr. Thayer's. I was looking forward to going; I'd get to see the people I had worked with for years—real adults—and I considered the visit the last one of my pregnancy. After this, I was going to be a whole new woman.

Max fell asleep on the way to Dr. Thayer's, and when we pulled into the parking lot, I found myself holding my breath and gently disengaging my seat belt, praying he would not wake up. I even left the car door ajar, afraid that a slam would start him screaming. But Max seemed to be out for the long haul. I slung his car seat/carrier over my arm, as if he were a basket of harvested grapes, and headed up the familiar stone stairs of the OB/GYN office.

"Paige!" Mary, the receptionist who had replaced me, stood up the minute I walked in the door. "Let me give you a hand." She came up to me and lifted Max's carrier off my arm, poking her finger into his puffy red cheek. "He's adorable," she said, and I smiled.

Three of the nurses, hearing my name, swelled into the waiting room. They embraced me and wrapped me in the heady smell of their perfume and the brilliance of their clean white outfits. "You look fabulous," one said, and I wondered if she didn't see my tangled, hanging hair; my mismatched socks; the pasty wax of my skin.

Mary was the one to shoo them back behind the swinging wooden door. "Ladies," she said, "we've got an office to run here." She carried Max to an empty chair, surrounded by several very pregnant women. "Dr. Thayer's running late," she said to me. "So what's new?"

Mary ran back to the black lacquer desk to answer the phone, and I watched her go. I wanted to push her out of the way, to open the top drawer and riffle through the paper clips and the payment invoices, to hear my own steady voice say "Cambridge OB/GYN." Before Max was even born, Nicholas and I had decided I'd stay home with him. Art school was out of the question, since we couldn't afford both day care and tuition. And as for me working, well, the cost of decent day care almost equaled my combined salaries at Mercy and the doctors' office, so it just didn't pay. *You don't want a stranger taking care of him, do you?* Nicholas had said. And I suppose I had to agree. *One year,* Nicholas told me, smiling. *Let's give it one year, and then we'll see.*

And I had beamed back at him, running my palms over my still-swollen belly. One year. How bad could one single year be?

I leaned over and unzipped Max's sweater, opened the first few buttons of the jacket underneath. He was sweating. I would have taken them both off, but that would have awakened him for sure, and I wasn't ready for that. One of the pregnant women caught my eye and smiled. She had healthy, thick brown hair that fell in little cascades to her shoulders. She was wearing a sleeveless linen maternity dress and espadrilles. She looked down at Max and unconsciously rubbed her hands over her belly.

When I turned to look, most of the other women in the office were watching my baby sleep. They all had the same expression on their faces—kind of dreamy, with a softness in their eyes that I never remembered seeing in mine. "How old is he?" the first woman asked.

"Six weeks," I said, swallowing a lump in my throat. All the others turned at the sound of my voice. They were waiting for me to tell them something—anything—a story that would let them know it was worth the wait; that labor wouldn't be so horrible; that I had never been happier in my life. "It's not what you think," I heard myself saying, my words pouring thick and slow. "I haven't slept since he was born. I'm always tired. I don't know what to do with him."

"But he's so precious," another woman said.

I stared at her, her belly, her baby inside. "Consider yourself lucky," I said.

Mary called my name minutes later. I was set up in a small white examination room with a poster of a womb on the wall. I undressed and wrapped the paper robe around myself and opened the drawer to the little oak table. Inside was the tape measure and the Doppler stethoscope. I touched them and peeked at Max, still sleeping. I could remember lying on the examination table during my checkups, listening to the baby's amplified heartbeat and wondering what he would look like.

Dr. Thayer came into the room in a burst of rustling paper.

"Paige!" she said, as if she was surprised to see me there. "How are you feeling?"

She motioned me to a stool, where I could sit and talk to her before getting up on the table and into the humiliating position of an internal exam. "I'm all right," I said.

Dr. Thayer flipped open my file and scribbled some notes. "No pain? No trouble with nursing?"

"No," I told her. "No trouble at all."

She turned to Max, who slept in his carrier on the floor as though he were always an angel. "He's wonderful," she said, smiling up at me.

I stared at my son. "Yes," I said, feeling that choke again at the back of my throat. "He is." Then I put my head in my hands and started to cry.

I sobbed until I couldn't catch my breath, and I thought for sure I would wake up Max, but when I lifted my head he was still sleeping peacefully on the floor. "You must think I'm crazy," I whispered.

Dr. Thayer put her hand on my arm. "I think you're like every other new mother. What you're feeling is perfectly normal. Your body has just been through a very traumatic experience, and it needs time to heal, and your mind needs to get adjusted to the fact that your life is going to change."

I reached across her for a tissue. "I'm awful with him. I don't know how to be a mother."

Dr. Thayer glanced at the baby. "Looks like you're doing fine to me," she said, "although you might not have needed the sweatshirt *and* the sweater."

I winced, knowing that I had done something wrong again and hating myself for it. "How long does it take?" I asked, a thousand questions at once. How long before I know what I'm doing? How long before I feel like myself again? How long before I can look at him with love instead of fear?

Dr. Thayer helped me over to the examination table. "It will take," she said, "the rest of your life."

I still had silver lines on my cheeks when Dr. Thayer left, memories I couldn't wash away of acting like a fool in front of her. I walked out of the office without saying goodbye to the waiting pregnant women or to Mary, who called after me even as the door was closing. I lugged Max to the parking lot, his carrier becoming heavier with each step. The diaper bag cut into my shoulder, and I had a pain in my back from leaning heavily to one side. Max still slept, a miracle, and I found myself praying to the Blessed Mother, figuring she of all holy saints would understand. Just one more half hour, I silently begged, and then we'll be home. Just one more half hour and he can wake up and I'll feed him and we'll go back to our normal routine.

The parking attendant in the lot was a teenager with skin as black as pitch and teeth that gleamed in the sun. He carried a boom box on his shoulder. I gave him my validated ticket, and he handed me my keys. Very carefully, I opened the passenger door and secured the seat belt around Max's carrier. I shut the door more quietly than I would have imagined possible. Then I moved around to my side of the car.

At the moment I opened the door, the attendant switched on his radio. The hot pulse of rap music split the air as powerfully as a summer storm, rocking the car and the clouds and the pavement. The boy nodded his head and shuffled his feet, hip-hop dancing between the orange parking lines. Max opened his eyes and shrieked louder than I had ever heard him yell.

"Sssh," I said, patting his head, which was sweaty and red from the band of the sweater's hood. "You've been such a good boy."

I put the car in drive and started out of the lot, but that only made Max cry louder. He'd slept so long I had no doubt he was starving, but I didn't want to feed him here. If I could just get him home, everything would be all right. I curved around the line of parked cars and came to the driveway that led out to the street. Max, purpled with effort, began to choke on his own sobs.

"Dear God," I said, slamming the car into park and unfastening the seat belt around Max's carrier. I pulled my shirt out of my slacks and hoisted it up around my neck, fumbling with my bra to bare a breast. Max stiffened as I lifted him and held his hot little body against mine. The rough wool of his sweater chafed my skin; his fingers clawed at my ribs. Now I began to cry, and tears splashed onto the face of my son, running over his own tears and falling somewhere between his sweater and sweatshirt. The parking attendant swore at me and started to walk over to the car. I quickly pulled my shirt down over Max's face, hoping that I wouldn't smother him. I did not unroll the window. "You're blocking my driveway," the boy said, his lips twisted and angry against the hot glass.

The rap music throbbed in my head. I turned away from the boy, and I pulled Max tighter against me. "Please," I said, closing my eyes. "Please leave me alone."

≈≈≈

Dr. Thayer had told me to do something for myself. So when Max went to sleep at eight, I decided I'd take a long, hot bath. I found the baby monitor the Fogertys had given us, and I set it up in the bathroom. Nicholas wasn't due home until ten, and Max would probably sleep until midnight. I was going to be ready when my husband came home.

Nicholas and I had not made love since I was just five months pregnant, that night when it had hurt and I told him to stop. We never spoke about it—Nicholas didn't like to talk about things like that—and as I got bigger and more uncomfortable, I cared less and less. But I needed him now. I needed to know that my body was more than a birthing machine, a source of food. I needed to hear that I was beautiful. I needed to feel Nicholas's hands on me.

I ran the bathwater, stopping it three times because I thought I had heard Max making sounds. In the corner of the medicine cabinet I found a lilac bath cube, and I watched it disintegrate in the water. I pulled my sweatshirt over my head and shrugged my shorts off and stood in front of the mirror.

My body had become foreign. Strange—I was still expecting to see the big curve of my stomach, the heavy lines of my thighs. But this thinner body wasn't the way it used to be, either. I was mapped with purple lines. My skin was the color of old parchment and seemed to be stretched just as tight. My breasts were low and full, my belly soft and bowed. I had become someone else.

I told myself Nicholas would still like what he saw. After all, the changes were because I had borne his child. Surely there was something beautiful in that.

I slipped into the steaming water and ran my hands up and down my arms, over my feet and between my toes. I nodded off for a little while, catching myself as my chin went underwater. Then I stood and toweled dry and walked to the kitchen absolutely naked, leaving soft damp footprints on the seamless carpet.

I had set a bottle of wine to chill, and I took it from the refrigerator and brought it into the bedroom with two thick blue water glasses. Then I rummaged in my drawers for the white silk sheath I had worn on our wedding night, the only piece of sexy lingerie I had. I pulled it over my head, but it stuck at my chest—I'd never considered that it might not fit. By wriggling and tugging, I managed to get it over me, but it stretched at the bust and the hips as if I'd been poured into it. My stomach was highlighted, a soft white bowl.

I heard Nicholas's car crunch into the driveway. Dizzy, I ran around the bedroom, turning off the lights. I smiled to myself—it would be like the first time all over again. Nicholas opened the front door quietly and climbed the stairs, pausing for a moment at our bedroom door. He pushed it open and stared at me where I sat on the center of the bed. My knees were tucked underneath me, my hair fell into my eyes. I wanted to say something to him, but my breath caught. Even with his loosened tie, his five o'clock shadow, and his hunched shoulders, Nicholas was the most striking man I had ever seen.

He looked at me and exhaled. "I've had a really long day, Paige," he said quietly.

My fingers clenched on the comforter. "Oh," I said.

Nicholas sat on the edge of the bed. He slipped a finger underneath the thin strap of the negligee. "Where did you get this thing?" he said.

I looked up at him. "That's what you said the first time I wore it," I said.

Nicholas swallowed and turned away. "I'm sorry," he said. "But it's really late, and I have to be at the hospital by—"

"It's only ten," I told him. I unknotted his tie and pulled it from around his neck. "It's been a very long time," I said quietly.

For a moment I saw something in Nicholas—some little spark, something that lit his eyes from inside. He brushed his hand across my cheek and touched his lips to mine. Then he stood up.

"I need to shower," he said.

He left me sitting on the bed while he went into the bathroom. I counted to ten, and then I lifted my head and stood up. I walked to the bathroom, where the shower was already running. Nicholas was leaning into the stall to adjust the temperature of the water.

"Please," I whispered, and he jolted around as if he were hearing a ghost. The steam rose between us. "You don't know what it's like for me," I said.

The mirrors fogged over and the bathroom clouded, so that when Nicholas spoke, his word seemed to sink in the weight of the air. "Paige," he said.

I took a step toward him and tilted my head for a kiss. In the background, over the monitor, I could hear Max sighing in his sleep.

Nicholas slipped the negligee over my head. He placed his hands on my waist and skimmed his fingers over my ribs. At his touch, I moaned and stretched toward him. A thin arc of milk sprayed from my nipple onto the dark hair of his chest.

I stared down at myself, angry at my body for its betrayal. When I turned to Nicholas, I expected him to ignore what had happened, maybe to make a joke; I was not prepared for what I saw in his eyes. He took a step away from me, and his gaze roved up and down my body with horror. "I just can't," he said, almost choking. "Not yet."

He touched my cheek and then he quickly kissed my forehead, as if he had to get it over with before he changed his mind. He stepped into the shower, and I listened for a while to the quiet symphony of the falling water and the soap sliding over his shoulders and his thighs. Then I pulled the pool of satin from my feet, held it up to cover me, and walked into the bedroom.

I put on the oldest, softest nightgown I had, one that buttoned down the front and had small panda bears printed all over it. As I stepped into the hallway, Nicholas turned off the water in the shower. I carefully twisted the doorknob of the nursery, pitch black inside. Nicholas would not come for me. Not tonight. I felt my way through the dark in the room, holding on to the air as though it were something tangible. I stepped around the large stuffed red ostrich Marvela had sent, and I skimmed my hands over the terry-cloth top of the changing table. Stumbling, I hit my shin against the sharp edge of the rocker, knowing the sticky slip of my foot came from my own blood. I settled down to count Max's even breaths and waited for my son to call me.

chapter 17
Nicholas

"You're going to be late again? I don't understand why you can't arrange to be home just a little bit more."

"Paige, don't be ridiculous. I don't make my hours."

"But you don't know what it's like here, all day and all night, with him. At least you get to leave your office."

"Do you know what I'd give to come home one night and not hear you bitching about the kind of day *you've* had?"

"Pardon me, Nicholas, but I don't get too many other visitors to complain to."

"No one tells you to sit in the house."

"No one helps me when I leave it."

"Paige, I'm going to bed. I have to get up early."

"You always have to get up early. And you're the one that counts, of course, because you're the one with the job."

"Well, you're doing something just as important. Consider this *your* job."

"I do, Nicholas. But it wasn't supposed to be."

≈≈≈

The first thing that struck Nicholas was how many trees were already in bloom. He'd lived on this block for eighteen years of his life, but it had been so long since he'd even seen it that he assumed the Japanese maples and the crab apple trees formed their wide mauve awnings over the front yard at the *end* of June. He sat for a few minutes in the car, thinking about what he would say and how he would say it. He ran his fingers over the smooth polished wood of the stick shift, feeling instead the cool leather of a baseball, the soft inner pouch of his childhood mitt. His mother's Jaguar was parked in the driveway.

Nicholas had not been to his parents' home in eight years, not since the night when the Prescotts had made clear what they thought of his choice of Paige as a wife. He had been bitter enough to cut off his contact with his parents for a year and a half, and then a Christmas card had come from Astrid. Paige had left it with the bills for Nicholas to see, and when he did he had turned it over and over in his hands like an ancient relic. He'd run his fingertips over the neat block lettering of his mother's print, and then he had glanced up to see Paige across the room, trying to look as if she didn't care. For her benefit he'd thrown away Astrid's card—but the next day, from the hospital, he had called his mother.

Nicholas told himself he was not doing it because he forgave them, or because he thought they were right about Paige. In fact, when he spoke to his mother—twice a year now, on Christmas and on her birthday—they did not mention Paige. They did not mention Robert Prescott, either, because Nicholas vowed that in spite of the curiosity that drew him to his mother, he would never forget the image of his father bearing down on Paige eight years before, when she sat unsettled and engulfed by a wing chair.

He didn't tell Paige about these calls. Nicholas was inclined to believe that since his mother had never in eight years even asked about his wife, his parents had not changed their original impression of Paige. The Prescotts seemed to be waiting for Paige and Nicholas to have a falling-out, so they could point fingers and say "I told you so." Oddly enough, Nicholas never took this personally. He spoke to his mother just to keep hanging by a filial thread; but he divided his life into pre-Paige and post-Paige. Their conversations concentrated on Nicholas's life up till the fateful argument, as if days instead of years had passed. They spoke about the weather, about Astrid's treks, about Brookline's curbside recycling program. They did not mention his specialization in cardiac surgery, the purchase of his house, Paige's pregnancy. Nicholas did not offer any information that might widen the rift that still spread between them.

It didn't help to be sitting in front of his childhood home, however, and be thinking that all those years ago, his parents just might have had a point. Nicholas felt he'd been defending Paige forever, but he was beginning to forget why. He was starving, because Paige didn't make his lunch anymore. She was often awake at four-thirty in the morning, but usually Max was attached to her. Sometimes— not often—he blamed the baby. Max was the easiest target, the demanding thing that had taken his wife like a body snatcher and left in her place the sullen, moody woman he now shared a home with. It was hard to blame Paige herself. Nicholas would look into her eyes, raring for an argument, but all that gazed back at him was that vacant sky-stare, and he'd swallow his anger and taste raw pity.

He didn't understand Paige's problem. *He* was the one on his feet all goddamned day; *he* was the one with a reputation on the line; *he* was the one whose missteps could cost lives. If anyone had a right to be exhausted or short-tempered, it was Nicholas. All Paige did was sit in the house with a baby.

And from the time he'd spent with his son, it didn't seem so difficult. Nicholas would sit on the floor and pull at Max's toes, laughing when Max opened his eyes wide and stared around, trying to figure out who'd done that. A month or so ago, he'd been whirling Max around over his head and then hanging him from his feet—he loved that kind of thing—as Paige watched from a corner, her mouth turned down. "He's going to puke on you," she said. "He just drank." But Max had kept his eyes open, watching his world spin. When Nicholas had righted the baby and cradled him, Max turned his gaze up and stared directly at his father. Then a slow smile spread across his face, blushing into his cheeks and straightening his little shoulders. "Look, Paige!" Nicholas had said. "Isn't that his first real smile?" And Paige had nodded and looked at Nicholas in awe. She had left the room to find Max's baby book, so she could record the date.

Nicholas patted his breast pocket. They were still there, the pictures of Max he'd just had developed. He would leave one with his mother if he was feeling charitable by the time he left. He hadn't wanted to come in the first place. It was Paige who had suggested he call his parents and let them know they had a grandson. "Absolutely not," Nicholas had said. Of course, Paige still believed he hadn't talked to his parents in eight years, but maybe that was true. Speaking to someone was not the same as really talking. Nicholas didn't know if he was willing to be the one to back down first.

"Well," Paige had said, "maybe it's time for all of you to let bygones be bygones." He'd found this a little hypocritical, but then she had smiled at him and ruffled his hair. "Besides," she had said, "with your mom around, think of the fortune we'll save on baby pictures."

Nicholas leaned his head back against the car seat. Overhead, clouds moved lazily across the hot spring sky. Once, when their lives were still uncluttered, Paige and Nicholas had lain on the banks of the Charles and stared at the clouds, trying to find images in their shapes. Nicholas could see only geometric figures: triangles, thin arcs, and polygons. Paige had to hold his hand against the backdrop of blue, tracing the soft fleeced white edges with his finger. *There,* she'd said, *there's an Indian chief. And far to the left is a bicycle. And a thumbtack, a kangaroo.* At first Nicholas had laughed, falling in love with her all over again for her imagination. But little by little he'd begun to see what she was talking about. Sure enough, it wasn't a cumulonimbus but the thick flowing headdress of a Sioux chief. In the corner of the sky was a wallaby's joey. When he'd looked through her eyes, there were so many things he could suddenly see.

≈≈≈

"What's the matter with him?"

"I don't know. The doctor said it's probably colic."

"Colic? But he's practically three months old. Colic is supposed to end when they're three months old."

"Yes, I know. It's *supposed* to end. The doctor also told me that research says colicky babies grow up to be more intelligent."

"Should that make it easier to block out his screaming?"

"Don't take it out on me, Nicholas. I was just answering *your* question."

"Don't you want to get him?"

"I guess."

"Well, Christ, Paige. If it's such a big deal, I'll go get him."

"No. You stay. I'm the one who has to feed him. There's no point in you getting up."

"All right, then."

"All right."

≈≈≈

Nicholas counted the number of steps he took in crossing the street and reaching the path to his parents' house. Lining the neat slate stones were rows of tulips: red, yellow, white, red, yellow, white, in organized succession. His heart was pounding to the beat of his footsteps; his mouth was unnaturally dry. Eight years was a very long time.

He thought about ringing the bell, but he didn't want to face one of the servants. He pulled his key chain from his pocket and looked through the many hospital keys to find the old, tarnished one he'd kept on the brass ring since grade school. He had never thrown it away; he wasn't quite sure why. And he wouldn't have expected his parents to ask for it back. A lot might have passed between Nicholas Prescott and his parents, but in his family even bitter estrangements had to follow certain civil rules.

Nicholas was not prepared for the rush of heat that crept up his back and his neck the moment his key fit into the lock of his parents' home. He remembered, all at once, the day he'd fallen from the tree-house and snapped his leg bone through his skin; the time he'd come home drunk and weaved through the kitchen and into the house-keeper's bedroom by mistake; the morning he carried the world on his shoulders—his college graduation. Nicholas shook his head to force away the emotions and pushed himself into the massive foyer.

The black marble on the floor reflected a perfect image of his set face, and the fear in his eyes was mirrored in the high-polished frames of his mother's Endangered exhibit. Nicholas took two steps that sounded like primal thunder, certain that everyone now knew he was here. But no one came. He tossed his jacket onto a gilded chair and walked down the hall to his mother's darkroom.

Astrid Prescott was developing her photos of the Moab, nomads who lived among hills of sand, but she couldn't get her red right. The color of the ruby dust was still clouding her mind, but no matter how many prints she made, it wasn't the right shade. It didn't fix angry enough to whirl around the people, framing them in their nightmares. She put down the last set of photos and pinched the bridge of her nose. Maybe she would try again tomorrow. She pulled several contact sheets from her hanging line, and then she turned and saw the image of her son.

"Nicholas," his mother whispered.

Nicholas did not move a muscle. His mother looked older, frailer. Her hair was wound in a tight knot at the nape of her neck, and the veins on her clenched fists stood out prominently, marking her hands like a well-traveled map. "You have a grandchild," he said. His words were tight and clipped and sounded foreign on his tongue. "I thought you should know."

He turned to leave, but Astrid Prescott rushed forward, scattering the elusive prints of the desert onto the floor. Nicholas was stopped by the touch of his mother's hand. Her fingertips, coated with fixer, left traces of burns up the length of his arm. "Please stay," she said. "I want to catch up. I want to look at you. And you must need so much for the baby. I'd love to see him—her?—and Paige too."

Nicholas regarded his mother with all the cold reserve she'd proudly bred into him. He pulled a snapshot of Max from his pocket and tossed it onto the table, on top of a print of a turbaned man with a face as old as honesty. "I'm sure it isn't as good as yours," Nicholas said, staring down into the startled blue eyes of his son. When they'd taken that picture, Paige had stood behind Nicholas with a white sock pulled onto her hand. She had drawn eyes on the top of it and a long forked tongue and had hissed and made rattlesnake noises, pretending to bite Nicholas's ear. In the end, Max had smiled after all.

Nicholas pulled his arm away from his mother's touch. He knew he could not stand there much longer without giving in. He would reach for his mother, and by erasing the space between them, he would be wiping clean a slate listed with grievances that were already starting to fade. He took a deep breath and stood tall. "At one point you weren't ready to be part of my family." He stepped back, digging his heel into the melting fossil sunset of one Moab print. "Well, *I'm* not ready now." And he turned and disappeared through the shifting black curtain of the darkroom, leaving an outlined glow in the dim crimson light like the unrelenting face of a ghost.

≈≈≈

"I went today."

"I know."

"How did you know?"

"You haven't said three words to me since you got home. You're a million miles from here."

"Well, only about ten miles. Brookline's not so far. But you're just a Chicago girl; what could you know?"

"Very funny, Nicholas. So what did they say?"

"*She.* I wasn't going to go when my father was home. I went during my lunch break today."

"I didn't know you got lunch breaks—"

"Paige, let's not start this again."

"So—what did she say?"

"I don't remember. She wanted to know more. I left her a picture."

"You didn't talk to her? You didn't sit down and have tea and crumpets and all that?"

"We're not British."

"You know what I mean."

"No, we did not sit down and have tea. We didn't sit down at all. I was there for ten minutes, tops."

"Was it very hard? . . . Why are you looking at me like that? What?"

"How can you do it? You know, just cut to the heart of the matter like that?"

"Well, *was* it?"

"It was harder than putting together a heart-lung. It was harder than telling the parents of a three-year-old that their kid just died on the operating table. Paige, it was the hardest thing I've ever done in my life."

"Oh, Nicholas."

"Are you going to turn off that light?"

"Sure."

"Paige? Do we have a copy of that picture I left at my parents'?"

"The one of Max we got with the sock snake?"

"Yeah. It's a good picture."

"I can get a copy. I have the negative somewhere."

"I want it for my office."

"You don't have an office."

"Then I'll put it in my locker. . . . Paige?"

"Mmm?"

"He's a pretty attractive kid, isn't he? I mean, on the average, I don't think babies are quite as good-looking. Is that a pretentious thing to say?"

"Not if you're his father."

"But he's handsome, isn't he?"

"Nicholas, love, he looks exactly like you."

chapter 18
Paige

I was reading an article about a woman who had a bad case of the postpartum blues. She swung from depression to exhilaration; she had trouble sleeping. She became slovenly, wild-eyed, and agitated. She began to have thoughts about hurting her baby girl. She called these thoughts The Plan and told them, in fragments, to her co-workers. Two weeks after she began having these ideas, she came home from work and smothered her eight-month-old daughter with a couch pillow.

She had not been the only one. There was a woman before her who killed her first two babies within days of their births and who tried to kill the third before authorities stepped in. Another woman drowned her two-month-old and told everyone he'd been kidnapped. A third shot her son. Another ran her baby over with her Toyota.

This apparently was a big legal battle in the United States. Women accused of infanticide in England during the first year after birth could be charged only with manslaughter, not murder. People said it was mental illness: eighty percent of all new mothers suffered from the baby blues; one in a thousand suffered from postpartum psychosis; three percent of those who suffered from psychosis would kill their own children.

I found myself gripping the magazine so tightly that the paper ripped. What if I was one of them?

I turned the page, glancing at Max in his playpen. He was gumming a plastic cube that was part of a toy too advanced for his age. No one ever sent us age-appropriate baby gifts. The next article was a self-help piece. *Make a list,* the article suggested, *of all the things you can do.* Supposedly after fashioning such a list, you'd feel better about yourself and your abilities than when you started. I flipped over the grocery list and picked up a dull pencil. I looked at Max. *I can change a diaper.* I wrote it down, and then the other obvious things: *I can measure formula. I can snap Max's outfits without screwing up. I can sing him to sleep.* I began to wonder what talents I had that had nothing to do with my baby. Well, I could draw and sometimes see into people's lives with a simple sketch. I could bake cinnamon buns from scratch. I knew all the words to "A Whiter Shade of Pale." I could swim half a mile without getting too tired; at least I *used* to be able to do that. I could list the names of most of the cemeteries in Chicago; I knew how to splice electrical cords; I understood the difference between principal and interest payments on our mortgage. I could get to Logan Airport via the T. I could fry an egg and flip it in the pan without a spatula. I could make my husband laugh.

The doorbell rang. I stuffed the list into my pocket and tucked Max under my arm, especially unwilling to leave him alone after reading that piece on killer mothers. The familiar brown suit and cap of the UPS man was visible through the thin stained-glass pane of the door. "Hello," I said. "It's nice to see you again."

The UPS man had come very other day since Nicholas mentioned to his mother that she had a grandson. Big boxes filled with Dr. Seuss books, Baby Dior clothing, even a wooden hobbyhorse, were sent in an effort to buy Max's—and Nicholas's—love. I liked my UPS man.

He was young and he called me ma'am and he had soft brown eyes and a moony smile. Sometimes when Nicholas was on call he was the only adult I'd see for days. "Maybe you'd like to have some coffee," I said. "It's still pretty early."

The UPS man grinned at me. "Thanks, ma'am," he said, "but I can't, not on company time."

"Oh," I said, stepping back from the threshold. "I see."

"It must be tough," he said.

I blinked up at him. "Tough?"

"With a baby and all. My sister just had one and she used to be a teacher and she says one little monster is worse than a hundred and twenty seventh graders in springtime."

"Well," I said, "I suppose it is."

The UPS man hoisted the box into our living room. "Need help opening it?"

"I can manage." I shrugged and gave a small smile. "Thanks, though."

He tipped his worn brown hat and disappeared through the open doorway. I listened to the squat truck chug down the block, and then I set Max on the floor next to the box. "Don't go anywhere," I said. I backed my way into the kitchen, and then I ran to get a knife. When I came into the living room again, Max had pushed himself up on his hands, like the Sphinx. "Hey," I said, "that's pretty good." I flushed, pleased that I had finally seen a developmental marker before Nicholas.

Max watched as I cut the twine around the box and pulled out the staples. He caught a length of string in his fist and tried to work it into his mouth. I laid the knife beside the couch and pulled out of the box a little stool with cut-out yellow letters that spelled MAX and could be removed like a jigsaw puzzle. "Love, Grandma and Grandpa," read the note. Somewhere, Max had another grandpa and possibly another grandma. I wondered if he'd ever meet either.

I stood up to throw away the box, but a smaller, flat pink box caught my eye. It had been packed in the bottom of the larger one. I broke the gold-foil seals at its sides and opened it to reveal a beautiful silk scarf printed with linked brass horse bits and braided reins and U-shaped silver shoes. "For Paige," the card said, "because not only the baby deserves gifts. Mother." I thought about this. Astrid Prescott was not my mother; she never would be. For a moment my breath caught, and I wondered if it was possible that my real mother, wherever she was, had sent me this beautiful scarf through the Prescotts. I rumpled the thin silk and held it to my nose, breathing in the fragrance of a fine boutique. It was from Astrid, I knew that, and inside I was fluttering because she had thought of me. But just for today, I was going to pretend this had come from the mother I never got to know.

Max, who could not crawl, had wriggled himself over to the knife. "Oh, no you don't," I said, lifting him by his armpits. His feet kicked a mile a minute, and little bubbles of spit formed at the corners of his mouth. Standing, I held him to my chest, one arm out like a dance partner. I whirled into the kitchen, humming a Five Satins song, watching his unsteady head bob left and right.

We watched the bottle heat up in the saucepan—the only bottle of formula Max got each day, because in some ways I was still afraid that the La Leche woman would come back and find out and point a damning finger at me. I tested the liquid on my hand. We danced back to the couch in the living room and turned on Oprah, then I gently placed him on a pillow across the couch.

I liked to feed Max this way, because when I held him in my arms he could smell the breast milk and sometimes he refused to take the bottle. He wasn't a stupid little thing; he knew the real McCoy. I'd prop him on the pillow and tuck a cloth burping diaper under his chin to catch the runoff; then I'd even have a free hand to flip through channels with the remote or to scan the pages of a magazine.

Oprah had on women who had been pregnant and given birth without even knowing they'd been carrying a child. I shook my head at the screen. "Max, my boy," I said, "where could she even *find* six people like this?" One woman was saying that she had had a child already and then one night she felt a little gassy and she went to lie down in bed and ten minutes later she realized a squalling infant was between her legs. Another woman nodded her head; she'd been in the back seat of her friend's van and all of a sudden she just gave birth through her underwear and her shorts, and the baby was lying on the floor mat. "How couldn't they feel it kicking?" I said out loud. "How couldn't they notice a contraction?"

Max lifted his chin, and the diaper-bib fell to the floor, twisting over my leg to land behind me. I sighed and turned away for half a second to grab it, and that was when I heard the hard crack of Max's head striking the side of the coffee table as he rolled off the couch and onto the floor.

He lay on the pale-beige carpet, scant inches from the knife I'd used to cut the twine of the box. His arms and legs were flailing, and he was facedown. I could not breathe. I lifted him into my arms, absorbing his screams into the shallows of my bones. "Oh, God," I said, rocking him back and forth tightly as he howled with pain. "Dear God."

I lifted my head to see if Max was quieting down, and then I saw the blood, staining my shirt and a corner of the beautiful new scarf. My baby was bleeding.

I put him on the pale couch, not caring, running my fingers over his face and his neck and his arms. The blood was coming out of his nose. I had never seen so much blood. He didn't have any other cuts; he must have fallen face-first onto the hard oak of the table. His cheeks were puffed and beet red; his fists beat the air with the fury of a warrior. He would not stop bleeding. I did not know what to do.

I called the pediatrician, the number etched into my heart. "Hello," I said, breathless, over Max's cries. "Hello? No, I can't be put on hold—" But they cut me off. I pulled the phone into the kitchen, still trying to rock my child, and picked up Dr. Spock's book. I looked up Nosebleeds in the index. *Get on the phone,* I thought. *This is a goddamned emergency. I have hurt my child.* There . . . I read the whole paragraph, and at the end it said to tilt him forward so he wouldn't choke on the blood. I positioned Max and watched his face get even redder, his cries louder. I curled him into my shoulder again and wondered how I had done it wrong.

"Hello?" A voice returned to the pediatrician's line.

"Oh, God, please help me. My baby just fell. He's bleeding through his nose, and I can't make it stop—"

"Let me get you a nurse," the woman said.

"*Hurry,*" I shouted into the phone, into Max's ear.

The nurse told me to tilt Max forward, just like Dr. Spock said, and to hold a towel to his nose. I asked her if she'd hang on, and then I tried that, and this time the bleeding seemed to ebb. "It's working," I yelled into the receiver, lying on its side on the kitchen table. I picked it up. "It's working," I repeated.

"Good," the nurse told me. "Now, watch him for the next couple of hours. If he seems content, and if he's eating all right, then we don't need to see him."

At this, a flood of relief washed through me. I didn't know how I'd ever manage to get him to the doctor by myself. I could barely make it out of the neighborhood with him yet.

"And check his pupils," the nurse continued. "Make sure they aren't dilated or uneven. That's a sign of concussion."

"Concussion," I whispered, unheard over Max's cries. "I didn't mean to do it," I told the nurse.

"Of course," the nurse assured me. "No one does."

When I hung up the phone, Max was still crying so hard that he'd begun to gag on his sobs. I was shaking, rubbing his back. I tried to sponge the clotted blood around his nostrils so that he'd be able to breathe. Even after he was cleaned, faint red blotches remained, as if he'd been permanently stained. "I'm so sorry, Max," I whispered, my words rattling in my throat. "It was just a second, that's all I turned away for; I didn't know that you were going to move that fast." Max's cries waned and then became louder again. "I'm so sorry," I said, repeating the words like a lullaby. "I'm so sorry."

I carried him to the bathroom and ran the faucet and let him peek into the mirror—all the things that usually calmed him down. When Max didn't respond, I sat down on the toilet lid and rocked him closer. I had been crying too, high keening notes that tore through my body and ripped shrilly through Max's screams. It took me a moment to realize that suddenly I was the only one making a sound.

Max was still and quiet on my shoulder. I stood and moved to the mirror, afraid to look. His eyes were closed; his hair was matted with sweat. His nose was plugged with dried sienna blood, and two bruises darkened his skin just beneath his eyes. I shivered with the sudden thought: I was just like those women. I had killed my child.

Still hiccuping with sobs, I carried Max to the bedroom and placed him on the cool blue bedspread. I sighed with relief: his back rose and fell; he was breathing, asleep. His face, though brutally marked, held the peace of an angel.

I put my face into my hands, trembling. I had known that I wouldn't be a very good mother, but I assumed that my sins would be forgetfulness or ignorance. I didn't know I would hurt my own son. Surely anyone else would have lifted the baby to retrieve the diaper. I was too stupid to think of it. And if I had done it once, it could happen again.

I had a sudden memory of my mother the night before she disappeared from my life. She wore a pale-peach bathrobe and fuzzy bunny slippers. She sat on the edge of my bed. "You know I love you, Paige-boy," she said, because she thought I was asleep. "Don't you let anyone tell you otherwise."

I laid my hand on my son's back, smoothing out his ragged breathing. "I love you," I said, tracing the letters of his name on his cotton playsuit. "Don't let anyone tell you otherwise."

≈≈≈

Max woke up smiling. I was leaning over his crib, as I had been for the hour he'd been asleep, praying for the first time since he was born that he'd wake up soon. "Oh, sweetie," I said, reaching for his chubby fingers.

I changed his diaper and took out his little bathtub. I sat him in it fully clothed but filled the basin with Baby Magic and warm water.

Then I washed off his face and his arms where they were still splat-
tered from the nosebleed. I changed his outfit, rinsing the old one as
best I could and hanging it over the shower rod to dry.

I gave him the breast instead of the bottle he'd never finished,
figuring he deserved a little pampering. I cuddled him close, and he
smiled and rubbed his cheek against me. "You don't remember a
thing, do you?" I said. I closed my eyes and leaned my head against
the couch. "Thank heaven."

Max was so good-natured for the rest of the afternoon that I knew
God was punishing me. I wallowed in my guilt, tickling Max's belly,
blowing wet kisses onto his fat thighs. When Nicholas came home,
a knot tightened in my stomach, but I did not get up off the floor
with the baby. "Paige, Paige, Paige!" Nicholas sang, stepping into
the hallway. He sashayed into the living room with his eyes half
closed. He'd been on call for thirty-six straight hours. "Don't mention
the words Mass General to me—don't even say the word *heart*. For
the next twenty-four glorious hours I'm going to sleep and eat greasy
food and be a sloth right here in my own house." He walked down
the hall toward the stairs, his voice trailing behind. "Did you get to
the cleaners?" he called.

"No," I whispered. I had an excuse this time for not leaving the
house, but he wouldn't want to hear it.

Nicholas reappeared in the living room, holding his shirt by the
collar. His good mood had vanished. He'd asked me to go to the dry
cleaners two days ago, but I hadn't felt comfortable taking Max by
myself, and Nicholas hadn't been home to watch him, and I didn't
know how to even begin to find a baby-sitter. "It's a good thing I
have off tomorrow, then, since this is the last goddamned clean shirt
I had. Come *on,* Paige," he said, his eyes turning dark. "You can't
possibly be busy every minute of the day."

"I was thinking," I said, not looking up, "that maybe you'd watch
the baby while I go to the laundry and grocery shopping." I swallowed. "I was kind of waiting for you to get home."

Nicholas glared at me. "This is the first break I've had in thirty-
six hours and you want me to watch Max?" I did not say anything.

"For Christ's sake, Paige, it's my only day off in the past two weeks. *You're* here every single goddamned day."

"I can wait till you take a nap," I suggested, but Nicholas was already starting back down the hall.

I held Max's little fists in my hands and braced myself for what I knew was to come. Nicholas ran down the stairway with Max's bloody outfit, wet, wrapped around his fingers. "What the hell is this?" Nicholas said, his voice hot and low.

"Max had an accident," I said as calmly as I could. "A nosebleed. I didn't mean to do it. The diaper fell—" I looked up at Nicholas, at the storm in his eyes, and I started to cry again. "I twisted around for a second—well, not even; more like half a second—to get it, and Max rolled the wrong way and hit his nose on the table—"

"When," Nicholas said, "were you planning on telling me?"

He crossed the room in three long strides and picked Max up roughly. "Be careful," I said, and Nicholas made a strange sound in the back of his throat.

His eyes swept the kidney-shaped bruises below Max's eyes, the traces of blood on the pads of his nose. He looked at me for a moment, as if he were piercing through to my soul and knew I was marked for hell. He clutched the baby tighter in his arms. "You go," he said quietly. "I'll take care of Max."

His words, and the accusation behind them, stung me as violently as a slap to the face. I stood and walked to the bedroom, collecting the heap of Nicholas's shirts. I pulled them into my arms, feeling their sleeves wrap and bind my wrists. I pulled my purse and my sunglasses from the kitchen table, and then I stood in the doorway of the living room. Nicholas and Max looked up at the same time. They sat together on the pale couch, looking as if they were carved from the same block of marble. "I didn't mean to," I whispered, and then I turned away.

At the cash machine, I was crying so hard that I didn't realize I had pressed the wrong buttons until a thousand dollars came out, instead of the hundred I needed for grocery shopping and prepayment on Nicholas's shirts. I did not bother to redeposit it. Instead I tore out of the fire zone I'd parked in, rolled down all the windows, and headed to the nearest highway. It felt good to hear the wind scream in my ears and lighten the weight of my hair. The band in my chest began to ease, and my headache was disappearing. Maybe, I thought, what I needed all along was a little time alone. Maybe I just needed to get away.

The supermarket's flashing sign appeared at the horizon. And it struck me then that Nicholas was right to doubt me, to hold Max as far away from me as he could. Here I was smiling into the rushing air, thinking about my freedom, when just hours before I had watched my child bleed because of my own carelessness.

There had to be something wrong with me, deep down, that made me to blame for Max's fall. There had to be something that made me such an incompetent mother. Maybe it was the same reason my own mother had left—she was afraid of what more she could do wrong. It was possible that Max was better off the way he was, in the solid, strong arms of his father. It was possible that given the option, Max would do better with no mother at all.

At the very least, this much was true: I was no good to Max, or to Nicholas, the way I was right now.

As I drove straight past the market, the plan began to form in my head. I wouldn't be gone for long, just for a little while. Just until I had got a full night's sleep, and I felt good about myself and about being Max's mother, and I could make a long self-help list of all the things I could do, without running out of ideas. I would come back with all the answers; I would be a whole new person. I would call Nicholas in a few hours and tell him my idea, and he would agree and say in his calm, brook-steady voice, "Paige, I think it's just what you need."

I started to laugh, my spirit bubbling up from where it had been buried deep inside. It was really so easy. I could keep driving and driving and pretend that I had no husband, no baby. I could keep going and never look back. Of course I *would* go back, as soon as I had my life in order again. But right now, I deserved this. I was taking back the time I had been cheated of.

I drove faster than I'd ever driven in my life. I ran my fingers through my hair and grinned until the wind cracked my lips. My cheeks grew flushed and my eyes stung from the brisk rush of the air. One by one, I tossed Nicholas's shirts out the window, leaving behind on the highway a trail of white, yellow, pink, powder blue, like a fine string of pale scattered pearls.

Part II:
Growth
Summer 1993

chapter 19
Paige

*T*he thick sateen curtains at Ruby's House of Fate blocked out the hot midday sun. Ruby herself, a mountain of copper flesh, sat across from me. She held my hands in her own. Her cheeks reddened, her chins trembled. Suddenly her thick eyelids opened, to reveal startling green eyes that had, just minutes before, been brown. "Girl," Ruby said, "yo' future is yo' past."

I had come to Ruby's House of Fate out of hunger. Driving all day away from Cambridge had brought me to Pennsylvania—to Amish country. For a time I had parked the car and watched the neat black buggies, the fresh-capped girls. Something told me to keep on driving, in spite of the burning in the pit of my stomach. I hadn't eaten since breakfast, and it was now almost eight o'clock at night. So I had continued west, and at the outskirts of Lancaster I discovered Ruby. Her little row house was marked by a big billboard in the shape of a palm, covered with glittering moons and gold stars. RUBY'S HOUSE OF FATE, the sign read. YOUR PLACE TO FIND ANSWERS.

I wasn't certain what my questions were, but that didn't seem important. I wasn't a believer in astrology, but that also seemed to be beside the point. Ruby answered the door as if she had been expecting me. I was confused. What was a black woman doing reading fortunes in Amish country? "You'd be amazed," she said, as if I had spoken aloud. "So many people pass through."

Ruby did not tear her green eyes from mine. I had been driving aimlessly all day, but at Ruby's words I suddenly realized where I was headed. "I'm going to Chicago?" I asked softly, for confirmation, and Ruby grinned.

I tried to pull away from her grasp, but she held fast to my hand. She rubbed her smooth thumb over my palm and spoke quietly in a language I did not understand. "You'll find her," she said, "but she isn't what you think she is."

"Who?" I asked, although I knew she meant my mother.

"Sometimes," she said, "bad blood skips a generation."

I waited for her to explain, but she released my hand and cleared her throat. "That'll be twenty-five," she said, and I rummaged through my purse. Ruby walked me outside, and I swung open the hot, heavy door of the car. "You need to call him too," she said, and by the time I looked up at her, she was gone.

≈≈≈

"Nicholas?" I pulled at the collar of my shirt and ran my fingers over the smooth silk scarf from Astrid, trying to escape the phone booth's heat.

"My God, Paige. Are you hurt? I called the supermarket—I called six of them, because I didn't know where you'd gone, and I tried the nearest gas stations. Was there an accident?"

"Not really," I said, and I heard Nicholas draw in his breath. "How's the baby?" I asked, feeling tears prick the back of my throat. It was strange; for almost three months, all I'd thought about was getting away from Max, and now I couldn't stop thinking about him. He was always in the corner of my mind, clouding my vision, his gummy fists reaching toward me. I actually missed him.

"The baby's fine. Where are you? When are you coming home?"

I took a deep breath. "I'm in Lancaster, Pennsylvania."

"You're *where?*" In the background, I heard Max start to cry, and then the sounds became louder, so I knew Nicholas was jiggling the baby in his arms.

"I was headed to the Stop & Shop, and I kind of kept going. I just need a little time—"

"Well, hey, Paige, so does the rest of the free world, but we don't just up and run away!" Nicholas was yelling; I held the receiver away from my ear. "Let me get this straight," he said, "you left us on *purpose?*"

"I didn't run away," I insisted. "I'm coming back."

"When?" Nicholas demanded. "I have a life, you know. I have a job to get back to."

I closed my eyes and leaned my head against the glass of the phone booth. "I have a life too."

Nicholas did not answer, and for a moment I thought he'd hung up, but then I heard Max babbling in the background. "Your life," Nicholas said, "is right here. *Not* in Lancaster, Pennsylvania."

What I wanted to tell him was: I'm not ready to be a mother. I can't even be your wife, not until I patch together the pieces of my own life and fill in all the holes. I *will* come home, and we'll pick up where we left off. I won't forget you; I love you. But what I said to Nicholas was: "I'll be back soon."

Nicholas's voice was hoarse and low. "Don't bother," he said, and he slammed down the phone.

≈≈≈

I drove all night and all day, and by 4:00 P.M. I was on the Loop, heading into Chicago. Knowing that my father wouldn't be home for a couple of hours, I headed toward the old art supply store I used to go to. It felt strange driving through the city. When I had been here last, I had no car; I had always been escorted. At a stoplight I thought about Jake—the angles of his face and the rhythm of his breathing. Once, that was all it had taken to make him appear. I drove carefully when the light turned green, expecting him to be on the next street corner, but I was mistaken. That telepathy had been severed years ago by Jake, who knew we could never go back.

The owner of the art store was Indian, with the smooth brown skin of an onion. He recognized me right away. "Missy O'Toole," he said, his voice running over my name like a river. "What can I get for you?" He clasped his hands in front of himself, as if I had last stepped into the store a day or two before. I did not answer him at first. I walked to the carved statues of Vishnu and Ganesh, running my fingers over the cool stone elephant's head. "I'll need some conté sticks," I whispered, "a newsprint pad, and charcoal." The words came so easily, I might as well have been seventeen again.

He brought me what I had asked for and held out the conté sticks for my approval. I took them into my palm as reverently as I'd taken the Host at Communion. What if I couldn't do it anymore? It had been years since I'd drawn anything substantial.

"I wonder," I said to the man, "if maybe you would let me draw you."

Pleased, the man settled himself between the Hindu sculptures of the Preserver of Life and the God of Good Fortune. "What better place for me to be sitting myself," he chattered. "If you please, missy, this place would be very good, very good indeed."

I swallowed hard and picked up the newsprint pad. With hesitant lines I drew the oval of the man's face, the fierce glitter of his eyes. I used a white conté stick for relief shading, creating a fine web of wrinkles at his temples and his chin. I mapped the age of his smile and the slight swell of his pride. When I finished, I stepped away from the pad and observed it critically. I was a little off on the likeness, but it was good enough for a first try. I peered into the background and the shadows of his face, expecting to see one of my hidden pictures, but there was nothing except for the calm brush of charcoal. Maybe I had lost my other talent, and I thought that this might not be so bad.

"Missy, you have finished? You do not want to keep such work all to yourself." The man scurried toward me and beamed at my sketch. "You will leave it here for me, yes?"

I nodded. "You can have it. Thank you."

I handed him the sketch, and a twenty to pay for the supplies, but he waved me away. "You give me a gift," he said, "I give you one in return."

I drove to the lake and parked illegally. Carrying my pad and my box of charcoal under my arm, I went to sit on the shore. It was a cool day, and not many people were in the water, just some children with bubble floats around their waists, whose mothers watched with lioness stares in case they drifted away. I sat on the edge of the water and brought Max to mind, trying to conjure a clear enough image to draw him. When I couldn't, I was shocked. No matter how hard I tried, I couldn't catch in his eyes the way he looked at the world, the way everything was a series of first times. And without that, a picture of Max just wasn't a picture of Max. I tried to imagine Nicholas, but it was the same. His fine aquiline nose, the thick sheen of his hair— they appeared and receded in waves, as if I were looking at him lying on the bottom of a rippled pond. When I touched the charcoal to the paper, nothing happened at all. It struck me how strong the slam of that phone might have been. As Jake had done once before, it was possible that Nicholas had broken all of our connections.

Determined not to start crying, I stared across the dappled surface of the lake and began to move the charcoal over the blank page. Diamonds of sunlight and shifting currents appeared. Even though the picture was black and white, you could clearly see how blue the water was. But as I continued, I realized that I was not drawing Lake Michigan at all. I was drawing the ocean, the Caribbean ring that banded Grand Cayman Island.

When I was twelve I had gone with my father to Grand Cayman for an Invention Convention. He used up most of our savings for the plane ticket and the rental condo. He was setting up a booth of rocks, the fake ones he'd created that held a secret compartment for a key and could be placed on the dirt right outside your front door just in case. The convention lasted for two days, during which I was left at the condo to roam the beach. I made snow angels in the white sand and I snorkeled around the reefs and dove to grab at fire-colored coral and neon-streaked angelfish. The third day, our last, my father sat on a chaise longue on the beach. He didn't want to go into the water with me, because, he said, he'd barely even seen the sun. So I went in alone, and to my surprise, a sea turtle came swimming beside me. It was two feet long and had a tag under its armpit. It had black beaded eyes and a leathery smile; its shell was curved down like a topaz horizon. It seemed to grin at me, and then it swam away.

I followed. I was always a few strokes behind. Finally, when the turtle disappeared behind a wall of coral, I stopped. I floated on my back and rubbed the stitch in my side. When I opened my eyes, I was at least a mile away from where I'd started.

I breast-stroked back, and by that time my father was frantic. He asked where I'd gone, and when I told him he said it had been a stupid thing to do. But I went into the ocean again anyway, hoping to find that sea turtle. Of course it was a big ocean and the turtle was long gone, but I had known—even at twelve—that I had to take the chance.

I laid down the drawing. A familiar breathlessness came when I finished the sketch, as if I'd had a spirit channeling through me and was only just returning now. In the middle of Lake Michigan I'd drawn that vanishing turtle. Its back was made up of a hundred hexagons. And very faintly, in every single polygon, I had drawn my mother.

≈≈≈

I knew before I even turned onto my old block that I would not be staying long enough to remember all the things about my childhood that I'd trapped in some dark corner of my mind. I would not be able to remember the bus route to the Institute of Art. I would not have time to recall the name of the Jewish bakery with fresh onion bagels. I would stay only until I had gathered the information I needed to find my mother.

I realized that in a way I'd always been trying to find her. Except I hadn't been chasing her; she'd been chasing me. She was always there when I looked over my shoulder, reminding me of who I was and how I got to be that way. Until today I had believed she was the reason I had lost Jake, the reason I'd run from Nicholas, the reason I'd left Max. I saw her at the root of every mistake I'd ever made. But now I wondered if she really *was* the enemy. After all, I seemed to be following in her footsteps. She had run away too, and maybe if I knew her reasons I'd understand mine. For all I knew, my mother could be just like me.

I walked up the steps to my childhood home, my feet falling into the sunken brick patterns. Behind me lay Chicago, winking at dusk and spread like a destiny. I knocked on the front door for the first time in eight years.

My father opened it. He was shorter than I remembered, and his hair, streaked with gray, fell over his eyes. "May," he whispered, frozen. "*Á mhuírnán.*"

My love. He had spoken in Gaelic, which he almost never did, an endearment I remembered him saying to my mother. And he had called me by my mother's name.

I did not move. I wondered if this was an omen. My father blinked several times and took a step backward, and then he stared at me again. "*Paige,*" he said, shaking his head as if he still could not believe it was me. My father held out his hands and, with them, everything he could offer. "Lass," he said, "you're the image of your mother."

chapter 20

Nicholas

Who the hell did she think she was? She picked up and vanished for hours, and then she phoned from goddamned Lancaster, Pennsylvania, and all the time that he'd been pacing and calling hospital emergency rooms she'd been running away. In one fell swoop, Paige had overturned his entire life. This was not the way Nicholas liked things. He liked neat sutures, very little bleeding, OR schedules that did not waver. He liked organization and precision. He did not enjoy surprises, and he *hated* being shocked.

He was not sure whom he was more pissed off at: Paige, for running away, or himself, for not seeing it coming. What kind of woman *was* she, anyway, to abandon a three-month-old baby? A shudder ran across Nicholas's shoulders. Surely this was not the woman he'd fallen in love with eight years ago. Something had happened, and Paige was not what she used to be.

This was inexcusable.

Nicholas glanced at Max, still chewing on the piece of telephone cord that dipped into his playpen. He picked up the telephone and called the twenty-four-hour emergency number of the bank. Within minutes he'd put a hold on his assets, frozen his checking account, and revoked Paige's charge cards. This made him smile, with a feeling of satisfaction that snaked all the way down to his belly. She wasn't going to get very far.

Then he called Fogerty's office at the hospital, expecting to leave a message for Alistair to call him later that evening. But to Nicholas's surprise, it was Fogerty's brusque, icy voice that answered the phone. "Well, hello," he said, when he heard Nicholas. "Shouldn't you be sleeping?"

"Something's come up," Nicholas said, swallowing the bitterness that lodged in his mouth. "It seems that Paige is gone."

Alistair didn't respond, and then Nicholas realized he probably thought Paige was dead. "She's left, I mean. She just sort of picked up and disappeared. Temporary insanity, I think."

There was silence. "Why are you telling me this, Nicholas?"

Nicholas had to think about that. Why *was* he calling Fogerty? He turned to watch Max, who had rolled onto his back and was biting his own feet. "I need to do something with Max," Nicholas said. "If I have surgery tomorrow I'll need someone to watch him."

"Perhaps the past seven years haven't clarified my position at the hospital for you," Fogerty said. "I'm the head of cardiothoracic, not day care."

"Alistair—"

"Nicholas," Fogerty said, "this is *your* problem. Good night." And he hung up the phone.

Nicholas stared at the receiver in his hand in disbelief. He had less than twelve hours to find a baby-sitter. "Shit," he said, rummaging through the kitchen drawers. He tried to find an address book of Paige's, but there seemed to be nothing around. Finally, tucked against the microwave, he found a thin black binder. He opened it and riffled through the pages, alphabetically thumb-indexed. He looked for unfamiliar female names, friends of Paige's he might prevail upon. But there were only three numbers: Dr. Thayer, the obstetrician; Dr. Rourke, the pediatrician; and Nicholas's beeper number. It was as if Paige didn't know anyone else.

Max began to cry, and Nicholas realized he hadn't changed the baby's diaper since Paige disappeared. He carried him into the nursery, holding him away from his chest as if he might get soiled. Nicholas pulled at the crotch of the playsuit until the snaps all freed themselves, and then he untaped the disposable diaper. He went to reach for another and was holding it in the air, trying to determine if the little Mickey and Donald faces went in the front or the back, when he felt something warm strike him. A thin arc of urine jetted from between Max's kicking legs and soaked Nicholas's neck and collar.

"God damn you," Nicholas said, looking squarely at his son but speaking to Paige. He loosely tacked on the new diaper and left the playsuit to hang free, unwilling to bother with the snaps. "We're going to feed you," Nicholas said, "and then you're going to sleep."

Nicholas didn't realize until he reached the kitchen that Max's primary source of food was hundreds of miles away. He seemed to remember Paige mentioning formula. He put Max into the high chair wedged into a corner of the kitchen and pulled cereals, pasta, and canned fruit from the cabinets in an effort to find the Enfamil.

It was a powdered mix. He knew something should be sterilized, but there wasn't time for that now. Max was starting to cry, and without even checking him, Nicholas put the water up to boil and found three empty plastic bottles that he assumed were clean. He read the back of the Enfamil bucket. One scoop for every two ounces. Surely in this kitchen he could find a measuring cup.

He looked under the sink and over the refrigerator. Finally, under a collection of spatulas and slotted spoons he found one. He tapped his foot impatiently, willing the teakettle to whistle. When it did he poured eight ounces of water into each bottle and added four scoops of powder. He did not know that a baby Max's age could not finish an eight-ounce bottle in one sitting. All that Nicholas cared about was getting Max fed, getting Max to go to sleep, and then crawling into bed himself.

Tomorrow he'd find a way to keep Max at the hospital with him. If he showed up at the OR with a baby on his shoulder, *someone* would give him a hand. He couldn't think about it now. His head was pounding, and he was so dizzy he could barely stand.

He stashed two bottles in the refrigerator and took the third to Max. Except he couldn't find Max. He'd left him in the high chair, but suddenly he was gone. "Max," Nicholas called. "Where'd you go, buddy?" He walked out of the kitchen and ran up the stairs, so wiped out he half expected his son to be standing at the bathroom sink, shaving, or in the nursery getting dressed for a date. Then he heard the cries.

It had never occurred to him that Max couldn't sit up well enough to go into a high chair. What the hell was the thing doing in the kitchen, then? Max had slipped down in the seat until his head was wedged under the plastic tray. Nicholas tugged at the tray, unsure which latch would release it, and finally pulled hard enough to dislodge the whole front section. He tossed it across the room. As soon as he picked up his son, the baby quieted, but Nicholas couldn't help noticing the red welted pattern pressed into Max's cheek by the screws and grooves of the high chair.

"I only left him for half a second," Nicholas muttered, and in the back of his mind he heard Paige's soft, clear words: *That's all it takes.* Nicholas hiked the baby higher on his shoulder, hearing Max's muffled sigh. He thought about the nosebleed and the way Paige's voice shook when she told Nicholas about it. Half a second.

He took the baby into the bedroom and fed him the bottle in the dark. Max fell asleep almost immediately. When Nicholas realized that the baby's lips had stopped moving, he pulled away the bottle and adjusted Max so that he was cradled in his arms. Nicholas knew that if he stood up to bring Max to his crib, he'd wake up. He had a vision of Paige nursing Max in bed and falling asleep. *You don't want him to get used to sleeping here,* he'd told her. *You don't want to create bad habits.* And she'd stumble into the nursery, holding her breath so the baby wouldn't wake.

Nicholas unbuttoned his shirt with one hand and settled a pillow under the arm that held Max. He closed his eyes. He was bone tired; he felt worse after taking care of Max than he did after performing open-heart surgery. There were similarities: both required quick thinking, both required intense concentration. But he was good at one, and as for the other, well, he didn't have a clue.

This was all Paige's fault. If it was her idea of some stupid little lesson, she wasn't going to get away with it. Nicholas didn't care if he never saw Paige again. Not after she'd pulled this stunt.

Out of nowhere, he remembered being eleven years old, his lip split by a bully in a playground fight. He had lain on the ground until the other kids left, but he would not let them see him cry. Later, when he'd told his parents about it, his mother had held her hand against his cheek and smiled at him.

He would not let Paige see him cry, or complain, or be in any way inconvenienced. Two could play the same game. And he'd do what he did to that bully—he'd ignored him so completely in the days following the fight that other children began to follow Nicholas's lead, and in the end the boy had come to Nicholas and apologized, hoping he'd win back his friends.

Of course, that was a kids' competition. This was his life. What Paige had done was somewhere beyond forgiveness.

Nicholas expected to toss and turn, racked by black thoughts of his wife. But he was asleep before he reached the pillow. He did not remember, the next morning, how quickly sleep had come. He did not remember the dream he had of his first Christmas with Paige, when she'd given him the children's game Operation! and they'd played for hours. He did not remember the coldest part of the night, when out of pure instinct Nicholas had pulled his son closer and given him his heat.

chapter 21
Paige

My mother's clothes didn't fit. They were too long in the waist and tight at the chest. They were made for someone taller and thinner. When my father brought up the old trunk filled with my mother's things, I had held each musty scrap of silk and cotton as if I were touching her own hand. I pulled on a yellow halter top and seersucker walking shorts, and then I peeked into the mirror. Reflected back was the same face I'd always seen. This surprised me. By now my mother and I had grown so similar in my mind, I believed in some ways I had *become* her.

When I came back down to the kitchen, my father was sitting at the table. "This is all I have, Paige," he said, holding up the wedding photo I knew so well. It had sat on the night table beside my father's bed my whole life. In it, my father was looking at my mother, holding her hand tightly. My mother was smiling, but her eyes betrayed her. I had spent years looking at that photo, trying to figure out what my mother's eyes reminded me of. When I was fifteen, it had come to me. A raccoon trapped by headlights, the minute before the car strikes.

"Dad," I said, running my finger over his younger image, "what about her other stuff? Her birth certificate and her wedding ring, old photos, things like that?"

"She took them. It isn't as if she died, you know. She planned leavin', right on down to the last detail."

I poured myself a cup of coffee and offered some to him. He shook his head. My father moved uncomfortably in his chair; he did not like the topic of my mother. He hadn't wanted me to look for her—that much was clear—but when he saw how stubborn I was about it, he said he'd do what he could for me. Still, when I asked him questions, he wouldn't look up at me. It was almost as if after all these years he blamed himself.

"Were you happy?" I said quietly. Twenty years was a long time, and I had been only five. Maybe there had been arguments I hadn't heard behind sealed bedroom doors, or a physical blow that had been regretted even as it found its mark.

"I was very happy," my father said. "I never would have guessed May was goin' to leave us."

The coffee I'd been drinking seemed suddenly too bitter to finish. I poured it down the sink. "Dad," I said, "how come you never tried to find her?"

My father stood up and walked to the window. "When I was very little and we were livin' in Ireland, my own father used to cut the fields three times each summer for haying. He had an old tractor, and he'd start on the edge of one field, circlin' tighter and tighter in a spiral until he got almost dead center. Then my sisters and I would run into the grass that still stood and we'd chase out the cottontails that had been pushed to the middle by the tractor. They'd come out in a flurry, the lot of them, jumpin' faster than we could run. Once —I think it was the summer before we came over here—I caught one by the tail. I told my da I was going to keep it like a pet, and he got very serious and told me that wouldn't be fair to the rabbit, since God hadn't made it for that purpose. But I built a hutch and gave it hay and water and carrots. The next day it was dead, lyin' on its side. My father came up beside me and said that some things were just meant to stay free." He turned around and faced me, his eyes brilliant and dark. "That," he said, "is why I never went lookin' for your mother."

I swallowed. I imagined what it would be like to hold a butterfly in your hands, something bejeweled and treasured, and to know that despite your devotion it was dying by degrees. "Twenty years," I whispered. "You must hate her so much."

"Aye." My father stood and grasped my hands. "At least as much as I love her."

≈≈≈

My father told me that my mother was born Maisie Marie Renault, in Biloxi, Mississippi. Her father had tried to be a farmer, but most of his land was swamp, so he never made much money. He died in a combine accident that was heavily questioned by the insurance company, and when she was widowed, Maisie's mother sold the farm and put the money in the bank. She went to Wisconsin and worked for a dairy. Maisie began calling herself May when she was fifteen. She finished high school and got a job in a department store called Hersey's, right on Main Street in Sheboygan. She had stolen her mother's emergency money from the crock pot, bought herself a linen dress and alligator pumps, then told the personnel director at Hersey's that she was twenty-one and had just graduated from the University of Wisconsin. Impressed by her cool demeanor and her smart outfit, they put her in charge of the makeup department. She learned how to apply blusher and foundation, how to make eyebrows where there were none, how to make moles disappear. She became an expert in the art of deception.

May wanted her mother to move to California. Years of leading the cows to the milking machines had chapped her mother's hands and permanently bent her back. May brought home pictures of Los Angeles, where lemons could grow in your backyard and where there wasn't any snow. Her mother refused to go. And so at least three times a year, May would start to run away.

She would take all her money out of the bank and pack her bag with only the most important things and put on what she called her traveling outfit: a halter top and tight white shorts. She bought bus tickets and railroad tickets and went to Madison, Springfield, even Chicago. At the end of the day she always turned around and went back home. She'd redeposit her money in the bank and unpack her suitcase and wait for her mother to return from work. As if it had all been just a lark, she'd tell her mother where she'd gone. And her mother would say, *Chicago. Now, that's farther than you went the last time.*

It was on one of these excursions to Chicago that she met my father in a diner. Maybe she'd never finished her journey because she just needed an extra push. Well, that's what my father gave her. She used to tell the neighbors that the day she laid eyes on Patrick O'Toole, she knew she was looking at her destiny. Of course she never mentioned if that was good or bad.

She married my father three months after she met him at the diner, and they moved into the little row house I would grow up in. That was 1966. She took up smoking and became addicted to the color TV they had bought with the money they got at their wedding. She watched *The Beverly Hillbillies* and *That Girl* and told my father repeatedly that her calling was to be a script writer. She practiced, writing comic routines on the backs of the brown paper grocery bags when she'd unpacked the week's food. She told my father that one day she was going to hit it big.

Because she thought she had to start somewhere, she took a job at the *Tribune*, writing the obituaries. When she found out that year that she was pregnant, she insisted on keeping the job, saying she'd go back after she had her maternity leave, because they needed the money.

She took me to the office with her three times a week, and the other two days I was watched by our next-door neighbor, an old woman who smelled of camphor. My father said May was good as a

mother, but she never talked to me like I was a baby or did baby
things like play patty-cake or hide-and-seek. When I was only nine
months old, my father had come home to find me sitting at the
threshold of the front door, wearing a diaper and a string of pearls,
my eyes and lips colored with violet eye shadow and rouge. My
mother had come running out of the living room, laughing. "Doesn't
she look perfect, Patrick?" she'd said, and when my father shook his
head, all the life had gone out of her eyes. Things like that happened
often when I was a baby. My father said she was trying to make me
grow up faster so she'd have a good, close friend.

May left us without saying goodbye on May 24, 1972. My father
said that what bothered him most about my mother's disappearance
was that he hadn't seen it coming. He'd been married to her for six
years, and he'd known so many details: the order in which she removed her makeup at night, the salad dressings she hated, the shifting
color of her eyes when she needed to be held. But she had completely
surprised him. For a while he bought the Los Angeles papers at an
international newsstand, thinking she would certainly show up in
Hollywood writing sitcoms and he'd get wind of it. But as the years
went on, he began to suspect this: Surely anyone who could vanish
without a trace could have been lying all those years. My father believed that the whole time they were married, she'd been getting
together a plan. He resolved that if she ever did come back he
wouldn't let her in, because he had been wounded beyond repair.
Unfortunately, he still found himself wondering from time to time if
she was alive, if she was all right. It was not that he expected to find
word of her anymore; he had lost his faith in love. After all, it had
been twenty years. If she appeared on his doorstep, she'd have been
no more than a stranger.

≈≈≈

My father came into my bedroom that night when the stars were
starting to lose themselves in the yawn of the morning. "You're
awake, aren't you," he said, his brogue thick from a lack of sleep.

"You knew I would be," I said. He sat down, and I took his hand in my own and looked up at him. Sometimes I could not believe all he had done for me. He had tried so hard.

"What will you do when you find her?" he said.

I sat up, pulling the covers with me. "I may not ever get that far," I said. "It's been twenty years."

"Oh, you'll find her, all right," he said. "That's the way it should be." My father was a great believer in Fate, which he had twisted to mean Divine Wisdom. As far as he was concerned, if God meant for me to find May Renault, I would find her. "When you do find her, though, you shouldn't be tellin' her things she doesn't need to know." I stared at him, unsure of what he meant. "It's too late, Paige," he said.

Then I realized that maybe for the past two days I had been harboring a rosy image of my father, my mother, and me all living again under this roof in Chicago. My father was letting me know that wouldn't happen, not on his end. And I knew that it couldn't happen on my end, either. Even if my mother packed her bags and followed me home, my home was no longer Chicago. My home was miles away, with a very different man.

"Dad," I said, pushing away the thought, "tell me a story again."

I had not heard my father's stories in years, not since I was four-teen and decided I was too old to thrill to the exploits of muscled Black Irish folk heroes possessing wit and ingenuity.

My father smiled at my request. "I suppose you'll be wantin' a love story," he said, and I laughed.

"There aren't any," I said. "There are only love stories gone wrong." The Irish had a story for every infidelity. Cuchulainn—the Irish equivalent to Hercules—was married but seduced every maiden in Ireland. Angus, the handsome god of love, was the son of Dagda —king of the gods—and a mistress, Boann, while her husband was away. Deirdre, forced to marry the old king Conchobhar to avoid a prophecy of nationwide sorrow, eloped instead with a handsome young warrior named Naoise to Scotland. When messengers tracked and found the lovers, Conchobhar had Naoise killed and commanded Deirdre to marry him. She never smiled again, and eventually she dashed her brains out on a rock.

I knew all these stories and their embellishments well enough to tell them to myself, but all of a sudden I wanted to be tucked under the covers in my childhood bedroom, listening to the tumbling brogue of my father's voice as he sang me the stories of his homeland. I settled under my blankets and closed my eyes. "Tell me the story of Dechtire," I whispered.

My father placed his cool hand on my forehead. "'Twas always your favorite," he said. He lifted his chin and stared out at the sun coming over the edge of the buildings across the street. "Well, Cuchulainn was no ordinary Irishman, and he had no ordinary birth. His mother was a beautiful woman named Dechtire, with hair as bright as king's gold and eyes greener than rich Irish rye. She was married to an Ulster chieftain, but she was too beautiful to escape the notice of the gods. And so one day she was turned into a bird, an even more beautiful creature than she had been before. She had feathers white as snow and wore a wreath braided from the pink clouds of mornin'; only her eyes were that same emerald green. She flew with fifty of her handmaidens to an enchanted palace on a lush isle in the sky, and there she sat, surrounded by her women, rufflin' and settlin' her wings.

"So nervous she was at first that she did not notice that she had been changed back into the beautiful woman she had been; nor did she notice the sun god, Lugh, standing before her and fillin' up her sky. When she turned her head and looked at him, at the rays of light spillin' from him in a bright halo, she immediately fell in love. She lived there with Lugh for many years, and there she bore him a son—Cuchulainn himself—but she eventually took her boy and went back home."

I opened my eyes, because this was the part I liked best, and even before my father said it, I realized for the first time as an adult why this story had always held such power for me.

"Dechtire's chieftain husband, who had spent years starin' into the sky and just waitin', welcomed her back, because after all, you never really stop lovin' someone, now, and he raised Cuchulainn as his own."

In all the years I had been listening, I had pictured my mother as Dechtire and myself as Cuchulainn, victims of Fate living together on a magical glittering isle. And yet I had also seen the wisdom of the waiting Ulster chieftain. I had never stopped thinking that maybe one day my mother was coming back to us too.

My father finished and patted my hand. "I've missed you, Paige," he said. He stood up then and left. I blinked at the pale ceiling. I wondered what it was like to have the best of both worlds. I wondered what it might be like to feel the smooth tiles of the sun god's palace beneath my running feet, to grow up in his afterglow.

≈≈≈

Armed with the wedding photo and all of my mother's history, I waved goodbye to my father and got into my car. I waited until he disappeared behind the peach door curtain, and then I sank my head against the wheel. Now what was I going to do?

I wanted to find a detective, someone who wouldn't laugh at me for picking up a missing persons search twenty years after the fact. I wanted to find someone who wouldn't charge me too much. But I didn't have the slightest idea where to look.

As I drove down the street, Saint Christopher's loomed on my left. I had not been into a church in eight years; Max hadn't even been baptized. This had surprised Nicholas at the time. "I thought you were just a lapsed Catholic," he said, and I told him I no longer believed in God. "Well," he had said, raising his eyebrows. "For once we see eye to eye."

I parked the car and pulled myself up the smooth stone steps of the church. Several older women were in the left aisle, waiting for a confessional to become vacant. As the minutes passed, the curtains drew back one at a time, spitting out sinners who had yet to cleanse their souls.

I walked down the central aisle of the church, the one I'd always believed I'd walk down as a bride. I sat in the first pew. The stained glass cast a rippled puddle at my feet, the dappled image of John the Baptist. I frowned at it, wondering how I had seen only the splendor of the blues and greens when I was growing up, how I never noticed that the window really blocked out the sun.

I had given up my religion, just as I told Nicholas, but that didn't mean it had given up on me. It was a two-way street: just because I chose not to pray to Jesus and the Virgin Mary didn't mean they were going to let me go without a fight. So even though I didn't attend Mass, even though I hadn't been to confession in almost a decade, God was still following me. I could feel Him like a whisper at my shoulder, telling me it wasn't as easy as I thought to renounce my faith. I could hear Him smiling gently when, in moments of crisis—like Max's nosebleed—I automatically called out to Him. It only made me angrier to know that no matter how forcefully I pushed Him out of my head, I had little choice in the matter. He was still charting my course; He was still pulling the strings.

I knelt, thinking I should look the part, but I did not let prayers form on my lips. Almost directly in front of me was the statue of the Virgin I'd wreathed as May Queen.

The mother of Christ. There aren't that many blessed women in Catholicism, so when I was a child she was my idol. I always prayed to her. And like every other little Catholic girl, I figured that if I was perfectly good for the twelve or so years left in my childhood, I'd grow up to be just like her. Once on Halloween I had even dressed up as her, wearing a blue mantle and a heavy cross, but nobody knew who I was supposed to be. I imagined Mary to be very peaceful and very beautiful—after all, God had chosen her to bear His son. But the thing I loved best about her was that her place in heaven was guaranteed simply because she'd been the mother of someone very special, and sometimes I'd borrow her from Jesus, pretending that she was sitting on the edge of my bed at night, asking me what I'd done in school that day.

I seemed to know so much about mothers in the abstract. I remembered when I had learned during a social studies unit in fifth grade that baby monkeys, given the choice, picked terry-cloth figures to cling to, rather than wire ones. Once, in a doctor's waiting room, I had read of coyotes, who howl if their cubs get lost, knowing they will find their way home by the signal. I wondered if Max would be able to find safety in my voice. I wondered if after all these years I'd be able to pick out my mother's.

Out of the corner of my eye I saw a familiar priest heading toward the altar. I did not want to be recognized and shamed into penance. I ducked my head and pushed past him in the aisle, shivering as my shoulder caught the strength of his faith.

I drove away from Saint Christopher's to the place where I knew I'd have to go before I left to find my mother. Even as I approached the Mobil station, I could see him from a distance. Jake was handing a credit card back to a buttoned-down lawyer type, taking care not to brush his blackened hand against his customer's. The man drove away in his Fiat, leaving a space for me.

Jake did not move as I pulled my car up beside the unleaded tank and got out. "Hello," I said. He clenched and then unclenched his fingers. He was wearing a wedding band, and this made my stomach burn, even though I was wearing one too. It was all right for *me* to go on, but I somehow had expected Jake to be just the way he had been when I left.

I swallowed and put on my brightest smile. "Well," I said, "I can tell you're overwhelmed to see me."

Jake spoke then, his voice running and low as I had remembered it. "I didn't know you were back," he said.

"I didn't know I was coming." I took a step away from him, shielding my eyes from the sun. The façade of the garage had been updated with fresh paint and a sign that said, "Jake Flanagan, Proprietor." I turned back to Jake.

"He died," Jake said quietly, "three years ago."

The air between us was humming, but I kept my distance. "I'm sorry," I said. "No one told me."

Jake looked at the car, which was dusty from its long drive. "How much do you want?" he said, lifting the nozzle from its cradle.

I stared at him blankly. He unscrewed the cap. "Oh, the car," I said. "Fill it."

Jake nodded and started the pump. He leaned against the hot metal door, and I watched his hands, restrained in their strength. Grease had settled into the creases in his palms, the way it used to. "What are you doing now?" he asked. "Still drawing?"

I smiled at the ground. "I'm an escape artist," I said.

"Like Houdini?"

"Yeah," I said, "but the knots and cuffs are stronger."

Jake didn't look at me when the pump switched off. He held out his hand, and I gave him my credit card.

I had expected the familiar physical jolt that had always flared between us when our fingers touched. But nothing happened. Nothing at all. I wasn't looking for passion, and I knew I wasn't in love with Jake. I was married to Nicholas. I was where I was supposed to be. But somehow I expected there to be a little something left from before. I looked into Jake's face, and his aqua eyes were cool and reserved. *Yes,* he seemed to be saying, *between us, it is over.*

When he came back a minute later, he asked if I'd come into the office for a moment. My heart caught; maybe he was going to say something to me or let down his guard. But he took me to the machine that validated credit cards. My American Express card had been rejected. "That's impossible," I murmured, and I handed him a Visa. "Try this."

The same thing happened. Without asking Jake's permission, I picked up the telephone and dialed the emergency 800 number on the back of my credit card. The operator informed me that Nicholas Prescott had voided his old Visa card and that a new one, with a new number, was being sent to his address. I put the receiver down on the counter and shook my head. "My husband," I said. "He just cut me off."

I mentally ran through the amount of cash I had left, the chances of my checks being accepted out-of-state. What if I didn't have enough to find my mother? What if I *could* find her but then was too broke to get to her? Suddenly Jake's arm was around my shoulders. He led me to a worn orange plastic window seat. "I'm gonna move your car," he said. "I'll be right back." I closed my eyes and slipped into the familiar feeling. This time, I told myself, Jake would be able to rescue me.

When he came back he sat beside me. There was gray in his hair now, just at the temples, and it still hung over his eyes and curled at the edges of his ears. He lifted my chin, and in his touch I felt that easy camaraderie I had felt when I was his favorite little sister. "So, Paige O'Toole," he said, "what brings you back to Chicago?"

As he drew the outline I filled in with chiseled images and stories the past eight years of my life. I had just told him about Max falling off the couch and getting a nosebleed, when the glass door jingled and a young woman came in. She had dark, exotic skin and eyes that tilted up. She was wearing a tie-died cotton jumper, and she carried a big bag of Fritos in her left hand. "Dinner!" she sang, and then she saw Jake sitting with me. "Oh." She smiled. "I can wait out back."

Jake stood and wiped his hands on his jeans. He put his arm around the woman's shoulders. "Paige," he said, "this is my wife, Ellen."

Ellen's dark eyes opened wider at the sound of my name. I waited a second, expecting a flare of jealousy to streak her smile. But she just took a step forward and held out her hand. "After all these years of hearing about you, it's nice to finally meet you," she said, and I could see it in her gaze—she was being honest. She slipped her arm around Jake's waist and squeezed lightly, hooking her thumb into the belt loop of his jeans. "How about I leave the Fritos," she said. "I'll catch up with you at home." And as easily as she'd interrupted, she disappeared.

When she left the small glass business office, taking with her the halo of energy that hovered around her, the air seemed to be sucked away as well. "Ellen and I have been married for five years," Jake said, staring after her. "She knows about everything. We can't—" His voice tripped, and then he started again. "We haven't been able to have any kids yet." I turned away; I did not trust myself to meet his eyes. "I love her," he said softly, watching her drive onto Franklin.

"I know."

Jake squatted down on the floor in front of me. He picked up my left hand and rubbed his thumb over my wedding band, leaving a stripe of grease that he did not try to erase. "Tell me why he cut off your charge cards," he said.

I tilted back my head and thought about the days when Jake

would be getting ready for a date with another girl; all the nights I had eaten with his family and pretended that I really belonged and spun such complicated tales about my mother's death that I sometimes wrote them down just to keep track. I remembered Terence Flanagan's buckled grin as he pinched his wife's backside while she served the potatoes. I remembered Jake coming to me after midnight, to dance in the moonlit kitchen. I thought of Jake's arms around me as he carried me to my bedroom, still bleeding from the loss of a life. I thought of his face coming in and out of my pain; of the impossible ties he cut to say goodbye. "I've run away," I whispered to Jake, "again."

chapter 22
Nicholas

"This is the deal," Nicholas said, juggling Max on his hip and the diaper bag on his shoulder. "I'll pay you whatever you ask. I'll do everything in my power to get you off the next two graveyard shifts. But you've got to watch my kid."

LaMyrna Ratchet, the nurse on duty in orthopedics, twisted a strawberry-blond curl around her finger. "I don't know, Dr. Prescott," she said. "I could get in a shitload of trouble for this."

Nicholas gave her his most winning smile. He was watching the heavy clock above her head, which said that even if he left right now he'd be fifteen minutes late to surgery. "I'm trusting you with my son, LaMyrna," he said. "I've got to go. I've got a patient waiting. I'll bet you can figure something out."

LaMyrna chewed on a fingernail and finally reached out for Max, who grabbed at her Coke-bottle glasses and her stringy hair. "He doesn't cry, does he?" she called after Nicholas, who was running down the hall.

"Oh, no," Nicholas yelled over his shoulder. "Not a bit."

Nicholas had arrived at the hospital at five in the morning, a half hour earlier than usual. He'd actually had the pleasure of waking up his son, who had awakened him three times during the night to drink and to be changed. Max, still half asleep, had fussed the whole time Nicholas tried to jam him into a fuzzy yellow playsuit. "Yeah, well," he'd said, "how do *you* like it?"

Nicholas had expected to put Max in whatever sort of staff day care the hospital had, but there *was* no damn program on site. If Nicholas wanted to use Mass General's child care facility, he'd have to drive to fucking *Charlestown,* and—as if that weren't inconvenient enough—it didn't open until 6:30 A.M., when Nicholas would already be scrubbing for surgery. He'd asked the OR nurses to watch Max, but they had looked at him as though he had two heads. They couldn't, they said, not when at least six times a day there was no one behind the desk because of short staffing. They suggested the general patient floors, but the only nurses on the early shift were bleary from being up all night, and Nicholas didn't quite trust them. So he'd headed up to the orthopedics floor, and he'd found LaMyrna, a homely girl with a good heart whom he remembered from his internship.

"Dr. Prescott," he heard, and he whipped around. He'd missed the door to the operating suite, that's how exhausted he was. The nurse held the swinging door for him. He turned on the steaming water in the industrial sinks, scouring under his fingernails until the pads of his fingers were pink and raw. When he pushed his way backward into the operating suite, he saw that everyone else had been waiting.

Fogerty leaned closer to the unconscious patient. "Mr. Brennan," he said, "it seems Dr. Prescott has decided to grace us with his presence after all." He turned toward Nicholas and then toward the door. "What," he said, "no stroller? No Porta-Crib?"

Nicholas pushed him out of the way. "Just when did you develop a sense of humor, Alistair?" he said. He turned to the head OR nurse. "Prep him."

≈≈≈

He was tired and sweating and badly needed a shower, but the only thing in his mind when he finished surgery was Max. He knew he needed to round his patients; he hadn't a clue about his schedule for tomorrow. He rode up five flights in the cool green elevator. Maybe he'd go home today, and Paige would be there, and this would have been a lousy nightmare.

LaMyrna Ratchet was nowhere to be found. Nicholas stuck his head into the back room at the nurses' station, but no one seemed to know whether she was still on duty. Nicholas began to peer into different patient rooms. He poked through a bouquet of balloons because he thought he saw a short white skirt, but LaMyrna was not in the room. The patient, a woman of about fifty, clung to Nicholas's arm. "No more blood," she cried. "Don't let them take no more blood."

LaMyrna was not in any of the patient rooms. Nicholas even checked the women's staff bathroom, startling a couple of nurses and a female resident, but LaMyrna was not at the sink. He ducked down, peering at the shoes in the stalls. He called her name.

Finally, he went back to the nurses' station in the center of the orthopedic floor. "Look," he said, "this nurse has disappeared, and she's taken my baby."

An unfamiliar nurse handed him a pink telephone message note that had been folded like a Chinese football. "Why didn't you say so?" the woman said.

Dr. Prescott, the note read, *I had to leave because my shift was over and they told me you were still in OR so I left Mike with the people in the volunteer lounge. LaMyrna.*

Mike?

Nicholas couldn't even remember where the volunteer lounge was. They had built it sometime during his residency; it was a general meeting area with lockers and a sign-in sheet for the candy stripers and older hospital volunteers. He asked for directions at the hospital's front desk. "I can take you," a girl said. "I'm on my way there."

She was no older than sixteen and wore a jeans jacket with an airbrushed rendering of Nirvana on the back. She carried a small Eddie Bauer refrigerated cold-pack, and her peppermint-stick uniform protruded from a plain white tote bag. She saw Nicholas staring at the bag. "I wouldn't be caught dead leaving school in it," she said, and she cracked a gum bubble, loud.

There was no one in the volunteer lounge. Nicholas ran his fingers over the page of signed-in volunteers, but found nothing to indicate that one of them was watching a baby. Then, propped in the corner, he saw his diaper bag.

Nicholas sagged against the wall, flooded with relief. "How do I find out what candy stripers are on what rotations?" The girl looked at him blankly. "Where do you all work?"

The girl shrugged. "Check the front of the book," she said, flipping to the sign-in page. He saw a list of volunteers, organized by the day they worked and their staff assignments. There were at least thirty volunteers in the hospital at that moment. Nicholas pinched the bridge of his nose. He could not do this. He just could not do this.

He left the volunteer lounge with the diaper bag on his shoulder and for the first time noticed a secretary sitting at the makeshift desk outside. "Dr. Prescott," she said, smiling up at him.

He did not question how she knew his name; many people at the hospital had heard about the wunderkind of cardiac surgery. "Have you seen a baby?" he said.

The woman pointed down the hall. "Dawn had him, last I saw. She took him to the cafeteria. They didn't need her so badly in ambulatory care today."

Nicholas heard Max's laughter before he saw him. Beyond the thick line of residents and nurses and sullen hospital visitors waiting to be served, he spotted his son's spiky black hair through hazy red cubes of jello. When he reached the table where a candy striper was bouncing Max on her knee, he dropped the diaper bag. The girl was feeding his three-month-old son an ice cream bar.

"What the hell do you think you're doing?" he yelled, grabbing his son away. Max reached his hand toward the ice cream, but then realized his father had returned and burrowed his sticky face into the neck of Nicholas's scrubs.

"You must be Dr. Prescott," the girl said, unruffled. "I'm Dawn. I've been with Max since noon." She opened the diaper bag and held up the one bottle Nicholas had brought to the hospital, now bone dry. "He finished this at ten this morning, you know," she chided. "I had to take him to the milk bank."

Nicholas had a fleeting image of Holsteins, wearing pearls and cat's-eye glasses, acting as tellers and counting out cash. "The milk bank," he repeated, and then he remembered. In the preemie pediatric ward, new mothers pumped their own milk for strangers' babies born too early.

He assessed the girl again. She was smart enough to find food for Max; hell, she had even known he was hungry, which *he* couldn't tell for sure. He sat down across from her at the table, and she folded the remains of the ice cream sandwich into a napkin. "He liked it," she said defensively. "A little bit can't hurt him, not once he's hit three months."

Nicholas stared at her. "How do you know these things?" he asked. Dawn looked at him as if he were crazy. Nicholas leaned forward conspiratorially. "How much do you make for candy striping?"

"Money? We don't make money. That's why we're called volunteers."

Nicholas grabbed her hand. "If you come back tomorrow, I'll pay you. Four bucks an hour, if you'll watch Max."

"I don't candy-stripe on Thursdays. Only on Mondays and Wednesdays. I have band on Thursdays."

"Surely," Nicholas said, "you have friends."

Dawn stood up and shied away from the two of them. Nicholas held his hand out in the air as if that might stop her. He wondered what he looked like through her eyes: a weary, mussed surgeon, sweaty and wild-eyed, who probably wasn't even holding his baby the right way. He wondered what *was* the right way.

For a second, Nicholas thought he was going to lose control. He saw himself breaking down, his face in his hands, sobbing. He saw Max rolling to the floor and striking his head on the beveled edge of the chair. He saw his career destroyed, all his colleagues turning their heads away in embarrassment. His only salvation was the girl in front of him, an angel half his age. "Please," he murmured to Dawn. "You don't understand what it's like."

Dawn held her arms out for Max and tugged the diaper bag onto her thin shoulder. She put her hand on the back of Nicholas's neck. The hand was gloriously cool, like a waterfall, and gentle as a breath. "Five bucks," she said, "and I'll see what I can do."

chapter 23
Paige

*I*f Jake hadn't been with me, I would have run from Eddie Savoy's without ever going inside. His office was thirty miles outside Chicago, in the heartland of the country. The building was little more than a brown weathered shack attached to a chicken farm. The stench of droppings was overpowering, and there were feathers stuck to the wheels of my car when I got out. "Are you sure?" I asked Jake. "You know this guy?"

Eddie Savoy burst out of the door at that point, knocking it off its hinges. "Flan-man!" he yelled, wrapping Jake in a bear hug. They broke away and did some funny handshake that looked like two birds mating.

Jake introduced me to Eddie Savoy. "Paige," he said, "me and Eddie were in the war together."

"The war," I repeated.

"The Gulf War," Eddie said proudly. His voice was as rough as a grindstone.

I turned to Jake. The Gulf War? He had been in the army? The sun slanted off his cheekbones and lightened his eyes so that they appeared transparent. I wondered how much more about Jake Flanagan I had missed.

When I told Jake about leaving Nicholas and Max, and then about wanting to find my mother, I'd expected him to be surprised —maybe even angry, since I'd been telling him all those years that my mother had died. But Jake just smiled at me. "Well," he said, "it's about time." I could tell by the brush of his hands that he had known all along. He told me he had a friend who might be able to help, and then he asked one of his mechanics to watch the station.

Eddie Savoy was a private investigator. He'd been getting started in the business, working as a lackey for another detective, and then he'd joined the army when the war broke out in the Persian Gulf. When he came back he felt he'd had enough of taking orders; he started his own agency.

He led us into a small room that looked as if it had been a meat storage refrigerator in a different life. We sat on the floor on tasseled Indian cushions, and Eddie sat across from us, behind a low parsons bench. "Hate chairs," he explained. "They do things to my back."

He was not much older than Jake, but his hair was completely white. It had been shaved in a crew cut and stood away from his scalp as if each individual piece was very frightened. He had no mustache but the beginnings of a beard, which also seemed to stick straight out from his chin. He reminded me of a tennis ball. "So you haven't seen your ma for twenty years," he said, tugging the old wedding photo from my hand.

"No," I said, "and I've never tried to find her before." I leaned closer. "Do I have a chance?"

Eddie leaned back and pulled a cigarette out of his sleeve. He struck a match against his low desk and drew in deeply. When he spoke, his words came out in smoke. "Your mother," he said to me, "did not disappear off the face of the earth."

Eddie told me it was all in the numbers. You couldn't escape your numbers, not for that long a time. Social Security, Registry of Motor Vehicles, school records, work records. Even if people intentionally changed their identity, eventually they'd collect a pension or welfare, or file taxes, and the numbers would lead you to them. Eddie told me how the previous week he'd found in half a day the kid a mother gave up for adoption.

"What if she's changed her Social Security number?" I said. "What if her name isn't May anymore?"

Eddie smirked. "If you change your Social Security number, it's recorded as being changed. And the address and age of the person changing the number is listed too. You can't just walk in and get someone else's, either. So if your mother is using someone else's number—say her own mom's—we'll still be able to find her."

Eddie took down the family history that I knew. He was particularly concerned about genetic illnesses, because he had just wrapped up a missing persons case that involved diabetes. "This woman's whole family has the sugar," he says, "so I chase her for three years and I know she's in Maine, but I can't get the exact location. And then I figure she's about the age all her relatives start dying. So I call up every hospital in Maine and see what patients have the sugar. Sure enough, there she is, getting her last rites."

I swallowed, and Eddie reached across the table and took my hand. His skin felt like a snake's. "It's very difficult to disappear," he said. "It's all a matter of public records. The hardest people to find are the ones who live in tenements, because they move around a lot. But then you get them through welfare."

I had an image of my mother on welfare, living on the streets, and I winced. "What if my mother isn't my mother anymore?" I asked. "It's been twenty years. What if she's found a new identity?"

Eddie blew smoke rings that expanded and settled around my neck. "You know, Paige," he said, pronouncing my name *Pej,* "people just ain't creative. If they get a new identity, they do something stupid like flip their first and middle names. They use their maiden names or the last name of their favorite uncle. Or they spell their same name different or change one digit in their Social Security number. They aren't willing to completely give up what they're leaving behind." He leaned forward, almost whispering. "Of course, the really sharp ones get a whole new image. I found a guy once who'd taken a new identity by striking up a conversation at a bar with a fellow who looked like him. He got the other guy to compare IDs, just for kicks, and he memorized the number on the driver's license and then got himself a copy by saying it had been stolen. It ain't so hard to become someone else. You look in the local papers and find the name of someone who died within the past week who was about your own age. That gives you a name and an address. Then you go to the place where the death occurred, and it's on public record, and bingo, you got a date of birth. Then you go to Social Security and make up a wacko story about your wallet being filched and you get a new card with this new name—the death records are usually slow in getting over to Social Security, so nothing seems out of the ordinary. And then you pull the same shit at the RMV and you get a new driver's license. . . ." He shrugged and stubbed out his cigarette on the floor. "The thing is, Paige, I know all this stuff. I got connections. I'm one step ahead of your mother."

I thought about my mother's obituaries; how easy it would have been for her to find someone close to her age who had died. I thought of how connected she got to those people, how she'd visit the graves as if they were old friends. "What are you going to do first?" I asked.

"I'm gonna start with the scraps of the truth. I'm gonna take all this information you gave me and the picture, and I'm gonna walk around your neighborhood in Chicago, seeing if anyone remembers her. Then I'm gonna run a driver's license check and a Social Security check. If that don't work, I'm gonna look up twenty-year-old obit pages of the *Trib*. And if *that* don't work, I'm gonna dig in my brain and ask myself, 'Where the hell can I turn now?' I'm gonna hunt her down and get an address for you. And then if you want I'll go to her house and I'll get her garbage before the town picks it up and I'll be able to tell you anything you want to know about her: what she eats for breakfast, what she gets in the mail, if she's married or livin' with someone, if she has kids."

I thought of my mother holding another baby, a different daughter. "I don't think that will be necessary," I whispered.

Eddie stood up, letting us know the meeting was over. "Fifty bucks an hour is my fee," he said, and I paled. I couldn't possibly afford to pay him for more than three days.

Jake stepped up behind me. "That's fine," he said. He squeezed my shoulder, and his words fell softly behind my ear. "Don't worry about it."

≈≈≈

I left Jake waiting in the car and called Nicholas from a pay phone on the way back to Chicago. It rang four times, and I was thinking about what kind of message I could leave, when Nicholas answered, hurried and breathless. "Hello?"

"Hello, Nicholas," I said. "How are you?"

There was a beat of silence. "Are you calling to apologize to me?"

I clenched my fists. "I'm in Chicago now," I said, trying to keep my voice from wavering. "I'm going to find my mother." I hesitated and then asked what was on my mind, what I couldn't get off my mind. "How's Max?" I said.

"Apparently," Nicholas said, "you don't give a damn."

"Of course I do. I don't understand you, Nicholas. Why can't you just think of this as a vacation, or a visit to my father? I haven't been back here in eight years. I *told* you I'd come home." I tapped my foot against the pavement. "It's just going to take a little longer than I thought."

"Let me tell you what I did today, *dear*," Nicholas said, his voice icy and restrained. "After getting up with Max three times during the night, I took him to the hospital this morning. I had a quadruple bypass scheduled, which I almost didn't complete because I couldn't stay on my feet. Someone could have died because of your need for a—what did you call it?—a *vacation*. And I left Max with a stranger because I didn't have any idea who else could baby-sit for him. And you know what? I'm doing this all again tomorrow. Aren't you jealous, Paige? Don't you wish you were me?" The static on the line grew as Nicholas fell silent. I had never thought about all that; I had just left. Nicholas's voice was so bitter that I had to hold the receiver away from my ear. "Paige," he said, "I don't want to see your face again." And then he hung up.

I leaned my forehead against the side of the telephone booth and took deep breaths. Out of nowhere, that list I had written of my accomplishments just days before came to mind. *I can change a diaper. I can measure formula. I can sing Max to sleep.* I closed my eyes. *I can find my mother.*

I walked out of the phone booth, shading my eyes from the judgment of the sun. Jake grinned at me from the passenger seat of my car. "How's Nicholas?" he asked.

"He misses me," I said, forcing a smile. "He wants me to come home."

≈≈≈

In honor of my return to Chicago, Jake took what he called a well-deserved vacation, and insisted I spend time with him while Eddie Savoy found my mother. So the next morning I drove to Jake and Ellen's apartment, which was across the street from where Jake's mother still lived. It was an unassuming little brick building, with a cast-iron fence around the tiny blotched yard. I rang the bell and was buzzed in.

Even before I reached Jake's apartment, on the first floor, I knew which one was his. The familiar smell of him—green spring leaves and honest sweat—seeped through the cracks of the old wooden door. Ellen opened it, startling me. She held a spatula in her hand and wore an apron that said across her chest, KISS MY GRITS. "Jake says Eddie's going to find your mother," she said, not even bothering with "hello." She drew me in with her excitement. "I bet you can't wait. I can't imagine not seeing my mother for twenty years. I wonder how long it—"

"Jeez, El," Jake said, coming down the hall. "It's not even nine o'clock." He had just showered. His hair was still dripping at the ends, leaving little pockmarks on the carpet. Ellen reached over and made a part with her spatula.

The apartment was nearly bare, dotted with mismatched sofas and armchairs and an occasional plastic cube table. There weren't many knickknacks, except for a few grade-school art class ceramic candy bowls, probably made years before by Jake's siblings, and a statuette of Jesus on the Cross. But the room was warm and homey and smelled like popcorn and overripe strawberries. It looked happily wrapped and comfortably lived-in. I thought about my Barely White kitchen, my skin-colored leather couch, and I was ashamed.

Ellen had made French toast for breakfast, and fresh-squeezed orange juice and corned beef hash. I hovered at the edge of the speckled Formica table, looking at all the food. I hadn't made breakfast in years. Nicholas left at four-thirty in the morning; there wasn't time for a spread like this. "When do you have to get up to do all this?" I asked.

Jake curled his arm around Ellen's waist. "Tell her the truth," he said, and then he looked up at me. "Breakfast is all Ellen *can* do. My mother had to teach her how to turn on the oven when we got married."

"Jake!" Ellen slapped his hand away, but she was smiling. She slipped a piece of French toast onto a plate for me. "I told him he's more than welcome to move back home, but then he'd have to do his own laundry again."

I was mesmerized by them. They made it look so easy. I could not remember the last time there had been a gentle touch or a relaxed conversation between Nicholas and me. I couldn't remember if Nicholas and I had *ever* been like this. Things had happened so quickly for us, it was as though our whole relationship had been fast-forwarded. I wondered for a moment what might have happened if *I* had married Jake. I pushed that thought away. I had given my life to Nicholas, and we could have been like this, I knew we could, if Nicholas had been around just a little more. Or if I had given him something to stick around for.

I watched Jake pull Ellen onto his lap and kiss her senseless, as if I weren't even there. He caught my eye. "Flea," he said, grinning, "you *aren't* going to watch, are you?"

"For God's sake," I said, smiling back at Jake. "What's a girl got

to do to get breakfast in this house?" I stood up and opened the
refrigerator, looking for the maple syrup. I watched Jake and Ellen
from behind the door. I saw their tongues meet. *I promise you this,
Nicholas,* I thought. *Once I get my act together, I'm going to make it up to
you. I'm going to fall in love with you all over again. I'm going to make
you fall in love with me.*

Ellen left for work minutes later, without eating anything she'd
prepared. She worked for an advertising agency downtown, in Relo-
cation. "When people move to different branches in the country," she
had said, "I get them started all over again." She draped a long
multicolored scarf over her shoulders and kissed Jake on the neck and
waved to me.

Over the next two days, Jake and I went food shopping together,
ate lunch together, watched the evening news. I spent all day with
him, waiting to hear from Eddie Savoy. At seven o'clock, when Ellen
came home, I would get up off her sofa and turn Jake over to her.
I'd drive home to my father's, sometimes pulling off into a dark,
rustling alley to imagine what they were doing.

The third day I was in Chicago, the temperature soared to one
hundred degrees. "Get yourself to the lake," the morning radio DJ
said when I was on my way over to Jake's place. When I opened his
door, he was standing in the middle of the living room in his boxer
shorts, packing a wicker basket. "It's a picnic kind of day," he said,
and he held up an orange Tupperware bowl. "Ellen made three-bean
salad," he told me, "and she left you a bathing suit to borrow."

I tried on Ellen's bathing suit, feeling very uncomfortable in the
bedroom where Jake slept with his wife. There was nothing on the
white walls except the old sampler that had hung over Jake's childhood bed, with the Irish blessing that he had left in my knapsack
when I walked away from my life. Most of the room was taken up
by an enormous four-poster bed, carved out of golden oak. Each post
depicted a different scene from the Garden of Eden: Adam and Eve
in a gentle embrace; Eve biting into the forbidden fruit; the Fall from
Grace. The serpent wound itself over the fourth post, which I was
using to balance myself as I stepped into Ellen's maillot. I looked

into the mirror and smoothed my hands over the places where my bust did not fill up the cups and where the material strained at my waist, thicker because of Max. I wasn't the slightest bit like Ellen.

In the corner of the mirror I saw Jake come to stand in the doorway. His eyes lingered on my hands as I traced them over my body, lost and unnatural in his wife's clothing. Then he looked up and held my reflection, as if he was trying to say something but could not find the words. I turned away to break the spell, and put my hand on the serpent's carved neck. "This is some bed," I said.

Jake laughed. "Ellen's mom gave it to us as a wedding gift. She hates me. I think this was her way of telling me to go to hell." He walked to a chipped armoire in the corner of the room and took out a T-shirt, tossing it to me. It hung to the middle of my thighs. "You all set?" he said, but he was already leaving.

Jake and I parked in the lot for a private golf club and walked beneath the highway overpass to the shores of Lake Michigan. He had pulled the wicker basket and a cooler of beer out of the trunk, and as I was about to lock it up, I pulled out my sketch pad and conté sticks on impulse.

In early July, the lake was still cold, but the humidity and the heat rolling off its surface softened the shock of wading in. My ankles throbbed and then little by little became numb. Jake splashed by me, diving in headfirst. He surfaced about six feet away and tossed his hair, spraying me with tiny iced drops that made my breath catch. "You're a wimp, Flea," he said. "You move out East and look what happens."

I thought about Memorial Day the year before, when it was unseasonably hot and I had begged Nicholas to take me to the beach in Newburyport. I'd waded into the water, ready to swim. The ocean was no more than fifty degrees, and Nicholas had laughed and said it never gets swimmable until the end of August. He'd practically carried me back up the beach, and then he held his warm hands over my ankles until my teeth stopped chattering.

Jake and I were the only ones on the beach, because it was barely nine in the morning. We had the whole lake to ourselves. Jake did the butterfly and then the backstroke, and he purposely came close

so that he'd splash me. "I think you should move back here permanently," he said. "What the hell. Maybe I'll just never go back to
work."

I sank into the water. "Isn't that the beauty of being the owner,
though? You can delegate responsibility and walk away and still make
a profit."

Jake dove under and stayed there for so long I began to get worried. "Jake," I whispered. I splashed around with my hands to clear
the deep water. "Jake!"

He grabbed my foot and pulled hard, and I didn't even have a
chance to take a breath before I went under.

I came to the surface, sputtering and shivering, and Jake smiled
at me from several feet away. "I'm going to kill you," I said.

Jake dipped his lips to the water and then stood up and spurted
a fountain. "You could," he said, "but then you'd have to get wet
again." He turned and started to swim farther away from the shore.
I took a deep breath and went after him. He had always been a better
swimmer; I was out of breath by the time I reached him. Gasping, I
grabbed at his bathing suit and then at the slippery skin of his back.
Jake treaded water with one hand and held me under the armpit with
the other. He was winded too. "Are you okay?" he said, running his
eyes over my face and the cords of my neck.

I nodded; I couldn't really speak. Jake supported both of us until
my breathing came slow and even. I looked down at his hand. His
thumb was pressed so tightly against my skin that I knew it would
leave a mark. The straps of Ellen's bathing suit, too long to begin
with, had fallen off my shoulders, and the fabric sagged, leaving a
clear line of vision down my chest. Jake pulled me closer, scissor-
kicking between my own legs, and he kissed me.

It was no more than a touch of our lips, but I pushed away from
Jake and began swimming as hard as I could back to the shore,
terrified. It was not what he had done that scared me so; it was what
was missing. There had been no fire, no brutal passion, nothing like
what I remembered. There had been only the quiet beat of our pulses
and the steady lap of the lake.

I was not upset that Jake was no longer in love with me; I'd known that since the day I took a bus east and started my second life. But I had always wondered *What if?*, even after I was married. It wasn't that I didn't love Nicholas; I just assumed a little piece of me would always love Jake. And maybe that was what had me so shaken: I knew now that there was no holding on to the past. I was tied, and always would be, to Nicholas.

I lay down on the towel Jake had brought and pretended to be asleep when he came out of the water and dripped over me. I did not move, although I wanted to sprint miles down the beach, tearing over the hot sand until I couldn't breathe. Running through my mind were the words of Eddie Savoy: *I'm gonna start with the scraps of the truth.* I was starting to see that the past might *color* the future, but it didn't *determine* it. And if I could believe that, it was much easier to let go of what I'd done wrong.

When Jake's steady breathing told me he had fallen asleep, I sat up and opened my sketch pad to a fresh page. I picked up my conté stick and drew his high cheekbones, the flush of summer across his brow, the gold stubble above his upper lip. There were so many differences between Jake and Nicholas. Jake's features held a quiet energy; Nicholas's had power. I had waited forever for Jake; I got Nicholas in a matter of days. When I pictured Jake I saw him standing beside me, at eye level, although he really had half a head on me. Nicholas, though—well, Nicholas had always seemed to me to be twenty feet tall.

Nicholas had come into my life on a white stallion, had handed me his heart, and had offered me the palace and the ball gown and the gold ring. He had given me what every little girl wanted, what I had long given up hope of having. He could not be blamed just because no one ever mentioned that once you closed the storybook, Cinderella still had to do laundry and clean the toilet and take care of the crown prince.

An image of Max flooded the space in front of me. His eyes were wide open as he rolled from belly to back, and a smile split his face in two when he realized he was seeing the world from a whole different angle. I was beginning to understand the wonder in that, and it was better late than never. I stared at Jake, and I knew what was the greatest difference: with Jake I had taken a life; with Nicholas I had created one.

Jake opened his eyes one at a time just as I was finishing his portrait. He turned onto his side. "Paige," he said, looking down, "I'm sorry. I shouldn't have done that."

I looked squarely at him. "Yes, you should have. It's okay." Now that his eyes were open, I sketched in his pale, glowing pupils and the tiger's stripe of gold around them.

"I had to make sure," he said. "I just had to make sure." Jake tipped down the edge of my pad so that he could see. "You've gotten so much better," he said. He ran his fingers along the edge of the charcoal, too light to smudge.

"I've just gotten older," I said. "I guess I've seen more." Together we stared at the penciled lines of surprise in his eyes, the beating heat of the sun reflecting off the white page. He took my hand and touched my fingers to a spot on the paper where damp curls met the nape of his neck. There I had drawn, in silhouette, a couple embracing. In the distance, reaching toward the woman, was a man who looked like Nicholas; reaching toward the man was a girl with Ellen's face.

"It worked out the way it should have," Jake said.

He put his hand on my shoulder, and all I felt was comfort. "Yes," I murmured. "It has."

≈≈≈

We sat on Eddie Savoy's throw pillows, poring through a soiled manila folder that pieced together the past twenty years of my mother's life. "Piece of cake," Eddie said, picking his teeth with a letter opener. "Once I figured out who she was, she was a cinch to track down."

My mother had left Chicago under the name Lily Rubens. Lily had died three days before; my mother had written the obituary for the *Tribune.* She was twenty-five, and she'd died—according to my mother's words—of a long, painful illness. My mother had copies of her Social Security card, driver's license, even a birth certificate from the Glenwood Town Hall. My mother had not gone to Hollywood. She'd somehow gotten to Wyoming, where she'd worked for Billy DeLite's Wild West Show. She had been a saloon dancer until Billy DeLite himself spotted her cancan and talked her into playing Calamity Jane. According to Billy's fax, she'd taken to riding and target shooting as if she'd been doing it since she was a tadpole. Five years later, in 1977, she disappeared in the middle of the night with the most talented rodeo cowboy in the Wild West show and most of the previous day's earnings.

Eddie's records blanked out here for a while, but they picked up again in Washington, D.C., where my mother worked for a while doing telemarketing surveys for consumer magazines. She saved up enough commission money to buy a horse from a man named Charles Crackers, and because she was living in a Chevy Chase condo at the time, she boarded the horse at his stable and came to ride three times a week.

The pages went on to record my mother's move from Chevy Chase to Rockville, Maryland, and then a switch of jobs, including a brief stint at a Democratic senator's campaign office. When the senator didn't win reelection, she sold her horse and bought a plane ticket to Chicago, which she did not use at the time.

In fact, she hadn't traveled for pleasure at all over the past twenty years, except once. On June 10, 1985, she *did* come to Chicago. She stayed at the Sheraton and signed in as Lily Rubens. Eddie watched over my shoulder as I read that part. "What happened on June tenth?" he said.

I turned to Jake. "My high school graduation." I tried to remember every detail: the white gowns and caps all the girls of Pope Pius had worn, the blazing heat of the sun burning the metal rims of our folding chairs, Father Draher's commencement address about serving God in a sinful world. I tried to see the hazy faces of the audience seated on the bleachers of the playing field, but it had been too long ago. The day after graduation, I left home. My mother had come back to see me grow up, and she had almost missed me.

Eddie Savoy waited until I came to the last page of the report. "She's been here for the last eight years," he said, pointing to the circle on the map of North Carolina. "Farleyville. I couldn't get no address, though, not in her name, and there ain't a phone listing. But this here's the last recorded place of employment. It was five years ago, but something tells me that in a town no bigger than a toilet stall, you ain't gonna have any trouble tracking her down." I looked at the scribbled humps of Eddie's shorthand. He grimaced and then sat down behind his low desk. He held out a piece of ripped paper on which he'd written "Bridal Bits" and a phone number. "It's some boutique, I guess," he said. "They knew her real well."

I thought about my mother, apparently single except for that rodeo cowboy, and wondered what would compel her to move to the hills of North Carolina to work in a bridal salon. I imagined her walking around the tufts of Alençon lace, the thin blue garters and the satin beaded pumps, touching them as if she had a right to wear them. When I looked up, Jake was pumping Eddie Savoy's hand. I dug into my wallet and pulled out his four-hundred-dollar fee, but Eddie shook his head. "It's already been taken care of," he said. Jake led me outside and didn't say a word as we settled into our respective seats in my car. I drove slowly down the rutted road that led to Eddie's, spraying bits of gravel left and right and flustering the chickens that had gathered in front of the fender. I pulled over less than a hundred yards from Eddie's and put my head down on the steering wheel to cry.

Jake pulled me into his arms, awkwardly twisting my body around the center console. "Now what do I do?" I said.

He ran his hands over my ponytail, tugging just a little. "You go to Farleyville, North Carolina," he said.

Finding her had been the easy part. I was terrified of meeting my mother, a woman I'd remade in the image of myself. I didn't know what was worse: stirring up memories that might make me hate her at first sight, or finding out that I was exactly like her, destined to keep running, too unsure of myself to be somebody's mother. That was the risk I was taking. In spite of what I had promised myself or pleaded to Nicholas, if I really had turned out like May O'Toole, I might never feel whole enough to go home.

I looked up at Jake, and the message was clear in my eyes. He smiled gently. "You're on your own now."

I remembered the last time he'd said that to me, silently, in slightly different words. I lifted my chin, resolved. "Not for long," I said.

chapter 24

Nicholas

W hen her voice came over the line, crackling at the edges, the bottom dropped out of Nicholas's world. "Hello, Nicholas," Paige said. "How are you?"

Nicholas had been changing Max, and he had carried him to the phone in the kitchen with his snaps all undone. He placed the baby on the kitchen table, cradling his head on a stack of napkins. At the cadence of his wife's voice, he had suddenly become very still. It was as if the air had stopped circulating, as if the only motion was the quick kick of Max's legs and the insistent pounding of blood behind Nicholas's ears. Nicholas tucked the phone in the crook of his neck and laid the baby facedown on the linoleum. He pulled the cord as far as it could stretch. "Are you calling to apologize to me?"

When she didn't answer at first, his mouth became dry. What if she was in trouble? He had cut off her money. What if she'd had a problem with the car, had had to hitchhike, was running away from some lunatic with a knife? "I'm in Chicago," Paige said. "I'm going to find my mother."

Nicholas ran his hand through his hair and almost laughed. This was a joke. This did not happen to real people. This was something you'd see on the Sunday Movie of the Week or read about in a *True Confessions* magazine. He had always known that Paige was haunted by her mother; she was so guarded when speaking about her that she gave herself away. But why now?

When she didn't say anything, Nicholas stared out the tiny kitchen window and wondered what Paige was wearing. He pictured her hair, loose and framing her face, rich with the colors of autumn. He saw the ragged pink tips of her bitten fingernails and the tiny indentation at the base of her neck. He opened the refrigerator and let the cool gust of air clear her image from his mind. He did not care. He simply would not let himself.

When he heard her ask about Max, his anger started to boil again. "Apparently you don't give a damn," he said, and he walked back toward Max, planning to slam down the phone. She was babbling about how long she'd been away from Chicago, and suddenly Nicholas was so tired he could not stand. He sank into the nearest chair and thought of how today could possibly have been the worst day of his life. "Let me tell you what I did today, *dear*," Nicholas said, biting off each word as if it were a bitter morsel. "After getting up with Max three times during the night, I took him to the hospital this morning. I had a quadruple bypass scheduled, which I almost didn't complete because I couldn't stay on my feet." He spit out the rest of his words, barely even hearing them himself. "Someone could have died because of your need for a—what did you call it?—a *vacation*." He held the receiver away from his mouth. "Paige," he said softly, "I don't want to see your face again." And closing his eyes, he put the phone back in its cradle.

When the phone rang again, minutes later, Nicholas picked it up and yelled right into it, "Goddammit, I'm not going to say it again."

He paused long enough to catch his breath, long enough for Alistair Fogerty's control to snap on the other end of the line. The sharp edge of his voice made Nicholas take a step backward. "Six o'clock, Nicholas. In my office." And he hung up.

By the time Nicholas drove back to the hospital, he had a splitting headache. He had forgotten to bring a pacifier, and Max had yelled the entire way. He trudged up the stairs to the fifth floor, the administrative wing, because the elevator from the parking garage was broken. Fogerty was in his office, systematically spitting into the spider plants that edged his window. "Nicholas," he said, "and, of course, Max. How could I forget? Everywhere Dr. Prescott goes, the little Prescott isn't far behind."

Nicholas continued to look at the potted plant that Alistair had been leaning over. "Oh," Fogerty said, dismissing his actions with a wave of his hand. "It's nothing. For unexplained reasons, my office flora react favorably to sadism." He stared at Nicholas with the predatory eyes of a hawk. "What we are here to talk about, however, is not me, Nicholas, but you."

Nicholas had not known what he was going to say until that moment. But before Alistair could open his mouth about the hospital not being a day care facility to meet Nicholas's whims, he sat in a chair and settled Max more comfortably on his lap. He didn't give a damn about what Alistair had to tell him. The son of a bitch didn't have a heart. "I'm glad you wanted to see me, Alistair," he said, "since I'll be taking a leave of absence."

"A *what?*" Fogerty stood and moved closer to Nicholas. Max giggled and reached out his hand toward the pen in Fogerty's lab coat pocket.

"A week should do it. I can have Joyce reschedule my planned surgeries; I'll double up the next week if I have to. And the emergencies can be handled by the residents. What's-his-name, that little skunky one with the black eyes—Wollachek—he's decent. I won't expect pay, of course. And"—Nicholas smiled—"I'll come back better than ever."

"Without the infant," Fogerty added.

Nicholas bounced Max on his knee. "Without the infant."

Saying it all out loud lifted a tremendous pressure from Nicholas's chest. He had no idea what he'd do in the span of a week, but surely he could find a nanny or a full-time sitter to stay in the house. At the very least, he could figure Max out—which cry meant he was hungry and which meant he was tired; how to keep his undershirts from riding up to his armpits; how to open the portable stroller. Nicholas knew he was grinning like an idiot, and he didn't give a damn. For the first time in three days, he felt on top of the world.

Fogerty's mouth contorted into a black, wiry line. "This will not reflect well upon your record," he said. "I had expected more from you."

I had expected more from you. The words brought back the image of his father, standing over him like an impenetrable basilisk and holding out a prep school physics exam bearing the only grade lower than an A that Nicholas had received in his whole life.

Nicholas grabbed Max's leg so tightly that the baby started to cry. "I'm not a goddamned machine, Alistair," he yelled. "I can't do it all." He tossed the diaper bag over his shoulder and walked to the threshold of the office. ALISTAIR FOGERTY, it said on the door. DIRECTOR, CARDIOTHORACIC SURGERY. Maybe Nicholas's name would never make it to that door, but that wasn't going to change his mind. You couldn't put the cart before the horse. "I'll see you," he said quietly, "in a week."

≈≈≈

Nicholas sat in the park, surrounded by mothers. It was the third day he'd come, and he was triumphant. Not only had he discovered how to open the portable stroller; he'd figured out a way to hook on the diaper bag so that even when he lifted Max out, it wouldn't tip over. Max was too little to go into the sandbox with the other kids, but he seemed to like the sturdy infant swings. Nikki, a pretty blond woman with legs that went on forever, smiled up at him. "And how's our little Max doing today?" she said.

Nicholas didn't understand why Paige wasn't like these three women. They all met in the park at the same time and talked animatedly about stretch marks and sales on diapers and the latest gastrointestinal viruses running through the day care centers. Two of them were on maternity leave, and one was staying home with the kids until they went to school. Nicholas was fascinated by them. They could see with the backs of their heads, knowing by instinct when their kid had swatted another in the face. They could pick out their own child's cry from a dozen others. They effortlessly juggled bottles and jackets and bibs, and their babies' pacifiers never fell to the dirt. These were skills, Nicholas believed, that he could never learn in a million years.

The first day he'd brought Max, he had been sitting alone on a chipped green bench, watching the women across the way spoon sand over the bare legs of the toddlers. Judy had spoken to him first. "We don't get many dads," she had said. "And never on weekdays."

"I'm on vacation," Nicholas had replied uncomfortably. Max then let forth a burp that shook his entire body, and everyone laughed.

That first day, Judy and Nikki and Fay had set him straight about day care and nanny services. "You can't buy good help these days," Fay had said. "A British nanny—and that's the one you want—they take six months to a year to get. And even so, didn't you see *Donahue?* The ones with the highest references could still drop your kid on the head or abuse her or God knows what."

Judy, who was going back to work in a month, had found a day care center when she was six months pregnant. "And even then," she had said, "I was only on a waiting list."

And so Nicholas's week was almost up, and he still didn't know what to do with the baby when Monday came. On the other hand, it had been worth it—these women had taught him more about his own son in the span of three days than he had ever hoped to know. When Nicholas went home from the park, he almost felt as if he was in control.

Nicholas pushed Max higher on the swing, but he was whining. He'd been crabby for the past three days. "I called your baby-sitter," he told Nikki, "but she's got a summer job as a counselor and said she can't sit for me until the end of August, when camp lets out."

"Well, I'll keep asking around for you," Nikki said. "I bet you can find somebody." Her little girl, a thirteen-month-old with wispy strawberry-blond bangs, fell on her face in the sandbox and came up crying. "Oh, Jessica." Nikki sighed. "You've got to figure out this walking thing."

He liked Nikki best. She was funny and smart, and she made being a mother seem as easy as chewing gum. Nicholas pulled Max out of the swing and sat down on the edge of the sandbox, letting Max squish the sand through his toes. Max looked up at Judy and began to scream. She held out her hands. "Let me," she said.

Nicholas nodded, secretly thrilled. He was amazed when people asked to hold the baby. He would have given him to a complete stranger, the way he'd been acting these past few days; that's how big a relief it was to see him in someone else's arms. Nicholas traced his initials in the soft, cool sand and, from the corner of his eye, watched Max perched over Judy's shoulder.

"I fed him cereal for the first time yesterday," Nicholas said. "I did it the way you said, mostly formula, but he kept pushing out his tongue like he couldn't figure out what a spoon was. And no matter what you told me, he did *not* sleep through the night."

Fay smiled. "Wait till he's having more than a teaspoon a day," she said. "Then come back so I can say, 'I told you so.' "

Judy walked toward them, still bouncing Max. "You know, Nicholas, you've really come along. Hell, if you were my husband, I'd kiss your feet. Imagine having someone who could take care of the kids and not ask every three minutes why they're crying." She leaned close to Nicholas and batted her eyelashes, smiling. "You give me a sign, and I'll get a divorce lawyer."

Nicholas smiled, and the women fell quiet, watching their children overturn plastic buckets and build free-form castles. "Tell me if this bothers you," Nikki said hesitantly. "I mean, we haven't really known you very long, and we barely know anything about you, but I have this friend who's divorced, with a kid. and I was wondering if sometime you might . . . you know . . ."

"I'm married." The words came so quickly to Nicholas's lips that they surprised him more than the mothers. Fay, Judy, and Nikki exchanged a look. "My wife . . . she isn't around."

Fay smoothed her hand over the edge of the sandbox. "We're sorry to hear that," she said, assuming the worst.

"She's not dead," Nicholas said. "She sort of left."

Judy came to stand behind Fay. "She left?"

Nicholas nodded. "She took off about a week ago. She, well, she wasn't very good at this—not like you all are—and she was a little overwhelmed, I think, and she cracked under the pressure." He looked at their blank faces, wondering why he felt he had to make explanations for Paige when he himself couldn't forgive her. "She never had a mother," he said.

"*Everyone* has a mother," Fay said. "That's the way it happens."

"Hers left her when she was five. Last I heard, actually, she was trying to find her. Like that might give her all the answers."

Fay pulled her son toward her and restrapped the hanging front of his overalls. "Answers, jeez. There aren't any answers. You should have seen me when he was three months old," she said lightly. "I had scared away all my friends, and I was almost declared legally dead by my family doctor."

Nikki sucked in her breath and stared at Nicholas, her eyes wide and liquid with pity. "Still," she whispered, "to leave your own *child.*"

Nicholas felt the silence crowding in on him. He didn't want their stares; he didn't want their sympathy. He looked at the toddlers, wishing for one of them to start crying, just to break the moment. Even Max was being quiet.

Judy sat down beside Nicholas and balanced Max on her lap. She touched Nicholas's wrist and lifted his hand to the baby's mouth. "I think I've found out what's making him such a monster," she said gently. "There." She pressed Nicholas's finger to the bottom of Max's gums, where a sharp triangle of white bit into his flesh.

Fay and Nikki crowded closer, eager to change the subject. "A tooth!" Fay said, as animated as if Max had been accepted to Harvard; and Nikki added, "He's just over three months, right? That's awfully early. He's in a hurry to grow up; I bet he crawls soon." Nicholas stared at the downy crown of black hair on his son's head. He pressed down with his finger, letting Max bite back with his jaws, with his brand-new tooth. He looked up at the sky, a day without clouds, and then let the women run their fingers over Max's gums. *Paige would have wanted to be here,* he thought suddenly, and then he felt anger searing through him like a brush fire. *Paige* should *have wanted to be here.*

chapter 25

Paige

I had never been there, but this was the way I had pictured Ireland from my father's stories. Rich, rolling hills the deep green of emeralds; grass thicker than a plush rug, farms notched into the slopes and bordered by sturdy stone walls. Several times I stopped the car, to drink from streams cleaner and colder than I had ever imagined possible. I could hear my father's brogue in the cascade and the current, and I could not believe the irony: my mother had run away to the North Carolina countryside, a land my father would have loved.

If I hadn't known better, I would have assumed the hills were virgin territory. Paved roads were the only sign that anyone else had been here, and in the three hours I'd been driving across the state, I hadn't passed a single car. I had rolled down all the windows so that the air could rush into my lungs. It was crisper than the air in Chicago, lighter than the air in Cambridge. I felt as if I were drinking in the endless open space, and I could see how, out here, someone could easily get lost.

Since leaving Chicago, I had been thinking only of my mother. I ran through every solid memory I'd ever had and froze each of them in my mind like an image from a slide projector, hoping to see something I hadn't noticed before. I couldn't come up with an image of her face. It drifted in and out of shadows.

My father had said I looked like her, but it had been twenty years since he'd seen her and eight since he'd seen me, so he might have been mistaken. I knew from her clothes that she was taller and thinner. I knew from Eddie Savoy how she'd spent the past two decades. But I still didn't think I'd be able to spot her in a crowd.

The more I drove, the more I remembered about my mother. I remembered how she tried to get ahead of herself, making all my lunches for the week on Sunday night and stowing them in the freezer, so that my bologna and my turkey and my Friday tuna fish were never fully thawed by the time I ate them. I remembered that when I was four and got the mumps on only the right side of my face, my mother had fed me half-full cups of Jell-o and kept me in bed half the day, telling me that after all, I was half healthy. I remembered the dreary day in March when we were both worn down by the sleet and the cold, and she had baked a devil's food cake and made glittery party hats, and together we celebrated Nobody's birthday. I remembered the time she was in a car accident, how I had come downstairs at midnight to a room full of policemen and found her lying on the couch, one eye swollen shut and a gash over her lip, her arms reaching out to hold me.

Then I remembered the March before she left, Ash Wednesday. In kindergarten, we had a half day of school, but the *Tribune* was still open. My mother could have hired the baby-sitter to take care of me until she came home, or told me to wait next door at the Manzettis'. But instead she'd come up with the idea that we would go out to lunch and then make afternoon Mass. She had announced this over the dinner table and told my father that I was smart enough to take the bus all by myself. My father stared at her, not believing what he had heard, and then finally he grabbed my mother's hand and pressed it to the table, hard, as if he could make her see the truth through the pain. "No, May," he'd said, "she's too young."

But well after midnight, the door to my room opened, and in the slice of light that fell across my bed I saw the shadow of my mother. She came in and sat in the dark and pressed into my hand twenty cents, bus fare. She held out a route map and a flashlight and made me repeat after her: *Michigan and Van Buren Street, the downtown local. One, two, three, four stops, and Mommy will be there.* I said it over and over until it was as familiar as my bedtime prayers. My mother left the room and let me go to sleep. At four in the morning, I awoke to find her face inches away from mine, her breath hot against my lips. "Say it," she commanded, and my mouth formed the words that my brain could not hear, stuffed as it was with sleep. *Michigan and Van Buren Street,* I murmured. *The downtown local.* I opened my eyes wide, surprised by how well I had learned. "That's my girl," my mother said, cupping my cheeks in her hands. She pressed a finger to my lips. "And don't tell your daddy," she whispered.

Even I knew the value of a secret. Through breakfast, I avoided my father's gaze. When my mother dropped me off at the school gates, her eyes flashed, feverish. For a moment she looked so different that I thought of Sister Alberta's lectures on the devil. "What's it all for," my mother said to me, "without the risk?" And I had pressed my face against hers to kiss her goodbye the way I always did, but this time I whispered against her cheek: *One, two, three, four stops. And you'll be there.*

I had swung my feet back and forth under my chair that morning, and I colored in the pictures of Jesus outside the lines because I was so excited. When Sister let us out at the bell, blessing us in a stream of rushed words, I turned to the left, the direction I never went. I walked until I came to the corner of Michigan and Van Buren and saw the pharmacy my mother had said would be there. I stood underneath the Metro sign, and when the big bus sighed into place beside the curb, I asked the driver, "Downtown local?"

He nodded and took my twenty cents, and I sat in the front seat as my mother had said, not looking beside me because there could be bums and bad men and even the devil himself. I could feel hot breath on my neck, and I squeezed my eyes shut, listening to the roll of the wheels and the lurch of the brakes and counting the stops. When the door opened for the fourth time, I bolted from my seat, peeking into the one beside mine just that once, to see only blue vinyl and the lacy grate of the air conditioner. I stepped off the bus and waited for the knot of people to clear, shielding my eyes from the sun. My mother knelt, her arms open, her smile red and laughing and wide. "Paige-boy," she said, folding me into her purple raincoat. "I knew you'd come."

$$\approx \approx \approx$$

I had asked a man with spare tufts of gray hair, who'd been sitting on a milk can at the side of the road, if he'd heard of Farleyville. "Yuh," he said, pointing in front of me. "You almost there now."

"Well," I said, "maybe you've heard of a salon called Bridal Bits?"

The man scratched his chest through his worn chambray shirt. He laughed, and he had no teeth. "A sa-*lon*," he said, mocking my words. "I don't know 'bout that."

The corners of my mouth turned down. "Could you just tell me where it is?"

The man grinned at me. "If it be the same place I'm thinking of, and I'm bettin' it ain't, then you want to take the first right at the 'baccy field and keep goin' till you see a bait shop. It's three miles past that, on the left." He shook his head as I stepped back into the car. "You said Farleyville," he said, "di'n't you?"

I followed his directions, messing up only once, and that was because I couldn't tell a tobacco from a corn field. The bait shop was nothing but a shack with a crude fish painted on a wooden sign in front of it, and I wondered why people would come all the way out here to buy wedding gowns. Surely Raleigh would be a better place. I wondered if my mother's shop was secondhand or wholesale, how it could even stay in business.

The only building three miles down on the left was a neat pink cement-block square, without a sign to herald it. I stepped out of the car and pulled at the front door, but it was locked. The big show window was partially lit by the setting sun, which had come up behind me as I drove, to wash over the tops of the tobacco plants like hot lava. I peered inside, looking for a seed-pearl headpiece or a fairy-tale princess's gown. I couldn't see beyond the showcase itself, and it took me a minute to realize that set proudly behind the glass was a finely stitched saddle with gleaming stirrups, a furry halter, a spread wool blanket with the woven silhouette of a stallion. I squinted and then I moved back to the door, to the handwritten sign I hadn't noticed the first time. BRIDLES & BITS, it said. CLOSED.

I sank to the ground in front of the threshold and drew up my knees. I rested my head against them. All this time, all these miles, and I'd come for nothing. My thoughts came in waves: my mother wasn't working here; she was supposed to be at a completely different kind of store; I was going to have Eddie Savoy's head. Pink clouds stretched across the sky like fingers, and at that moment the final streak of sun left in the day lit the inside of the tack shop. I had a clear view of the mural on the ceiling. It matched like a twin the ceiling I remembered, the one I'd painted with my mother and had lain beneath for hours, hoping that those fast-flying horses might champion us far away.

chapter 26
Nicholas

*A*strid Prescott was sure she was seeing a ghost. Her hand was still frozen on the brass door handle where she'd pulled it open, silently cursing because Imelda had disappeared in search of the silver polish and so Astrid had been disturbed from her study. And consequently she'd come face-to-face with the same ghost that had haunted her for weeks, after making it perfectly clear that the past was not to be forgiven. Astrid shook her head slightly. Unless she was imagining it, standing on the threshold were Nicholas and a black-haired baby, both of them frowning, both of them looking like they might break down and cry.

"Come in," Astrid said smoothly, as if she'd seen Nicholas more than once during the past eight years. She reached toward the baby, but Nicholas shrugged the diaper bag off his shoulder and gave it to her instead.

Nicholas took three resounding steps into the marble hall. "You should know," he said, "I wouldn't be here if I wasn't at the end of my rope."

Nicholas had been awake most of the night, trying to come up with an alternate plan. He'd been on unpaid leave for a full week, and in spite of his best efforts, he hadn't found quality day care for his son. The British nanny service had laughed when he said he needed a woman within six days. He had almost hired a Swiss au pair—going so far as to leave her with the baby while he went grocery shopping—but he'd returned home to find Max wailing in his playpen while the girl entertained some biker boyfriend in the living room. The reputable child care centers had waiting lists until 1995; he didn't trust the teenage daughters of his neighbors who were looking for summer employment. Nicholas knew that if he was going to return to Mass General as scheduled, the only option open to him was to swallow his pride and go back to his parents for help.

He knew his mother wouldn't turn him away. He'd seen her face when he'd first told her of Max. He'd lay odds she kept the photo of Max—the one he had left behind—right in her wallet. Nicholas pushed past his mother into the parlor, the same room he'd pulled Paige from indignantly eight years before. He found his eyes roaming over the damask upholstery, the burnished wood tables. He waited for his mother's questions, and then the accusations. What had his parents been able to see that he'd been so blind to?

He put Max down on the rug and watched him roll over and over until he landed beneath the sofa, reaching for a thin carved leg. Astrid hovered uneasily at the door for a moment and then put on her widest diplomat's smile. She had charmed Idi Amin into granting her free press access to Uganda; surely this couldn't be any more difficult. She sat down on a Louis XIV love seat, which afforded her the best view of Max. "It's so good to see you, Nicholas," she said. "You'll be staying for lunch?"

Nicholas did not take his eyes off his son. Astrid watched her son, too large for the chair he sat upon, and realized he did not look right in this room at all. She wondered when that had happened.

Nicholas shifted his gaze to his mother, a challenge. "Are you busy?" he asked.

Astrid thought about the photographs spread across her study, the old Ladakhi women with heavy feather necklaces, the bare brown children playing tag in front of ancient Buddhist monasteries. She had been writing the introduction to her latest book of photos, centering on the Himalayas and the Tibetan plateau. She was three days late on her deadline already, and her editor was going to call first thing Monday morning to badger her again. "As a matter of fact," Astrid said, "I haven't a thing to do all day."

Nicholas sighed so gently that even his mother did not notice. He sank against the stiff frame of the chair, thinking of the blue-and-white-striped overstuffed love seats Paige had found at a fire sale for the living room in their old apartment. She had sweet-talked a drummer she met on the street outside the diner into helping her bring the couches home in his van, and then she spent three weeks asking Nicholas whether they were too much sofa for such a little room. *Look at those elephant legs,* she had said. *Aren't they all wrong?* "I need your help," Nicholas said softly.

Whatever hesitation Astrid might still have had, whatever warnings she had been trying to heed to go slowly, all of that shattered when Nicholas spoke. She stood and walked over to her son. Silently, she folded him in her arms and rocked back and forth. She had not held Nicholas like this since he was thirteen and had taken her aside after she'd embraced him at a school soccer match and told her he was too old for that.

Nicholas did not try to push her away. His arms came up to press against the small of her back; and he closed his eyes and wondered where his mother, brought up with afternoon tea parties and Junior League balls, had got all her courage.

Astrid brought iced coffee and a cinnamon ring and let Nicholas eat, while she kept Max from chewing on the fireplace tools and loose electrical cords. "I don't understand," she said, smiling down at Max. "How could she have left?"

Nicholas tried to remember a time when he would have defended

Paige to the end, railed at his mother and his father, and sacrificed his right arm before letting them criticize his wife. He opened his mouth to make an excuse, but he could not think of one. "I don't know," he said. "I really don't know." He ran his finger around the edge of his glass. "I can't even tell you what the hell she was *thinking,* to be honest. It's like she had this whole different agenda that she never bothered to mention to me. She could have said something. I would have—" Nicholas broke off. He would have what? Helped her? Listened?

"You wouldn't have done a damn thing, Nicholas," Astrid said pointedly. "You're just like your father. When I fly off for a shoot, it takes him three days to notice I'm gone."

"This isn't my fault," Nicholas shouted. "Don't blame this on me."

Astrid shrugged. "You're putting words in my mouth. I was only wondering what reasons Paige gave you, if she's planning on coming back, that sort of thing."

"I don't give a damn," Nicholas muttered.

"Of course you do," Astrid said. She picked up Max and bounced him on her lap. "You're just like your father."

Nicholas put his glass down on the table, taking a small amount of satisfaction in the fact that there was no coaster and that it would leave a ring. "But *you* aren't like Paige," he said, "*You* would never have left your own child."

Astrid pulled Max closer, and he began to suck on her pearls. "That doesn't mean I didn't think about it," she said.

Nicholas stood abruptly and took the baby out of his mother's arms. Nothing was going the way he had planned. His mother was supposed to have been so overwhelmed with gratitude to see Max that she wouldn't ask these questions, that she would beg to watch her grandson for the day, the week, whatever. His mother was *not* supposed to make him think about Paige, was *not* supposed to take her goddamned side. "Forget it," he said. "We're going. I thought you'd be able to understand what I was getting at."

Astrid blocked his exit. "Don't be an idiot, Nicholas," she said. "I know exactly what you're getting at. I didn't say Paige was right for leaving, I just said I'd considered it a couple of times myself. Now give me that gorgeous child and go fix hearts."

Nicholas blinked. His mother pulled the baby out of his arms. He hadn't told her his plan; hadn't even mentioned that he needed her to baby-sit while he worked. Astrid, who had started to carry Max back to the parlor, turned around and stared at Nicholas. "I'm your *mother*," she said by way of explanation. "I know how you think."

Nicholas closed the top of the baby grand piano and spread out the plastic foam pad from the diaper bag, forming a makeshift changing table. "I use A&D on him," he said to Astrid. "It keeps him from getting diaper rash, and powder dries out his skin." He explained when Max ate, how much he took, the best way to keep him from spitting strained green beans back in your face. He brought in Max's car seat/carrier and said it would work for a nap. He said that if Max decided to sleep at all, it would be between two and four.

He left Astrid his beeper number in case of emergency. She and Max walked him to the door. "Don't worry," she said, touching Nicholas's sleeve. "I've done it before. And I did a damn good job." She reached up to kiss Nicholas on the cheek, remembering the change in course her life had taken on the day her once-little son was able to look her in the eye.

Nicholas set off down the slate path, unencumbered. He did not turn back to wave to Max or even bother to kiss him goodbye. He rolled the muscles bunched in his shoulders from the cutting straps of the diaper bag and the uneven weight of an eighteen-pound baby. He was amazed at how much he knew about Max, how much he'd been able to tell his mother about the routine. He began to whistle and was so proud of his accomplishments that he didn't even think about Robert Prescott until he reached his car.

With his hand still touching the warm metal of the door handle, he turned back to face his mother. She and Max were standing in the doorway, dwarfed by the enormity of the house behind them. Meeting his mother had been fairly simple after all the tentative phone conversations. But in all that time, Robert Prescott hadn't even been mentioned. Nicholas had no idea if his father would be thrilled to see the child who would carry on his name, or if he would disown Max as effortlessly as he had disowned his son. He had no idea what his father was like anymore. "What will Dad say?" he whispered.

His mother could not possibly have heard him at such a distance, but she seemed to understand his question. "I imagine," she said, stepping into a neat square of the brilliant afternoon, "he'll say, 'Hello, Max.' "

≈≈≈

Nothing could have surprised Nicholas more than the scene that met him when he arrived at his parents' close to midnight to pick up the baby. Filling the parlor was a tumbled clutter of educational toys, a Porta-Crib, a playpen, a baby swing. A big green quilt with a dinosaur head sewn on to its corner was spread across the floor. A panda mobile replaced the trailing spider plant that had hung over the piano. Stacked on the piano, beside the foam pad Nicholas had placed there earlier for diapering, was the largest vat of A&D ointment Nicholas had ever seen and a carton of Pampers. And in the middle of it all was Nicholas's father—taller than he remembered and thinner too, with a shock of now-white hair—asleep on the spindled sofa, with Max curled over his chest.

Nicholas drew in his breath. He had anticipated many things about this first meeting with his father: awkward silence, condescension, maybe even a shred of hate. But Nicholas had not expected his father to be so old.

He stepped back quietly to close the door to the room, but his foot tripped over a jangling terry-cloth ball. His father's eyes opened, bright and alert. Robert Prescott did not sit up, knowing that would wake Max. But he did not tear his gaze away from his son.

Nicholas waited for his father to say something—anything. He remembered the first time he'd lost a crew race in high school, after a three-year winning streak. There had been seven other rowers in the boat, and Nicholas had known that the six-man wasn't pulling hard during the power tens. In no way was it Nicholas's fault the race was lost. But he had taken it that way, and when he met his father after the race, he had hung his head, waiting for the accusations. His father had said nothing, nothing at all, and Nicholas had always believed that stung more than any words his father could have uttered. "Dad," Nicholas said quietly, "how's he been?"

Not *How have* you *been*, not *What have I missed in your life*. Nicholas figured that if he kept the conversation limited to Max, the ache that rounded the bottom of his stomach might go away. He clenched his fists behind his back and looked into his father's eyes. There were shadows there that Nicholas could not read, but there were also promises. *Too much has happened; I will not bring it up*, Robert seemed to say. *And neither will you.*

"You've done well," Robert said, stroking Max's hunched shoulders. Nicholas raised his eyebrows. "We never stopped asking questions about you, Nicholas," he said gently. "We always kept tabs."

Nicholas remembered Fogerty's tight-lipped grin when he saw him enter the hospital today at noon without Max. "Oh," he had bellowed past Nicholas in the hall. "*Si sic omnia!*" Then he had come up to Nicholas, paternally gripping his shoulders with a strong arm. "I take it, Dr. Prescott," Fogerty said, "that you are once again of sound mind in sound body and that we won't have a repeat of that ridiculous debacle." Fogerty lowered his voice. "You are my protégé, Nicholas," he said. "Don't fuck up a sure thing."

Nicholas's father was well known in the Boston medical community; it wouldn't have been hard for him to track his son's quick rise in the cardiothoracic hierarchy at Mass General. Still, it unnerved Nicholas. He wondered what his father had asked. He wondered whom he had approached and who had been willing to answer.

Nicholas cleared his throat. "Was he good?" he repeated, gesturing toward Max.

"Ask your mother," Robert said. "She's in her darkroom."

Nicholas walked down the corridor to the Blue Room, where the circular black-curtained entrance to his mother's workplace was. He had just parted the first curtain when he felt the warm brush of his mother's fingers. He jumped back.

"Oh, Nicholas," Astrid said, pressing her hand to her throat. "I think I scared you as much as you scared me." She was carrying two fresh prints, still smelling faintly of fixer. She waved them, one in each hand, helping them to dry.

"I saw Dad," Nicholas said.

"And?"

Nicholas smiled. "And nothing."

Astrid laid the two prints on a nearby table. "Yes," she said, scanning them with her critical eyes, "it's amazing how several years can soften even the hardest heads." She stood up and groaned, kneading her hands into the small of her back. "Well, my grandson was as good as gold," she said. "You noticed we went shopping? A wonderful baby store in Newton, and then I *had* to go to F. A. O. Schwarz. Max didn't cry the whole time. Really rose to the occasion."

Nicholas tried to imagine his son sitting quietly in his infant seat, watching the rush of colors fly past a car window, and stretching his arms toward the panorama of toys at F. A. O. Schwarz. But in his experience, Max had never gone more than an hour without pitching a fit. "Maybe it's me," he murmured.

"Did you say something?" Astrid said.

Nicholas pinched the bridge of his nose. It had not been an easy day: a quadruple bypass, and then he got word that his last heart transplant patient had rejected the organ. He had a valve replacement at seven the next morning; if he was lucky—if Max was cooperative —he could get about five hours of sleep.

"I took some pictures of Max," Nicholas heard his mother say. "Quite a good little subject—he likes the flash of the light meter. Here." She thrust one of the photographs toward Nicholas.

He had never understood how his mother did it. He was too impatient for photography. He relied on an autofocus camera, and he could usually get a person's image without cutting off the top of the head. But his mother not only recorded a moment; she also stole its soul. Max's downy blue-black hair capped his head. One hand was held out in front of him, reaching toward the camera, and the other was draped across the gray plastic edge of his infant seat, devil-may-care. But it was his eyes that really made the picture. They were wide and amused, as if someone had just told him he was going to have to stay in this world for a good deal longer.

Nicholas was impressed. He had seen his mother capture the pain of grieving military widows, the horror of maimed Romanian orphans, even the rapture and calm piety of the Pope. But this time she had done something truly amazing: she had taken Nicholas's own son and trapped him in time, so that at least here he would never grow up. "You're so damn good," he murmured.

Astrid laughed. "That's what they tell me."

Something twitched at the back of Nicholas's mind. He had been just as impressed by Paige, by her haunted drawings and the secrets that spilled out of her like prophecies she couldn't seem to control. Paige, like his mother, did not just capture an image. Paige drew directly from the heart.

"What is it?" Astrid asked. "You're a million miles away."

"It's nothing," Nicholas said. What had happened to Paige's art stuff? He hadn't been able to move three feet in the apartment without tripping over a spray fixative or crushing a box of charcoal. But Paige hadn't really drawn in years. He had once complained because she'd hung her sketches over the curtain rod of the shower while the fixative was drying. He remembered watching her from behind, when she didn't know he was there, marveling as her fingers flew over the smooth vanilla paper to coax images out of hiding.

Astrid held out the other photo she had carried from her dark-room. "Thought you might like this too," she said. She passed him a candid portrait, and for a moment the dim light in the room caught only the white glare of the damp photographic paper. Then he realized he was staring at Paige.

She was sitting at a table, looking at something off to the left. It was a black-and-white, but Nicholas could clearly see the color of her hair. When he envisioned Cambridge, he pictured it as the shade of Paige's hair—deep and rich, the red of generations.

"How did you get this?" he whispered. Paige's hair was shorter here, just to her shoulders, not long as it had been when she'd met Astrid years before. This was a recent photo.

"I saw her once in Boston, and I couldn't resist. I took it with a telephoto lens. She never saw me." Astrid moved closer to Nicholas and touched her finger to the top of the photograph. "Max has her eyes."

Nicholas did not know why he hadn't noticed it before; it was so obvious. It wasn't the shape or the color as much as the demeanor. Like Max, Paige was looking at something Nicholas could not see. Like Max, her expression was one of blameless surprise, as if she had just been told she was going to have to stay for a while longer.

"Yes," Astrid said, pulling the photo of Max to sit beside the one of Paige. "Definitely his mother's eyes."

Nicholas tucked the picture of Paige behind the one of Max. "Let's hope," he said, "that's all he inherits from her."

chapter 27
Paige

F ly By Night Farm was not really a farm at all. In fact, it was part of a larger complex called Pegasus Stables, and that was the only sign visible from the road. But when I had parked the car and wandered past the lazy stream and the dancing paddocked horses, I noticed the small carved maple plaque: FLY BY NIGHT. LILY RUBENS, PROPRIETOR.

That morning, the woman who owned the tack shop with my mother's horses running across the ceiling had given me directions. My mother had painted the mural eight years before, when she first moved to Farleyville. She had traded her commission for a used saddle and something called draw reins. Lily was well known on the circuit, according to this woman. In fact, when people came for lesson referrals, she always pointed them toward Fly By Night.

I walked into the cool, dark stable, kicking at a tuft of straw with my feet. When my eyes adjusted to the dim light, I found myself just inches away from a horse, its fermenting breath hot on my ear. I put my hand against the wire mesh gate that separated the horse's stall from the main aisle of the stable. The horse whinnied, and its jaundiced teeth curved around the chain links, trying to bite at the flesh of my palm. As its lips brushed my skin, they left behind a green slime that smelled faintly of hay.

"I wouldn't do that if I were you," a voice said, and I whipped around. "But then again, I am you, and you are me, and that's the beauty." A kid no older than eighteen stood propped on a strange skinny rake beside a wheelbarrow piled with manure. He wore a T-shirt colored by a fading portrait of Nietzsche, and his dirty-blond hair was pulled away from his face. "Andy's a biter," he said, coming forward to stroke the horse's nose.

He disappeared as quickly as he'd come, behind the cage door of a different stall. The barn was about half filled with horses, each of them different from the others. There was a chestnut, with hair the same shade as mine; a bay, with a coarse black mane. There was a white Thoroughbred, straight out of a fairy tale; and one tremendous, majestic horse hovering in the shadows, the color of a pitch-dark night.

I walked the length of the aisle, passing the boy, who was heaving wet tufts of hay into the wheelbarrow. It was clear that my mother was not in this barn, and I sighed in relief. I turned to a small table at the end of the aisle. It held a wooden chest and—of all things— an Astrid Prescott photo desk calendar, opened to the current date. I ran my fingers over the misty image of Mount Kilimanjaro, wondering why my mother couldn't have escaped the way Nicholas's mother had—months at a time, but always with a promise to return. Sighing, I turned to the facing page. Neatly lettered beside the printed hours were female names: Brittany, Jane, Anastasia, Merleen. The hand-writing was my mother's.

I remembered it from before, although when she left I hadn't been able to read it. I remembered the way her letters all sloped to the left, in spite of the fact that every other written word I'd ever seen leaned a little to the right. After all, that's what the sisters taught me later in penmanship class. Even when she wrote, my mother bucked the system.

I did not know what I planned to do once I had found her. I did not have a speech ready. On the one hand, I wanted to stare her down and yell at her, one minute for every year since she'd left me. On the other hand, I wanted to touch her, to feel that the substance of her skin was as warm as mine. I wanted to believe I had grown up like her, in spite of the circumstances. I wanted this so badly it hurt, but I knew better than to hedge my bets. After all, I was not sure if, when it came down to it, I would throw myself into her arms or spit at her feet.

I became aware of the blood in my body, which surged down my arms, down my sides. When I remembered well enough how to move again, I pushed through the fear that hung like a net and walked to the boy in the stall. "Excuse me," I said. "I don't mean to bother you."

He did not look up at me or break his rhythmic shoveling. "What are you," he said, "but a speed bump on the autobahn of life?"

I did not know if he expected an answer, so I took a step into the stall, feeling the damp, soft hay give way under my heel. "I'm looking for Lily Rubens," I said, trying out her name on my tongue. "I've come to see Lily Rubens."

The boy shrugged. "She's around," he said. "Check the ring."

The ring. The ring. I nodded to the boy's back and walked down the stable's aisle again, staring at the telephone tucked against the wall and waiting a moment for magic to happen. What did he mean by the ring?

I slipped out of the dark barn and stepped into such bright sun that for a moment the world was only white. Then I saw the brook, running on this side of the stable as well, and a big metal hangar that reminded me of a roller-skating rink in Skokie that had been turned into a flea market. Right beside the barn I had been in was another barn, and down the bend of a little hill was a third barn, built into the slope of a terraced field. There were two gravel paths, which split to either side of the hangar. One seemed to go across a field where a big horse was bucking, and the other sidelined the little brook. I took a deep breath and set off down that one.

The path forked again at a sturdy wooden fence. It either continued up a heathered hill or let you through a gate into a big oval littered with fences and bars and redwood barricades. Riding along the edge of the oval, toward me, was a woman on a horse. I could not see her face, but she was tall and thin and seemed to know what she was doing. The horse shook his head from left to right. "Jeez, Eddy," she said as she came by me, "take it easy. Everyone's got to deal with the bugs. You think you've got a monopoly on them?"

I listened carefully, trying to remember my mother's voice, but I honestly wouldn't have been able to pick it out from others. This could be my mother—if I could just see her face. But she had rounded the curve and was now riding away from me. The only other person there was a man, kind of short, wearing jeans and a big polo shirt and a tweed newsboy's cap. I could not hear his voice, but he was calling out to the woman riding.

The woman kicked the horse, and he began flying around the edge of the track. He jumped a thick blue wall, and then another high rail, and suddenly he was coming a hundred miles an hour directly toward me. I could hear the heavy breath of the rider and see the flared nostrils of the horse as he thundered closer. He wasn't going to stop. He was going to take the gate next, and I was right in his way.

I crouched down and covered my head with my arms just as the horse came to a dead halt inches in front of me. His heavy head was above the gate, his nose grazed my fingers. In the background, the man called something out. "Yes," the woman said, looking down at me. "It was the best line yet, but I think we've scared someone half to death." She smiled at me, and I could see that her hair was blond and her eyes were brown and that her shoulders were much wider than any I'd ever seen on a woman; that she wasn't my mother at all.

I mumbled an apology and headed up the other fork of the path. It opened into a vast field that was sprinkled with buttercups and wild daisies, with grass growing higher than my thighs. Before I saw

them, I heard the rhythm of their hooves—*da da dum, da da dum*—
two horses tearing across the field as if they were being chased by the
devil. They jumped a brook and ran up to the fenced edge of the
pasture. They lowered their heads to graze, their tails switching back
and forth in metronome time like the long swinging hair of exotic
dancers.

By the time I returned, there was no one riding in the little oval.
I headed back toward the barn where that boy had been, figuring I
could ask for better directions. As I walked up the hill, I saw the
man who had been calling out the things I couldn't hear, holding
tight to a thick leather strap that was clipped to Eddy's halter. He
held a dripping sponge in his other hand, but as soon as he touched
it to Eddy's flank, the horse twisted away violently. I kept my distance, half hidden. The man dripped the sponge over the horse's back,
and again it bucked to the left. The man dropped the sponge and
lightly whipped the horse twice across the neck with the strap, then
tucked it over the nose and through the muzzle of the halter. The
horse quieted and bowed his head, and the man began to talk softly,
running his hand over the horse's spine.

I decided to ask this man about my mother, so I stepped forward.
He put down the sponge and lifted his head, but his back was to me.
"Excuse me," I said quietly, and he spun around so fast that his hat
came off and a thick tumble of dark-red hair fell down.

This was not a man. This was my mother.

She was taller than I was, and leaner, and her skin was the color
of honey. But her hair was like mine, and her eyes were like mine,
and there was no mistaking it. "Oh, my God," she said.

The horse snorted over her shoulder, and water dripped off his
mane to form a puddle on my mother's shirt. She did not seem to
notice. "I'm Paige," I said, stiffly, and impulsively I held out my
hand to shake hers. "I'm, um, your daughter."

My mother began to smile, and it melted her from her head to
her feet, making her able to move again. "I know who you are," she
said. She did not take my hand. She shook her head and knotted her
fingers around the leather lead. She fidgeted, scuffing the toes of her

boots in the loose gravel. "Let me get rid of Eddy," she said. She pulled on the lead and then stopped to turn back to me. Her eyes were huge and pale, the eyes of a beggar. "Don't go anywhere," she said.

I followed a few steps behind the horse she led. She disappeared into a stall—the one the boy had been cleaning—and slid the halter off the horse's head. She stepped out, latched the mesh gate, and hung the leather contraption on a nail pegged to the right of the stall. "Paige," she said, breathing my name as if it were forbidden to speak aloud.

She reached toward me and touched her palm to my shoulder. I could not help it; I shivered and stepped back. "I'm sorry," I said, looking away.

At that moment the boy who had been working the stable earlier appeared out of nowhere. "I'm done for the day, Lily," he said, although it was only noon.

My mother dragged her gaze away from me. "Josh," she said, "this is Paige. My daughter, Paige."

Josh nodded at me. "Cool," he said. He turned to my mother. "Aurora and Andy need to be brought in. I'll see you tomorrow. Although," he said, "tomorrow is just the flip side of today."

As he walked down the long aisle of the barn, my mother turned to me. "He's a little bit Zen," she said, "but he's all I can afford right now."

Without another word, my mother walked out of the barn and headed down the gravel path toward the field that ran to the left. When she reached the field she propped her elbows against the wooden gate and watched the horse at the far end. Even at this distance he was one of the largest horses I had ever seen. He was sleek and sable-colored, with the exception of his two front legs. They turned pure white halfway down, as if he'd only just stepped into heaven. "How did you find me?" my mother asked nonchalantly.

"You didn't make it easy," I snapped. I was fuming. My mother didn't seem the tiniest bit put out by my appearance. I was more rattled than she was. Sure, there had been that shock of surprise, but now she was acting cool and relaxed, as if she'd known I was coming. This was not the way I'd thought she would be. I realized that at the very least, I'd expected her to be curious. At the very most, I had wanted her to care.

I turned to her, waiting for a splinter of real recognition to hit me—some gesture or smile or even the lilt of her voice. But this was an entirely different woman from the one who had left me when I was five years old. I had spent the past few days—the past twenty years—conjuring up comparisons between us, making assumptions. I knew we would bear a resemblance to each other. I knew that we had both been driven away from our homes, although I didn't know why she had left. I imagined that I would meet her and she would reach out her arms for me and there I would be, in the place where I always knew I would fit best. I imagined that we would sound the same, walk the same, think the same. But this was her world, and I knew nothing about it. This was her life, and it had gone smoothly without me around. The truth was that I barely knew her when she left and that I did not know her now. "A friend of mine introduced me to a private eye, and he tracked you to Bridles & Bits," I said, "and then I saw the ceiling."

"The ceiling," my mother whispered, her thoughts far away. "Oh—the *ceiling*. Like Chicago."

"Just like," I said, my words clipped and bitten.

My mother turned abruptly. "I didn't mean to leave you, Paige," she said. "I only meant to *leave*."

I shrugged as if I did not care at all. But something sparked inside me. I thought of Max's round little face and flat chin, and of Nicholas, pulling me against the hot line of his chest. I had not meant to leave them; I had only meant to leave. I wasn't running away from them; I was only running away. I peered at my mother from the corner of my eye. Maybe this went deeper than appearances. Maybe, after all, we had more in common than it seemed.

As if she knew I needed proof, my mother whistled to the horse at the far end of the field. He exploded toward us, running at a breakneck pace, but slowed as he approached my mother. Gentling, he circled until he was calm. He nodded and tossed his head, and then he leaned down and nuzzled my mother's hand.

He was easily the most beautiful animal I had ever seen. I wanted to draw him, but I knew I'd never be able to capture his energy on paper. "This is my best show horse," my mother said. "Worth over seventy-five thousand dollars. This whole thing"—here she swept her hand across the vast farm—"my lessons and my training and everything else I do, is just to support him, so I can show him on weekends. We show in the elite shows, and we've even come in first in our division."

I was impressed, but I did not understand why she was telling me this now when there were so many other things that needed to be said. "I don't own this land," my mother continued, slipping the halter over the horse's head. "I rent from Pegasus Stables. I rent my house and my trailer and my truck from them. This horse is just about the only thing I can really say is mine. Do you understand?"

"Not really," I said impatiently, stepping back as the horse lifted his head to dodge a fly.

"This horse is named Donegal," my mother said, and the word brought back what it always had—the name of the county in Ireland where my father had been born, the place he never stopped telling us about when I was little. *Tumbling clover like emeralds; stone chimneys brushing the clouds; rivers as blue as your mother's eyes.*

I remembered Eddie Savoy saying that people can't ever wholly give up what they've left behind. "Donegal," I repeated, and this time as my mother held out her arms, I stepped into their quiet circle, amazed that the vague wisps of old memories could crystallize into such warmth, such flesh and blood.

≈≈≈

"I spent years hoping you would come," my mother said. She led me up the steps to the farmer's porch of the small white clapboard house. "I used to watch the little girls walk down to the stable for their lessons, and I kept thinking, This one will pull off her riding helmet, and it's going to be Paige." At the screen door, she turned to me. "It never was, though."

My mother's house was clean and neat, almost Spartan. The porch was empty, except for a white wicker rocking chair, which blended into the background paint, and a bright-pink hanging begonia. The front hall had a faded Oriental runner and a thin maple table, on top of which was a set of Shaker boxes. To the right was a tiny living room; to the left, a staircase. "I'll get you settled in," my mother said, although I had never said I would be staying. "But I've got some lessons this afternoon, so I won't be around much."

She took me up to the second floor. Straight ahead at the top of the staircase was the bathroom, and the bedrooms were to the right and the left. She turned to the right, but I got a glimpse of her own room—pale and breezy, with gauze curtains billowing over the white of the bed.

When I stepped into the doorway of the other room, I drew in my breath. The wallpaper was a busy tumble of huge pink flowers. The bed was a frothy canopy, and on a chest against the wall were two porcelain dolls and a stuffed green clown. It was the room of a little girl. "You have another daughter," I said. It wasn't a question really, but a statement.

"No." My mother walked forward and brushed the cool cheek of one of the dolls. "One of the reasons I decided to lease this stable was because of this room. I kept thinking how much you would have liked it here."

I looked around the room at the sugar-candy decoration, the suffocating wallpaper. I *wouldn't* have liked it as a child. I thought about my bedroom at home in Cambridge, which I didn't like, either, with its milk-colored carpet, the near-white walls. "I was eighteen when you got this place," I pointed out. "A little old for dolls."

My mother shrugged easily. "You were kind of stuck in my mind at five years old," she said. "I kept thinking I'd go back and get you, but I couldn't do that to your father, and besides, if I went back I knew it would be to stay. Before I knew it, you were all grown up."

"You came to my graduation," I said, sitting down on the bed. It was a hard mattress, unforgiving.

"You saw me?"

I shook my head. "Private eye," I said. "Very thorough."

My mother sat down beside me. "I spent ten hours in Raleigh-Durham, trying to make up my mind about getting on that plane. I could, then I couldn't. I even sat down on one flight and ran off before they closed the door."

"But you came," I said, "so why didn't you try to talk to me?"

My mother stood up and smoothed away the wrinkles on the bedspread so that it looked as though she'd never sat down. "I didn't go there for you," she said. "I went there for *me.*"

My mother checked her watch. "Brittany's coming at two-thirty," she said. "Cutest little kid you've ever seen, but she's never going to make it as a rider. Feel free to come down and watch, if you like." She looked around as if something were missing. "You have a bag?"

"Yes," I said, knowing that even if I wanted to I could not make myself stay at a motel. "It's in my car."

My mother nodded and started to walk out, leaving me on the bed. "There's food in the fridge if you're hungry, and be careful because the toilet lever sticks a little, and if you need me in a hurry there's a sticker on the phone with a number that goes straight to Pegasus's barn, and they can get me."

It was so easy to talk to her. It came effortlessly; I could have been doing it forever. I supposed I had, but she hadn't been answering. Still, I wondered how she could be this matter-of-fact, as if I were the kind of visitor she got every day. Just thinking about her made a headache come behind my eyes. Maybe she knew better and was doing this to skip all the gutted history in between. When you don't keep looking back, it's that much easier not to trip and fall.

My mother stopped at the threshold of the door and held her hand against the wooden frame. "Paige," she said, "are you married?"

A sharp pain ran straight down my spine, a sick ache that came from her being able to talk about phone lines and lunch but not knowing the things a mother is supposed to know. "I got married in 1985," I told her. "His name is Nicholas Prescott. He's a cardiac surgeon."

My mother raised her eyebrows at this and smiled. She started to walk out of the room. "And," I called after her, "I have a baby. A son, Max. He's three months old."

My mother stopped, but she did not turn around. I might even have imagined the quiet tremble of her shoulders. "A baby," she murmured. I knew what was going through her mind: *A baby, and you left him behind, and once upon a time I left you.* I lifted my chin, waiting for her to turn around and admit to the cycle, but she didn't. She shifted her weight until she was moving down the stairs, humbled and silent, with the parallel lines of our past running cluttered through her mind.

≈≈≈

She was standing in the center of the oval—the ring—and a girl on a pony danced around her. "Transitions, Brittany," she called. "First you're going to take him to a trot. Squeeze him into it; don't lean forward. Sit up, sit up, push those heels down." The girl was leggy and small. Her hair hung in a thick blond tail from beneath the black riding helmet. I leaned against the rail where I'd stood earlier, watching the squat brown horse jaunt its way around in a circle.

My mother walked to the edge of the ring and adjusted one of the redwood rails so that it was lower to the ground. "Feel when he's going too fast and too slow," she yelled. "You need to ride every step. Now I want you to cross the diagonal. . . . Keep stretching down in your heels."

The girl steered the horse—at least I thought she did—coming out of the corner and making an X across the ring. "Okay, sitting trot," my mother called. The girl stopped bouncing up and down and sat heavy in the saddle, wiggling a little from side to side with every step of the horse. "Half seat!" my mother called, and the girl bounced up once, freezing in the position that held her out of the saddle, hanging on to the horse's mane for dear life. My mother saw me and waved. "Let's cross the diagonal again, and you're going to go right over this cavalletti," she said. "Ride him right into the woods." She crouched down, her voice tense and her body coiled, as if she could will the horse to do it correctly. "Eyes up, eyes up . . . leg, leg, leg!" The horse did a neat hop over the low rail and slowed down to a quiet walk. The little girl stretched her legs out in front of her, feet still in the stirrups. "Good girl," my mother called, and Brittany smiled. "We can end with that."

A woman had come up beside me. She pulled out her checkbook. "Are you taking lessons with Lily?" she asked, smiling.

I did not know how to answer. "I'm thinking about it," I said.

The woman scrawled a signature and ripped off the check. "She's the best there is around here."

Brittany had dismounted, neatly sliding off the saddle. She walked up to the fence, leading the horse by the reins. My mother glanced at me, looking from my head to my shoulders to my walking shorts and sneakers. "Don't worry about tacking Tony down," she said. "I think I need him for another lesson." She held out her hands for the reins and watched as Brittany and her mother disappeared up the hill toward the barn.

"My three-thirty has the flu," she said, "so how'd you like a lesson for free?"

I thought of the horse that morning taking the jumps with the power of a locomotive, and then I looked at this little horse. It had long dark eyelashes and a white patch on its forehead in the shape of Mickey Mouse. "I don't think so," I said. "I'm not the type."

"I never was, either," my mother said. "Just try it. If you don't feel comfortable, you can get off." She led me toward the little red-wood rail and paused, holding the horse's reins. "If you really want to know about me, you should try riding. And if you really want me to know about you, I can learn a hell of a lot just by watching you in the saddle."

I held the horse's reins while my mother adjusted the stirrup lengths and pointed out the names of things: blanket, pad, and English saddle; bit, bridle, martingale, girth, reins. "Step on the caval-letti," my mother said, and I looked at her blankly. "The *red* thing," she said, kicking the rail with her foot. I stepped onto it with my right foot and then tucked my left foot into the stirrup. "Hang on to the mane and swing yourself over. I'm holding Tony; he isn't going anywhere "

I knew as soon as I was sitting that I looked ridiculous. A little girl might have looked cute on a pony, but I was a fully grown woman. I was certain my legs almost touched the ground. I might as well have been riding a burro. "You're not going to kick him," my mother said. "Just urge him into walking."

I touched my foot gently to the horse's flanks, but nothing happened. So I did it again, and the horse shot off, bouncing me from left to right until I leaned forward and wrapped my arms around its neck. "Sit up!" my mother yelled. "Sit up and pull back." I summoned all my strength and did what she said, sighing when the horse slowed to a quiet walk that barely jogged me at all. "*Never* lean forward," my mother said, smiling, "unless you're planning to gallop."

I listened to my mother's calm directions, letting all the words run together and feeling the simple meter of the horse's movements and the scratch of its hide against my bare calves. I was amazed at the power I had. If I pushed my right leg against Tony's side, he moved to the left. If I pushed my left leg against him, he moved right. He was completely under my control.

When my mother urged the horse to a trot by clucking at him, I did what she said. I kept my shoulders, my hips, and my heels in a straight line. I posted up and down, letting the horse's rhythm lift me out of the saddle and holding the beat until the next hoof fell. I kept my back erect and my hands quiet on Tony's withers. I was completely out of breath when she told me to sit back and let the horse walk, and I turned to her immediately. It wasn't until then that I saw how much I wanted her approval.

"That's enough for today," she said. "Your legs are going to kill you tonight."

She held the reins while I slid out of the saddle, patting Tony on the side of his neck. "So what do you know about me now that you didn't know before?" I asked.

My mother turned, her hands on her hips. "I know that at least twice during that half hour you pictured yourself galloping across a field. And that if you had fallen the first time Tony pulled away a little fast, you would have got right back on. I know you're wondering what it's like to jump, and I know that you're more of a natural at this than you think." She tugged on the reins so that the horse separated us. "All in all," she said, "I can see that you are very much like me."

≈≈≈

It was my job to make the salad. My mother was simmering spaghetti sauce, her hands on her hips in front of the old stove. I glanced around the neat kitchen, wondering where I would find a salad bowl, tomatoes, vinegar.

"The lettuce is on the bottom shelf," my mother said, her back to me.

I stuck my head into the refrigerator, pushing past nectarines and Bartles & Jaymes wine coolers to find the head of iceberg lettuce. My father believed you could tell a lot about people from their kitchens. I wondered what he'd have to say about this one.

I started to peel the leaves off the lettuce and rinse them in the sink, and looked up to find my mother watching me. "Don't you core it?" she asked.

"Excuse me?"

"You know," my mother said. "Take the core out." She rammed the heel of the lettuce against the counter and neatly twisted it out. The lettuce fell open in a series of petals. "Your father never taught you that?" she said lightly.

My spine straightened at the criticism. *No,* I wanted to tell her. *He was too busy doing other things. Like guaranteeing my moral conscience, and showing me how to trust other people, and letting me in on the unfair ways of the world.* "As a matter of fact," I said quietly, "he did not."

My mother shrugged and turned back to the stove. I began tearing the lettuce into a bowl, ripping it furiously into tiny pieces. I peeled a carrot and diced a tomato. Then I stopped. "Is there anything you don't take?" I asked. My mother looked up. "In your salad, I mean."

"Onion," she said. She hesitated. "What about you?"

"I eat everything," I told her. I chopped cucumber, thinking how ridiculous it was that I did not know what vegetables my own mother would eat in a tossed salad. I couldn't prepare her coffee, either, or conjure her shoe size, or tell a stranger which side of the bed she slept on. "You know," I said, "if our lives had been a little different, I wouldn't be asking these things."

My mother did not turn around, but her hand stopped stirring the sauce for the span of a breath. "Our lives weren't a little bit different, though, were they?" she said.

I stared at her back until I could not stand it anymore. Then I threw the carrots, the tomatoes, and the cucumber into the bowl, while the rough anger and the disappointment pressed back-to-back and settled heavy on my chest.

≈≈≈

We ate on the porch, and afterward we watched the sun go down. We drank cold peach wine coolers from cognac glasses that still had price stickers on their bottoms. My mother pointed out the mountains in the background, which rose in swells so close they seemed within reach. I concentrated on physical things: the bones of our knees, the curve of our calves, the placement of freckles, all so similar. "When I first moved here," my mother said, "I used to wonder if it was at all like Ireland. Your father was always saying he'd take me there, but it never happened." She paused. "I miss him very much, you know."

I stared at her, softening. "He told me you were married three months after you'd met." I took a large gulp of wine and smiled tentatively. "It was love at first sight, he said."

My mother leaned back her head so that her throat was straight and white and vulnerable. "It could have been," she said. "I can't remember all that well. I know I couldn't wait to get out of Wisconsin, and then Patrick magically appeared, and I always felt a little sorry that he had to suffer when I found out it hadn't been about Wisconsin at all."

I saw this as my lead-in. "When I was little," I said, "I used to dream up these scenarios that had made you leave. I figured once that you were connected to a gang and you'd slipped up and they threatened the safety of your family. And another time I figured that you maybe had fallen in love with someone else and run off with him."

"There was someone else," my mother said frankly, "but it was *after* I left, and I never loved him. I wasn't going to take that away from Patrick too."

I put the glass down beside me, tracing its edge with my fingertip. "What made you leave, then?" I asked.

My mother stood up and rubbed her upper arms. "Damn mosquitoes," she said. "I swear they're here all year. I'm going to check on the barn." She started to turn away. "You can stay or you can come."

I stared at her, astonished. "How can you do that?"

"Do what?"

"Just change the subject like that?" I hadn't come all this distance just to be pushed farther away. I walked down the two steps of the porch until we were standing eye-to-eye. "It's been twenty years, *Mom*," I said. "Isn't it a little late to be dodging the question?"

"It's been twenty years, *dear*," my mother shot back. "What makes you think I remember the answer?" She broke her stare, looking down at her shoes, and then she sighed. "It was not the mob, and it was not a lover. It wasn't anything like that at all. It was something much more normal."

I lifted my chin. "You still haven't given me a reason," I said, "and you are far from what is considered normal. Normal people do not vanish in the middle of the night and never speak to their families again. Normal people do not spend two decades using a dead person's name. Normal people do not meet their daughter for the first time in twenty years and act like it's an ordinary visit."

My mother took a step back, anger and pride making violet slashes in her eyes. "If I had known you were coming," she said, "I would have taken my goddamned red carpet out of storage." She started off toward the barn, and then she stopped and faced me. When she spoke, her voice was more gentle, as if she'd realized too late what she had said. "Don't ask me why *I* left, Paige, until you can tell yourself why *you* left."

Her words burned, flaming my cheeks and my throat. I watched her slip up the hill toward the barn.

I wanted to run after her and tell her it was her fault that I'd left; that I knew I had to take this opportunity to learn all the things I had never learned from her: how to look pretty; how to hold a man; how to be a mother. I wanted to tell her that I never would have left *my* husband and *my* child under any other circumstances and that, unlike her, I was going back. But I had a feeling that she would have laughed at me and said, *Yes, that's the way it begins.* And I had a feeling that I would not be telling the complete truth.

I had left before I had any inkling that I wanted to find my mother. I had left without giving my mother a second thought. No matter what I had brainwashed myself to believe by now, I hadn't even considered going to Chicago until I was several hundred miles away from my home. I needed to see her; I wanted to see her—I understood what had prompted me to hire Eddie Savoy. But it was only *after* I'd left Max and Nicholas that I thought of coming here. It wasn't the other way around. The truth was that even if my mother had lived just down the street, I would have wanted to get away.

Back then I had blamed it on Max's nosebleed—but that had just been the spark that set off the fire. The real reason was that my confusion ran too deep to sort out at home. I *had* to go. I didn't have any other choice. I didn't leave out of anger, and I didn't want to leave forever—just long enough. Long enough to feel that I wasn't doing it all wrong. Long enough to feel that *I* mattered, that I was more than a necessary extension of Max's or Nicholas's life.

I thought of all the magazine articles I'd read on mothers who worked and constantly felt guilty about leaving their children with someone else. I had trained myself to read pieces like that and silently say to myself, *See how lucky you are?* But it had been gnawing at me inside, that part that didn't quite fit, that I never let myself even *think* about. After all, wasn't it a worse kind of guilt to be *with* your child and to know that you wanted to be anywhere but there?

I saw a light flash on in the barn, and all of a sudden I knew why my mother had left.

I went up to the bathroom and undressed. I ran hot water in the claw-footed tub and thought about how good it would feel on the clenched muscles of my thighs. Riding had made me aware of places on my body that I hadn't known existed. I brushed my teeth and stepped neatly into the tub. I leaned my head back against the enamel rim, closed my eyes, and tried to will away thoughts of my mother.

Instead I pictured Max, who would be exactly three and a half months old the next day. I tried to remember the milestones he should have been reaching now, according to that *First Year* book Nicholas had brought me. Solid foods, that was the only one I could remember, and I wondered what he thought of bananas, applesauce, strained peas. I tried to imagine his tongue pushing out against a spoon, that unfamiliar object. I smoothed one hand over the other and tried to remember his silky powdered touch.

When I opened my eyes, my mother was standing over the bathtub, wearing a yellow wrapper. I tried to cross my arms over my chest and to twist my legs, but it was too small a tub. A flush of embarrassment ran from my belly up to my cheeks. "Don't," she said. "You've turned out quite beautiful."

I stood up abruptly, grabbing a towel and sloshing water all over the floor in my hurry. "I don't think so," I murmured, and I threw open the bathroom door. I ran to my little-girl room, letting the steam steal down the hall to veil my image from my mother.

≈≈≈

When I first woke up, before I was fully conscious, I thought that they were at it again. I could so clearly hear in my imagination the voices of my mother and father attacking, tangling, retreating.

They were not fights; they were never really fights. They were triggered by the simplest things: a burned soufflé, a priest's sermon, a supper my father came home to late. They were only half-arguments, started by my mother and quelled by my father. He never picked up the gauntlet. He'd let her scream and accuse, and then, when the sobs came, his soft words would cover her like a soft blanket.

It didn't scare me. I used to lie in bed and listen to the scene that had been replayed so many times I knew the dialogue by heart. *Slam:* that was my mother at the bedroom door, and seconds later it would open again, once my father came upstairs. In the months after my mother left, when I was doing my remembering, I thought of the arguments and I added the pictures I could never see, fashioning them like actors in a grainy black-and-white film. So, for example, here I envisioned my parents back-to-back, my mother tugging a brush through her hair and my father unbuttoning his shirt. "You don't understand," my mother said, her words always hitched and high, always the same. "I can't do it all. You expect me to do everything."

"Sssh, May," my father murmured. "You take it so hard." I imagined him turning to her and grasping her shoulders, like Bogart in *Casablanca.* "Nobody expects anything."

"Yes you do," my mother screamed, and the bed creaked as she stood. I could hear her pacing, footsteps like rain. "I can't do anything right, Patrick. I'm tired. I'm just bone-tired. Dear God, I just wish —I want—"

"What do you want, *á mhuírnán?*"

"I don't know," my mother said. "If I knew, I wouldn't be here."

Then she would start crying, and I would listen to the gentle sounds that drifted through the wall: the butterfly kisses and the slip of my father's hands over my mother's skin and the charged quiet that I later learned was the sound of making love.

Sometimes there were variations—like when my mother begged my father to go away with her, just the two of them, sailing in a dugout canoe to Fiji. Another time she scratched and clawed at my dad and made him sleep on the couch. Once she said that she still believed the world was flat and that she was hanging at the edge.

My father was an insomniac, and after these episodes he'd get up in the dead of the night and creep down to his workshop. As if on cue, I'd tiptoe out of my room, and I would crawl under the covers of their big bed. It was like that in our family; someone was always filling in for someone else. I'd press my cheek against my mother's back and hear her murmur my name, and I held her so close my own body trembled with her fear.

I had heard the cries again tonight; that's what made me wake so suddenly. But my father's voice was missing. For a moment I couldn't place the crowded wallpaper, the intruding moon. I slipped out of bed and turned in at the bathroom, then I redirected myself and walked till I stood at the threshold of my mother's room.

I hadn't dreamed it. She was curled beneath the covers, her fists pressed to her eyes. She was crying so hard she couldn't catch her breath.

I shifted from one foot to the other, nervously wringing the sleeve of my nightshirt. I just couldn't do it. After all, so much had happened. I wasn't a four-year-old child, and she was no more than a stranger. She was practically nothing to me.

I remembered how I had flinched at her touch this afternoon, and how annoyed I had been when she took my arrival as easily as she'd take an afternoon tea. I remembered seeing my face reflected in her eyes when she was talking about my father. I considered the room, that god-awful room, that she had had waiting for me.

Even as I crossed the floor I was listing all the reasons I shouldn't. *You don't know her. She doesn't know you. She shouldn't be forgiven.* I crawled under the covers. With a sigh that unraveled the years, I put my arms around my mother and willingly slid back to where I'd started.

chapter 28
Nicholas

Nicholas Prescott was already unofficially engaged to Paige O'Toole when they went out on their fourth date. Nicholas picked her up at that waitress Doris's apartment, a small flea-ridden building in Porter Square. He'd left a message while she was working, telling her to wear something along the lines of haute couture because he was taking her to the top that night. He did not know that she spent an hour asking Doris, the neighbors, and finally the reference librarian at the Boston Public Library what haute couture meant.

She was wearing a simple black sleeveless sheath. Her hair was piled on top of her head in a loose knot; her eyes were wide and luminescent. Her shoes were fake alligatorskin, with spike heels—the kind of shoes his college friends had called fuck-me pumps—although with someone like Paige wearing them, that term would never have come to mind.

At the end of their other three dates, Nicholas had gone no further than gently cupping her breasts, and from her quiet trembling he knew that was enough. In spite of the fact that she'd run away from home, that she was not college educated, and that she was a waitress in a diner, to Nicholas, Paige O'Toole was as chaste as they came. When he pictured her, he thought of the image of Psyche from the White Rock ginger ale label, a girl-woman kneeling on a boulder, staring at her reflection as if she was surprised to see it in the water below. The way Paige was shy to smile, the instinctive habit she had of covering her body when Nicholas touched her—it all added up. They had never spoken of it; Nicholas wasn't like that. But he believed in the strength of coincidence, and surely there was a reason he had been in Mercy when she had begun to work there: Paige did not know it, but she had been waiting for him all her life.

"You look wonderful," Nicholas said, kissing the spot below her left ear. They were waiting for the elevator.

Paige smoothed her hands over the dress, tugging as if it didn't fit her like a second skin. "This is Doris's," she admitted. "I didn't have any couture, so we went through her closet. Would you believe this is from 1959? We spent the whole afternoon taking in the seams."

"And the shoes?" The bell rang, and Nicholas took Paige's elbow to lead her into the elevator.

Paige looked straight at him, challenging. "I bought them. I figured I deserved something new."

Nicholas was sometimes surprised by the fury she held in check. When she believed she was right, she would fight to the end to make you see her side, continuing emphatically even after she had proof that she was wrong.

When the elevator touched ground level, Nicholas waited for Paige to step out first, as he'd been taught in eighth grade. But when she didn't, he turned to face her, and he saw again the expression she often had when looking at Nicholas. It was as if he filled up her entire world; as if there was nothing he could do wrong. "What is it?" Nicholas said, taking her hand.

Paige shook her head. "It's just you." She took two steps and then looked back at him, smiling. "If you had lived in Chicago, you would have passed me on the street."

"No I wouldn't," Nicholas said.

Paige laughed. "You're absolutely right. You wouldn't have been caught *dead* on Taylor Street."

Nicholas couldn't convince Paige that it didn't matter to him where she had come from, where she was working, whether she had a diploma. The one important thing was where she was going, and Nicholas was planning to make sure that she would go there with him. It was one of the reasons he'd told her to dress to the nines and had booked a reservation at the Empress in the Hyatt Regency on the river. They'd head up to the Spinnaker afterward, the revolving bar, and then he'd take her home and they'd sit beneath the street-lights of Porter Square, kissing until their lips were swollen and bruised. Then Nicholas would drive back to his own apartment in Cambridge, and he would lie naked beneath the ceiling fan in the bedroom, lazily tracing circles on the sheets and imagining the silk of Paige's skin underneath his fingers.

"Where are we going?" Paige asked as she slipped into the car.

Nicholas grinned at her. "A surprise," he said.

Paige fastened her seat belt and smoothed the wrinkles out of the black skirt stretched over her lap. "Probably not McDonald's," she said. "They've relaxed the dress code."

The tuxedoed maître d' at the restaurant bowed to Nicholas and led the way to a tiny corner table that abutted a wall of glass. The basin of the Charles River was bathed in the fuchsia and orange of sunset. Playing across the surface like skittering butterflies were the distant billowed sails of the MIT sailing club. Paige drew in her breath and pressed her palms to the glass for a second, leaving a neat steamed print when she took them away. "Oh, Nicholas," she said, "this is great."

Nicholas picked up the black matchbook in the crystal ashtray, embossed with Paige's initials in gold lettering. It was one of the reasons he'd chosen the Empress instead of Café Budapest or the Ritz-

Carlton; this was one of their touches. Nicholas handed the matches to Paige. "You might want to hang on to these," he said.

Paige smiled. "You know I don't smoke," she said. "Doris doesn't even have a fireplace." She tossed them back into the ashtray, and then she noticed the letters, PMO. Nicholas sat back, watching Paige's eyes darken and grow wide. Then, like a little kid, she glanced around and sneaked to an empty table next to them. She lifted the matchbook out of the ashtray and her face fell, but only for a second. "It's just this one," she said, breathless. "But how do they *know?*"

As the meal progressed, Nicholas began to question his motive for an elegant dinner. Paige had urged him to order, since she hadn't had any of the dishes before, and he'd done that. The appetizer—a bird's nest filled with chicken and vegetables—had been delicious, but Paige had no more than touched a straw mushroom to her mouth when her lip began to swell like a balloon. She had held ice to it with her napkin, and it subsided a little, but she must have been allergic. Then when the waiter had brought the complimentary palate-cleansing sorbet, frothed in dry ice that spilled over onto your lap like the mist of a Scottish moor, Paige had argued with the man, insisting that since they hadn't ordered it, they shouldn't have to pay. She had watched Nicholas eating throughout the entire meal, refusing to pick up one of the three forks or spoons until he did. More than once Nicholas caught her with her guard down, staring at her dish as if it were another wall to scale in an obstacle course.

When the check came, the waiter brought Paige a long-stemmed rose, and she smiled across the table at Nicholas. She looked exhausted. Nicholas couldn't believe he hadn't thought of it from this angle: to Paige, this had all been work, almost a kind of test. After Nicholas's credit card had been returned, Paige bolted from her chair before he could even pull it out for her. She walked quickly through the path of least resistance toward the door, head down, not looking at the other diners she passed.

When she was in the hallway by the elevator, she leaned against the wall and closed her eyes. Nicholas stood beside her, his hands jammed into his trousers pockets. "I guess a drink upstairs is out of the question," he murmured.

Paige opened her eyes, momentarily confused, as if Nicholas were the last person she'd expected to find beside her. A smile fixed itself on her face. "It was delicious, Nicholas," she said, and Nicholas couldn't help it, he kept staring at the puffy outline of her still-swollen lower lip, which made her look like a 1930s screen siren. She covered her mouth with her hand.

Nicholas grabbed her fingers and pulled them down to her side. "Don't do that," he said. "Don't ever do that." He slipped his suit jacket over her shoulders.

"Do what?"

Nicholas paused for a fraction of a second and then picked up again. "Lie to me."

He expected her to deny it, but Paige turned to him. "It was awful," she admitted. "I know you didn't mean it, Nicholas, but that isn't really my speed."

Nicholas didn't believe it was really *his* speed, either, but he'd been doing it for so long he had never really considered anything else. He rode down the fourteen stories in the elevator in silence, holding Paige's hand, thinking about what Taylor Street in Chicago might look like and whether, in fact, he *wouldn't* be caught dead on it.

It wasn't that he doubted Paige; in spite of his parents' reaction, he knew that they were going to get married. But he wondered how very different two worlds had to be before they kept people apart. His parents had come from opposite sides of the proverbial tracks, but that didn't count, since they'd wanted to swap places anyway. In Nicholas's mind, that sort of equalized them. His mother had married his father to thumb her nose at society, and his father had married his mother to gain entry into a tight circle of wealth that all the new money in the world couldn't buy. He really didn't know how—or *if*—love ever figured into it, and that was the biggest difference between his parents' relationship and the feelings he had for Paige. He loved Paige because she was simple and sweet, because her hair was the color of an Indian summer, and because she could do an impression of Elmer Fudd that was nearly flawless. He loved her because she had made it to Cambridge on less than a hundred dollars, because she knew how to say the Lord's Prayer backward without stopping, because she could draw exactly what he could never quite put into words. With an overwhelming fervor that surprised Nicholas himself, he believed in her ability to land on her feet; in fact, Paige was the closest thing to a religion he'd had in years. He didn't give a damn whether or not she could tell a fish knife from a salad fork, if she'd be able to pick a waltz from a polka. That wasn't what marriage was about.

But on the other hand, Nicholas couldn't help but remember that marriage was a man-made thing, a statute created by society itself. Two souls that were meant to be together—and Nicholas wasn't saying that was the case with him; he was too scientific to be so romantic—well, two people like that could just mate for life with no need for a paper certificate. Marriage didn't really seem to be about love; it was about the ability to *live* together for a long period of time, and that was something completely different. That was something he just wasn't sure about when it came to him and Paige.

He stared at her profile when he pulled up at a red light. Tiny nose, shining eyes, classic lips. Suddenly she turned to him, smiling. There had to be a happy medium. "What are you thinking about?" she asked.

"I was thinking," Nicholas said, "that I wish you could show me what Taylor Street is like."

chapter 29
Paige

*M*y mother had seven geldings, and with the exception of Donegal, they were named for men she had turned down. "I don't date," she had told me. "Very few men think that the perfect end to an evening of seduction is a ten o'clock check through the stable." Eddy and Andy were chestnuts, Thoroughbreds. Tony was a mixed-breed pony she had saved from starvation. Burt was a quarter horse that was older than dirt, and Jean-Claude and Elmo were three-year-olds that had come from the racetrack and were in the process of being broken.

While she took Jean-Claude or Elmo down to the ring to work on a lunge line, Josh and I mucked the stalls and spread sweet bedding and scrubbed the water buckets. It was hard work, which knotted my back and my calf muscles, but I found that I could rake through an entire stable sometimes without thinking about Nicholas or Max. In fact, almost anything I did in association with the horses took my mind off the family I had left behind, and I began to see what held my mother's fascination.

I was filling the black beveled buckets in Aurora's stall, and as usual she was trying to bite my back every time I turned away. She was the eighth horse my mother owned, the white fairy-tale mare. She had said that she bought her on impulse, because she'd been hoping Prince Charming would come with the deal, but she'd regretted the purchase ever since. Aurora was bitchy and foul-tempered and stubborn to train. "I've done Aurora's water," I called to Josh, who was mucking farther down in the same barn. I liked him—he was a little weird, but he made me smile. He did not eat meat because "somewhere, cows are sacred." He had let me know the second day I was here that he was already halfway down the eightfold path to nirvana.

I picked up the wheelbarrow Josh had filled with manure and went to the dump pile that composted under the hot Carolina sun. I lifted my face and felt the grime collecting on the back of my neck although it was only eight-thirty.

"Paige!" Josh yelled, "Get here quick! And bring a halter!"

I threw the wheelbarrow aside and raced back, grabbing the halter hanging beside Andy's stall. From the far end of the barn I heard Josh's soothing words. "Come closer," he whispered to me, "and walk slow."

When I peeked out the far door, he had Aurora by the mane. "It's customary to lock the stall when you finish," he said, grinning.

"I did!" I insisted, and I worked the little clip, just to prove it. But one of the chain-link spokes had broken, and I realized I had probably fastened the clip over that one, and the door had sprung free. "Sorry," I said, and I took Aurora by the halter. "Maybe you should have just let her go," I said.

"I don't know," Josh said. "I don't owe Lily any favors this month."

We took a break and went to watch my mother lunging Jean-Claude. She stood in the center of the ring, letting the horse buck and gallop in circles around her. This time, he had a saddle on his back, simply to get used to the feeling. "Look at his conformation," she'd said. "He's a born jumper—nice sloping shoulders, short back."

"And," Josh had said, "an ass like a truck."

My mother had patted him on the cheek with the same tenderness she showed her horses. "Just as long as you don't say that about me," she said.

We watched the muscles in my mother's arms cord and bunch as she tugged on the line that Jean-Claude was valiantly trying to shake free. "How long has she been doing this?" I asked.

"Jean-Claude?" Josh said. "He's only been here a month. But Jesus, Donegal's her first horse, and he's a champion, and he's only seven." Josh bent down and pulled a stalk of grass from the ground and settled it between his front teeth. He began to tell me the story of my mother and Fly By Night Farm.

She had been working as a personal secretary to Harlan Cozackis, a Kentucky millionaire who had made his fortune in corrugated cardboard. He was very involved in the racing circuit and bought a couple of horses who placed well in the Derby and the Preakness. When he got pancreatic cancer, his wife left him for his business partner. He had told Lily she ought to go too; who gave a damn if his company was in order, since the co-owner was banging his own wife? But Lily hadn't left. She stopped keeping the books and started to feed Harlan barley soup in bed; she recorded the times he'd taken his painkillers. He tried chemotherapy for a while, and Lily stayed with him the nights after the treatments, holding damp washcloths to his wrinkled chest and mopping up his vomit.

When he started to die, Lily sat for hours at his side, reading him the odds for local horse races and placing bets over the phone. She told him stories of her days as Calamity Jane in the rodeo, and that was probably what had given him the idea. When he died, he did not leave her any money but instead gave her the colt that had been born just a month before, sired by a stallion with bloodlines to Seattle Slew.

Josh said my mother had laughed long and hard over this one: she had a nearly priceless horse and not a red cent to her name. She drove to Carolina, all the way to Farleyville, until she found a stable she wanted to lease. She brought Donegal out here and for a long time he was the only one in the barn, but she paid her rent just the same. Little by little, by giving lessons to people on their own horses and farms, she saved enough money to buy Eddy, and also Tony, and then Aurora and Andy. She bought a horse named Joseph right from the track, like Aurora, and trained him for a year and then sold him for $45,000—three times her buying price. That was when she started to show Donegal, and his prize money began to pay for his blue-blood care: hundred-fifty-dollar plastic shoes, shots every three months, expensive hay with more clover than timothy. "But we still lost ten thousand dollars last year," Josh said.

"You lost *ten thousand dollars*," I whispered. "You don't even turn a profit? Why does she keep doing this?"

Josh smiled. In the distance, my mother spoke softly to Jean-Claude and then lifted herself into the saddle bound over his back. She held her reins steady until the horse stopped whinnying and tossing from side to side. She lifted her face to the sky and laughed into the wind. "It's her karma," Josh said. "Why else?"

≈≈≈

It got easier every day. I would ride for an hour in the morning after we'd turned out the other horses and mucked the stalls. I rode Tony, the gentlest horse my mother owned. Under her careful direction, I improved. My legs stopped feeling like tightly stretched bands. I could second-guess the horse, who had a habit of ducking out to the right of a jump. Even the canter, which at first had seemed so quick and uncontrollable, had settled. Now Tony would take off so neatly I could close my eyes and pretend that I was running on the voice of the wind.

"What do you want to do now?" my mother called from the center of the ring.

I had slowed Tony to a walk. "Let's jump," I said. "I want to try a vertical." I knew now that the fences were called gymnastics; that a straight-across bar was a vertical and an "X" was called a cross-rail.

Because Tony was only about fourteen hands, he couldn't jump very high, but he could easily take a two-foot vertical if he was in the mood.

I loved the feeling of a jump. I loved the easy lead up to it, the squeeze of my thighs and calves pressuring the horse's hind end, the remarkable power with which he pushed off the ground. As Tony started to come up, I'd lift myself into the half-seat position, suspended in midair until the horse's back rose up to meet me. "Don't look down—look across the jump," my mother had told me over and over, and I would, seeing the rich berry-twisted brush that edged the stream. It never failed to surprise me that within seconds, we actually touched down on everyday earth.

My mother set up a course of six jumps for me. I patted Tony's neck and gathered up my reins for a canter. My mother shouted corrections at me, but I could barely hear her. We flew around the ring so gracefully I wasn't sure that the horse's legs were striking the ground. Tony took the first jump long, throwing me back in the saddle. He picked up speed, and I knew that I should be sitting back to slow him, but somehow my body wasn't doing what I wanted it to. As he landed the next jump, he raced around the corner of the ring. He leaned strangely to one side, and I fell off.

When I opened my eyes, Tony was gnawing on the grass along the edge of the ring and my mother was standing above me. "It happens to everyone," she said, reaching out her hand to help me up. "What do you think you did wrong?"

I stood and dusted off the britches I'd borrowed from her. "Besides the fact that he was running a hundred miles an hour?"

My mother smiled. "Yeah, it was a little faster than a usual canter," she said.

I rubbed my hand over the back of my neck and readjusted the black velvet helmet. "He was off center," I said. "I knew I was going to fall off before it happened."

My mother pulled Tony back by the reins and held him while I mounted again. "Good girl," she said. "That's because when you come across a diagonal, you've changed your direction. When you canter, a horse should have the inside lead, right?" I nodded; I remembered this lesson well because it had taken me forever to figure it out: when a horse cantered, or galloped, for that matter, the leg on the innermost side of the ring should be the first to fall; it kept them balanced. "When you change your direction, the horse needs to switch leads. Tony won't do it naturally—he's too dumb for that; he'll just run around off kilter, wearing himself out until he trips or throws you off. You've got to tell him, really, that you want him to try a new trick in his repertoire. You break him down to a trot and then pick up the canter again—it's called a simple change of lead."

I shook my head. "I can't remember all this," I said.

"Yes you can," my mother insisted. She clucked Tony into a trot. "Do a figure eight," she said, "and don't stop. He's not going to do what you want him to unless you guide him into it. Keep going across your diagonals and do your simple changes."

By the time we turned down the first diagonal, I had Tony moving quietly toward the middle of the jump. I looked at his hooves, and Tony was on the same lead he'd been on before the jump, only now, because we'd changed direction, it was his outside leg. I pulled back on the reins until he broke his stride, and then I turned his head toward the woods and kicked him into a canter again. "Good," my mother yelled, and I squeezed Tony over the next line of jumps. I did the same pattern over and over until I thought I was breathing harder than Tony, and I slowed him to a walk without my mother's command.

I leaned over Tony's neck, sighing into his coarse mane. I knew about running fast, and knowing you were off balance, and not understanding how to fix yourself. "You don't see how lucky you have it," I said. I thought about how easy it would be to take an unfamiliar course if I had someone pushing me in the right direction; a gentle, knowing pressure that let me break down the pace until I was ready to run again.

≈≈≈

"When do I get to ride Donegal?" I asked, as we led him to the field where my mother liked to ride him. His mane whipped from left to right as he strained against the leather lead to his halter.

"You could sit him right now," my mother said, "but you wouldn't be riding him; he'd be riding you." She handed me the reins while she adjusted the chin strap of her riding helmet. "He's a phenomenal horse, he'll take any jump you put in front of him and automatically change his leads, but he'd just be making you look good. If you're learning to ride, you should do it on someone like Tony, a workhorse with an attitude."

I saw my mother swing herself into the saddle and take off at a trot; then I sat down on the grass and watched her ride. I opened the pad I'd brought and took out a stick of charcoal. I tried to draw the spirit that seemed to run straight from my mother's spine through the flanks and powerful hind legs of Donegal. She didn't even have to touch the horse; it seemed that she communicated her changes and transitions by willing them into Donegal's mind.

I drew the crimped jet mane and the arch of the horse's neck, the steam rising from his sides and the rhythm of his labored breathing. I sketched the rippled muscles of Donegal's legs, from the line of the blue shin and ankle boots to the raw force that throbbed in check beneath the sheen of his haunches. My mother leaned low over his neck, whispering words I could not hear. Her shirt flew out behind her, and she moved faster than light.

When I drew her, she seemed to come right out of the horse, and it was impossible really to tell where he ended and she began. Her thighs were wrapped tight around Donegal's flanks, and his legs seemed to move across the page. I drew them over and over on the same piece of paper. I was working so furiously that I never noticed my mother getting off Donegal, tying him up to the fence, and coming to sit beside me.

She peered over my shoulder and stared at her image. I had drawn her repeatedly, but the final effect was that of motion: her head and Donegal's were bent low at several different angles and positions, all rooted to the same flying body. It seemed mythical and sensual. It was as if my mother and Donegal had started off several times but couldn't decide where they wanted to go.

"You're amazing," my mother said, resting her hand on my shoulder.

I shrugged. "I'm okay," I said. "I could be better."

My mother touched her fingertips to the edge of the paper. "Can I have it?" she asked, and before I handed it over I peered into the hollows and shadows of the picture, trying to see what else I might have revealed. But this time, in spite of all the secrets that lay between us, there was absolutely nothing.

"Sure," I said. "Consider it yours."

Dear Max,

Enclosed is a sketch of one of the horses here. Her name is Aurora, and she looks like the one in your picture book of Snow White, the one you always tried to eat when I read it to you. Oh, I suppose you don't know—"here" is your grandmother's place. It's a farm in North Carolina, and it's very green and very beautiful. When you are older one day maybe you'll come down here and learn how to ride.

I think of you quite a lot—I wonder if you are sitting up yet and if you have your bottom teeth. I wonder if you'll recognize me when you see me. I wish I could explain why I left the way I did, but I am not sure I could put it into words. Just keep believing me when I say I'm coming back.

I don't know when yet.

I love you.

Do me a favor, will you? Tell your daddy I love him.

Mom

At the end of August I went with my mother to an AHSA "A" list horse show in Culpeper, Virginia. We packed Donegal into the trailer and drove for six hours. I helped my mother lead him into the makeshift stalls under the blue-and-white tent. That night, we paid to practice on the four-foot jumps, which Donegal took easily after being cooped up for so long. My mother tacked him down and gave him a warm bath. "We'll see you tomorrow, Don," she said, "and I'm planning on going home with a champion."

The next day I watched, wide-eyed, as judging went on in three rings at once. Men and women competed together, one of the few

sports where they were equal. My mother's class was Four Foot Working Hunter, the highest show class. She seemed to know everyone
there. "I'm going to change," she said, and when she returned, she
was wearing tan britches, tall polished boots, a high-necked white
blouse, and a blue wool blazer. She had jammed her hair into fifteen
little barrettes all around her head, and she asked me to hold a mirror
while she stuffed her helmet on over them. "Points off," she told me,
"if any hair is sticking out."

There were twenty-one horses in her class, the last event of the
day. She was the third rider up. While Donegal pranced around
the warm-up ring, I watched from the bleachers, keeping an eye on
the man jumping the largest stallion I'd ever seen, over fences that
were nearly as tall as me. My mother's number was forty-six, tied on
her back on a crinkled piece of yellowed card. She smiled at the man
who had finished the course, passing him on her way in.

The judge sat off to the side. I tried to make out what he was
writing, but it was impossible at this distance. Instead I concentrated
on my mother. It took only seconds. I watched Donegal come down
the final line on the outside of the ring. As he reared up, his front
legs were tight, his knees were high. He didn't take the jump long
or chip it; it was right in stride. I saw my mother sit back, holding
Donegal slow until the next jump rose in front of them, and then
she pulled into her half-seat, chin high, eyes burning straight ahead.
It was only when they finished the course that I realized I had been
holding my breath.

The woman sitting beside me had on a copper-colored polka-
dotted dress and a wide-brimmed white straw hat, as if she'd been
expecting Ascot. She held a program, and on the back she was writing
the numbers of the riders she believed would win. "I don't know,"
she murmured to herself. "I think the first man was much better."

I turned to her, angry. "You've got to be joking," I said. "His
horse took every jump long." The woman sniffed and tapped her
pencil against her chin. "I'll give you five dollars if forty-six doesn't
beat that guy," I said, pulling a fold of cash from my back pocket.

The woman stared at me, and for a moment I wondered if this

was illegal, but then a smile spread across her onion features and she held out a gloved hand. "You're on," she said.

Nobody else in the class was as good as my mother on Donegal. Several of the horses ducked out at the jumps, or dumped their riders and were disqualified. When the results were announced, the blue ribbon went to number forty-six. I stood up in the bleachers and cheered, and my mother twisted her head around to look at me. She jogged the horse back into the ring so Donegal could be judged sound, then fixed her blue ribbon on the loop of Donegal's bridle. The woman beside me sniffed loudly and held out a crisp five-dollar bill. "One thirty-one was better," she insisted.

I took the money from her palm. "Maybe," I said, "but forty-six is my mother."

≈≈≈

At my mother's suggestion, we celebrated the end of summer by camping out in the backyard. I didn't think I would like it. I figured the ground would be lumpy and I'd be worried about ants crawling up my neck and into my ears. But my mother found two old sleeping bags the owners of Pegasus had used in Alaska, and we stretched out on them in the field where my mother rode Donegal. We watched for falling stars.

It had been unbearably hot in August, and I had become used to seeing blisters on the backs of my hands and my neck—the parts that were exposed to sun all the time. "You're a country girl, Paige," my mother said, reaching her arms up behind her head. "You wouldn't have lasted this long if you weren't."

There were things to be said about North Carolina. It was nice to see the sinking sun cool itself against the face of a mountain instead of the domes of Harvard; there was no pavement to breathe beneath your feet. But sometimes I felt so secluded that I stopped to listen, to make sure I could hear my pulse over the singing black flies and the rumble of hoofbeats.

My mother rolled toward me, propping herself on an elbow. "Tell me about Patrick," she said.

I looked away. I could tell her what my father had looked like or that he hadn't wanted me to search for her, but either one would hurt. "He's still building pipe dreams in the basement," I said. "A couple have actually sold." My mother held her breath, waiting. "His hair is gray now, but he hasn't really lost any of it."

"It's still there, isn't it? That look in his eyes?"

I knew what she meant: it was this glow that came over my father when he saw a masterpiece even though he was looking at a concoction of spit and glue. "It's still there," I said, and my mother smiled.

"I think that's what made me fall for him," she said, "that and the way he promised to show me Ireland." She rolled onto her back and closed her eyes. "And what does he think of the fine Dr. Prescott?"

"He's never met him," I blurted, cursing myself for making such a stupid mistake. I decided to tell her a half-truth. "I've just barely kept in touch with Dad. I ran away from Chicago when I graduated from high school."

My mother frowned. "That doesn't sound like Patrick. Patrick only wanted you to go to college. You were going to be the first Irish Catholic woman President."

"It wasn't college," I told her. "I was planning on going to the Rhode Island School of Design, but something else came up." I held my breath, but she did not pressure me. "Mom," I said, eager to change the subject, "what about that rodeo guy?"

She laughed. "That rodeo guy was Wolliston Waters, and we ran around together with the money we stole from the Wild West show. I slept with him a couple of times, but only to remember what it was like to feel another person next to me. It wasn't love, you know; it was sex. You've probably seen the difference." I turned away, and my mother touched my shoulder. "Oh, come on, now. There had to be a high school guy who broke your heart."

"No," I said, avoiding her eyes. "I didn't date."

My mother shrugged. "Well, the point is I never got over your father. Never really wanted to. Wolliston and I, well, more than anything we were in business together. Until one morning I woke up and he'd taken all our cash and savings, plus the toaster oven and even the stereo. Just disappeared, like that."

I rolled onto my back and remembered Eddie Savoy. "People don't just disappear," I told her. "You of all people should know that."

Overhead, stars shifted and winked against the dark night sky. I opened my eyes wide and tried to see the other galaxies that hid at the edges of ours. "There was nobody else?" I asked.

"No one worth mentioning," my mother said.

I looked at her. "Don't you—you know—miss it?"

My mother shrugged. "I have Donegal."

I smiled into the darkness. "That's not really the same," I said.

My mother frowned, as if she was thinking about this. "You're right; it's more fulfilling. See, I'm the one who trained him, so I'm the one who can take credit for whatever Donegal does. With a horse I've made a name for myself. With a husband I was nobody." Barely moving a muscle, my mother covered my hand with her own. "Tell me what Nicholas is like," she said.

I sighed and tried to do with words what I would ordinarily do in a sketch. "He's very tall, and he has hair as dark as Donegal's mane. His eyes are the same color as yours and mine—"

"No, no, no," my mother interrupted. "Tell me what Nicholas is *like.*"

I closed my eyes, but nothing came clearly to mind. I seemed to be seeing my life with him through shadows, and even after eight years I could barely hear the patterns of his voice or feel the touch of his hands on me. I tried to picture those hands, their long, surgeon's fingers, but couldn't even imagine them holding the base of a stethoscope. I felt a hollow pit in the base of my chest, where I knew these memories should be, but it was as if I had married someone a long time ago and hadn't kept contact since. "I really don't know what Nicholas is like," I said. I could feel my mother's eyes on me, so I tried to explain. "He's just a different man these days; he works extremely hard, and that's important, you know, but because of that I don't get to see him all that much. A lot of the time when I do see him I'm not at my best—I'm at a fund-raising dinner table and he's sitting beside a Radcliffe girl making comparisons, or I've been up half the night with Max and I look like the wild woman of Borneo."

"And that's why you left," my mother finished for me.

I sat up abruptly. "That's *not* why I left," I said. "I left because of you."

It was a what came first, the chicken or the egg dilemma. I had left because I needed time to catch my breath and get my bearings and start with a clean slate. But obviously, this tendency had been bred into me. Hadn't I known all along I would grow up to be just like my mother? Hadn't I worried about this very thing happening when I was pregnant with Max—and with my other baby? I still believed these events were all linked together. I could honestly say that my mother was the reason I'd run away, but I wasn't sure if she had been the cause or the consequence of my actions.

My mother crawled into her sleeping bag. "Even if that was true," she said, "you should have waited until Max was older."

I rolled away from her. The scent of the pine trees on the ridge behind us was so overwhelming I was suddenly dizzy. "That's the pot calling the kettle black," I murmured.

From behind me came my mother's voice. "When you were born, they were just starting to let men in the delivery room, but your father didn't want any part of it. He actually wanted me to give birth at home, like his mother had, but I vetoed that. So he took me to the hospital, and I begged him not to leave me. Told him I couldn't go through with it. I was all alone for twelve hours, until you decided to make your appearance. It was another hour until they let him in to see you and me together—it took that long for the nurses to comb my hair and give me my makeup so I'd look like I hadn't been doing anything at all for the past day." My mother was so close I could feel her breath against my ear. "When your father came in and saw you, he stroked your cheek and said, 'Now, May, now that you've got her, where's the sacrifice?' And do you know what I told him? I looked at him and I said, 'Me.' "

My heart constricted as I remembered staring at Max and wondering how he could possibly have come from inside me and what I could do to make him go back. "You resented me," I said.

"I was terrified of you," my mother said. "I didn't know what I'd do if you didn't like me."

I remembered that the year I was enrolled in Bible preschool my mother had bought me a special coat for Easter, as pink as the inside lip of a lily. I had bothered her and begged and pleaded to wear it to school after Easter. "Just once," I had cried, and finally she let me. But it rained on the way home from school, and I was afraid she'd be angry if the coat got wet, so I took it off and stuffed it into a little ball. The neighbor's daughter, who walked me home every day because she was nine years old and responsible, helped me jam the coat inside my Snoopy book bag. "You little fool," my mother had said when my friend left me at the door, "you're going to catch pneumonia." I had run up to my room and thrown myself on the bed, angry that I had disappointed her yet again.

But then again, this was the woman who let me take a bus across downtown Chicago when I was five because she thought I was trust-worthy. She had tinted clear gelatin with blue food coloring because that was my favorite color. She taught me how to dance the Stroll and how to hang from the monkey bars with my hem tucked a certain way so that my skirt didn't fall up over my head. She had given me my first crayons and coloring book, and had held me when I messed up, assuring me that the lines were for people with no imagination. She had turned herself into someone who was larger than life; someone whose gestures I practiced at night in the bathroom; someone I wanted to be when I grew up.

The night closed around us like a choked throat, suffocating the twitched sounds of the squirrels and the whistling grass. "You weren't all that bad as a mother," I said.

"Maybe," my mother whispered. "Maybe not."

chapter 30
Nicholas

For the first time in years, Nicholas's gloved hands shook as he made the incision in the patient's chest. A neat red line of blood spilled into the hollow left by the scalpel, and Nicholas swallowed the bile that rose in his throat. Anything but this, he thought to himself: climbing Everest, memorizing a dictionary, fighting a war from the front line. Anything had to be easier than doing a quadruple bypass on Alistair Fogerty himself.

He did not have to look under the sterile drapes to know the face connected with the hideously swabbed orange body. Every muscle and line had been etched into his mind; after all, he'd spent eight years absorbing Fogerty's insults and rallying to meet his boundless expectations. And now the man's life was in his hands.

Nicholas picked up the saw and switched it to life. It vibrated in the circle of his hands as he touched it to the sternum, carving through the bone. He spread the ribs and he checked the solution in which the leg veins, already harvested, were floating. He imagined

Alistair Fogerty standing in the background of the operating suite, his presence hovering at Nicholas's neck like the stale breath of a dragon. Nicholas looked up at his assisting resident. "I think we're all set," he said, watching his words puff out his blue paper mask as if they had meaning or substance.

≈≈≈

Robert Prescott was on his hands and knees on the Aubusson rug, rubbing Perrier into a round yellow spot that was part vomit and part sweet potatoes. Now that Max could sit up by himself—at least for a few minutes—he was more likely to spit up whatever he'd last eaten or drunk.

Robert had tried using his baby-sitting time to go over patient files for the next morning, but Max had a habit of pulling them off the couch and wrinkling the papers into his palms. He had gummed one manila binder so thoroughly it fell apart in Robert's hands.

"Ah," he said, sitting back on his heels to survey his work. "I don't think it looks any different from the rosettes." He frowned at his grandson. "You haven't done any more of that, have you?"

Max squealed to be picked up—that was his latest thing, that and a razz sound that sprayed everything within three feet. Robert thought he had lifted his arms too, but that might have been wishful thinking. According to Dr. Spock, whom he'd been rereading in between patients, that didn't come until the sixth month.

"Let's see," he said, holding Max like a football under his arm. He looked around the little parlor, redecorated as a substitute nursery/playroom, and found what he had been looking for, an old stethoscope. Max liked to suck on the rubber tubes and to hold the cold metal base against his gums, swollen from teething. Robert stood up and passed the toy to Max, but Max dropped it and puckered his lips, getting ready to cry. "Drastic measures," he said, wheeling Max in a circle over his head. He switched on a *Sesame Street* cassette he'd bought at the bookstore and started to do a jaunty tango over the clutter of toys on the floor. Max laughed—a wonderful sound, really, Robert thought—every time they whipped around at the corner.

Robert heard the jingle of keys in the door and jumped over the walker so that he could push the Stop button on the tape deck. He slipped Max into the Sassy Seat that was balanced on the edge of the low walnut coffee table and handed him a colander and a plastic mixing spoon. Max stuck the spoon in his mouth and then dropped it on the floor. "Don't say anything that might give me away," Robert warned, leaning close to Max, who grabbed his grandfather's finger and pulled it into his mouth.

Astrid walked into the room, to find Robert thumbing through a patient file and Max sitting quietly with a colander on his head. "Everything's all right?" she asked, sliding her pocketbook onto the nearest chair.

"Mmm," Robert said. He noticed that the file he was supposed to be reading was upside down. "Not a peep out of him the whole time."

≈≈≈

When the hospital grapevine made it known that Fogerty had collapsed while doing an aortic valve replacement, Nicholas postponed his afternoon rounds and went straight to his chief's office. Alistair had been sitting with his feet propped up on the radiator, facing out the window toward the stacks and bricks of the hospital's incinerator. He was absentmindedly breaking the spiked leaves off his spider plant. "I've been thinking," he said, not bothering to turn around. "Hawaii. Or maybe New Zealand, if I can stand the flight." He swiveled in the wide leather chair. "Do call out the eighth-grade English teachers. Definition of *irony:* getting into a car accident while you're putting on your seat belt. Or the cardiac surgeon discovering he needs a quadruple bypass."

Nicholas sank down into the chair that sat across from the desk. "What?" he murmured.

Alistair smiled at him, and Nicholas suddenly realized how very old he seemed. He didn't know Alistair at all, out of this context. He didn't know if he golfed, or if he took his Scotch neat; he didn't know if he had cried at his son's graduation or his daughter's wedding. Nicholas wondered if anyone knew Alistair that well; if, for that matter, anyone knew *him,* either. "Dave Goldman ran the tests," Fogerty said. "I want you to do the surgery."

Nicholas swallowed. "I—"

Fogerty held up a hand. "Before you humble yourself, Nicholas, keep in mind that I'd rather do it myself. But since I can't and since you're the only other asshole I trust in this entire organization, I wonder if you might pencil me into your busy schedule."

"Monday," Nicholas said. "First thing."

Fogerty sighed and leaned his head against the chair. "Damn right," he said. "I've seen you in the afternoon; you're sloppy." He ran his thumbs over the armrests of the chair, worn smooth by the habit. "You'll take on as many of my patients as you can," he said. "There will have to be a leave of absence."

Nicholas stood. "Consider it done."

He watched as Alistair Fogerty turned his chair to the window again, charting the rise and fall of the chimney smoke. His echo was simply a whisper. "Done," he said.

≈≈≈

Astrid and Robert Prescott sat on the floor of their dining room under the magnificent cherry table that, with all the leaves in place, could seat twenty. Max seemed to like it under there, as if it were some kind of natural cave that deserved exploration. Spread in front of his chubby feet was an array of eight-by-ten glossies, laminated so that his saliva wouldn't stain the surfaces. Astrid pointed to the smiling picture of Max himself. "Max," she said, and the baby turned toward her voice. "Ayee," he said, drooling.

"Close enough." She patted his shoulder and pointed to the picture of Nicholas. "Daddy. Daddy."

Robert Prescott straightened abruptly and slammed his head on the underside of the table. "Shit," he said, and Astrid poked him with an elbow.

"Your language," she snapped. "That's *not* the first word I want to hear from him." She picked up the portrait of Paige she had shot from a distance, the one Nicholas had balked at the first day he'd left

Max. "This is your mommy," she said, running her fingertips over Paige's delicate features. "Mommy."

"Muh," Max said.

Astrid turned to Robert, her mouth wide. "You did hear that, didn't you? Muh?"

Robert nodded. "It could have been gas."

Astrid scooped the baby into her arms and kissed the folds of his neck. "You, my love, are a genius. Don't listen to your dotty old grandfather."

"Nicholas would pitch a fit if he knew you were showing him Paige's picture, you know," Robert said. He stood and straightened, rubbing the small of his back. "I'm too damn old for this," he said. "Nicholas should have had Max ten years ago, when I could really enjoy him." He held out his arms for Max, so that Astrid could pull herself up. She gathered together the photos. "Max isn't all yours, Astrid," he said. "You really should get Nicholas's go-ahead."

Astrid pulled the baby back into her arms. Max pressed his lips to her neck and made razzing sounds. She slid him into the high chair that sat at the head of the table. "If we'd always done what Nicholas wanted," she said, "he'd have been a teenage vegetarian with a crew cut who bungee-jumped from hot-air balloons."

Robert opened two jars of baby food, pear-pineapple and plums, and sniffed at them to see which might taste better. "You have a point," he said.

≈≈≈

Nicholas had planned to do the entire operation, with the exception of the vein harvest, from start to finish, out of deference to Alistair. He knew that if the positions were reversed, he would want it that way. But by the time he had threaded the ribs with wire, he was unsteady on his feet. He had been concentrating too hard too long. The placement of the veins had been perfect. The sutures he'd made around Alistair's heart were microscopically minute. He just couldn't do any more.

"You can close," he said, nodding to the resident who had been assisting him. "And you'd better do the best goddamned job of your surgical career." He regretted the words as soon as he'd said them, seeing the slight tremor in the girl's fingers. He leaned down below the sterile drapes that hid Alistair's face. There was a lot he had planned to say, but just seeing him there with the life temporarily drained out of him reminded Nicholas too much of his own mortality. He held his wrist against Alistair's cheek, careful not to mark him with his own blood. He felt the tingle coming back to Fogerty's skin as the unobstructed heart began to do its work again. Satisfied, he left the room with all the dignity Fogerty had told him he would one day command.

≈≈≈

Robert didn't like it when Astrid took Max into the darkroom. "Too many wires," he said, "too many toxic chemicals. God only knows what gets into his system in there." But Astrid wasn't stupid. Max couldn't crawl yet, so there was no danger of his getting into the stop bath or the fixer. She didn't do any developing when he was around; she just scanned contact sheets for the prints she'd make later. If she placed him just right, on a big striped beach towel, he was perfectly content to play with his chunky plastic shapes and the electronic ball that made farm animal noises.

"Once upon a time," Astrid said, telling the story over her shoulder, "there was a girl named Cinderella, who hadn't lived the most charmed life but had the good fortune to meet a man who had. The kind of man, by the way, you're going to grow up to be." She leaned down and handed him a rubber triangle he'd inadvertently tossed away. "You're going to open doors for girls and pay for their dinners and do all the chivalrous things men used to do before they slacked off under the excuse of equal rights."

Astrid circled a tiny square with her red grease pen. "This one's good," she murmured. "Anyway, Max, as I was saying . . . oh, yes, Cinderella. Well, someone else will probably tell you the story at a later date, so I'm just going to skip ahead a little. You see, a book doesn't always end at the final page." She squatted down until she was sitting across from Max, and then she took his hands in her own, kissing the tips of his stubby wet fingers.

"Cinderella had liked the idea of living in a castle, and she was actually rather good at being a princess until one day she started to think about what she might be doing if she hadn't gotten married to the handsome prince. All her old friends were kicking up their heels at banquet halls and entering Pillsbury Bake-Offs and dating Chippendale's dancers. So she took one of the royal horses and traveled to the far ends of the earth, taking photographs with this camera she'd gotten from a peddler in exchange for her crown."

The baby hiccuped, and Astrid pulled him to a standing position. "No, really," she said, "it wasn't a rip-off. After all, it was a Nikon. Meanwhile, the prince was doing everything he could to get her out of his mind, because he was the laughingstock of the royal community for not being able to keep a leash on his wife. He went hunting three times a day and organized a croquet tournament and even took up taxidermy, but staying busy all the time still couldn't occupy his thoughts. So—"

Max waddled forward, supported by Astrid's hands, just as Nicholas appeared at the darkroom's curtain. "I don't like when you take him in here," he said, reaching for Max. "What if you turn your back?"

"I don't," Astrid said. "How was your surgery?"

Nicholas hoisted Max onto his shoulder and smelled his bottom. "Jeez," he said. "When did Grandma change you last?"

Standing, Astrid frowned at her son and plucked Max off his shoulder. "It only takes him a minute," she said, walking past Nicholas from her darkroom into the muted light of the Blue Room.

"The surgery was fine," Nicholas said, picking at a tray of olives and cocktail onions that Imelda had set out for Astrid hours before. "I'm just here to check in because I know I'll be late. I want to be there when Fogerty wakes up." He stuffed three olives into his mouth and spit the pimentos into a napkin. "And what was that trash you were telling Max?"

"Fairy tales," Astrid said, unsnapping Max's outfit and pulling free the tapes of the diaper. "You remember them, I'm sure." She swabbed Max's backside and handed Nicholas the dirty bundle to dispose of. "They all have happy endings."

≈≈≈

When Alistair Fogerty awoke from a groggy sleep in surgical ICU, the first words he uttered were, "Get Prescott."

Nicholas was paged. Since he had been expecting this summons, he was at Fogerty's bedside in minutes. "You bastard," Alistair said to him, straining to shift his weight. "What have you done to me?"

Nicholas grinned at him. "A very tidy quadruple bypass," he said. "Some of my best work."

"Then how come I feel like I have an eighteen-wheeler on my chest?" Fogerty tossed against the pillows. "God," he said. "I've been listening to patients tell me that for years, and I never really believed them. Maybe we should all go through open heart, like psychiatrists have to be analyzed. A humbling experience."

His eyes began to close, and Nicholas stood up. Joan Fogerty was waiting at the door. He crossed to speak to her, to tell her that all the preliminary signs were very good. She had been crying; Nicholas could tell by the raccoon rings of mascara under her eyes. She sat beside her husband and spoke softly, words Nicholas could not hear.

"Nicholas," Fogerty whispered, his voice barely audible above the steady blip of the cardiac monitor. "Take care of my patients, and don't fuck with my desk."

Nicholas smiled and walked out of the room. He took several steps down the hall before he realized what Alistair had been telling him: that he was now the acting chief of cardiothoracic surgery at Mass General. Without realizing it, he took the elevator to the floor where Fogerty's office was located, and he turned the unlocked door. Nothing had changed. The files were still piled high, their coded edges bright like confetti. The sun fell across the forbidding swivel chair, and Nicholas was almost certain he could see Alistair's impression on the soft leather.

He walked to the chair and sat down, placing his hands on the arms as he had seen Fogerty do so many times. He turned to face the window but closed his eyes to the light. He didn't even hear Elliot Saget, Mass General's chief of surgery, enter. "And the seat isn't even cold yet," Saget said sarcastically.

Nicholas whipped around and stood up, sending the chair flying into the radiator behind. "I'm sorry," he said. "I was just down checking on Alistair—"

Saget held up a hand. "I'm only here to make it official. Fogerty's on six months leave. You're the acting director of cardiothoracic. We'll let you know what kind of meetings and committees we'll be cluttering your evenings with, and I'll get your name on the door." He turned to leave and then paused at the threshold of the door to smile. "We've known about your skills for a long time, Nicholas. You've got quite a reputation for spit and fire. If you're the one who gave Alistair his heart trouble, then God help me," he said, and he walked out.

Nicholas sank back into Alistair's leather wing chair—*his* leather wing chair—and wheeled himself in circles like a little kid. Then he put his feet down and soberly organized the papers on the desk into neat, symmetric piles, not bothering to read the pages, not yet. He picked up the phone and dialed for an outside line, but realized he had no one to call. His mother was taking Max to a petting zoo, his father was still at work, and Paige, well, he didn't know where she was at all. He leaned back and watched the billowed smoke blowing from Mass General toward Boston. He wondered why, after years of wanting to stand at the very top, he felt so goddamned empty.

chapter 31

Paige

M y mother said there was no connection, but I knew that Donegal colicked because she had broken her ankle.

It hadn't been his feed or water; those had been consistent. There hadn't been any severe temperature changes that could have caused it. But then my mother had been tossed from Elmo over a jump, right into the blue wall. She had landed a certain way and was now wearing a cast. I thought Donegal's colic was a sort of sympathy pain.

My mother, who had been told not to move by the doctor who'd set her ankle, hopped the whole way from the house to the barn on her crutches. "How is he?" she said, falling to her knees in the stall and running her hands over Donegal's neck.

He was lying down, thrashing back and forth, and he kept looking back at his sides. My mother pulled up his lip and looked at his gums. "He's a little pale," she conceded. "Call the vet."

Josh walked to the phone, and I sat by my mother. "Go back to bed," I told her. "Josh and I can take care of this."

"Like hell you can," my mother said. "Don't tell me what to do." She sighed and rubbed her face against her shirt sleeve. "In the chest on the table up there you'll find a syringe of Banamine," she said. "Would you get it for me?"

I stood up, clenching my jaw. I only wanted to help her, and she wasn't doing herself any good hobbling around a sick horse that was flailing all over the place and likely to hit her. "I hope to God he hasn't got a twisted gut," she murmured. "I don't know where I'll get the money for an operation."

I sat on the other side of Donegal while my mother gave him the shot. We both stroked him until he quieted. After a half hour, Donegal suddenly neighed and wriggled his legs beneath him and shuddered to his feet. My mother scooted out of the way on her hands, into a urine-soaked pile of hay, but she didn't seem to care. "That's my boy," she said, beckoning Josh to help her stand.

Dr. Heineman, the traveling vet, arrived with a pickup truck stocked with two treasure chests full of medicine and supplies. "He's looking good, Lily," he said, checking Donegal's temperature. " 'Course, you look like hell. Whaddya do to your foot?"

"I didn't do it," my mother said. "It was Elmo."

Josh and I held Donegal in the center aisle of the barn as the vet put a twitch on his nose—a metal clothespin-like thing—and then, when he was distracted by that pain, threaded a thick plastic catheter down his nostril and into his throat. Dr. Heineman waved his nose over the free end and smiled. "Smells like fresh green grass," he said, and my mother sighed, relieved. "I think he's going to be just fine, but I'll give him a little oil just in case." He began to pump mineral oil from a plastic gallon tub through the tube, blowing the last bit down with his own mouth. Then he unthreaded the catheter, letting loose phlegm splatter at Donegal's feet. He patted the horse's neck and told Josh to lead him back into the stall. "Watch him for the next twenty-four hours," he said, and then he turned to me. "And it couldn't hurt to watch her as well."

My mother waved him away, but he was laughing. "You tried out that cast yet, Lily?" he said, walking down the barn's aisle. "Does it fit into your stirrup?"

My mother leaned against my side and watched the vet go. "I can't believe I pay him," she said.

I walked slowly with my mother back to the house, getting her to promise she'd at least stay on the couch downstairs if I sat in the barn with Donegal. While Josh did the afternoon chores, I ran back and forth between the stable and the house. When Donegal slept, I helped my mother do crossword puzzles. We turned on the TV and watched daytime soaps, trying to figure out the story lines. I cooked dinner and tied a plastic bag around my mother's foot when she wanted to bathe, and then I tucked her into bed.

I woke up suddenly, breathless, at midnight, realizing that of all nights, tonight I had forgotten to do a ten o'clock check. How did my mother remember all these things? I ran down the stairs and threw the door open. I raced the whole way to the barn in my bare feet. I switched on the light and panted, catching my breath as I walked down the stalls. Aurora and Andy, Eddy and Elmo, Jean-Claude and Tony and Burt. All the horses were sitting, their legs folded neatly beneath them. They were in varying states of consciousness, but none startled at my appearance. The last stall in the barn was Donegal's. I took a deep breath, thinking I would never forgive myself if anything had happened to him. I could never make something like that up to my mother. I held my hands against the chain-link door. Curled against the belly of the snoring horse was my mother, fast asleep, her cast gleaming in the slanted square of moonlight, her fingers twitching in the wake of a dream.

≈≈≈

"Now remember," my mother said, balancing precariously on her crutches at the gate to the field, "he hasn't been turned out in two days. We're going to ease into this; we're not going to run him ragged. Understand?"

I nodded, looking down at her from what seemed like a tremendous height when in fact I was only on Donegal. I was terrified. I kept remembering what my mother had said two months before, that even an inexperienced rider could sit on Donegal and look good. But he had been sick, and I had never galloped across an open field, and the only horse I'd ridden was twenty years older than this one and knew the routine better than I did.

My mother reached up and squeezed my ankle. She adjusted the stirrup so it rested further up by my toes. "Don't worry," she said. "I wouldn't have asked you to ride him if I didn't think you could do it." She hallooed and slapped Donegal's hind leg, and I sat level in the saddle as he cantered off.

I couldn't see Donegal's legs for the tall grass, but I could feel his strength between my thighs. The more I gave him the reins, the gentler the rhythm of his run became. I fully expected that I was going to take off, that he would step on the lowest clouds and carry me over the swollen blue peaks of the mountains.

I leaned in toward Donegal's neck, hearing my mother's voice in my mind from that very first day: "Never lean forward unless you're planning to gallop." I had never galloped, not really, unless you counted a pony's quick strides at a canter. But Donegal shifted into a faster run, so smooth that I barely lifted in the saddle.

I sat very still and closed my eyes, letting the horse take the lead. I tuned in to the pounding sound of Donegal's hooves and the matching beat of my own pulse. I opened my eyes just in time to see the brook.

I hadn't known there was another stream, one that ran across this field, but then again I'd never ridden in it, never even walked all the way across it. As Donegal approached the stream he tensed the muscles in his hindquarters. I released my hands to slide up his neck, adding leg to help him off the ground. We soared over the water, and although it couldn't have been more than half a second, I could have sworn I saw each glistening rock, each rush and surge of current.

I pulled back on the reins, and Donegal tossed his head, breathing heavily. He stopped at the fence a few feet away from the brook and turned toward the spot where we had left my mother as if he knew he had been putting on a show all along.

At first I could not hear it over the tumble of water and the gossip of the robins, but then the sound came: slow, growing louder, until even Donegal became perfectly quiet and pricked up his ears. I patted his neck and praised him, all the while listening to the proud beat of my mother's clapping.

≈≈≈

My mother came into my bedroom late that night when the heaviest stars had dripped like a chain of diamonds over the sill of my window. She put her hand over my forehead, and I sat up and thought for a moment that I was five years old and that this was the night before she left. *Wait,* I tried to tell her, but nothing came out of my throat. *Don't do it again.* Instead I heard myself say, "Tell me why you left."

My mother lay down beside me on the narrow bed. "I knew this was coming," she said. Nearby, the face of the porcelain doll gleamed like a Cheshire cat. "For six years I believed in your father. I bought into his dreams and I went to Mass for him and I worked at that stinking paper to help pay the mortgage. I was the wife he needed me to be and the mother I was supposed to become. I was so busy being everything he wanted that there was too little left of Maisie Renault. If I didn't get away, I knew I'd lose myself completely." She wrapped her arms around my shoulders and pulled me back against her chest. "I hated myself for feeling that way. I didn't understand why I wasn't like Donna Reed."

"I didn't understand that, either," I said quietly, and I wondered if she thought I was talking about her or about me.

My mother sat up and crossed her legs. "You're happy here," she said. "And you fit. I saw it in the way you rode Donegal. If you lived here you could teach some of the beginner kids. If you want, you could even start to show." Her voice trailed off as she stared out the window, and then she turned her gaze back to me. "Paige," she said, "why don't you just stay here with me?"

Just stay here with me. As she spoke, something inside me burst and coursed warm through my veins, and I realized that all along I must have been a little bit cold. Then that rush stopped, and there was nothing. This was what I had wanted, wasn't it? Her stamp of approval, her need for me. I'd waited twenty years. But something was missing.

She said she wanted me to stay, but I was the one who'd found her. If I did stay, I'd never know the one thing I really wanted to know. Would she ever have come looking for me?

It was a choice, a simple choice. If I stayed, I would not be with Nicholas and Max. I wouldn't be around when Max threw his first loopy pitch; I wouldn't run my fingers over the plaque on Nicholas's office door. If I stayed, it was for good; I would never be going home.

Then it struck me for the first time: the meaning of the words I'd been saying over and over since I'd arrived. I really *did* have to go home, although I was only now beginning to believe it. "I have to go back," I said. The words fell heavy, a wall between my mother and myself.

I saw something flicker across my mother's eyes, but just as quickly it was gone. "You can't undo what's done, Paige," she said, squaring her shoulders the same way I did when I fought with Nicholas. "People forgive, but they never forget. I made a mistake, but if I had come back to Chicago, I never would have been able to live it down. You always would have been throwing that up at me, like you are now. What do you think Nicholas is going to do? And Max, when he's old enough to understand?"

"I didn't run away from them," I said stubbornly. "I ran to find you."

"You ran to remind yourself you still *had* a self," my mother said, getting up from the bed. "Be honest. It's about *you*, isn't it?"

She stood beside the window, blocking out the reflected light so that I was left in almost total darkness. All right, I was at my mother's horse farm and we were catching up and all that was good, but it hadn't been the reason I'd left home. In my mind, both actions were tangled together, but one hadn't caused the other. Still, no matter what, leaving home had to do with more than just me. It may have started out that way, but I was beginning to see how many chain reactions had been set off and how many people had been hurt. If the simple act of my disappearance could unravel my whole family, I must have held more power—been more important—than I'd ever considered.

Leaving home was all about *us*. I realized this was something that my mother had never stopped to learn.

I stood up and rounded on her so quickly she fell back against the pale glass of the window. "What makes you think it's that simple?" I said. "Yes, you walk out—but you leave people behind. You fix your life—but at someone else's expense. I waited for you," I said quietly. "I needed you." I leaned closer. "Did you ever wonder what you missed? You know, all the little things, like teaching me to put on mascara and clapping at my school plays and seeing me fall in love?"

My mother turned away. "I would have liked to see that," she said softly. "Yes."

"I guess you don't always get what you want," I said. "Do you know that when I was seven, eight, I used to keep a suitcase, all packed and ready, hidden in my closet? I used to write to you two or three times a year, begging you to come and get me, but I never knew where to send the letters."

"I wouldn't have taken you away from Patrick," my mother said. "It wouldn't have been fair."

"Fair? By whose standards?" I stared at her, feeling worse than I had in a very long time. "What about me? *Why didn't you ever ask me?*"

My mother sighed. "I couldn't have forced you to make that kind of choice, Paige. It was a no-win situation."

"Yes. Well," I said bitterly, "I know all about those." Suddenly I was so tired that all the rage rushed out of my body. I wanted to sleep for months; for, maybe, years. "There are some things you can't tell your father," I said, sinking onto the bed. My voice was even and matter-of-fact, and in a moment of courage I lifted my eyes to see, quicksilver, my soul fly out of hiding. "I had an abortion when I was eighteen," I said flatly. "You weren't there."

Even as my mother reached for me, I could see her face blanch. "Oh, Paige," she said, "you should have come to me."

"You should have been there," I murmured. But really, what difference could it have made? My mother would have believed it was her duty to tell me of the choices. She might have whispered about the certain smell of a baby, or reminded me of the spell we had woven, mother and daughter, lying beside each other on a narrow kitchen table, wrapping our future around us like a hand-worked shawl. My mother might have told me the things I didn't want to hear back then and could not bear to hear right now.

At least my baby never knew me, I thought. *At least I spared her all that pain.*

My mother lifted my chin. "Look at me, Paige. You can't go back. You can't *ever* go back." She moved her hands to rest on my shoulders like gripped clamps. "You're just like me," she said.

Was I? I had spent the past three months trying to find all the easy comparisons—our eyes, our hair, and the less obvious traits, like the tendency to run and to hide. But there were some traits I didn't want to admit I shared with her. I had given up the gift of a child because I was so scared that my mother's irresponsibility would be passed on in my bloodline. I had left my family and chalked it up to Fate. For years I had convinced myself that if I could find my own mother, if I could just see what might have been, I would possess all the answers.

"I'm not like you," I said. It wasn't an accusation but a statement, curled at the end in surprise. Maybe I had expected to be like her, maybe I had even secretly hoped to be like her, but now I wasn't going to lie down and just let it happen. This time I was fighting back. This time I was choosing my own direction. "I'm not like you," I said again, and I felt a knot tighten at the base of my stomach, now that all of a sudden I had no excuse.

I stood up and walked around the little-girl's bedroom, already knowing what I was going to do. I had spent my life wondering what I could have done wrong that made the one person I loved more than anything leave me behind; I wasn't going to pin that blame like a scarlet letter on Nicholas or Max. I pulled my underwear out of a drawer. I stuffed my jeans, still covered with hay and manure, into the bottom of the small overnight bag I'd arrived with. I carefully wrapped up my sticks of charcoal. I started to envision the quickest route home, and I counted off the hours in my mind. "How can you even ask me to stay?" I whispered.

My mother's eyes glowed like a mountain cat's. She shook with the effort of holding her tears at bay. "They won't take you back," she said.

I stared at her, and then I slowly smiled. "*You* did," I said.

chapter **32**

Nicholas

*M*ax had his first cold. It was amazing that he'd made it this long—the pediatrician said it had something to do with breast-feeding and antibodies. Nicholas had got almost no sleep in the past two days, which were supposed to be his time off from the hospital. He sat helpless, watching Max's nose bubble and run, scrubbing clean the cool-mist vaporizer, and wishing he could breathe for his son.

Astrid was the one to diagnose the cold. She had taken Max to the pediatrician because she thought he'd swallowed a willow pod—which was an entirely different story—and she wanted to know if it was poisonous. But when the doctor listened to his chest and heard the upper-respiratory rattle and hum, he'd prescribed PediaCare and rest.

Nicholas was miserable. He hated watching Max choke and sputter over his bottle, unable to drink since he couldn't breathe through his nose. He had to rock him to sleep, a lousy habit, because Max couldn't suck on a pacifier and if he cried himself to sleep he wound up soaked in mucus. Every day Nicholas called the doctor, a colleague at Mass General who'd been in his graduating class at Harvard. "Nick," the guy said over and over, "no baby's ever died of a cold."

Nicholas carried Max, who was blessedly quiet, to the bathroom to check his weight. He placed Max on the cool tile and stood on the digital scale, getting a reading before he stepped back onto it holding Max. "You're down a half pound," Nicholas said, holding Max up to the mirror so he could see himself. He smiled, and the mucus in his nostrils ran into his mouth.

"This is disgusting," Nicholas muttered to himself, tucking the baby under his arm and carrying him to the living room. It had been an endless day of carrying Max when he cried, cuddling him when he got frustrated and batted at his nose, washing his toys in case he could reinfect himself.

He propped Max up in front of the TV, letting him watch the evening news. "Tell me what the weather's going to be like this weekend," Nicholas said, walking upstairs. He needed to raise one end of the crib and to get the vaporizer going so that if, God willing, Max fell asleep, he could carry him into the dark nursery without waking him. He was bound to fall asleep. It was almost midnight, and Max hadn't napped since morning.

He finished in the nursery and came back downstairs. He leaned over Max from behind. "Don't tell me," he said. "Rain?"

Max reached up his hands. "Dada," he said, and then he coughed.

Nicholas sighed and settled Max into the crook of his arm. "Let's make a deal," he said. "If you go to sleep within twenty minutes I'll tell Grandma you don't have to eat apricots for the next five days." He uncapped the bottle that had been leaking onto the couch and rubbed it against Max's lips until his mouth opened like a foundling's. Max could take three strong sucks before he had to break away and breathe. "You know what's going to happen," Nicholas said. "You're going to get all better, and then *I'm* going to get sick. And I'll give it back to you, and we'll have this damn thing until Christmas."

Nicholas watched the commentator talk about the consumer price index, the DJIA, and the latest unemployment figures. By the time the news was over, Max had fallen asleep. He was cradled in Nicholas's arms like a little angel, his arms resting limp over his stomach. Nicholas held his breath and contorted his body, pushing himself up from the heels, then the calves, then the back, finally snapping his head up. He tiptoed up the stairs toward the nursery, and then the doorbell rang.

Max's eyes flew open, and he started to scream. "Fuck," Nicholas muttered, tossing the baby against his shoulder and jiggling him up and down until the crying slowed. The doorbell rang again. Nicholas headed back down the hall. "This better be an emergency," he muttered. "A car crash on my front lawn, or a fire next door."

He unlocked and pulled open the heavy oak door and came face-to-face with his wife.

At first Nicholas didn't believe it. This didn't really look like Paige, at least not as she had looked when she left. She was tanned and smiling, and her body was trim. "Hi," she said, and he almost fell over just hearing the melody wrapped around her voice.

Max stopped crying, as if he knew she was there, and stretched out his hand. Nicholas took a step forward and extended his palm, trying to ascertain whether he would be reaching toward a vision, coming up with a handful of mist. His fingertips were inches away from her collarbone, and he could see the pulse at the base of her throat, when he snapped his wrist back and stepped away. The space between them became charged and heavy. What had he been thinking? If he touched her, it would start all over again. If he touched her, he wouldn't be able to say what had been building inside him for three months; wouldn't be able to give her her due.

"Nicholas," Paige said, "give me five minutes."

Nicholas clenched his teeth. It was all coming back now, the flood of anger he'd buried under his work and his care of Max. She couldn't just step in as though she'd been on a getaway weekend and play the loving mother. As far as Nicholas was concerned, she didn't have the right to be there anymore at all. "I gave you three months," he said. "You can't just breeze in and out of our lives at your pleasure, Paige. We've done fine without you."

She wasn't listening to him. She reached forward and touched her hand to the baby's back, brushing the side of Nicholas's thumb. He turned so that Max, asleep again on his shoulder, was out of reach. "Don't touch him," he said, his eyes flashing. "If you think I'm going to let you walk back in here and pick up where you left off, you've got another thing coming. You aren't getting into this house, and you're not getting within a hundred feet of this baby."

If he decided to talk to Paige, *if* he let her see Max, it would be in his own sweet time, on his own agenda. Let her stew for a little while. Let her see what it was like to be powerless all of a sudden. Let her fall asleep fitfully, knowing she had absolutely no idea what tomorrow held in store.

Paige's eyes filled with tears, and Nicholas schooled himself not to move a muscle. "You can't do this," she said thickly.

Nicholas stepped back far enough to grab the edge of the door. "Watch me," he said, and he slammed it shut in his wife's face.

Part III:
Delivery
Fall 1993

chapter 33

Paige

*T*he front door has grown larger overnight. Thicker, even. It is
the biggest obstacle I've ever seen. And I should know. For
hours at a time, I focus all my concentration on it, waiting
for a miracle.

It would almost be funny, if it didn't hurt so much. For four years
I walked in and out of that door without giving it a second thought,
and now—the first time I've really *wanted* to, the first time I've *chosen*
to—I can't. I keep thinking, *Open sesame.* I close my eyes and I picture
the little hallway, the Chinese umbrella stand, the Persian runner.
I've even tried praying. But it doesn't change anything; Nicholas and
Max are on one side, and I'm stuck on the other.

I smile when I can to my neighbors as they go by, but I am very
busy. Such concentration takes all my energy. I repeat Nicholas's
name silently, and I picture him so vividly I almost believe I can
conjure him—magic!—inches from where I sit. And still nothing

happens. Well, I will wait forever, if it comes to that. I have made my decision. I want my husband to come back into my life. But I will settle for finding a chink in his armor, so that I can slip back into *his* life and prove that we can go back to normal.

I don't find it strange that I would give my right arm to be *inside* the house, watching Max grow up before my eyes—doing, really, the things that made me so crazy three months ago. I'd just been going through the motions then, acting out a role that I couldn't really remember being cast in. Now I'm back by my own free will. I *want* to spread chutney on Nicholas's turkey sandwiches. I *want* to stretch socks over Max's sunburned feet. I *want* to find all my art supplies and draw picture after picture with pastels and oils and hang them on the walls until every dull, pale corner of that house is throbbing with color. God, there is such a difference between living the life you are *expected* to live and living the life you *want* to live. I just realized it a little late, is all.

Okay, so my homecoming hasn't gone quite the way I'd planned. I figured on Nicholas welcoming me with a small parade, kissing me until my knees gave out beneath me, telling me that come hell or high water, he'd never let me go again. Truth is, I was so excited about slipping back into the routine that fit me like a soft old shoe, I never considered that the circumstances might have changed. I had learned the lesson already this past summer, with Jake, but I never thought to apply it here. But of course, if *I* am different, I shouldn't expect that time has stood still for Nicholas. I understand that he's been hurt, but if I can forgive myself, surely Nicholas can forgive me too. And if he can't, I'll have to make him try.

Yesterday I accidentally let him get away. I never thought of following him; I assumed that he'd found someone to watch Max at home when he went to work. But at 6:30 A.M., there he had been, toting the baby and a diaper bag, stuffing both into his car with the carelessness that comes from constant practice. I was very impressed. I could never carry both Max *and* the diaper bag—in fact, I could barely summon enough courage to take Max out of the house. Nicholas—well, Nicholas made it look so easy.

He had come out the front door and pretended I wasn't there. "Good morning," I had said, but Nicholas didn't even nod his head. He got into his car, sitting for a minute behind the wheel. Then he unrolled the window on the passenger side and leaned toward it. "You will be gone," he said, "by the time I get home."

I assumed he was going to the hospital, but I wasn't about to go there looking the way I did. Embarrassing Nicholas in his own front yard was one thing; making him look bad in front of his superiors was another. That I knew he would never forgive. And I *had* looked awful yesterday. I'd driven seventeen hours straight, slept on my front lawn, and skipped showers for two days. I would slip into the house, wash up, change my clothes, and then go to Mass General. I wanted to see Max without Nicholas around, and how difficult could it be to find the day care facility there?

After Nicholas left, I crawled into the front seat of my car and fished my keys from my pocketbook. I felt sure that Nicholas had forgotten about those. I opened the front door and stepped into my house for the first time in three full months.

It smelled of Nicholas and Max and not at all of me. It was a mess. I didn't know how Nicholas, who loved order, could live like this, much less consider it sanitary for Max. There were dirty dishes piled on every pristine surface in the kitchen, and the Barely White tiles on the floor were streaked with muddy footprints and scribbles of jelly. In the corner was a dead plant, and fermenting in the sink was half a melon. The hallway was dark and littered with stray socks and boxer shorts; the living room was gray with dust. Max's toys— most of which I'd never seen before—were covered with tiny smudged handprints.

My first instinct had been to clean up. But if I did that, Nicholas would know I had been inside, and I didn't want him yelling again. So I made my way to the bedroom and pulled a pair of khaki pants and a green cotton sweater out of my closet. After a quick shower, I put them on and threw my dirty clothes into the bathroom hamper.

When I thought I heard a noise, I ran out of the bathroom, stopping only in the nursery to get a quick scent of Max—soiled diapers and baby powder and sweet milky skin. I slipped out the back door just in case, but I didn't see anybody. With my hair still wet, I drove to Mass General and inquired about staff child care, but they told me there was no facility on the hospital grounds. "Good Lord," I said to the receptionist at the information desk. "Nicholas has him in a day care center." I laughed out loud then, thinking about how ridiculous this had all turned out. If Nicholas had agreed to consider day care before the baby was born, I wouldn't have been home all day with him. I would have been taking classes, maybe drawing again—I would have been doing something for *myself*. If I hadn't been home with Max, I might never have needed to get away.

I wasn't about to search through the Boston phone book for day care centers, so I had gone home and resigned myself to the fact that I'd lost a day. Then Nicholas showed up and told me again to get the hell off his lawn. But late last night, he had come outside. He wasn't angry, at least not as angry as he had been. He stepped down to the porch, sitting so close that I could have touched him. He was wearing a robe I had not seen before. As I watched him, I pretended that we were different, that it was years ago, and we were eating bagels and chive cream cheese and reading the real estate listings of the Sunday *Globe*. For a moment, just a moment, something passed behind the shadows in his eyes. I could not be sure, but I thought it took the shape of understanding.

That's why today I am bright-eyed and bushy-tailed, ready to follow Nicholas to the ends of the earth. He's late—it's past seven o'clock—and I'm already in the car. I have moved out of the driveway and parked down the block, because I want him to think I have disappeared. When he drives away I am going to tail him, like in the movies, always keeping a couple of cars between us.

He walks out the front door with Max tucked beneath his arm like a Federal Express package, and I start the engine. I unroll my window and stare, just in case Nicholas does anything I can use as a clue. I hold my breath as he locks the door, saunters to his car, and settles Max into the car seat. It's a different car seat now, facing forward, instead of the little bucket that faced the back. On the plastic bar across the car seat is a circus of plastic animals, each holding a different jingling bell. Max giggles when Nicholas buckles him in, and he grabs a yellow rubber ball that hangs from an elephant's nose. "Dada," he says—I swear I can hear it—and I smile at my baby's first word.

Nicholas looks over the top of the car before he slips into his seat, and I know he is trying to find me. I have an unobstructed view of him: his glinting black hair and his sky-colored eyes. It has been quite a while since I've really looked at him; I have been making up images from a composite of memories. Nicholas really is the most handsome man I have ever seen; time and distance haven't changed that. It isn't his features as much as their contrast; it isn't his face as much as his ease and his presence. When he puts the car in gear and begins to drive down the block, I count, whispering out loud. "One Mississippi, two Mississippi," I say. I make it to five, and then I start to follow him.

As I expected, Nicholas doesn't take the turn to Mass General. He takes a route that I recognize from somewhere but that I can't quite place. It is only when I hide my car in a driveway three houses down from Nicholas's parents' house that I realize what has happened while I've been away.

I can see Astrid only from a distance. Her shirt is a blue splotch against the wood door. Nicholas holds out the baby to her, and I feel my own arms ache. He says a few words, and then he walks back to the car.

I have a choice: I can follow Nicholas to wherever he's going next, or I can wait until he leaves and hope that I have the advantage of surprise and try to get Astrid Prescott to let me hold my baby, which I want more than anything. I see Nicholas start the car. Astrid closes the heavy front door. Without thinking about what I am doing, I pull out of the neighbor's driveway and follow Nicholas.

I realize then that I would have come back to Massachusetts no matter what. It has to do with more than Max, with more than my mother, with more than obligation. Even if there were no baby, I would have returned because of Nicholas. *Because of Nicholas. I'm in love with Nicholas.* In spite of the fact that he is no longer the man I married; in spite of the fact that he spends more time with patients than with me; in spite of the fact that I have never been and never will be the kind of wife he should have had. A long time ago, he dazzled me; he saved me. And out of every other woman in the world, Nicholas chose *me.* We may have changed over the years, but these are the kinds of feelings that last. I *know* they're still there in him, somewhere. Maybe the part of his heart that he's using now to hate me used to be the part that loves.

Suddenly I am impatient. I want to find Nicholas immediately, tell him what I now know. I want to grab him by the collar and kiss my memory into his bloodstream. I want to tell him I am sorry. I want to hear him set me free.

I lean my hand out the window as I drive, cupping the firm knob of air that I can't see. I laugh out loud at my discovery: I had been restless for so long that, like an idiot, I ran for miles and miles just to realize that what I really wanted was right here.

Nicholas parks in the Mass General garage, the uppermost level, and I park four spaces away from him. I think about the police shows I've seen on TV as I hide behind the concrete pylons, keeping my distance in case Nicholas decides to turn around. I start to sweat, wondering how I'll be able to keep him from noticing me on an elevator, but Nicholas takes the stairs. He goes down one level into the hospital building and walks down a hall that does not even remotely resemble a surgical floor. There is blue commercial carpeting and a line of wooden doors with the names of doctors spread across them on brass plaques. At one point, when he turns to fit a key into a lock, I pull myself into a doorway. "May I help you?" a voice says behind the half-open door, and I feel the blood drain out of my face, even as I curl my way back into the hall.

Nicholas has closed the door behind himself. I walk up to it and read the plaque. DR. NICHOLAS J. PRESCOTT, ACTING CHIEF OF CAR-DIOTHORACIC SURGERY. When did that happen? I lean against the frame of the smooth varnished door and rub my fingers over the recessed letters of Nicholas's name. I would have liked to be here for that, and even as I think this, I am wondering what the circumstances were. I see Alistair Fogerty, pants pillowed around his ankles, in a compromising position with a nurse in the supply closet. Maybe he is sick, or even dead. What else would make that pompous old goat give up his position?

The twitch of the doorknob startles me. I turn to the bulletin board and pretend to be engrossed in an article about endorphins. Nicholas walks past without noticing me. He has taken off his jacket and is wearing his white lab coat. He stops at an empty circular desk near the elevator bank and riffles through a clipboard's papers.

When he disappears behind the doors of the elevator, I panic. This is a big hospital, and the chances of my finding him again are next to nothing. But I must have followed him here for a reason, whatever it might be, and I'm not ready to give up yet. I press my fingers to my temples, thinking of Sherlock Holmes and Nancy Drew, of clues. How did Nicholas spend his day? Where would a doctor be likely to go? I try to run through my mind snippets of conversation we've had when he mentioned places in the hospital, even specific floors. Nicholas could have gone to the patient rooms, the laboratory, the lockers. Or he could be headed where a cardiac surgeon should be headed.

"Excuse me," I say quietly to a janitor emptying a trash container. *"No hablo inglés."* The man shrugs.

I try again. "Operation," I say. "I'm looking for the operations." *"Sí, operación."* The man makes a jagged line across his stomach. He bobs his head, smiling.

I shake my head and try to remember the *Sesame Street* Spanish I'd heard when I turned it on for Max. *"Uno,"* I say, holding my hand close to the floor. I move it up an inch. *"Dos."* I move it again. *"Tres, cuatro . . .* operation?"

The man claps his hands. *"Sí, sí, operación."* He holds up three fingers. *"Tres,"* he says.

"Gracias," I murmur, and I jam my finger repeatedly into the elevator call button, as if this might make it come faster.

Sure enough, the operating rooms are on three, and as the elevator doors part I get a glimpse of Nicholas rushing by, now in his blue scrubs. Everything on him is covered, except for his face, but I would have been able to spot him from a distance simply by the stately manner of his walk. He looks over my head at a wall clock, then he disappears behind a double panel of doors.

"If you're a relative," a voice says behind me, "you'll have to go to the waiting room." I turn to see a pretty, petite nurse in a crisp white uniform. "Only patients are allowed in here," she says.

"Oh," I say. "I must have gotten lost." I give a quick smile and then ask her if Dr. Prescott has arrived yet.

Nodding, she takes my elbow, as if she knows this is a ploy and wants me out immediately. "Dr. Prescott is always ten minutes early," she says. "We set our watches by him." She stands beside the elevator with me. "I'll tell him you were here," she says. "I'm sure he'll come to see you when the operation is over."

"No!" I say, a little too loud. "You don't have to tell him anything." For the past half hour, I've had the upper hand. I'm where I want to be, and Nicholas doesn't know. I *like* being anonymous and watching him. After all, I've never really seen him work, and maybe this is part of the reason I felt compelled to follow him to the hospital. Another hour or two, and I'll come into the open. But not now, not yet. I'm still learning.

I look at the nurse, considering a string of different excuses. I knot my hands together in front of me. "I . . . I don't want him to be distracted."

"Of course," she says, and she propels me into the yawning mouth of the elevator.

When Nicholas comes back up to his office, he is still wearing scrubs, but they are dark with sweat, pressed against his back and under his arms. He unlocks his door and leaves it open, and I creep from my hiding spot behind a row of sleeping wheelchairs to sit on the floor beside the doorway. "Mrs. Rosenstein," Nicholas is saying, "this is Dr. Prescott."

His voice makes my stomach flip. "I'm calling to let you know that the procedure went well. We did four grafts, as expected, and he came off the bypass machine nicely. Everything is going just fine, and he should be waking up in a few hours." I listen to the calm currents running under his words and wonder if he uses that tone to put Max to sleep. I remember Nicholas telling me about making postoperative phone calls when he was a beginning resident. "I never say 'How are you,' because I know damn well how they are. How else could you be if you've been sitting next to the phone for six hours, waiting to hear if your husband is alive or dead?"

I lose Nicholas for a little while after that, because he meets with some residents and fellows in a small room where there is nowhere for me to hide. I am impressed. He hasn't stopped yet. Everywhere he goes in the hospital, people know his name, and nurses fall over each other to hand him charts and schedules before he even thinks to ask. I wonder if that is because he is a surgeon or because he is Nicholas.

≈≈≈

When I see Nicholas again, he is with a younger man, probably a resident, walking through the halls of surgical ICU. I knew he'd make a swing through here, even if he was planning to head to other floors first, because he'd have to check on that morning's patient. His name is Oliver Rosenstein, and he is sleeping peacefully, breathing in time with the steady beats of the heart monitor. "We make patients sicker than they are when they come to us," Nicholas is saying to the resident. "We *elect* to make them sicker in hopes that they'll be better in the long run. That's part of why you're put up on a pedestal. If you trust your car to a mechanic, you look for someone who's good. If you trust your life to a surgeon, you look for someone who's God." The resident laughs and looks up at Nicholas, and it is clear that he thinks Nicholas is as mythic as they come.

Just as I am wondering why I have never seen Nicholas work during the eight years we've been married, he is paged over the loud-speaker. He murmurs something to the resident and bolts up the nearest staircase. The resident leaves Oliver Rosenstein's room and walks off in the other direction. Because I don't know where to go, I stay where I am, at the open doorway to the room.

"Uhh," I hear, and Oliver Rosenstein stirs.

I bite my lower lip, not certain what to do, when a nurse breezes past me into the room. She leans close to Oliver and adjusts several tubes and wires and catheters. "You're doing fine," she soothes, and then she pats his yellow, veined hand. "I'm going to page your doctor for you." She leaves as briskly as she entered, and because of that I am the only person who hears Oliver Rosenstein's first postsurgical words. "It isn't easy," he says, barely audible, "not easy to go through this. . . . It's real, real hard." He rolls his head from side to side, as if he is looking for something, and then he sees me and smiles. "Ellie," he says, his voice a rough sandpaper snap. He clearly thinks I am someone else. "I'm here, *kine ahora*," he says. "For a WASP, that Prescott is a mensch."

≈≈≈

It is another hour before I find Nicholas again, and that is only by accident. I am wandering around the post-op floor, when Nicholas blusters out of the elevator. He is reading a file and eating a Hostess cupcake. A nurse laughs at him as he passes the central desk. "You gonna be the next cardiac surgeon around these parts with blocked arteries," she scolds, and Nicholas tosses her the second cupcake, still packaged.

"If you don't tell anyone," he says, "this is yours."

I marvel at this man, whom everyone seems to know, who seems so controlled and so calm. Nicholas, who could not tell you where I keep the peanut butter in his own kitchen, is completely in his element at this hospital. It hits like an unexpected slap: This is really Nicholas's home. These people are really Nicholas's family. This doctor, whom everyone seems to need for a signature or a quiet word or an answer, does not need anyone else, especially me.

Nicholas stuffs the chart he has been reading into the box glued to the door of room 445. He enters and smiles at a young resident in a white coat, her hands jammed in her pockets. "Dr. Adams tells me you're all set for tomorrow," he says to the patient, pulling up a chair next to the bed. I scoot to the other side of the doorway so that I can peek in, unseen. The patient is a man about my father's age, with the same round face and faraway look in his eyes. "Let me tell you what we're going to do, since I don't think you're going to remember much of it," Nicholas says.

I cannot really hear him, but little drifts of dialogue float out to me, words like *oxygenation, mammary arteries, intubate.* The patient does not seem to be listening. He is staring at Nicholas with his mouth slightly open, as if Nicholas is Jesus Himself.

Nicholas asks the man if he has any questions. "Yes," the patient says hesitantly. "Will I know you tomorrow?"

"You might," Nicholas says, "but you're going to be groggy by the time you see me. I'll check in when you're up in the afternoon."

"Dr. Prescott," the patient says, "in case I'm too doped up to tell you—thanks."

I do not hear Nicholas respond to the patient, so I don't have time to retreat before he comes out the door. He barrels into me, apologizes, and then notices whom he has run into. With a narrowed look, he grabs my upper arm and starts to pull me down the hall. "Julie," he says to the resident who has been in the room with him, "I'll see you after you round." Then he curses through his clenched teeth and drags me into a tiny room off the side of the hall, where patients can get ice chips and orange juice. "What the hell do you think you're doing here?"

My breath catches in my throat, and for the life of me I cannot answer. Nicholas squeezes my arm so hard that I know he is leaving behind a bruise. "I—I—"

"You *what?*" Nicholas seethes.

"I didn't mean to bother you," I say. "I just want to talk to you." I start to tremble and wonder what I will say if Nicholas takes me up on my offer.

"If you don't get the hell out of here," Nicholas says, "I'll have security throw you out on your ass." He releases my arm as if he's been touching a leper. "I told you not to come back," he says. "What else do I have to do to show you I mean it?"

I lift my chin and pretend I haven't heard anything he's said. "Congratulations," I say, "on your promotion."

Nicholas stares at me. "You're crazy," he says, and then he walks down the hall without turning back.

I watch him until his white coat is a blur against a distant wall. I wonder why he cannot see the similarity between me and his patients, whom he keeps from dying of broken hearts.

≈≈≈

At the Prescotts' Brookline mansion, I sit for seven minutes in the car. I let my breath heat up the interior and wonder if there is an etiquette for begging mercy. Finally, driven by an image of Max, I push myself up the slate path and rap on the door with the heavy brass lion knocker. I am expecting Imelda, the short, plump maid, but instead Astrid herself—and my son—opens the door.

I'm immediately struck by the contrast between Astrid and my own mother. There are the simple things—Astrid's silk and pearls as compared to my mother's flannel shirts and chaps; Astrid's antiques set against my mother's stables. Astrid thrives on her fame; my mother goes to great lengths to protect her identity. But on the other hand, Astrid and my mother are both strong; they are both proud to a fault. They have both fought the system that bound them, and re-created themselves. And from the look of things, Astrid—like my mother—is beginning to admit to her mistakes.

Astrid doesn't say anything. She looks at me—no, actually she looks *into* me, as if she is sizing me up for the best lighting and direction and angle. Max is balanced on her hip. He watches me with eyes that the color blue must have been named for. His hair is matted with sweat on the side of his head, and a crinkled line from a sheet is imprinted on his cheek.

Max has changed so much in just three months.

Max is the image of Nicholas.

He figures out that I am a stranger, and he burrows his face in Astrid's blouse, rubbing his nose back and forth on the ribbing.

Astrid makes no move to give him to me, but she also doesn't shut the door in my face. To make sure of this, I take a tiny step forward. "Astrid," I say, and then I shake my head. *"Mom."*

As if the word has triggered a memory, which I know is impossible, Max lifts his face. He tilts his head, as his grandmother did at first, and then he reaches out one balled fist. "Mama," he says, and the fingers of the fist open one by one like a flower, stretching and coming to rest on my cheek.

His touch—it's not what I've expected, what I've dreamed. It is warm and dry and gentle and brushes like a lover. My tears slip down between his fingers, and he pulls his hand away. He puts it back into his mouth, drinking in my sorrow, my regrets.

Astrid Prescott hands Max to me so that his arms wrap around my neck and his warm, solid form presses the length of my chest. "Paige," she says, not at all surprised to see me. She steps back so that I can enter her home. "Whatever took you so long?"

chapter 34
Nicholas

*P*aige has single-handedly ruined Nicholas's day. Nicholas knows he has nothing else to complain about—his surgery went well enough; his patients are bearing up—but discovering Paige tripping along at his heels has unnerved him. It is a public hospital, and she has every right to be inside it; his threat about calling security was only that—a threat. Seeing her outside his patient's door rattled him, and he never gets rattled at the hospital. For several minutes after he walked away from her, he had felt his pulse jumping irregularly, as if he'd received a shock to the system.

At least she wouldn't find Max. She hadn't followed him to the hospital; surely he would have noticed. She must have showed up later. Which meant that she didn't know Max was at his parents', and never, never would she guess that Nicholas had swallowed his pride and in fact was starting to enjoy having Robert and Astrid Prescott back in his life. On the outside chance that Paige *did* go over there, well, his mother certainly wouldn't let her in, not after all the pain she'd caused to Astrid's own son.

Nicholas stops at his office to pick up his suit jacket before heading home. In spite of the name on the door and the fact that he has his own secretary, it is still really Alistair's place. The art on the walls is not what Nicholas would have picked; the nautical paraphernalia like that sextant and the brass captain's wheel are not his style. He would like a forest-green office with fox-and-hound prints, a banker's shaded lamp on his desk, an overstuffed cranberry damask couch. Anything but the pale white and beige that predominate in his house—which Paige, with her predilection for color, has always hated and which, all of a sudden, Nicholas is starting to see that he doesn't like himself.

Nicholas rests his hand on the brass wheel. Maybe one day. He is doing a good job as chief of cardiac surgery; he knows that. Saget has as much as told him that if Alistair decides to cut back his schedule or retire completely, the position is Nicholas's for keeps. It is a dubious honor. Nicholas has wanted it for so long that he has slipped into the schedule naturally, joining the proper hospital committees and giving lectures to the residents and visiting surgeons. But all the extra hours and the grueling pressure to succeed keep him apart from Max and from Paige.

Nicholas shakes his head. He *wants* to be apart from Paige. He doesn't need her anymore; he wants her to choke on a taste of her own medicine. Setting his jaw, he pulls together the files he needs to review before tomorrow and locks his office door behind him.

At eight o'clock, there isn't much traffic on Storrow Drive, and Nicholas makes it to his parents' house in fifteen minutes. He lets himself in and steps into the hall. "Hello," he calls, listening to his echo in the cupola above. "Where are you guys?"

He wanders into the parlor, which is primarily a playroom now, but no one is there. He peeks into the library, where his father usually spends the evenings, but the room is dark and cool. Nicholas starts up the stairs, his feet falling onto the worn track of the Oriental runner. "Hello," he says again, and then he hears Max giggle.

When Max laughs, it rumbles out of his belly, and it overcomes him so thoroughly that by the time the sound bubbles up through his throat, his little shoulders are shaking and his smile is like the sun. Nicholas loves the sound, just as much as he hates Max's piercing crabby whine. He follows the giggle around the hall and into one of the extra bedrooms, the one that Astrid has redecorated into a gingham nursery. Just outside, Nicholas drops to his hands and knees, thinking to surprise Max by crouching like a tiger. "Max, Max, Maximilian," Nicholas growls, pawing his way into the half-open door.

Astrid is sitting on the only chair in the room, an oversize white rocker. Max is in the middle of the pale-blue carpeted floor, tugging at tufts of the rug with one fist. His free hand is used for balance and is propped comfortably against Paige's knee.

Although Astrid looks up, Paige doesn't seem to notice that Nicholas has crawled into the room. She reaches for Max's bare toes and pulls them one by one, the pinkie last, and then runs her fingers up the length of his leg. He squeals and giggles again, leaning back his head so that he can see her upside down. "More?" she says, and Max slaps his hands against her thighs.

Somewhere in the back of Nicholas's mind, behind the red haze, something snaps. He stares at Paige, dumbfounded that she is actually in the same room as *his son*. She looks impossibly young, with her red hair spilling down over her shoulders and her shirt untucked in the back, her sneakered feet just out of Max's reach. It wasn't supposed to happen this way. But Max, who wails when the UPS man comes to the door these days, has taken to Paige as if she's been there all his life, instead of only half. And Paige makes it look so easy. Nicholas remembers the nights he had to walk up and down the halls of the house, letting Max cry in his arms because he didn't know how else to put him to sleep. He even took books out of the library to learn the words to "Patty-Cake" and "Three Blind Mice." But Paige walks in from nowhere, sits down, spreads her legs in a circular playground for Max, and she's got him crowing.

Out of the blue, a vision of Paige flashes across Nicholas's mind —Paige with her hand in the Miracle Whip jar, scraping together the last of the stuff for his sandwich. It was four-thirty in the morning, and he was leaving for surgery, but she, as always, had got up to make his lunch. "Well," she said, ringing the knife against the empty jar, "we can call this one quits." And she looked around the kitchen for a dish towel and couldn't find one and wiped her hands on the soft white cotton of her angel's nightgown when she thought, incorrectly, that Nicholas wasn't looking.

Paige hasn't made his lunch since Max was born, and although he isn't about to blame a newborn or admit to jealousy, he suddenly realizes that Paige hasn't been *his* since Max was born. He clenches his fists in the carpet, just like Max. Paige hasn't come back here for him; she's come for Max. She probably traced Nicholas to the hospital only to make sure he wouldn't be around when she found Max. And although this shouldn't bother him, because he's pushed away all his feelings for her, it still smarts.

Nicholas takes a deep breath, waiting for brilliant anger to replace the pain. But it is slow in coming, especially when he looks at Paige, at the picture she makes with his son. He narrows his eyes and tries to remember what is familiar about this, and then he sees the connection. The way Max looks at her—as if she is a deity—is exactly the way Paige used to look at Nicholas.

Nicholas jumps to his feet and glares at his mother. "Who the hell told you to let her in here?" he seethes.

Astrid stands calmly. "Who the hell told me not to?" she says.

Nicholas runs a hand through his hair. "For Christ's sake, Mom, I didn't think I had to spell it out. I *told* you she was back. You *know* how I feel. You *know* what she's done." He points to Paige, still wrapped around the baby and tickling his sides. "How do you know she isn't going to steal him away when your back is turned? How do you know she isn't going to hurt him?"

Astrid lays a hand on her son's arm. "Nicholas," she says, "do you really think she's going to do that?"

At that, Paige looks up. She stands and pulls Max up on his feet. "I just had to see him, Nicholas. I'll go now. It's not your mother's fault." She scoops Max into her embrace, and he locks his dimpled arms around her neck.

Nicholas takes a step forward, so close he can feel the warm rush of Paige's breath. "I don't want to see your car at home," he says in his quiet, steely surgeon's voice. "I'll get a restraining order."

He expects Paige to turn and slink away, intimidated, like everyone else does when he speaks that way. But she stands her ground and rubs her hands over Max's back. "It's my house too," she says quietly, "and it's my son."

Nicholas explodes. He grabs the baby so roughly, Max begins to cry. "What the hell do you think you're going to do? Take the kid the next time you decide to bolt? Or maybe you already have a plan to leave."

Paige knots her hands in front of her. "I am *not* going to bolt. All I want is to be let back in my house again. I'm not going to run anywhere unless I'm forced to."

Nicholas laughs, a strange sound that comes through his nose. "Right," he says. "Just like last time. Poor Paige, driven away by a twist of Fate."

In that moment, Nicholas knows he has won. "How come you have to see it like that?" Paige whispers. "How come you can't just see that I came home?" She steps back, speaking through a broken smile. "Maybe you're perfect, Nicholas, and everything you do turns out right the first time. The rest of us ordinary humans have to try over and over again and hope that we'll keep getting second chances until we figure it out." She turns and runs out of the room before a single tear falls, and Nicholas can hear the heavy oak front door pulled shut behind her.

Max fidgets in Nicholas's arms, so he sets him down on the carpet. The baby stares out the open bedroom door as if he is waiting for Paige to come back. Astrid, whom Nicholas has forgotten about, reaches down to pull the dying leaf of a potted palm out of Max's hand. When she straightens, she looks Nicholas right in the eye. "I'm ashamed of you," she says, and she walks out of the room.

≈≈≈

Paige is at the house when Nicholas returns with Max. She sits quietly in front of the porch with her sketch pad and her charcoal.

In spite of his threat, Nicholas does not call the police. He does not even acknowledge that he sees her when he carries Max and his diaper bag and the files from the hospital into the house. From time to time that night when he is playing with Max on the living room floor he can see Paige peering in through the window, but he doesn't bother to close the drapes or to move Max into another room.

When Max has trouble falling asleep, Nicholas tries the one thing that always works. Dragging the vacuum cleaner out of the front hall closet, he sets it over the threshold of the nursery and flips the switch so that the whir of the motor drowns out the choked cries of Max's screams. Eventually Max quiets down and Nicholas pulls the vacuum away. It works because of the white noise that distracts Max, but Nicholas thinks it might be genetic. He can remember coming home from thirty-six-hour shifts, falling asleep to the hum of the vacuum as Paige cleaned the house.

Nicholas walks to the front hall and turns out the light. Then he steps to the window, knowing that he'll be able to see Paige without her being able to see him. Her face is silver in the moonlight, her hair a rich bronze glow. Puddled around her are scores of drawings: Max sitting, Max sleeping, Max rolling over. Nicholas can not see among them a single image of himself.

The wind blows a couple of the drawings up the steps of the porch. Before he can even think to stop himself, Nicholas opens the front door in time for them to fly into the hall. He picks them up —one of Max playing with a rattle, one of Max grabbing his own feet—and walks onto the porch. "I think these are yours," he says, coming to stand beside her.

Paige is on her hands and knees, trying to keep the other drawings from blowing away. She has secured a stack of them under a big rock and has pinned the rest with her elbow. "Thanks," she says, rolling awkwardly onto her side. She gathers the pictures up and stuffs them inside the front cover of her sketch pad, as if she is embarrassed. "If you want to stay out here," she says, "I can sit in the car."

Nicholas shakes his head. "It's cold," he says. "I'm going to go inside." He sees Paige draw in her breath, waiting for an invitation, but he's not about to let that happen. "You're very good with Max," he says. "He's going through this stranger thing now, and he doesn't take to just anybody."

Paige shrugs. "I think I've grown into him. This is more what I pictured when I thought of a baby—something that sits up and smiles and laughs with you, not just something that eats and sleeps and poops and completely ignores you." She peers up at him. "I think that *you're* the one who's very good with Max. Look at what he's turned into. He's like a whole different kid."

Nicholas thinks of many things he could say, but instead he just nods his head. "Thanks," he says. He leans against the step of the porch and stretches out his legs. "You can't stay here forever," he says.

"I hope I don't have to." Paige tilts her head back and lets the night wash over her face. "When I was in North Carolina, I slept outside with my mother." She sits up and laughs. "I actually liked it."

"I'll have to take you camping in Maine," Nicholas says.

Paige stares at him. "Yes," she says, "you'll have to."

A chill sweeps across the lawn, beading the dew and sending a shiver down Nicholas's spine. "You're going to freeze out here," he says, and he stands before he can say anything else. "I'm going to get you a coat."

He runs up the porch as if it is a refuge and pulls the first coat he can find out of the hall closet. It is a big woolen overcoat, one of his, and as he holds it out to Paige he sees it will sweep her ankles. Paige steps into the coat and pulls the lapels together. "This is nice," she says, touching Nicholas's hand.

Nicholas pulls away. "Well," he says, "I don't want you to get sick."

"No," Paige says, "I mean *this*." She gestures between herself and Nicholas. "Not yelling." When Nicholas does not say anything, she picks up her sketch pad and her charcoal, and as a second thought she offers a half-smile. "Give Max a kiss for me," she says.

When Nicholas steps into the safety of the house and stands in the folds of the dark hallway, he is momentarily disoriented. He has to lean against the doorframe and let the room settle before his memory returns. Maybe he believed that at some point he'd stop playing the game and let Paige back; but he can see that isn't going to happen. She's come for Max, only for Max, and something about that is driving him crazy. The feeling is like a fist being driven into his gut, and he knows exactly why. He still loves her. As stupid as it seems, as much as he hates her for what she has done, he can't quite stop that.

He peeks out the window and sees Paige settled in his overcoat and a sleeping bag she's borrowed from some goddamned neighbor. Part of him hates her for being given that comfort, and part of him hates himself for wanting to give her even more. With Paige, there have never been easy answers, only impulses, and Nicholas is beginning to wonder if it has all been a huge mistake. He can't keep doing this; not to himself and not to Max. There has to be a reconciliation or a clean break.

The moon slips under the front door, filling the hallway with a spectral glow. Suddenly exhausted, Nicholas pulls himself up the stairs. He will have to sleep on it. Sometimes things look different in the morning. He crawls into bed with his clothes still on and envisions Paige lying like a sacrifice beneath that stifling moon. His last conscious thought is of his bypass patients, of the moment during surgery when he stops their hearts from beating. He wonders if they ever feel it.

chapter 35
Paige

*A*nna Maria Santana, whom I had never met, was born and died on March 30, 1985. OUR FOUR HOUR ANGEL, the tombstone reads, still fairly new among the grave markers in the Cambridge graveyard I had last walked through when I was pregnant. I do not know why I didn't notice Anna Maria's grave back then. It is tidy and trimmed, and violets grow at the edges. Someone comes here often to see their little girl.

It does not pass my notice that Anna Maria Santana died at just about the same time I conceived my first child. Suddenly I wish I had something to leave—a silver rattle or a pink teddy bear—and then I realize that both Anna Maria and my own baby would have been eight now, growing out of baby gifts and into Barbies and bicycles. I hear my mother's voice: *You were stuck in my mind at five years old. Before I knew it, you were all grown up.*

Something has to come to a head soon. Nicholas and I can't keep stepping around each other, moving closer and then ripping apart as though we're following a strange tribal dance. I have not even attempted going to Mass General today, and I do not plan to go to the Prescotts' to see Max. I can't push Nicholas any more, because he is at the breaking point, but that makes me restless. I won't just sit around and let him decide my future the way I used to. But I can't make him see what I want him to see.

I am in the graveyard to clear my mind—it worked for my mother, so I hope it will work for me. But seeing Anna Maria's tombstone doesn't help much. I have told Nicholas the truth about leaving, but I still haven't really come clean. What if, when I get home, Nicholas is standing on the porch with open arms, willing to pick up where we left off? Can I let myself make the same mistakes all over again?

I read a "Dear Abby" column years ago in which a man had written about having an affair with his secretary. It had been over for years, but he had never told his wife, and although they had a happy marriage, he felt he should reveal what had happened. I was surprised by Abby's answer. *You're opening a can of worms,* Abby wrote. *What she does not know she cannot be hurt by.*

I do not know how long I can wait. I would never take Max and flee in the night, like I know Nicholas is thinking. I couldn't do it to Max, and I especially couldn't do it to Nicholas. Being with Max for three months has softened him around the edges. The Nicholas I left in July would never have crept around a corner on his hands and knees, pretending to be a grizzly bear to entertain his son. But practically, I cannot keep sleeping on the front lawn. It's mid-October, and already the leaves have come off the trees. We've had a frost at night. Soon there will be snow.

I walk to Mercy, hoping to get a cup of coffee from Lionel. The first familiar face is Doris's, and she drops two blue-plate specials at a booth and comes to hug me. "Paige!" She cries into the kitchen pass-through: "Paige is back again!"

Lionel runs in front and makes a big show of sitting me at the counter on a cracked red stool. The diner is smaller than I have remembered it, and the walls are a sickly shade of yellow. If I did not know the place, I would not feel comfortable eating here. "Where's that precious baby?" Marvela says, leaning in front of me so that her earbobs sway against the edges of my hair. "You got to have pictures, at least."

I shake my head and gratefully accept the cup of coffee that Doris brings. Lionel ignores the small line that has formed by the cash register and sits down beside me. "That doctor boy of yours came in here some months back. Thought you'd up and run off, and come to us for help." Lionel stares straight at me, and the line of his jagged scar darkens with emotion. "I tell him you ain't that kind of person," he says. "I know these things."

He looks for a moment as if he is going to hug me, but then he remembers himself and hoists his frame off the neighboring stool. "What you lookin' at?" he snaps at Marvela, who is wringing her hands beside me. "We got us a business, sweet pea," he says to me, and he stomps toward the cash register.

When the waitresses and Lionel have settled back into their routines, I let myself look around. The menus haven't changed, though the prices have. They have been rewritten on tiny fluorescent stickers. The men's bathroom is still out of order, as it was the last day I had worked there. And tacked above the cash register, dangling above the counter, are all the portraits I drew of the customers.

I cannot believe Lionel hasn't thrown them out. Surely some of the people have died by now. I scan the portraits: Elma the bag lady; Hank the chemistry professor; Marvela and Doris and Marilyn Monroe; Nicholas. *Nicholas.* I stand up, and then I crawl onto the countertop to get a closer look. I crouch with my hands pressed against Nicholas's portrait, feeling the stares of the customers. Lionel and Marvela and Doris, true friends, pretend they do not notice.

I remember this one very well. In the background I had drawn the face of a little boy, sitting in a twisted tree and holding the sun. At first I thought I'd drawn my favorite Irish legend, the one about Cuchulainn leaving the sun god's palace when his mother went home to her original husband. I did not understand why I would have drawn this particular scene, something from my own childhood, on Nicholas's portrait, but I thought it had something to do with my running away. I had stared at the drawing, and I imagined my father telling me the story while he smoked a bayberry pipe. At the time, I could easily see my father's hands, studded with glue and bits of twine from his workshop, waving in the air as he mimicked the passage of Cuchulainn back to ordinary earth. I wondered if Cuchulainn missed that other life.

Months afterward, when Nicholas and I were sitting in the diner and looking at his portrait, I told him the story of Dechtire and the sun god. He laughed. When I'd drawn it he had seen something completely different in the picture. He said he'd never even *heard* of Cuchulainn, but that as a kid he believed that if he climbed high enough he could truly catch the sun. *I guess,* he said, *in a way, we all do.*

≈≈≈

I unlock the house and spend a full hour pulling dirty socks and Onesies and fuzzy blanket sleepers from unimaginable places: the microwave, the wine rack, a soup tureen. When I have gathered a pile of laundry, I start a wash. In the meantime I dust the living room and the bedroom and scrub the white counters in the bathroom. I scour the toilet and vacuum the skin-colored rugs and try my best to get the jelly stains off the ivory tiles in the kitchen. I change the sheets on the bed and the ones in Max's crib, and I empty his diaper pail and spray perfume into the carpet so that some of the smell is masked. All the while, the TV is on, tuned to the soap operas I watched when my mother's ankle was first broken. I tell Devon to leave her husband and I cry when Alana's baby is stillborn and I watch, riveted, a love scene between a rich girl named Leda and Spider, a street-smart hustler. I am just setting the table for two when the telephone rings, and out of force of habit, I pick it up.

"Paige," the voice says. "I can't *tell* you how glad I am to find you."

"It's not what you think," I say, hedging, while I try to figure out who is on the other end.

"Aren't you coming to see Max? He's been waiting all day."

Astrid. Who else would call? I don't have any friends in this city. "I—I don't know," I say. "I'm cleaning the house."

"Nicholas didn't say that you'd moved back in," she says.

"I haven't."

"Paige," Astrid says, her voice as sharp as the edges of her black-and-white stills. "We need to have a little talk."

She is waiting for me at the front door with Max. He's dressed in Osh-Kosh overalls and is wearing the tiniest Nike sneakers I have ever seen. "Imelda has coffee waiting for us in the parlor," she says, handing Max over to me. She turns and walks into the imposing hall, expecting me to follow.

The parlor, just a room full of toys now, is much less intimidating than it was the first time I was there with Nicholas. If the rocking horse and the Porta-Crib had been there eight years ago, I wonder if things would have turned out this way. I set Max down on the floor, and he immediately gets onto his hands and his knees, rocking back and forth. "Look," I say, breathless. "He's going to crawl!"

Astrid hands me a cup and saucer. "Not to burst your bubble, but he's been doing that for two weeks. He can't seem to figure out the coordination." I watch Max bounce for a while; I accept cream and sugar. "I have a proposition for you," Astrid says.

I look up, a little afraid. "I don't know," I say.

Astrid smiles. "You haven't even heard it yet." She moves a fraction of an inch closer to me. "Listen. It's freezing these nights, and I know you can't stay much longer on your lawn. God only knows how long it's going to take my stubborn son to come to his senses. I want you to move in here. Robert and I have discussed it; we have more rooms than a small hotel. Now, out of deference to Nicholas, I'll have to ask you to leave during the day, so that Max is still in my care—he's a bit uptight about you being around him, as you've probably noticed. But I don't see why every now and then you and I and Max might not just cross paths."

I gape at Astrid, my mouth hanging open. This woman is offering me a gift. "I don't know what to say," I murmur, tugging my gaze away to rest on Max on the floor. A million things are running through my mind: *There has to be a catch. She's worked something out with Nicholas, something to prove that I'm an unfit mother, something to keep me even further away from Max. Or else she wants something in return. But what could I possibly give her?*

"I know what you're thinking," Astrid says. "Robert and I *owe* you. I was wrong in believing that you and Nicholas shouldn't be married. You're just what Nicholas needs, even if he's too stupid to realize it himself. He'll come around."

"I'm not what Nicholas needs," I say, still looking at Max.

Astrid leans forward so that her face is inches from mine and I am forced to turn to her. "You listen to me, Paige. Do you know what my first reaction was when Nicholas told me you'd left? I thought, *Hallelujah!* I didn't think you had it in you. When Nicholas brought you here originally, it wasn't your past or your life-style that I objected to. I won't speak for Robert, although he's far beyond that now. I wanted someone for Nicholas who had determination and tenacity—someone with a little bit of pluck. It rubs off, you know. But all I saw when I first looked at you was someone who idolized him, someone who tagged at his heels like a puppy and was willing to put her whole life in his hands. I didn't think you had the gumption to stand up in the wind, much less in a marriage. But he's had you running around for years at his beck and call, and finally you've given him a reason for pause. What you've gone through is not, in the long run, a tragedy—just a hiccup. You both will survive, and there will be two or three other little Maxes and a string of graduations and weddings and grandchildren. You're a fighter, every bit as much as Nicholas. I'd say, actually, that you're a very even match." She puts down her coffee cup and takes mine too. "Imelda is making up the room," she says. "Shall we go take a look?"

Astrid stands, but I do not. I knot my hands together in my lap and wonder if this is really what I want to do. It's going to make Nicholas furious. It's going to backfire in my face.

Max is making loud slurping noises and chewing on something that looks like a card. "Hey," I say, pulling it out of his hand. "Should you have this thing?" I wipe off the saliva and hand Max a different toy. Then I notice what I am holding. It is a key ring that holds three laminated photographs, eight-by-ten glossies. I know they are Astrid's work. The first is a picture of Nicholas giving his half-smile, his mind miles away. The second is a picture of Max taken about two months ago. I find myself staring at it greedily, drinking in the subtle changes that I have missed. Then I flip to the last card. It is a picture of me, fairly recent, although I don't know how Astrid could have taken it. I am sitting at an outdoor café at Faneuil Hall. I may even have been pregnant. I have a distant look in my eyes, and I know that even then I was plotting my escape.

"Mama," Max says, reaching for the card that I hold. On the back, written in permanent marker in Astrid's handwriting, is the word he's just spoken.

Imelda is just smoothing the bedspread when Astrid leads me into what will be my room. "Señora Paige," she says, smiling at me and then at Max when he grabs her long, dark braid. "This one, he has a bit of the devil in him," she says.

"I know," I say. "It comes from his father's side of the family."

Astrid laughs and opens an armoire. "You can keep your things here," she says, and I nod and look around. The room is simple by Prescott standards. It is furnished with a pale-peach sofa and a canopy bed; its sheets are the shades of a rainy Arizona sunset. The floor-length window curtains are Alençon lace, held back by brass pineapples. The mirror is an antique cheval glass and matches the armoire. "Is this all right?" Astrid asks.

I sink down on the bed and place Max next to me, rubbing his belly. I will miss the wet stars and the hydrangeas, but this will be just fine. I nod at her, and then I shyly stand and pass her the baby. "I think these were your terms," I say quietly. "I'll be back later."

"Come for supper," Astrid says. "I know Robert will want to see you."

She follows me down the steps and leads me to the front door. Max whimpers and reaches out when I start to leave, and she gives him to me for a moment. I trace the whorl of hair on the back of

Max's head and squeeze the spare flesh of his upper arms. "Why are you on my side?" I ask.

Astrid smiles. In the fading light, in just that instant, she reminds me of my mother. Astrid takes back my baby. "Why shouldn't I be?" she says.

≈≈≈

"Robert," Astrid Prescott says as we walk into the dining room, "you remember Paige."

Robert Prescott folds his newspaper and his reading glasses and stands up from his seat. I hold out my hand, but he ignores it and, after a moment's hesitation, sweeps me into his arms. "Thank you," he says.

"For what?" I whisper, unsure of what I've done now.

"For that kid," he tells me, and he smiles. I realize that in all the time I was taking care of Max, those were words Nicholas never said.

I sit down, but I am too nervous to eat the soup or the salad that Imelda brings from the kitchen. Robert sits at one end of the enormous table, Astrid at the other, and I am somewhere in between. There is an empty place setting across from me, and I stare at it anxiously. "It's just for balance," Astrid says when she sees me looking. "Don't worry."

Nicholas has already come for Max. He has a twenty-four-hour shift coming up and wanted to get to sleep early, according to Astrid. Usually during dinner, Max sits in a high chair next to Robert, who feeds him pieces of Parker House rolls.

"Nicholas hasn't told us very much about your trip," Robert says, making it sound as if I've been on the *QE2* for a holiday.

I swallow hard and wonder how much I can say without incriminating myself. After all, these *are* Nicholas's parents, however nice they are being. "I don't know if Nicholas ever told you," I say hesitantly. "I grew up without my mother. She left us when I was five, and somehow, when I wasn't doing a very good job taking care of Max, I figured if I could find her I'd automatically know how to do it all right."

Astrid clucks. "You did a fine job," she says. "In fact, you did all the hard work. You nursed, didn't you? Yes, I remember Nicholas found that out the hard way when Max was weaned in a day. We never bothered when you all were children. In our circles, nursing wasn't the proper thing to do."

Robert turns away and picks up the thread of the conversation. "Ignore Astrid," he says, smiling. "She sometimes spends weeks and months in huts without any other humans. She has a lot of practice talking only to herself."

"And sometimes," Astrid says pleasantly from the other end of the table, "I go away and I can't tell the difference between talking to myself and dinner conversation with you." She stands and walks toward Robert. She leans over him until he turns toward her. "Have I told you today that I love you?" she says, kissing his forehead.

"No, as a matter of fact," Robert says.

"Ah." Astrid pats his cheek. "So you *have* been listening." She looks up at me and grins. "I'm going to see what's happened to our steak."

It turns out that Robert Prescott actually knows of Donegal, my mother's horse. Well, not really of Donegal, but of his sire, the one with bloodlines to Seattle Slew. "She does this all by herself?" he asks.

"She rents space from a larger farm, and she has some kid come in to help her muck stalls," I say. "It's a beautiful place. So much green, and there are the mountains right behind her—it's a nice place to live."

"But you didn't stay," Robert points out.

"No," I say. "I didn't."

At that moment, when the conversation is starting to fit a little too tightly around me, Astrid comes back through the swinging door to the kitchen. "Another five minutes," she says. "Would you believe that after twenty years of living with us, Imelda still doesn't know that you like your steak burned to a crisp?"

"Well done," Robert says.

"Yes," Astrid says, laughing. "I *am* good, aren't I?"

Watching them, I feel my stomach tighten. I would never have expected this kind of warmth to exist between Nicholas's parents, and it makes me realize what I missed as a child. My father wouldn't remember how my mother prefers her steak; my mother couldn't tell you my father's favorite color or breakfast cereal. I had never seen my mother stand behind my father in the kitchen to kiss him upside down. I had never seen the jigsaw puzzle their hands made when they fit together, like Robert's and Astrid's, as if they'd been cut for each other.

The night that Nicholas asked me to marry him at Mercy, I did not really know him at all. I knew that I wanted his attention. I knew that he commanded respect wherever he went. I knew that he had eyes that took my breath away, the shifting color of the sea. I said yes because I thought he'd be able to help me forget about Jake, and the baby, and my mother, and Chicago. And in the long run I had blamed him because he lived up to all my expectations, making me forget about my old self so well that I panicked and ran again.

I said yes to Nicholas, but I did not know that I really wanted to marry him until the night we ran out of his parents' house after the argument about the marriage. That was the first time I noticed that in addition to my needing Nicholas, Nicholas needed me. Somehow I'd always just pictured him as the hero, the accessory to my plan. But that night, Nicholas had wavered beneath his father's words and turned his back on his family. Suddenly the man who had the world wrapped around his little finger found himself in absolutely unfamiliar territory. And to my surprise, it turned out to be a road *I* had traveled. For the first time in my life, someone needed my experience. It made me feel the way nothing ever had before.

That wasn't something that went away easily.

As I watch Astrid and Robert for the remainder of the meal, I think of all the things I know about Nicholas. I know that he absolutely will not eat squid or snails or mussels or apricot jam. I know that he sleeps on the right side of the bed and that no matter what precautions I take, the top sheet always becomes untucked on his side. I know that he won't come within a mile of a martini. I know that he folds his boxer shorts in half to fit into his dresser. I know that he can smell the rain a day before it comes, that he can sense snow by the color of the sky. I know that nobody else will ever know him as I do.

I also know that there are many facts Nicholas can list about me and still the most important truths will be missing.

≈≈≈

Bless me, Nicholas, for I have sinned. The words run through my mind with every footstep that leads me out of the Prescotts' house. I drive down the streets of Brookline and make familiar turns to our own house. For the last half mile I turn off the headlights and let the moon cut my path, wishing not to be seen.

I have not been to confession in eight and a half years. This makes me smile—how many rosaries would Father Draher pin on me to absolve me of my sins if it were him I was turning to instead of Nicholas?

My first confession was in fourth grade. We had been coached by the nuns, and we waited in line, saying our act of contrition before going into the confessional. The chamber was tiny and brown and gave me the sinking sense that the walls were coming in around me. I could hear the breathing of Father Draher, coming through the latticed metal that separated us. That first time, I said that I had taken the Lord's name in vain and that I had fought with Mary Margaret Riordan over who would get the last chocolate milk in the cafeteria. But when Father Draher didn't say anything, I began to make up sins: I had cheated on a spelling quiz; I had lied to my father; I had had an impure thought. At that last one Father Draher coughed, and I did not know why at the time, since I hadn't any idea what an impure thought was—it was a phrase I'd heard in a TV movie. "For your penance," he said, "say one Our Father and three Hail Marys." And that was that; I was starting with a clean slate.

How many years has it been since I have had to make up sins? How many years since I realized that an endless number of rosaries can't take away the guilt?

The lights are all off at the house, even in Nicholas's study. Then

I remember what Astrid said. He is trying to get a good night's sleep. I feel a pang of conscience: maybe this would be better done some other time. But I don't want to put it off anymore.

I stub my toe on Max's walker, which is stuffed into the corner of the hallway. Soundlessly I move up the stairs and tiptoe past the nursery to the door of our bedroom. It is ajar: Nicholas will be able to hear Max if he cries.

This is what I have planned: I will sit on the edge of the bed and fold my hands in my lap and poke Nicholas so that he wakes up. I will tell him everything he should have known from the start, and I will say that I couldn't let it go any longer and that I'll leave him now to think about it. And I'll pray for kindness the whole way home.

I am betting it all on one turn, I know that. But I don't see any other way out. Which is why when I creep into the bedroom and see Nicholas, half naked and wrapped in our pale-blue comforter, I don't just sit on the edge of the bed. I can't do that. If things don't work out for the best, at least I'll be able to know where his heart lies.

I kneel beside the bed and tangle my fingers in the thick sheaf of Nicholas's hair. I put my other hand on his shoulder, amazed at how warm his skin is to the touch. I slip my hand down to his chest and feel the hair spring against my palm. Nicholas groans and stretches, rolling over on his side. His arm falls across my own.

Moving very slowly, I touch my fingertips to his eyebrows, his cheekbones, his mouth. I lean forward until I can feel his breath on my eyelids. Then I inch closer until my lips brush his. I kiss him until he begins kissing me back, and before I can step away he wraps his arms around me and pulls me to him. His eyes fly open, but he does not seem surprised to find me there. "You cleaned my house," he whispers.

"*Our* house," I say. His hands are hot against me. I stiffen and pull away, sitting back on my heels.

"It's okay," Nicholas murmurs, propping himself against his pillows. "We're already married." He looks at me sideways and gives me a lazy smile. "I could get used to this," he says. "You sneaking into my bed."

I stand up and catch my reflection in the mirror. Then I rub my palms on the legs of my jeans and sit gingerly on the edge of the bed. I wrap my arms close, hugging myself tight. Nicholas sits next to me and slides an arm around my waist. "What's the matter?" he whispers. "You look like you've seen a ghost."

I shrug his hand away. "Don't touch me," I say. "You aren't going to want to touch me." I turn and sit cross-legged opposite him. Over his shoulder, I watch myself in the mirror. "Nicholas," I say, seeing my own lips move over words I never wanted to hear. "I had an abortion."

His back stiffens, and then his face sets, and finally he seems to be able to exhale. "You *what?*" he says. He moves closer, and the rage that darkens his features terrifies me. I wonder if he will grab me by the throat. "Is *that* where you were for three months? Getting rid of my child?"

I shake my head. "It happened before I met you," I say. "It wasn't your child."

I watch expressions flicker across his face as he remembers. Finally, he shakes his head. "You were a virgin," he says. "That's what you told me."

"I never told you anything," I say quietly. "That's what you wanted to believe." I hold my breath and tell myself that maybe it won't make a difference; after all, Nicholas had been living with his other girlfriend before he decided to marry me, and these days very few women come to marriage untouched. But then again, not all women are Nicholas's wife.

"You're Catholic," he says, trying to fit the pieces together. I nod. "That's why you left Chicago," he says.

"And that's why," I add softly, "I left Max. The day that I went—the day he fell off the couch and got that nosebleed—I figured I had to be the worst mother around. I had killed my first child; I had hurt my second. I figured no mother was better than someone like me."

Nicholas stands up, and I see in his eyes something I've never seen before. "You may be right about that," he says, speaking so loud I think the baby will wake. He grabs me by the shoulders and shakes me violently, so hard that my neck wrenches and I cannot see straight. "Get out of my house," he says, "and do not come back. What else do you want to get off your chest? Are you wanted for a murder rap? Are you hiding a lover in the closet?" He lets go of my arms, and even in the dark I can see the ten perfect bruises left by his clenched fingers, still glowing with his pain.

He sinks onto the edge of the bed as if his weight has suddenly become too much for him to bear. He bends down and holds his face in his hands. I want to touch him, to take away the ache. Looking at him, I wish I had never spoken. I reach out my hand, but Nicholas flinches before my skin brushes his. *Ego te absolvo.* "Forgive me," I say.

He takes the words like a brutal blow. When he lifts his head, his eyes are red-rimmed and brimming with fury. He stares at me, seeing me for what I really am. "God damn you," he says.

chapter 36

Nicholas

Whén Nicholas was a sophomore undergraduate at Harvard, he and his roommate, Oakie Peterborough, had got drunk and sprayed the fire extinguisher's foam all over their sleeping resident dorm adviser. They were put on probation for a year and then had gone their separate ways. When Nicholas entered Harvard Med, Oakie entered Harvard Law, and years before Nicholas had ever done surgery, Oakie was already an associate at a Boston law firm.

Nicholas takes a sip of his lemon water and tries to find the slightest resemblance between the Oakie he knew and the matrimonial attorney who sits across from him at the restaurant table. He was the one to call and ask about a lunch date, and Oakie, over the phone, said, "Hell, yeah," and penciled him in that afternoon. Nicholas thinks about Harvard and its connections. He watches the cool confidence of his old roommate as he settles his napkin on his lap, the shifting indifference of his eyes. "It's great to see you, Nicholas," Oakie says. "Amazing, isn't it, how you work in the same town and still never get the chance to see your old friends."

Nicholas smiles and nods. He does not consider Oakie Peterborough an old friend; he hasn't since he was nineteen and found him with a hand down Nicholas's own girlfriend's pants. "I'm hoping you can give me some answers," Nicholas says. "You practice family law, don't you?"

Oakie sighs and leans back. "Family law—what a crock. What I do doesn't keep families together. Sort of a contradiction in terms." He stares at Nicholas, and his eyes widen in realization. "You don't mean for yourself," he says.

Nicholas nods, and a muscle jumps at his jaw. "I want to find out about getting a divorce." Nicholas has lost a lot of sleep over this and has come to a decision with blinding clarity. He doesn't give a damn what it costs him, as long as he gets Paige out of his life and gets to keep Max. He is angry at himself for letting down his guard when Paige came into the bedroom last night. Her touch, the lilac smell of her skin—for a moment he was lost in the past, pretending she'd never left. He almost forgave the past three months. And then she told him the one thing he would never forget.

He starts shaking when he thinks of another man's hands on her body, another man's child in her womb, but he believes that with time the shock will pass. It's not really the abortion that upsets him. As a doctor, Nicholas spends so much time and effort saving lives that he can't personally support the decision to have an abortion, although he understands the motives of the pro-choice camp. No, what unnerves him is the secrecy. Even if he could listen to Paige's reasons for terminating a pregnancy, he couldn't understand hiding something like that from one's own husband. He had a right to know. It might have been *her* body, but it was *their* shared past. And in eight years, she never thought enough of him to mention the truth.

Nicholas spent the early morning trying to push from his mind the image of Paige begging for mercy. She had been shadowed by the mirror, so that there were two of her, her words and actions mocking her like a clown's silhouette. She had looked so fragile that Nicholas couldn't help but think of the wispy heads of dried dandelions, vulnerable to a breath. One word from him, and he knew she would fall apart.

But Nicholas had enough anger pulsing through his blood to block out any residual feelings. He was going to beat her at her own game, taking Max before she could use the poor kid to absolve her of guilt. He was going to get a divorce and drive her as far from him as possible, and maybe in five, in ten years, he wouldn't see her face every time he looked at his son.

Oakie Peterborough blots his meaty lips with his napkin and takes a deep breath. "Look," he says, "I'm a lawyer, but I'm also your friend. You ought to know what you're getting into."

Nicholas stares him down. "Just tell me what I have to do."

Oakie exhales, a sick sound like that of an overboiled kettle. "Well, Massachusetts is a state that permits fault in divorce cases. That means you don't have to prove fault to get a divorce, but if you can, the property and assets will be divided accordingly."

"She abandoned me," Nicholas interrupts. "And she lied for eight years."

Oakie rubs his hands together. "Was she gone for more than two years?" Nicholas shakes his head. "She wasn't the primary breadwinner, was she?" Nicholas snorts and throws his napkin on the table. Oakie purses his lips. "Well, then it's not desertion—at least not legally. And lying . . . I'm not sure about lying. Usually, just cause for fault is things like excessive drinking, beating, adultery."

"I wouldn't be surprised," Nicholas mutters.

Oakie does not hear him. "Fault would *not* include a change of religion, say, or moving out of the house."

"She didn't move," Nicholas clarifies. "She *left*." He stares up at Oakie. "How long is this going to take?"

"I can't know yet," he says. "It depends on whether we can find grounds. If not, you get a separation agreement, and a year later it can be finalized into a divorce."

"A *year*," Nicholas yells. "I can't wait a year, Oakie. She's going to do something crazy. She just up and left three months ago, remember—she's going to take my kid and run."

"A kid," Oakie says softly. "You didn't say there was a kid."

When Nicholas leaves the restaurant, he is seething. What he has learned is that although courts no longer assume that a woman should have custody, Max will go wherever his best interests lie. With Nicholas working so many hours a day, there is no guarantee of custody. He has learned that since Paige supported him through medical school, she is entitled to a portion of his future earnings. He has learned that this procedure will take much longer than he ever thought possible.

Oakie has tried to talk him out of it, but Nicholas is certain he has no choice. He cannot even think about Paige without feeling his spine stiffen or his fingers turn to ice. He cannot stand knowing that he has been played for a fool.

He walks into Mass General and ignores everyone who says hello to him. When he reaches his office, he shuts and locks the door behind him. With a sweep of his arm, he clears all the files off his desk. The one that lands on top of the pile on the floor is Hugo Albert's. That morning's surgery. It was also, he noted from the patient history, Hugo Albert's golden wedding anniversary. When he told Esther Albert that her husband was doing well, she cried and thanked Nicholas over and over, said that he would always be in her prayers.

He puts his head down on the desk and closes his eyes. He wishes he had his father's private practice, or that the association with surgical patients lasted as long as it does in internal medicine. It is too hard to deal with such intense relationships for such a short period of time and then move on to another patient. But Nicholas is starting to see that this is his lot in life.

With fierce self-control, he opens the top drawer and takes out a piece of the Mass General stationery that now bears his name. "Oakie wants a list," he mutters, "I'll give him a list." He starts to write down all the things that he and Paige own. The house. The cars. The mountain bikes and the canoe. The barbecue and the patio furniture and the white leather couch and the king-size bed. It is the same bed they had in the old apartment; it had too much of a history to justify replacement. Nicholas and Paige had ordered the handcrafted bed on the understanding that it would be theirs by the end of the week. But it was delayed, and they slept on a mattress on the floor for months. The bed had been burned in a warehouse fire and had to be built all over again. "Do you think," Paige said one night, curled against him, "God is trying to tell us this was all a mistake?"

When Nicholas runs out of possessions, he takes a blank sheet of paper and writes his name at the top left and Paige's name at the top right. Then he makes a grid. DATE OF BIRTH. PLACE OF BIRTH. EDUCATION. LENGTH OF MARRIAGE. He can fill it all in easily, but he is shocked at how much space his own schooling takes up and how little is written in Paige's column. He looks at the length of marriage and does not write anything.

If she had married that guy, would she have had the child?

Nicholas pushes away the papers, which suddenly feel heavy enough to threaten the balance of the desk. He leans his head back in the swivel chair and stares at the clouds manufactured by the hospital smokestacks, but all he sees are the lines of Paige's wounded face. He blinks, but the image does not clear. He half expects that if he whispers her name, she will answer. He thinks he must be going crazy.

He wonders if she loved this other guy, and why the question, still unspoken, makes him feel as if he will be sick.

≈≈≈

When he turns the chair around, his mother is standing in front of the desk. "Nicholas," she says, "I've brought you a present." She holds a large, flat, paper-wrapped square. Even before he pulls at the string, Nicholas knows it is a framed photograph. "It's for your office," she says. "I've been working on it for weeks."

"It isn't my office," Nicholas says. "I can't really hang anything up." But even as he is speaking, he finds himself staring at the photograph. It is a pliant willow tree on the shore of a lake, bent into an inverted U by an angry wind. Everything in the background is one shade or another of purple; the tree itself is molten red, as if it is burning at the core.

Astrid comes to his side of the desk and stands at his shoulder. "Striking, isn't it?" she says. "It's all in the lighting." She glances at the papers on Nicholas's desk, pretending not to notice what they say.

Nicholas runs his fingers across his mother's signature, carved at the bottom. "Very nice," he says. "Thanks."

Astrid sits on the edge of the desk. "I didn't come just to give you the photograph, Nicholas; I'm here to tell you something you aren't going to like," she says. "Paige has moved in with us."

Nicholas stares at her as if she has stated that his father was really a gypsy or that his medical diploma is a fraud. "You've got to be kidding," he says. "You can't do this to me."

"As a matter of fact, Nicholas," Astrid says, standing and pacing the room, "you have very little say as to what we do in our own house. Paige is a lovely girl—better to realize it late than never, I think—and she's a charming guest. Imelda says she even makes her own bed. Imagine."

Nicholas's fingers itch; he has a savage urge to strike out or to strangle. "If she lays a hand on Max—"

"I've already taken care of it," Astrid says. "She's agreed to leave the house during the day while I've got Max. She only comes back to sleep, since a car or a front lawn isn't really suitable."

Nicholas thinks that maybe he will remember this moment forever: the wrinkled empty smile of his mother; the flickering track light overhead; the scrape of wheels as something is rolled by the door. *This*, he will say to himself in years to come, *was the moment my life fell apart*. "Paige isn't what you think she is," he says bitterly.

Astrid walks to the far side of the office as if she hasn't heard him. She removes a yellowed nautical map from the wall, smoothing her fingers over the glass and tracing the whorls of eddies and currents. "I'm thinking about right here," she says. "You'll see it every time you look up." She crosses the room to put the old frame on the desk and picks up the picture of the willow. "You know," she says casually, reaching up on her toes to hang the picture correctly, "your father and I almost got a divorce. I think you remember her—she was a hematologist. I knew about it, and I fought him every step of the way, trying to be very difficult and spilling drinks on him to make a scene and threatening once or twice to run away with you. I thought that being quiet about the whole thing was the biggest mistake I could make, because then he'd think I was weak and he could walk all over me. And then one day I realized that I would have much more power if I decided to be the one to yield." Astrid straightens the picture and steps back. "There. What do you think?"

Nicholas's eyes are slitted, dark and angry. "I want you to throw Paige out of the house, and if she comes within a hundred feet of Max, I swear to God I'll have you brought up on charges. I want you to get out of my office and call me later and apologize profusely for butting into my life. I want you to put back that goddamned ocean map and leave me alone."

"Really, Nicholas," Astrid says lightly, although every muscle in her body is quivering. She has never seen him like this. "The way you're acting, I wouldn't recognize you as my son." She picks up the sailing chart and hooks it on the wall again, but she does not turn around.

"You don't know the half of it," Nicholas murmurs.

≈≈≈

By a twist of bad timing, Nicholas and Paige run into each other that afternoon at the Prescotts'. Because of a complication with a patient, Nicholas left the hospital late. He is just packing Max's toys into the duffel bag when Paige bursts into the parlor. "You can't do this to me," Paige cries, and when Nicholas lifts his head, his gaze has carefully been wiped clean of emotion.

"Ah," Nicholas says, picking up a Big Bird jingle ball. "My mother has been the bearer of bad news."

"You've got to give me a chance," she says, moving in front of him to catch his eye. "You aren't thinking clearly."

Astrid appears in the doorway, with Max in her arms. "Listen to her, Nicholas," she says quietly.

Nicholas tosses his mother a look that makes Paige remember the basilisk in Irish legend, the monster who killed with a glance. "I think I've listened enough," he says. "In fact, I've heard things I never wanted to hear." He stands and slings the diaper bag over his shoulder, roughly grabbing Max out of Astrid's arms. "Why don't you just run upstairs to your guest bedroom," he sneers. "Cry your little heart out, and then you can come downstairs for brandy with *my* goddamned parents."

"Nicholas," Paige says. Her voice breaks over the syllables. She takes a quick look at Astrid and runs through the hall after Nicholas, swinging open the door and yelling his name again into the street.

Nicholas stops just before his car. "You'll get a good settlement," he says quietly. "You've earned it."

Paige is openly crying now, clinging to the frame of the door as if she cannot keep upright by herself. "It isn't supposed to be this way," she sobs. "Do you think I really care about the money? Or about who lives in that stupid old house?"

Nicholas thinks about the horror stories he's heard from other surgeons, whose cutthroat, red-taloned wives have robbed them of half their Midas earnings and all their sterling reputations. He cannot picture Paige in a tailored suit, glaring from the witness stand, replaying a testimony that will support her for life. He can't truly see her caring about whether $500,000 per year will be enough to cover her cost of living. She'd probably hand him the keys to the house if he asked nicely. In truth, she isn't like the others; she never has been, and that's what Nicholas always liked.

Her hair has fallen over her face, and her nose is running; her shoulders are shaking with the effort to stop crying. She is a mess. "Mama," Max says, reaching out to her. Nicholas turns him away and watches Paige swipe the back of her hand across her eyes. He tells himself it can't turn out any other way, not with what he knows now; but he quite literally feels his chest burn, swollen tissue irreparably staked, as his heart begins to break.

Nicholas grimaces and shakes his head. He slips inside the car, fastening Max into his seat and then turning the ignition. He tries to trace the sequence, but he cannot figure out how they have made it to this point—the place where you cannot go back. Paige hasn't moved an inch. He cannot hear her voice over the purr of the engine, but he knows that she is telling him she loves him, she loves Max.

"I can't help that," he says, and he drives away without letting himself look back.

chapter 37
Paige

When I come down to breakfast in the morning, I am carrying my overnight bag. "I want to thank you for your hospitality," I say stiffly, "but I think I'm going to be leaving today."

Astrid and Robert look at each other, and it is Astrid who speaks first. "Where are you going?" she asks.

This question, the one I have been expecting, still throws me for a loop. "I don't know," I say. "I guess back to my mother's."

"Paige," Astrid says gently, "if Nicholas wants a divorce, he'll find you even in North Carolina."

When I do not say anything, Astrid stands up and folds her arms around me. She holds me even though I do not hold her back. She is thinner than I expected, almost brittle. "I can't change your mind?" she says.

"No," I murmur, "you can't."

She pulls away, keeping me at arm's length. "I won't let you leave without something to eat," she says, already moving toward the kitchen. "Imelda!"

She leaves me alone with Robert, who of all the people in this household makes me most uncomfortable. It isn't that he's been rude or even unkind; he has offered his house to me, he goes out of his way to compliment my appearance when I come down to dinner, he saves me the Living section of the *Globe* before Imelda clips the recipes. I suppose the problem is mine, not his. I suppose some things —like forgiveness—take time.

Robert folds his morning paper and motions for me to sit next to him. "What was the name of that colicky horse?" he says out of nowhere.

"Donegal." I smooth my napkin across my lap. "But he's fine now. Or he was when I left."

Robert nods. "Mmm. Incredible how they bounce back."

I raise my eyebrows, now understanding where this conversation is headed. "Sometimes they die," I point out.

"Well, yes, of course," Robert says, spreading cream cheese on a muffin. "But not the good ones. Never the good ones."

"You *hope* not," I say.

Robert jabs the muffin toward me, making his point. "Exactly." Suddenly he reaches across the table and covers my wrist with his free hand. His touch, unexpected, is cool and steady, just like Nicholas's. "You're making it very easy for him to forget about you, Paige. I'd think twice about that."

At that moment Nicholas strides into the dining room, carrying Max. "Where the hell is everybody?" he says. "I'm late."

He slips Max into the high chair beside Robert and makes a point of not looking at me. Astrid walks in with a tray of toast and fruit and bagels. "Nicholas!" she says, as if last night never happened. "You'll stay for breakfast?"

Nicholas glares at me. "You already have company," he says.

I stand up and watch Max bang the edge of Robert's plate with a sterling-silver spoon. Max has Nicholas's aristocratic face but most definitely my eyes. You can see it in his restlessness. He's always looking at the one place he cannot see. You can tell he will be a fighter.

Max sees me and smiles, and it makes his whole body glow. "I was just going," I say. With a quick look at Robert, I walk out the door, leaving my overnight bag behind.

≈≈≈

The volunteer lounge at Mass General is little more than a closet, tucked behind the ambulatory care waiting rooms. While I am waiting for Harriet Miles, the secretary, to find me an application form, I stare over her shoulder at the hall and wait to catch a glimpse of Nicholas.

I do not want to do this, but I see no other choice. If I'm going to make Nicholas change his mind about a divorce, I have to show him what he'll be missing. I can't do that when the only way I see him is by chance or in passing at his parents', so I'll have to spend all my time where he does—at the hospital. Unfortunately, I'm not qualified for most of the positions that would throw me together with him, so I try to convince myself that I've wanted to volunteer at the hospital all along but haven't had the time. Still, I know this isn't true. I hate the sight of blood; I don't like that antiseptic cloud of illness that you always smell in a hospital's halls. I wouldn't be here if I could think of any other way to cross Nicholas's path several times a day.

Harriet Miles is about four feet ten inches tall and almost as wide. She has to step on a little stool, fashioned in the shape of a strawberry, to reach the top drawer of the filing cabinet. "We don't have as many adult volunteers as we'd like," she says. "Most of the kids rotate through for a year or so just to beef up their college applications." She closes her eyes and stuffs her hand into a stack of papers and comes up with the right one. "Ah," she says, "success."

She settles back on her chair, which I could swear has a booster seat on it, but I am too embarrassed to lean over and check. "Now, Paige, have you had any medical training or been a volunteer at another hospital?"

"No," I say, hoping this won't keep them from accepting me.

"That's not a problem," Harriet says smoothly. "You'll attend one of our orientation sessions, and you can start working right after that—"

"No," I stammer. "I have to start *today.*" When Harriet stares at me, unnerved, I settle into the chair and clench my hands at my sides. *Careful,* I think. *Say what she wants to hear.* "I mean, I really *want* to start today. I'll do anything. It doesn't have to involve medical stuff."

Harriet licks the tip of her pencil and begins to fill in my application form. She doesn't blink when I give my last name, but then again, I suppose there are a lot of Prescotts in Boston. I give Robert and Astrid's address instead of my own, and just for kicks I fake my birth date, making myself three years older. I tell her I can work six days a week, and she looks at me as if I am a saint.

"I can put you in admitting," she says, frowning at a schedule on the wall. "You won't be able to do paperwork, but you can shuttle the patients up to their rooms in wheelchairs." She taps the pencil on the blotter. "Or you can work the book cart," she suggests, "on the patient floors."

Neither of which, I realize, will place me where I need to go. "I have a request," I say. "I'd like to be near Dr. Prescott, the cardiac surgeon."

Harriet laughs and pats my hand. "Yes, he's a favorite, isn't he? Those eyes! I think he's the reason for half the graffiti in the candy stripers' bathroom. Everyone wants to be near Dr. Prescott."

"You don't understand," I say. "He's my husband."

Harriet scans the application sheet and points to my last name. "So he is," she says.

I lick my lips and lean forward. I offer a quick, silent prayer that in this war between Nicholas and myself, no one else will be hurt. Then I smile and lie as I never have before. "You know, his hours are pretty awful. We never get a chance to see each other." I wink at Harriet conspiratorially. "I thought I'd do this as a kind of anniversary present. Try to be near him and all. I figured if I could get assigned close to him every day, kind of be his personal volunteer, he'd be happier, and then he'd be a better surgeon, and then everyone would win."

"What a romantic idea." Harriet sighs. "Wouldn't it be wonderful if all the other doctors' wives came in as volunteers?"

I give her a steady, sober look. I have never been on a conversational basis with those women, but if that is my penance I will swear to carry it out on penalty of death. Today I'd promise Harriet Miles the moon. "I'll do everything I can," I say.

Even as she smiles at me, Harriet Miles's eyes are melting. "I wish *I* was crazy in love," she says, and she picks up the telephone to dial an inside number. "Let's see what we can do."

≈≈≈

Astrid finds me sitting in the backyard under a peach tree, drawing. "What is it?" she asks, and I tell her I don't know. Right now it is just a collection of lines and curves; it will eventually form into something I recognize. I'm drawing because it is therapeutic. Nicholas almost didn't notice me today—even after I had helped wheel the stretcher with his recovering patient from surgical ICU to a semiprivate room, followed him with the book cart as he made his rounds, and stood behind him in the lunch line at the cafeteria. When he did finally recognize me as I refilled a water pitcher in the room of the patient he'd be operating on tomorrow, it was only because he had knocked against me and spilled water all over the front of my pale-pink volunteer pinafore. "I'm so sorry," he said, glancing at the stains on my lap and my chest. Then he looked at my face. Terrified, I didn't say a word. And although I expected Nicholas to storm out of the room and call for the chief of staff, he only raised his eyebrows and laughed.

"Sometimes I just draw," I say to Astrid, hoping that's enough of an explanation.

"Sometimes I just shoot," she says. I look up, startled. "A *camera*," she adds. She leans against the trunk of a tree and turns her face to the sun. I take in the firm set of her chin, the silver sweep of hair, the courage that hovers about her like expensive perfume. I wonder if there is anything in the world that Astrid Prescott would not be able to do if she set her mind to it.

"It would have been nice to have an artist in the family earlier," she says. "I always felt honor bound to pass along my talents." She laughs. "The photographic ones, anyway." She opens her eyes and smiles at me. "Nicholas was a nightmare with a camera. He never got the hang of f-stops, and he routinely overexposed his prints. He had the skill for photography, but he never had the patience."

"My mother was an artist," I blurt out, and then I freeze, my hand paused inches above my sketch pad. My first volunteered personal admission. Astrid moves closer to me, knowing that this unexpected chink in my armor is the first step toward getting inside. "She was a good artist," I say as carelessly as I can manage, thinking of the mural of horses in Chicago and then in Carolina. "But she fancied herself a writer instead."

I start to move my pencil restlessly over a fresh page, and not daring to meet Astrid's eyes, I tell her the truth. The words come fresh as a new wound, and once again I can clearly smell the Magic Markers in my tiny hand; feel my mother's fingers close around my ankles for balance on the stool. I can sense my mother's body pressed beside mine as we watch our unfettered stallions; I can remember the freedom of assuming—just *knowing*—that she would be there the next day, and the next.

"I wish my mother had been around to teach me how to draw," I say, and then I fall silent. My pencil has stopped flying over the page, and as I stare at it, Astrid's hand comes to cover mine where it lies. Even as I am wondering what has made me say these things to her, I hear myself speak again. "Nicholas was lucky," I say. "I wish I'd had someone like you around when I was growing up."

"Nicholas was doubly lucky, then." Astrid shifts closer to me on the grass and slips her arms around my shoulders. It feels awkward —not like my mother's embrace, which I fit into so neatly by the summer's end. Still, before I can stop myself, I lean toward Astrid. She sighs against my hair. "She didn't have a choice, you know." I close my eyes and shrug, but Astrid will not leave it be. "She's no different from me," Astrid says, and then she hesitates. "Or you."

Instinctively I pull away, putting the reason of distance between us. I open my mouth to disagree, but something stops me. *Astrid, my mother, myself.* I picture, like a collage, the grinning rows of white frames on Astrid's contact sheets; the dark press of hoofprints in my mother's fields; the line of men's shirts I'd flung from the car on the day I had to leave. The things we did, we did because we *had* to. The things we did, we did because we had a *right* to. Still, we each left markers of some kind—a public trail that either led others to us or became, one day, the road upon which we returned.

I exhale slowly. God, I'm more relaxed than I've been in days. To win over Nicholas, I may be fighting a force that is greater than myself, but I'm beginning to see that I'm *part* of a force that is greater than myself. Maybe I do have a chance after all.

I smile at Astrid and pick up the pencil again, quickly fashioning on paper the naked knot of branches that hangs above Astrid's head. She peers at the pad, then up at the tree, and then she nods. "Can you do me?" she asks, settling herself back in a pose.

I rip the top sheet off my pad and start to draw the slopes of Astrid's face, the gray strands laced with the gold in her hair. With her bearing and her expression, she should have been a queen.

The shadows of the peach tree color her face with a strange scroll-work that reminds me of the insides of confessionals at Saint Christopher's. The leaves that are starting to fall dance across my pad. When I am finished, I pretend that my pencil is still moving just so I can see what I have really drawn, before Astrid has a chance to look.

In each leaf-patterned shadow of her face, I have drawn a different woman. One looks to be African, with a thick turban wrapped around her head and gold hoops slicing her ears. One has the bottomless eyes and the black roped hair of a Spanish *puta*. One is a bedraggled girl, no older than twelve, who holds her hands against her swollen, pregnant belly. One is my mother; one is myself.

"Remarkable," Astrid says, lightly touching each image. "I can see why Nicholas was impressed." She cocks her head. "Can you draw from memory?" I nod. "Then do one of yourself."

I have done self-portraits before but never on command. I do not know if I can do it, and I tell her this. "You never know until you try," Astrid chides, and I dutifully turn to a blank page. I start with the base of my neck, working my way up the lines of my chin and my jaw. I stop for a second and see it is all wrong. I tear it off and turn to the next page, start at the hairline, working down. Again, I have to begin all over. I do this seven times, making each drawing a little more complete than the last. Finally, I put the pencil down and press my fingers against my eyes. "Some other time," I say.

But Astrid is leafing through the discarded drawings I've ripped off the pad. "You've done better than you think," she says, holding them out to me. "Look." I riffle through the papers, shocked that I didn't see this before. On every one, even the pictures made of threadbare lines, instead of myself I have drawn Nicholas.

chapter **38**

Paige

For the past three days Nicholas has been the talk of the hospital, and it's all because of me. In the morning when he arrives, I help ready his patient for surgery. Then I sit on the floor in front of his office in my pale pinafore and draw the portrait of the person he is operating upon. They are simple sketches that take only minutes. Each shows the patient far away from a hospital, in the prime of his or her life. I have drawn Mrs. Comazzi as a dance hall girl, which she was in the forties; I have drawn Mr. Goldberg as a dapper pin-striped gangster; I have drawn Mr. Allen as Ben-Hur, robust and perched on his chariot. I leave them taped to the door of the office, usually with a second picture, of Nicholas himself.

At first I drew Nicholas as he was at the hospital, on the telephone or signing a release form or leading a gaggle of residents into a patient's room. But then I started to draw Nicholas the way I wanted to remember him: singing "Sweet Baby James" over Max's bassinet, teaching me how to pitch a Wiffle ball, kissing me on the swan boat in front of everyone. Every morning at about eleven, Nicholas does the same thing. He comes back to his office, curses at the door, and rips both pictures off. He stuffs the one of himself in the trash can or his upper desk drawer, but he usually takes the one I've done of the patient and brings that during the postoperative checkup. I was offering magazines to Mrs. Comazzi when he gave the picture to her. "Oh, my stars," she exclaimed. "Look at me. Look at *me!*" And Nicholas, in spite of himself, smiled.

Rumors spread fast through Mass General, and everyone knows who I am and when I leave the drawings. At ten-forty, before Nicholas arrives, a crowd starts to gather. The nurses drift upstairs on their coffee break to see if they can figure out the likeness and to make cracks about the Dr. Prescott I tend to draw, the one they never see. "Jeez," I heard one profusionist say, "I wouldn't have guessed he even owned casual clothes."

I hear Nicholas's footsteps coming down the hall, quick and clipped. He is still wearing his scrubs, which might mean something has gone wrong. I start to scoot out of his way, but I am stopped by an unfamiliar voice. "Nicholas," the man says.

Nicholas stops, his hand on the doorknob. "Elliot," he says, more a sigh than a word. "Look," he says, "it's been a pretty bad morning. Maybe we can talk later."

Elliot shakes his head and holds up a hand. "Didn't come here to see you. I came to see what the fuss is with the artwork. Your door is becoming the hospital gallery." He looks down at me and beams. "Scuttlebutt has it that the phantom artist here is your wife."

Nicholas pulls the blue paper cap off his head and leans back against the door, closing his eyes. "Paige, Elliot Saget. Elliot, Paige. My wife." He exhales slowly. "For now."

If memory serves me right, Elliot Saget is the chief of surgery. I stand quickly and offer my hand. "A pleasure," I say, smiling.

Elliot pushes Nicholas out of the way and stares at the picture I've done of Mr. Olsen, Nicholas's morning surgery. Next to him is the image of Nicholas singing karaoke at an Allston bowling alley, something that to my knowledge he has never tried but that probably would do him good. "Quite a talent," he says, looking from the picture to Nicholas and back again. "Why, Nicholas, she almost makes you seem as human as the rest of us."

Nicholas mutters something under his breath and turns the key in the doorknob. "Paige," Elliot Saget says to me, "the hospital's communications director would like very much to talk to you about your artwork. Her name is Nancy Bianna, and she asked me to tell you to stop by when you aren't busy." He smiles then, and I know immediately that I can trust him if need be. "Nicholas," he says into the open doorway. He nods and then he lopes away down the hall.

Nicholas bends over, trying to touch his fingers to his toes. It helps his back; I've seen him do it before, after a very long day on his feet. When he looks up and sees that I am still here, he grimaces. He crosses to the door and rips off the two pictures I've drawn, crumples them into a ball, and tosses them into the garbage.

"You don't have to do that," I say, angry. The pictures—however simple they are—are my work. I hate watching my work be destroyed. "If you don't want yours, well, fine. But maybe Mr. Olsen would like to see his portrait."

Nicholas's eyes darken, and his fingers tighten on the doorknob. "This isn't a garden party, Paige. Mr. Olsen died twenty minutes ago on the operating table. Maybe *now*," he says quietly, "you can leave me alone."

≈≈≈

It takes me forty minutes to get back to the Prescotts', and when I do I am still shaking. I pull off my jacket and sag against a highboy, which jabs into my ribs. Wincing, I move away and stare at myself in an antique mirror. For the past week, no matter where I am, I've been uncomfortable. And deep down I know this has nothing to do with the sharp edges of the furniture, or with any other piece of decor. It's just that the cool hospital and the elegant Prescott mansion are not places where I feel at home.

Nicholas is right. I don't understand his life. I don't know the things that everyone else takes for granted, like how to read a doctor's mood after surgery, or which side to lean to when Imelda takes the dishes away. I'm killing myself to be part of a world where I'm always two steps behind.

A door opens, and classical music floods the hallway. Robert holds Max, letting him chew on the plastic CD case. I give my best smile, but I am still shivering. My father-in-law steps forward and narrows his eyes. "What's happened to you?" he asks.

The whole day, this past month, all of it crowds and chokes in my throat. The last person in the world I want to break down in front of is Robert Prescott, but still, I start to cry. "Nicholas," I sob.

Robert frowns. "Never did learn to pick on someone his own size," he says. He takes my elbow and guides me into his study, a dark room that makes me think of fox hunts and stiff British lords. "Sit down and unwind," he says. He settles into a huge leather chair and sets Max on the top of his desk to play with brass paperweights.

I lean back against the burgundy couch and obediently close my eyes, but I feel too conspicuously out of place to unwind. A crystal brandy decanter rests on a mahogany table beneath the frozen smile of a mounted buck. A set of dueling pistols, just for show, are crossed above the arch of the door. This room—dear God, this whole *house* —is like something straight out of a novel.

Real people do not live like this, surrounded by thousands of volumes of books and ancient paintings of pale women and thick silver varsity mugs. Real people do not take tea as seriously as if it were Communion. Real people do not make five-figure donations to the Republican party—

"Do you like Handel?"

At the sound of Robert's voice, my eyes fly open and every muscle in my body goes on the alert. I stare at him carefully, wondering if this is a test, a trap set for me so I'll slip up and show how little I understand. "I don't know," I say bitterly. "*Should* I?" I wait to see his eyes flare, or his mouth tighten, and when it doesn't, the fight goes out of me. *It's your own fault, Paige,* I think. *He's only trying to be nice.* "I'm sorry," I say. "I haven't had a very good day. I didn't mean to snap at you. It's just that when I was growing up, the only antique we had was my father's family Bible, and the music we listened to had words." I smile hesitantly. "This kind of life takes a little getting used to, although you couldn't really understand that—"

I break off, recalling what Nicholas told me years ago about his father, what I'd forgotten when I'd seen Robert, and all his trappings, again. Something flickers across his eyes—regret, or maybe relief— but just as quickly, it disappears. I stare at him, fascinated. I wonder how he could have come from my kind of background but still know, so easily, the right way to move and to act in a house like this.

"So Nicholas told you," Robert says, and he doesn't sound disappointed or furious; it's simply a statement of fact.

Suddenly I remember what had tugged at the corner of my mind when Nicholas said his father had grown up poor. Robert Prescott was the one who had objected to Nicholas's marrying me. Not Astrid—which I could understand—but Robert. *He* had been the one to drive Nicholas away. *He* had been the one who said Nicholas would be ruining his life.

I tell myself I'm not angry anymore, just curious. But I pick Max up anyway, taking him away from my father-in-law. "How *could* you?" I whisper.

Robert leans forward, resting his elbows on the desk. "I worked so hard for this. All of this." He gestures, sweeping his hands in the directions of the four walls. "I could never stand the thought of someone throwing it all away. Not Astrid, and especially not Nicholas."

Max squirms, and I set him down on the floor. "Nicholas didn't have to throw it all away," I point out. "You could have paid for his education."

Robert shakes his head. "It wouldn't have been the same. Eventually you'd have held him back. You could never move in these circles, Paige. You wouldn't be comfortable living like this."

It isn't the truth that stings; it is hearing Robert Prescott, once again, decide what is best for me. I curl my hands into fists. "How the hell can you be so sure?"

"Because *I'm* not," he says quietly. Shocked, I sink back into the couch. I stare at Robert's cashmere sweater, his neat white hair, the pride gracing his jaw. But I also notice that his hands are clenched tight together and that a pulse beats fast at the base of his neck. *He's terrified,* I think. *He's as scared of me as I've been of him.*

I think about this for a moment, and about why he is telling *me* something it obviously hurts him to discuss. I remember something my mother said in North Carolina when I asked her why she had never come back. "You make your own bed," she told me. "You have to lie in it."

I smile gently and sweep Max off the floor. I hand him to his grandfather. "I'll change for dinner," I say, and I start toward the hall.

Robert's voice stops me. His words trip over Handel's sweet violins and reaching flutes. "It's worth it," he says quietly. "I would do it all over again."

I do not turn around. "Why?"

"Why would *you?*" he says, and his question follows me up the stairs and slips into the cool quiet of my room. It demands an answer, and it knocks me off center.

Nicholas.

≈≈≈

Sometimes I sing Max to sleep. It doesn't seem to matter what I sing—gospel or pop, Dire Straits or the Beatles. I usually skip the lullabies, because I figure Max will hear those from everyone else.

We sit on the rocking chair in his room at the Prescotts'. Astrid lets me hold him whenever I want to now, as long as Nicholas isn't around and isn't about to show up. It's her way of getting me to stay, I think, although I don't consider leaving a real option anymore.

Max has just had his bath. The easiest way to give it, because he's so slippery in the bathtub, is just to get naked with him and set him between my legs. He has a Tupperware bowl and a rubber duck that he plays with in the water. He doesn't mind when I get baby shampoo in his eyes. Afterward I wrap him in the towel with me, pretending we share the same skin, and I think of wallabees and opossums and other animals that always carry around their young.

Max is getting very sleepy, rubbing his eyes with his little fists and yawning often. "Hang on a second," I say, sitting him up on the floor. I lean down and pop a pacifier into his mouth.

He watches me as I straighten his crib. I smooth the sheet and move the Cookie Monster and the rabbit rattle out of the way. When I turn around fast, he smiles, as if this is a game, and he loses his pacifier in the process. "You can't suck and smile at the same time," I tell him. I turn around to plug in the night-light, and when I face Max again he laughs. He holds up his arms to me, asking to be held.

Suddenly I realize that this is what I've been waiting for—a man who depends entirely on me. When I met Jake, I spent years trying to make him fall in love with me. When I married Nicholas, I lost him to the mistress of medicine. I dreamed for years of a man who couldn't live without me, a man who pictured my face when he closed his eyes, who loved me when I was a mess in the morning and when dinner was late and even when I overloaded the washing machine and burned out the motor.

Max stares up at me as if I can do no wrong. I have always wanted someone who treats me the way he does; I just didn't know that I'd have to give birth to him. I pick Max up, and immediately he wraps his arms around my neck and starts crawling up my body. This is the way he hugs; it is something he's just learned. I can't help but smile into the soft folds of his neck. *Be careful what you wish for,* I think. *It might come true.*

≈≈≈

Nancy Bianna stands in the long main founders' hallway, her finger pressed against her pursed lips. "Something," she murmurs. "I'm missing something." She swings her head back and forth, and her hair, blunt cut, moves like an Egyptian's.

Nancy has been the primary reason that my sketches of Nicholas's patients and some new ones, of Elliot Saget and Nancy and even Astrid and Max, now hang framed in the entrance to the hospital. Previously a row of unimaginative prints, imitations of Matisse, hung against the cinder-block walls. But Nancy says this will be the start of something big. "Who knew Dr. Prescott was so well connected?" she mused to me. "First you, and then maybe an exhibit by his mother."

That first day I met her, after I had left Nicholas in his office, she shook my hand vigorously and slid her thick black-rimmed glasses up her nose. "What patients want to see when they check into a hospital," she explained, "isn't a line of meaningless color. They want to see *people*." She leaned forward and gripped my shoulders. "They want to see *survivors*. They want to see *life*."

Then she stood up and walked casually in a circle around me. "Of course we understand you'd have the final say on placement and inclusion," she added, "and we'd compensate you for your work."

Money. They were going to give me money for the silly little pictures I drew to get Nicholas to notice me. My sketches were going to hang on the walls at Mass General, so that even when I wasn't around Nicholas, he couldn't help but be reminded.

I smiled at Nancy. "When can we start?"

Three days later, the exhibit is being set up. Nancy paces the hallway and switches a portrait of Mr. Kasselbaum with one of Max. "The juxtaposition of youth and age," she says. "Autumn and spring. I love it."

At the far end of the exhibit, near the admissions desk, is a small white card with my name printed on it. PAIGE PRESCOTT, it reads, VOLUNTEER. There is no biography, nothing at all about Nicholas or Max, and this is sort of nice. It makes me feel as though I have just appeared out of nowhere and stepped into the limelight; as if I have never had a history at all.

"Okay, okay . . . places," Nancy calls, grasping my hand. There are only two other people in the hall, custodians with ladders and wire-cutters, and neither of them speaks very good English. I don't really know who Nancy is talking to. She pulls me to the side and draws in her breath. "Ta-da!" she trills, although nothing has changed from a moment before.

"It's lovely," I say, because I know she is waiting.

Nancy beams at me. "Stop by tomorrow," she says. "We're thinking of changing our stationery, and if you're any good at lettering . . ." She lets her sentence trail off, speaking for itself.

When she disappears into an elevator, taking the workmen and the ladders with her, I stand in the hallway and survey my own work. It is the first time I have ever seen my skills on formal display. I am good. A sweet rush of success bubbles inside me, and I walk down the hall, touching each individual picture. I take away a shot of pride from each one and leave in its place the promise-marker of my fingerprints.

≈≈≈

One night when the house is as dark as a forest I go to the library to call my mother. I pass Astrid and Robert's room on the way and I hear the sound of lovemaking, and for some reason instead of being embarrassed I am frightened. When I reach the library, I settle in the big wing chair Robert likes best and I hold the heavy phone in my hands like a trophy.

"I forgot to tell you something," I say when my mother answers the phone. "We named the baby after you."

I hear my mother draw in her breath. "So you're speaking to me after all." She pauses, and then she asks me where I am.

"I'm staying with Nicholas's parents," I say. "You were right about coming back."

"I wish I didn't have to be," my mother says.

I didn't really want to call my mother, but I couldn't help it. In spite of myself, now that I had found her I needed her. I wanted to tell her about Nicholas. I wanted to cry about the divorce. I wanted her suggestions, her opinion.

"I'm sorry you left like that," she says.

"Don't be sorry." I want to tell her that no one is at fault. I think about the way the clean air in North Carolina would thrill to the back of my throat with the first breath of the morning. "I had a very nice time."

"For God's sake, Paige," she says, "that's the kind of thing you'd tell some Daughter of the American Revolution after a luncheon."

I rub my eyes. "Okay," I say, "I *didn't* have a very nice time." But I'm lying, and she knows it as well as I do. I picture the two of us, bracing Donegal when he could barely stand. I picture my arms around my mother's shoulders when she cried at night. "I miss you," I say, and instead of feeling sort of empty as the words leave my mouth, I start to smile. Imagine me saying that to my own mother after all these years, and meaning it, and no matter what I expected, the world hasn't shattered at my feet.

"I don't blame you for leaving," my mother says. "I know you'll be back."

"How do you know that?" I say sulkily, a little upset that she can pin me down so easily.

"Because," my mother says, "that's what's keeping me going."

I tighten my grip on the arm of Robert's chair. "Maybe I'm wasting my time," I say. "Maybe I should just come back now."

It would be so easy to be someplace where I am wanted, anyplace but here. I pause, waiting for her to take me up on the offer. But instead my mother laughs softly. "Do you know that your first word," she says, "even before *Mama* and *Dada,* was *goodbye?*"

She's right. It isn't going to do me any good to just keep running. I sink back against the chair and close my eyes, trying to picture the hairpin stream I jumped with Donegal, the ribbons of clouds lacing the sky. "Tell me what I'm missing," I say. I listen to my mother speak of Aurora and Jean-Claude, of the sun-bleached paint on the chipped wall of the barn, of a brisk seasonal change that creeps farther up the porch every night. After a while I don't bother to concentrate on her actual words. I let the sound of her voice wash over me, making itself familiar.

Then I hear her say, "I called your father, you know."

But I haven't spoken to my father since I've been back, so of course I could not have known. I am certain I've heard her wrong. "You *what?*" I say.

"I called your father. We had a good talk. I never would have called, but you sort of encouraged me. By leaving, I mean." There is silence for a moment. "Who knows," she murmurs. "Maybe one day I'll even see him."

I look around at the mutated, hunkering shapes of chairs and end tables in the dark library. I rub my hands over my shoulders. I am beginning to feel hope. Maybe, after twenty years, this is what my mother and I can do for each other. It is not the way other mothers and daughters are—we will not talk about seventh-grade boys, or French-braid my hair on a rainy Sunday; my mother will not have the chance to heal my cuts and bruises with a kiss. We cannot go back, but we can keep surprising each other, and I suppose this is better than nothing at all.

Suddenly I really believe that if I stick it out long enough, Nicholas will understand. It's just a matter of time, and I have a lot of that on my hands. "I'm a volunteer at the hospital now," I tell my mother proudly. "I work wherever Nicholas works. I'm closer than his shadow."

My mother pauses, as if she is considering this. "Stranger things have happened," she says.

≈≈≈

Max wakes up screaming, his legs bent close to his chest. When I rub his stomach, it only makes him scream harder. I think that maybe he needs to burp, but that doesn't seem to be the problem. Finally, I walk around with him perched on my shoulder, pressing his belly flush against me. "What's wrong?" Astrid says, her head at the nursery doorway.

"I don't know," I say, and to my surprise, uttering those words doesn't throw me into a panic. Somehow I know I will figure it out. "It might be gas."

Max squeezes up his face and turns red, the way he does when he's trying to go to the bathroom. "Ah," I say. "Are you leaving me a present?" I wait until he looks as if he's finished, and then I pull down his sweatpants to change his diaper. There is nothing inside, nothing at all. "You fooled me," I say, and he smiles.

I rediaper him and sit him on the floor with a Busy Box, rolling and turning the knobs until he catches on and follows. From time to time he screws up his face again. He seems to be constipated. "Maybe we'll have prunes for breakfast," I say. "That ought to make you feel better."

Max plays quietly with me for a few minutes, and then I notice that he isn't really paying attention. He's staring off into space, and the curiosity that flames the blue in his eyes seems to have dulled. He sways a little, as if he's going to fall. I frown, tickle him, and wait for him to respond. It takes a second or two longer than usual, but eventually he comes back to me.

He's not himself, I think, although I cannot put my finger on what the problem really is. I figure I will watch him closely. I tenderly rub his chunky forearms, feeling a satisfied flutter in my chest. *I know my own son,* I think proudly. *I know him well enough to catch the subtle changes.*

≈≈≈

"I'm sorry I haven't called," I tell my father. "Things have been a little crazy."

My father laughs. "I had thirteen years with you, lass. I think your mother deserves three months."

I had written my father postcards from North Carolina, just as I had written Max. I'd told him about Donegal, about the rye rolling over the hills. I told him everything I could on a three-and-a-half-by-five-and-a-half-inch card, without mentioning my mother.

"Rumor has it," my father says, "you've been sleepin' with the enemy." I jump, thinking he means Nicholas, and then I realize he is talking about living at the Prescotts'.

I glance at the Fabergé egg on the mantel, the Civil War Sharps carbine rifle hanging over the fireplace. "Necessity makes strange bedfellows," I say.

I wind the telephone cord around my ankles, trying to find a safe route for conversation. But there is little I *have* to say, and so much I *want* to. I take a deep breath. "Speaking of rumors," I say, "I hear Mom called."

"Aye."

My mouth drops open. "That's it? 'Aye'? Twenty-one years go by, and that's all you have to say?"

"I was expectin' it," my father says. "I figured if you had the fortune to find her, sooner or later she'd return the favor."

"The *favor?*" I shake my head. "I thought you wanted nothing to do with her. I thought you said it was too late."

For a moment my father is silent. "Paige," he says finally, "how did you find her to be?"

I close my eyes and sink back on the leather couch. I want to choose my words very carefully. I imagine my mother the way she would have wanted me to: seated on Donegal, galloping him across a field faster than a lie can spread. "She wasn't what I expected," I say proudly.

My father laughs. "May never was."

"She thinks she's going to see you someday," I add.

"Does she now," my father answers, but his thoughts seem very far away. I wonder if he is seeing her the way he did the first time he met her, dressed in her halter top and carrying her practice suitcase. I wonder if he can remember the tremor in his voice when he asked her to marry him, or the flash across her eyes as she said yes, or even the ache in his throat when he knew she was gone from his life.

It may be my imagination, but for the breadth of a moment everything in the room seems to sharpen in focus. The contrasting colors in the Oriental carpet become more striking; the towering windows reflect a devil's glare. It makes me question if, all this time, I haven't really been seeing clearly.

"Dad," I whisper, "I want to go back."

"God help me, Paige," my father says. "Don't I know it."

≈≈≈

Elliot Saget is pleased with my gallery at Mass General. He is so convinced that it is going to win some kind of humanitarian Best of Boston award that he promises me the stars on a silver platter. "Well, actually," I say, "I'd rather watch Nicholas in surgery."

I have never seen Nicholas truly doing his job. Yes, I have seen him with his patients, drawing them out of their fear and being more understanding with them than he has been with his own family. But I want to see what all the training is for; what his hands are so skilled at. Elliot frowns at me when I ask. "You may not like it very much," he says. "Lots of blood and battle scars."

But I stand my ground. "I'm much tougher than I look," I say.

And so this morning there will be no picture of Nicholas's patient tacked to his door. Instead I sit alone in the gallery above the operating suite and wait for Nicholas to enter the room. There are already seven other people: anesthesiologists, nurses, residents, someone sitting beside a complicated machine with coils and tubes. The patient, lying naked on the table, is painted a strange shade of orange.

Nicholas enters, still stretching the gloves on his hands, and all the heads in the room turn toward him. I stand up. There is an audio monitor in the gallery, so I can hear Nicholas's low voice, rustling behind his paper mask, greeting everyone. He checks beneath the sterile drapes and watches as a tube is set in the patient's throat. He says something to a nearby doctor, youngish-looking, his hair in a neat ponytail. The young doctor nods and begins to make an incision in the patient's leg.

All of the doctors wear weird glasses on their heads, which they flip down to cover their eyes when they bend over the patient. It makes me smile: I keep expecting this to be some kind of joke costume, with googly eyeballs popping out on springs. Nicholas stands to the side while two doctors work over the patient's leg. I cannot see very well what they are doing, but they take different instruments from a cloth-covered tray, things that look like nail scissors and eyebrow tweezers.

They pull a long purple spaghetti string from the leg, and when I realize it is a vein, I feel the bile rise in my throat. I have to sit down. The vein is placed in a jar filled with clear fluid, and the doctors working on the leg begin to sew with needles so small they seem invisible. One of them takes two pieces of metal from a machine and touches the leg, and I can swear I smell human flesh burning.

Then Nicholas moves to the center of the patient. He reaches for a knife—no, a scalpel—and traces a thin line down the orange area of the patient's chest. Almost immediately the skin is stained with dark blood. Then he does something I cannot believe: he pulls a saw out of nowhere—an actual saw, like a Black & Decker—and begins to slice through the breastbone. I think I can see chips of bone, although I can't believe Nicholas would let that happen. When I think I am surely going to faint, Nicholas hands the saw to another doctor and spreads the chest open, holding it in place with a metal device.

I don't know what I was expecting—maybe a red valentine heart. But what lies in the center of this cavity once the blood is mopped away looks like a yellow wall. Nicholas picks a pair of scissors off a tray, bends low toward the chest, and fiddles around with his hands. He takes two tubes that come from that complicated machine and attaches them to places I cannot quite see. Then he picks up a different pair of scissors and looks at the yellow wall. He begins to snip at it. He peels back the layer to reveal a writhing muscle, sort of pink and sort of gray, which I know is the heart. It twitches with every beat, and when it contracts it gets so small that it seems to be temporarily lost. Nicholas says, "Let's put him on bypass," to the man who is sitting at the machine, and in a quiet whir, red blood begins to run through the tubes. Below his mask, I think I see Nicholas smile.

He asks a nurse for cardioplegia, and she hands him a beaker filled with a clear solution. He pours it over the heart, and just like that, it stands still. *Dear Jesus,* I find myself thinking, *he's killed the man.* But Nicholas doesn't even stop for a moment. He picks up another pair of scissors and moves close to the patient again.

All of a sudden a spurt of blood covers Nicholas's cheek and the front of another doctor's gown. Nicholas's hands move faster than I can follow as he reaches into the open chest to stop the flow. I step back, breathing hard. I wonder how Nicholas can do this every single day.

The second doctor reaches into the jar I've forgotten about and takes out the vein from the leg. And then Nicholas, sweat breaking out on his brow, pulls a tiny needle repeatedly through the heart and through that vein, using tweezers to place the point and to retrieve it. The other surgeon steps back, and Nicholas taps the jellied heart with a metal instrument. Just like that, it starts to beat. It stops, and Nicholas asks for an internal defibrill-something. He touches it to the heart and shocks it into moving again. The second doctor takes the tubes from the top and bottom of the heart, and the blood stops coursing through the machine. Instead, the heart, still on display, begins to do what it was doing before—squeezing and expanding in a simple rhythm.

Nicholas lets the second surgeon do most of the work from that point—more sutures, including wire for the ribs and thick stitches through the orange skin that make me think of a Frankenstein monster. I press my hands against the sloped glass wall of the gallery. My face is so close that my breath clouds the window. Nicholas looks up and sees me. I smile hesitantly, wondering at the power he must feel to spend every morning giving life.

chapter 39

Nicholas

Nicholas remembers having heard once that the person who has started a relationship finds it easier to end it. Obviously, he thinks, that person did not know Paige.

He can't get rid of her. He has to give her credit—he never thought she'd take it this far. But it is distracting. Everywhere he turns, there she is. Arranging flowers for his patients, wheeling them out of surgical ICU, eating lunch across the cafeteria. It has reached the point where he actually misses her when she isn't around.

The drawings have got out of control. At first he ignored them, tacked crudely to his office door like kindergarten paintings on a refrigerator. But as people started to notice Paige's talent, he couldn't help but look at them. He brings the ones she does of his patients to their rooms, since it seems to brighten them up a little—some of his incoming patients have even heard of the portraits and ask for them at the pre-op exam. He pretends to throw out the ones she does of him, but in fact he has been saving them in the locked bottom drawer of the desk. When he has a minute, he pulls them out and looks at them. Because he knows Paige, he knows what to look for. And sure enough, in every single picture of him—even the ridiculous one of him singing in a bowling shirt—there is something else. Someone, actually. In the background of each drawing is a slight, barely noticeable portrait of Paige herself. Nicholas finds the same face over and over, and every time she is crying.

And now her pictures are all over the entrance hall of Mass General. The whole staff treats her like some kind of Picasso. Fans flock to his office door to see the latest ones, and he actually has to push through them to get into the room. The chief of staff—the goddamned chief of staff!—ran into Nicholas in the hall and complimented him on Paige's talent.

Nicholas does not know how she has managed to win so many people to her side in a matter of days. Now, *that's* Paige's real talent—diplomacy. Every time he turns around, someone is mentioning her name or, worse, she is standing there herself. It reminds him of the ad agencies' "block" strategy, where they run the same exact commercial at the same exact time on all three network stations, so that even if you flip channels you see their product. He can't get her out of his mind.

Nicholas likes to look at the portraits in his drawer just before he goes down to surgery—which, thank God, is the only place Paige hasn't been allowed into yet. The pictures clear his head, and he likes to have that kind of directed focus before doing an operation. He pulls out the latest drawing: his hands poised in midair as if they are going to cast a spell. Every line is deeply etched; his fingernails are blunt and larger than life. In the shadow of the thumb is Paige's face. The drawing reminds him of the photo his mother developed years before to save her marriage, the one of her own hands folded beneath his father's. Paige couldn't have known, and it strikes Nicholas as uncanny.

He leaves the portrait on the desk, on top of the scrawled sheets of assets he is supposed to be preparing for Oakie Peterborough. He has added nothing since the day he met the lawyer for lunch, a week ago. He keeps thinking that he must call to set up a consultation, but he forgets to mention it to his secretary and he is too busy to do it himself.

The operation this morning is a routine bypass, which Nicholas thinks he could do with his eyes closed. He walks briskly to the locker room, although he is not in a hurry; he changes into the soft laundered blue scrubs. He pulls on paper booties and a paper cap and winds a mask around his neck. Then he takes a deep breath and goes to scrub, thinking about the business of fixing hearts.

It's strange being the chief of cardiac surgery. When he enters the operating suite the patient is already prepped and the easy conversation between the residents and the nurses and the anesthesiologist comes to a dead halt. "Good morning, Dr. Prescott," someone says finally, and Nicholas can't even tell who it is because of the stupid masks. He wishes he knew what to do to put them all at ease, but he hasn't had enough experience at it. As a surgical fellow, he spent so much time clawing his way to the top, he never bothered to consider whom he was crawling over to get there. Patients are one thing: Nicholas believes that if someone is going to trust you with his life and shell out $31,000 for five hours' work, he or she deserves to be listened to and laughed with. He has even sat on the edges of beds and held his patients' hands while they prayed. But doctors are a different breed. They are so busy looking behind them for an encroaching Brutus that everyone becomes a potential threat. Especially a superior like Nicholas: with one written criticism, he has the power to end a career. Nicholas wishes he could look over the blue edge of a mask just once and see a pair of smiling eyes. He wishes Marie, the stout, serious OR nurse, would put a whoopee cushion under the patient, or set rubber vomit on the instrument tray, or play some other practical joke. He wonders what would happen if he walked in and said, "Have you heard the one about the rabbi, the priest, and the call girl?"

Nicholas speaks softly as the patient is intubated, and then he directs a resident, a man his own age, to harvest the leg vein. His hands move by themselves, making the incision and opening the ribs, dissecting out the aorta and the vena cava for the bypass machine, sewing up and cauterizing blood vessels that are accidentally cut.

When the heart has been stopped—an action that never loses its effect for Nicholas, who holds his breath as if his own body has been affected—Nicholas peers through magnifying spectacles and begins to cut away the diseased coronary arteries. He sews on the leg vein, turned backward, to bypass the obstructions. At one point, when a blood vessel begins spurting blood all over Nicholas and his first assistant, Nicholas curses. The anesthesiologist looks up, because he's never seen Dr. Prescott—the famous Dr. Prescott—lose his cool. But even as he does so, Nicholas's hands are flying quickly, clamping the vessel as the other doctor sews it up.

When it is all over and Nicholas steps back to let his assistant close, he does not feel as if five hours have passed. He never does. He is not a religious man, but he leans against the tiled wall and beneath his blue mask he whispers a prayer of thanks to God. In spite of the fact that he knows he is skilled, that his expertise comes from years of training and practice, Nicholas cannot help but believe a little bit of luck has been thrown in, that someone is looking out for him.

That's when he sees the angel. In the observation gallery is the figure of a woman, her hands pressed to the window, her cheek flush against the glass. She is wearing something loose that falls to her calves and that glows in the reflected fluorescent light of the operating suite. Nicholas cannot help himself; he takes a step forward and lifts his hand a fraction of an inch as if he might touch her. He cannot see her eyes, but somehow he knows this is only an apparition. The angel glides away and disappears into the dark background of the gallery. Nicholas knows that even if he has never seen her before, she has always been with him, watching over his surgeries. He wishes, harder than he has ever wished for anything in his life, that he could see her face.

≈≈≈

After such a spiritual morning, it is a letdown for Nicholas to find Paige in all his patients' rooms when he is doing afternoon rounds. Today she has pulled her hair away from her face in a braid that hangs down to her shoulder blades and moves like a thick switch when she leans over to refill a water pitcher or to plump pillows. She's not wearing makeup, she rarely does, and she looks about as old as a candy striper.

Nicholas flips over the metal cover of Mrs. McCrory's chart. The patient is a woman in her late fifties who had a valve replacement done three days ago and is almost ready to go home. He skims a finger across the vitals recorded by one of the interns. "I think we're getting ready to kick you out of here," he says, grinning down at her.

Mrs. McCrory beams and grabs Paige's hand, which is the nearest one. Paige, startled, gasps and almost overturns a vase of peonies. "Take it easy," Nicholas says dryly. "I don't have room in my agenda for an unscheduled heart attack."

At this unexpected attention, Paige turns. Mrs. McCrory eyes her critically. "He doesn't bite, dear," she says.

"I know," Paige murmurs. "He's my husband."

Mrs. McCrory claps her hands together, thrilled by this news. Nicholas mutters something unintelligible, amazed at how easily Paige can ruin his good mood. "Don't you have somewhere else to be?" he says.

"No," Paige says. "I'm supposed to go wherever you go. It's my job."

Nicholas tosses the chart down on Mrs. McCrory's bed. "That is *not* a volunteer's assignment. I've been here long enough to know the standard rounds, Paige. Ambulatory, patient transport, admitting. Volunteers are never assigned to doctors."

Paige shrugs, but it looks more like a shiver. "They made an exception."

For the first time in minutes, Nicholas remembers Mrs. McCrory. "Excuse us," he says, grabbing Paige's upper arm and dragging her out of the room.

"Oh, stay!" Mrs. McCrory exclaims after them. "You're better than Burns and Allen."

Reaching the hallway, Nicholas leans against the wall and releases

Paige. He wanted to yell and to complain, but suddenly he can't remember what he was going to say. He wonders if the whole hospital is laughing at him. "Thank God they don't let you in surgery," he says.

"They did. I watched you today." Paige touches his sleeve gently. "Dr. Saget arranged it for me, and I was in the observation room. Oh, Nicholas, it's incredible to be able to do that."

Nicholas does not know what makes him more angry: the fact that Saget let Paige watch him doing surgery without his consent, or the fact that his imagined angel was really just his wife. "It's my job," he snaps. "I do it every day." He looks at Paige, and that expression is back in her eyes—the one that probably made him fall in love with her. Like his patients, Paige is seeing him as someone who is flawless. But he has a sense that unlike them, she would have been just as impressed if she'd watched him mopping the hospital's halls.

The thought chafes around his neck. Nicholas pulls at his collar and thinks about going right back to his office and calling Oakie Peterborough and getting this over. "Well," Paige says softly, "I wish *I* were that good at fixing things."

Nicholas turns and walks down the hall to see another patient, a transplant recipient from last week. When he is half inside the room, he glances around, to find Paige at the door. "*I'll* change the damn water," he says. "Just get out of here."

Her hands are braced on either side of the doorway, and her hair is working its way out of her braid. Her volunteer uniform, two sizes too big, billows around her waist, falls to her shins. "I wanted to tell you," she says, "I think Max is getting sick."

Nicholas laughs, but it comes out as a snort. "Of course," he says, "you're an expert."

Paige lowers her voice and peeks into the hallway to make sure no one is around. "He's constipated," she says, "and he spit up twice today."

Nicholas smirks. "Did you give him creamed spinach?" Paige nods. "He's allergic."

"But there aren't any welts," Paige says, "and anyway it's more than that. He's been crabby, and, well, Nicholas, he just isn't himself."

Nicholas shakes his head at her and takes a step into the patient's room. As much as he doesn't want to admit it, when he sees Paige standing in the doorway, arms outstretched as if she is being crucified, she looks very much like an angel. "He's not himself," Nicholas repeats. "How the hell would you know?"

chapter 40

Paige

When Astrid hands Max over to Nicholas that night, something still is wrong. He has been crying on and off all day. "I wouldn't worry," Astrid says to me. "He's been a colicky baby." But it is not his crying that bothers me. It's the way the fight has gone out of his eyes.

I stand on the staircase while Nicholas takes Max. He hoists the diaper bag and some favorite toys over his free arm. He ignores me until he reaches the door, about to leave. "You might want to get a good lawyer," he says. "I'm meeting with mine tomorrow."

My knees give out under me, and I stumble against the banister. I feel as if I have been swiftly punched. It isn't his words that hurt so much; it is knowing that I have been too late. I can run in circles until I drop, but I cannot change the course of my life.

Astrid calls out to me as I pull myself up the stairs to my room, but I do not listen. I think about phoning my father, but he'll only lecture me on God's will, and that won't give me any comfort. What if I don't happen to like God's will? What if I want to keep the end from coming?

I do what I always do when I am in pain; I draw. I pick up my sketch pad and I draw image after image on the same page until it is nothing more than a dismal black knot. I flip the page and do this all over again, and I keep on doing this until little by little some of the rage leaves my body, seeping through my fingertips onto the page. When I no longer feel I am being eaten alive from the inside, I put down my charcoal and I decide to start over.

This time I draw in pastels. I rarely use them because I'm a lefty and they get all over the side of my hand and make me look strangely bruised. But right now I want color, and that is the only way I can think of getting it. I find that I am drawing Cuchulainn's mother, Dechtire, which seems natural after thinking of my father and the whims of the gods. Her long sapphire robes mist around her sandaled feet, and her hair flies behind her in a sleek arc. I draw her suspended in midair, somewhere between heaven and earth. One arm reaches down to a man silhouetted against the ground, one arm reaches up toward Lugh, the powerful god who carries the sun.

I make her fingers brush those of her husband below, and as I do it I get a physical jolt. Then I lengthen her other arm, seeing her torso twist and stretch on the page as she reaches into the sky. It takes all the effort in my fingers to make Dechtire's hand touch the sun god's, and when it does I begin to draw furiously, obliterating Dechtire's porcelain face and the solid body of her husband and the bronze arm of Lugh. I draw flames that cover all the characters, erupting in fiery sparks and bursting across the sky and the earth. I draw a blaze that feeds on itself, that shimmers and flares and sucks away all the air. Even as I cannot breathe anymore, I see that my picture has turned into a holocaust, an inferno. I throw the scorching pastels across the room, red and yellow and orange and sienna. I stare sadly at the ruined image of Dechtire, amazed that I have never before seen the obvious: when you play with fire, you are likely to get burned.

I fall asleep fitfully that night, and when I wake, sleet is rattling against the window. I sit up in bed and try to remember what has awakened me, and I get a sinking feeling in the pit of my stomach. I know what is coming. It is like that feeling I used to have about Jake, when we were so closely connected that I could sense when he stepped into his home at night, when he thought of my name, when he needed to see me.

I jump out of bed and pull on the pants and shirt I wore yesterday. I don't even think to find socks, tying up my sneakers over bare feet. I gather my hair into a tangled ponytail and secure it with the rubber band from a bag of gummy fish. Then I pull my jacket off the doorknob and run downstairs.

When I open the door, Nicholas stands before me, assaulted by the ice and the rain. Just beyond him, in the yellow interior light of his car, I can see Max, oddly silent, his mouth in a raw red circle of pain. Nicholas is already closing the door behind me and pulling me into the storm. "He's sick," Nicholas says, "Let's go."

chapter 41
Nicholas

*H*e watches the hands of people he does not know poke and prod at his son's body. John Dorset, the resident pediatrician on call last night, stands over Max now. Every time his fingers brush Max's abdomen, the baby shrieks in pain and curls into a ball. It reminds Nicholas of the sea anemones he played with on Caribbean beaches as a child, the ones that folded around his finger at the slightest touch.

Max hadn't gone to sleep easily last night, although that wasn't cause in itself for alarm. It was the way he kept waking up every half hour, screaming as if he were being tortured, fat clear tears rolling down his face. Nothing helped. But then Nicholas had gone to change the diaper, and he'd almost passed out at the sight of so much jellied blood.

Paige trembles beside him. She grabbed his hand the minute Max was brought into the emergency room, and she hasn't let go since.

Nicholas can feel the pressure of her nails cutting into his skin, and he is grateful. He needs the pain to remind him that this isn't a nightmare after all.

Max's regular pediatrician, Jack Rourke, gives Nicholas a warm smile and steps into the examination room. Nicholas watches the heads of the two doctors pressed together in consultation over the kicking feet of his son. He clenches his fists, powerless. He wants to be in there. He should be in there.

Finally, Jack steps out into the pediatric waiting room. It is now morning, and the staff nurses are starting to arrive, pulling out a box of Big Bird Band-Aids and sunny smiley-face stickers for the day's patients. Nicholas knew Jack when they were at Harvard Med together, but he hasn't really kept in touch, and suddenly he is furious at himself. He should have been having lunch with him at least once a week; he should have talked to him about Max's health before anything like this ever happened; he should have caught it on his own.

He should have caught it. That is what bothers Nicholas more than anything else—how can he call himself a physician and not notice something as obvious as an abdominal mass? How can he have missed the symptoms?

"Nicholas," Jack says, watching his colleague pick up Max and sit him upright. "I have a good idea of what it might be."

Paige leans forward and catches at the sleeve of Jack's white coat. Her touch is light and insubstantial, like a sprite's. "Is Max all right?" she asks, and then she swallows back her tears. "Is he going to be all right?"

Jack ignores her questions, which infuriates Nicholas. Paige is the baby's mother, for Christ's sake, and she's worried as hell, and that isn't the way to treat her. He is about to open up his mouth, when John Dorset carries Max past them. Max, seeing Paige, reaches out his arms and starts to cry.

A sound comes out of Paige's throat, a cross between a keen and a wail, but she doesn't take the baby. "We're going to do a sonogram," Jack says to Nicholas, Nicholas only. "And if I can verify the mass—I think it's sausage-shaped, right at the small bowel—we'll do a barium enema. That might reduce the intussusception, but it depends on the severity of the lesion."

Paige tears her gaze away from the doorway where Max and the doctor have disappeared. She grabs Jack Rourke's lapels. "Tell *me*," she shouts. "Tell me in normal words."

Nicholas puts his arm around Paige's shoulders and lets her bury her face against his chest. He whispers to her and tells her what she wants to know. "It's his small intestine, they think," Nicholas says. "It kind of telescopes into itself. If they don't take care of it, it ruptures."

"And Max dies," Paige whispers.

"Only if they can't fix it," Nicholas says, "but they can. They always can."

Paige looks up to him, trusting him. "Always?" she repeats.

Nicholas knows better than to give false hope, but he puts on his strongest smile. "Always," he says.

He sits across from her in the pediatric waiting room, watching healthy doddering toddlers fight each other for toys and crawl all over a big blue plastic ladder and slide. Paige goes up to ask about Max, but none of the nurses have been given any information; two don't even know his name. When Jack Rourke comes in hours later, Nicholas jumps to his feet and has to restrain himself from throwing his colleague against the wall. "Where is my son?" he says, biting off each word.

Jack looks from Nicholas to Paige and back to Nicholas. "We're prepping him," he says. "Emergency surgery."

≈≈≈

Nicholas has never sat in Mass General's surgical waiting room. It is dingy and gray, with red cubes of seats that are stained with coffee and tears. Nicholas would rather be anywhere else.

Paige is chewing the Styrofoam edge of a coffee cup. Nicholas has not seen her take a sip yet, and she's been holding it for a half hour. She stares straight ahead at the doors that lead to the operating suites, as if she expects an answer, a magical ticker-tape billboard.

Nicholas had wanted to be in the operating room, but it was against medical ethics. He was too close to the situation, and honestly he didn't know how he would react. He would renounce his salary and his title, just to get back the detachment about surgery that he had only yesterday. What had Paige said after the bypass? He was *incredible*. Good at *fixing*. And yet he couldn't do a damn thing to help Max.

When Nicholas was standing over a bypass patient whom he hardly knew, it was very easy to put life and death into black-and-white terms. When a patient died on the table, he was upset but he did not take it personally. He couldn't. Doctors learn early that death is only a part of life. But parents shouldn't have to.

What are the chances of a six-month-old making it through intestinal surgery? Nicholas racks his brain, but he can't come up with the statistics. He does not even know the doctor operating in there. He's never heard of the damn guy. It strikes Nicholas that he and every other surgeon live a lie: The surgeon is not God, he is not omnipotent. He cannot create life at all; he can only keep it going. And even that is touch and go.

Nicholas stares at Paige. *She has done what I can never do,* Nicholas thinks. *She has given birth.*

Paige has put down the Styrofoam cup and suddenly stands. "I'm going to get some more coffee," she announces. "Do you need anything?"

Nicholas stares at her. "You haven't touched the coffee you just bought."

Paige crosses her arms and rakes her fingernails into her skin, leaving raw red lines that she doesn't notice at all. "It's cold," she says, "way too cold."

A collection of nurses walks by. They are dressed in simple white uniforms but wear felt ears in their hair, and their faces are made up with whiskers and fur. They stop to talk to the devil. He is some kind of physician, a red cape whirling over his blue scrubs. He has a forked tail and a shiny goatee and a hot chili pepper clipped to his stethoscope. Paige looks at Nicholas, and for a second Nicholas's mind goes blank. Then he remembers that it is Halloween. "Some of the people dress up," he explains. "It cheers up the kids in pediatrics." *Like Max,* he thinks, but he does not say it.

Paige tries to smile, but only half her mouth turns up. "Well," she says. "Coffee." But she doesn't move. Then, like the demolition of a building, she begins to crumble from the top down. Her head sinks and then her shoulders droop and her face sags into her hands. By the time her knees give way beneath her, Nicholas is standing, ready to catch her before she falls. He settles her into one of the stiff canvas seats. "This is all my fault," she says.

"This isn't your fault," Nicholas says. "This could have happened to any kid."

Paige doesn't seem to have heard him. "It was the best way to get even," she whispers, "but He should have hurt me instead."

"Who?" Nicholas says, irritated. Maybe there *is* someone responsible. Maybe there *is* someone he can blame. "Who are you talking about?"

Paige looks at him as if he is crazy. "God," she says.

When he had changed Max's diaper and seen the blood, he didn't even stop to think. He bundled Max in a blanket and ran out the door without a diaper bag, without his wallet. But he hadn't driven straight to the hospital; he'd gone to his parents'. Instinctively, he had come for Paige. When it came right down to it, it didn't matter why Paige had left him, it didn't matter why she had returned. It didn't matter that for eight years she'd kept a secret from him he felt he had every right to know. What mattered was that she was Max's mother. That was their truth, and that was their starting point to reconnect. At the very least, they had that connection. They would *always* have that connection.

If Max was all right.

Nicholas looks at Paige, crying softly into her hands, and knows that there are many things that depend on the success of this operation. "Hey," he says. "Hey, Paige. Honey. Let me get you that coffee."

He walks down the hall, passing goblins and hoboes and Raggedy Anns, and he whistles to keep out the roaring sound of the silence.

≈≈≈

They should have come out to report on the progress. It has been so long that the sun has gone down. Nicholas doesn't notice until he goes outside to stretch his legs. On the street he hears the catcalls of trick-or-treaters and steps on crushed jewel-colored candy. This hospital is like an artificial world. Walk inside and lose all track of time, all sense of reality.

Paige appears at the door. She waves her hands frantically, as if she is drowning. "Come inside," she mouths against the glass.

She grabs at Nicholas's arm when he gets through the doorway. "Dr. Cahill said it went okay," she says, searching his face for answers. "That's good, isn't it? He wouldn't hold anything back from me?"

Nicholas narrows his eyes, wondering where the hell Cahill could have gone so fast. Then he sees him writing notes at the nurses' station around the corner. He runs down the hall and spins the surgeon around by the shoulder. Nicholas does not say a word.

"I think Max is going to be fine," Cahill says. "We tried to manually manipulate the intestines, but we wound up having to do an actual resection of the bowel. The next twenty-four hours will be critical, as expected for such a young child. But I'd say the prognosis is excellent."

Nicholas nods. "He's in recovery?"

"For a while. I'll check him in ICU, and if all is well we'll move him up to pediatrics." Cahill shrugs, as if this case is just like any other. "You might want to get some sleep, Dr. Prescott. The baby is sedated; he's going to sleep for a while. You, on the other hand, look like hell."

Nicholas runs a hand through his hair and rubs his palm over his unshaven jaw. He wonders who bothered to call off his surgery this morning; he forgot it entirely. He is so tired that time is passing in strange chunks. Cahill disappears, and suddenly Paige is standing beside him. "Can we go?" she asks. "I want to see him."

That is what shocks Nicholas into clarity. "You don't want to go," he says. He has seen babies in the recovery room, stitches snaked over half their swollen bodies, their eyelids blue and transparent.

Somehow they always look like victims. "Wait awhile," Nicholas urges. "We'll go up as soon as he's in pediatrics."

Paige pulls away from Nicholas's grasp and stands squarely in front of him, eyes flashing. "You listen to me," she says, her voice hard and low. "I've waited an entire day to find out if my son was going to live or die. I don't care if he's still bleeding all over the place. You get me to him, Nicholas. He needs to know that I'm here."

Nicholas opens his mouth to say that Max, unconscious, will not know if she is in the recovery room or in Peoria. But he stops himself. He's never been unconscious, so what does he know? "Come with me," he says. "They usually don't let you in, but I think I can pull strings."

As they make their way to the recovery room, a string of children in pajamas parades through the hall, wearing papier-mâché masks of foxes and geisha girls and Batman. They are led by a nurse whom Nicholas has seen once before; he thinks she baby-sat for Max what seems like years ago. They are singing "Camptown Races," and when they see Paige and Nicholas they break out of their line and puddle in a crowd around them. "Trick or treat," they chant, "trick or treat. Give me something good to eat."

Paige looks to Nicholas, who shakes his head. She stuffs her hands into the pockets of her jeans and turns them inside out to reveal an unshelled pecan, three nickels, and a ball of lint. She picks up each object as if it is coated in gold and presses the treasures one by one into the palms of the waiting children. They frown at her, disappointed.

"Let's go," Nicholas says, pushing her through the tangle of costumed kids. He goes the back way, coming from the service elevator, and walks straight to the nurses' station. It is empty, but Nicholas steps behind the desk as if it is his right and flips through a chart. He turns to tell Paige where Max is, but she has already moved away.

He finds her standing in the recovery room, partially obscured by the thin white curtains. She is absolutely rigid as she stares into the oval hospital crib that holds Max.

Nothing could have prepared Nicholas for this. Underneath the sterile plastic dome, Max is lying perfectly still on his back, arms pointed over his head. An IV needle stabs into him. A thick white bandage covers his stomach and chest, stopping at his penis, which is blanketed with gauze but not restricted by a diaper. A nasogastric tube feeds into a mask that covers his mouth and nose. His chest rises and falls almost imperceptibly. His hair looks obscenely black against the alabaster of his skin.

If Nicholas didn't know better, he would think that Max was dead.

He has forgotten that Paige is there too, but then he hears a choked sound beside him. Tears are streaming down her face when she steps forward to touch the side rail of the crib. Reflected light bathes her face in silver, and with her ringed, haggard eyes she looks very much like a phantom when she turns to Nicholas. "You liar," she whispers. "This is not my son." And she runs out of the room and down the hall.

chapter 42
Paige

They've killed him. He's so still and pale and tiny that I know it beyond a doubt. Once again there has been a baby and it did not live and it is all because of me.

I run out of the room where they've laid Max out, down the hall and the staircase and through the nearest door I can find. I am suffocating, and when the automatic door slides open I gulp in the night air of Boston. I can't get enough. I fly down Cambridge Street, passing teenagers dressed in bright neon rags and lovers entwined—Rhett and Scarlett, Cyrano and Roxanne, Romeo and Juliet. An old woman with wrinkled skin the shade of a prune stops me with a withered hand on my arm. She holds out an apple. "Mirror, mirror on the wall," she says. "Take it, dearie."

The whole world has changed while I have been inside. Or maybe I'm not where I think I am. Maybe this is purgatory.

The night sweeps from the sky to wrap my feet. When I laugh

because my lungs are bursting, the dark streets echo my shrieks. Surely, I think, I am going to hell.

Somewhere in the back of my mind I am aware of the place I've come to. It is in the business district of Boston, filled with pin-striped executives and sweaty hot dog carts during the day; but at night, Government Center is nothing more than a flat gray wasteland, a stage for the dance-crazed wind. I am the only person here. In the background I hear the flutter of the wings of pigeons, beating like a heart.

I have come here with a purpose in mind. I am thinking of Lazarus and of Christ Himself. It isn't right for Max to die for my sins. Nobody ever asked me. Tonight, in return for a miracle, I am willing to sell my own soul.

"Where are You?" I whisper, choking on my words. I close my eyes against the gusts that blow across the plaza. "Why can't I see You?"

I spin wildly. "I grew up with You," I cry. "I believed in You. I even trusted You. But You are not a forgiving God." As if in answer, the wind whistles over the glowing windows of an office building. "When I needed Your strength, You were never there. When I prayed for Your help, You turned away. All I ever wanted was to understand You," I shout. "All I ever wanted were the answers."

I fall to my knees and feel the unforgiving cement, wet and cold. I lift my face to the scrutiny of the sky. "What kind of God are You?" I say, sinking lower to the pavement. "You took away my mother. You made me give up my first baby. You've stolen my second." I press my cheek against the rough concrete surface and know the moment it scrapes and bleeds. "I never knew any of them," I whisper. "Just how much can one person take?"

I can feel Him before I raise my head. He is standing inches behind me. When I see Him, haloed by my pure white faith, it suddenly makes sense. He calls my name, and I fall right into the arms of the man who, I know, has always been my savior.

chapter 43
Nicholas

"*P*aige," Nicholas says, and she turns around slowly. Her shadow, stretching ten skinny feet in front of her, approaches him first. Then she comes forward and falls right against him. For a moment Nicholas does not know what to do. His arms, acting on their own, fold around her. He buries his face in her hair. It is fragrant and warm and jumps at the ends, as if there are live sparks. He is amazed that after all this time, she fits so well.

The only way he can get her to walk is by bracing her against his side, one arm locked around her shoulders. He is really just dragging her. Paige's eyes are open, and she seems to be looking at Nicholas but not seeing him. Her lips move, and when Nicholas leans close enough he can hear the hot whisper of her breath. He thinks she is saying a prayer.

The streets of Boston are dotted with costumed clusters of people—Elvira and the Lone Ranger and PLO terrorists and Marie

Antoinette. A tall man dressed as a scarecrow hooks his arm into Paige's free one and starts to skip, pulling Paige and Nicholas off to the left. "Follow the yellow brick road," he sings at the top of his lungs, until Nicholas shrugs him off. Sputtering lamps cast shadows that creep down the alleys on the backs of dead October leaves. Nicholas can smell winter.

When he reaches the parking garage at Mass General, he picks Paige up in his arms and carries her to his car. He sets her down on her feet while he slides Max's car seat over to one side, pushing a little terry-cloth clown rattle and a sticky pacifier. Then he helps Paige into the back seat, laying her on her side and covering her with his jacket. As he pulls the collar up under her neck, she grabs his hand and holds it with the strength of a vise. She is staring over his shoulder, and that's when she begins to scream.

Nicholas turns around and comes face-to-face with Death. Standing beside the door is an impossibly tall person in the flowing black robes of the Grim Reaper. His eyes are hidden in the folds of his hood, and the point of his tinfoil scythe just grazes Nicholas's shoulder. "Get out of here," Nicholas says, and then he shouts the words. He pushes at the cloak, which seems as insubstantial as ink. Paige stops screaming and sits up, struggling to get out. Nicholas closes her door and pulls himself into the car. He drives past the gaping face into the tangled streets of Boston, toward the sanctuary of his home.

"Paige," Nicholas says. She doesn't answer. He peeks into the rearview mirror, and her eyes stare wide. "Paige," he says again, louder. "Max is going to be fine. He's going to be *fine.*"

He watches her eyes as he says this, and he thinks he can see a glimmer of recognition, but that might just be the murky light in the car. He wonders what pharmacies are open in Cambridge, what he could prescribe that might snap Paige out of this. Normally he'd suggest Valium, but Paige is calm now. Too calm, really. He wants to see her scratching and crying out again. He wants to see a sign of life.

When he pulls into the driveway, Paige sits up. Nicholas helps her out of the car and starts to walk up the steps of the porch, expecting her to follow. But as he puts the key into the lock of the front door, he realizes that Paige is not standing beside him. He sees her walking across the front lawn to the blue hydrangeas, the place where she slept when she was camping outside the house. She lies down on the grass, melting the early frost with the heat of her skin.

"No," Nicholas says, moving toward her. "Come inside, Paige." He reaches out his hand. "Come with me."

At first she doesn't budge, but then Nicholas notices her fingers twitching where they lay at her sides. He realizes this is a case where he will have to go more than halfway. He kneels on the cold ground and pulls Paige into a sitting position, then up to her feet. As he leads her into the house, he looks back beneath the blue hydrangeas. The spot where Paige's body was lying is as clearly defined as a chalked murder outline. Her silhouette is obscenely green against the frost, as if she has left in her wake an artificial spring.

Nicholas leads her into the house, grinding wet mud into the light carpeting. As he peels off Paige's coat and towels her hair dry with a clean dishcloth, he looks over the smudged footprints and decides he likes them; they make him feel as if he knows where he's been. He tosses Paige's coat onto the floor, and then her damp shirt and her jeans. He watches each piece of clothing fall like a bright jewel against the sickly palette of the rug.

Nicholas is so fascinated by the splashes of color blooming across the living room that he does not notice Paige at first. She shivers in front of him, wearing only her underwear. When Nicholas turns to her, he is amazed by the contrasts of color: the tanned line of Paige's neck against the milky skin of her chest; the severe imprint of a birthmark against the whiteness of her belly. If Paige notices his scrutiny, she says nothing. Her eyes stay lowered, and her hands rub up and down her crossed arms. "Say something to me," Nicholas urges. "Say anything."

If she is really in shock, the last thing she should be doing is to stand half naked in the middle of a cold room. Nicholas thinks about bundling her in the old wedding-ring quilt they keep somewhere in the damn house, but he has no idea which closet it's in. He puts his arms around her, and the chill of her skin shudders down his own spine.

Nicholas leads her upstairs to the bathroom. He closes the door and runs the hottest water into the tub, letting the steam cloud the mirrors. When the water fills the tub halfway, he unhooks Paige's bra and slips off her underpants. He helps her into the tub and watches her teeth chatter and the mist rise around her. He stares beneath the ripple of the water at the stretch marks on her hips, now painted an airy silver, as if giving birth is really nothing more than a distant memory.

Automatically, Nicholas picks up the dinosaur-print washcloth and begins to soap Paige as he does Max. He starts with her feet, leaning half into the tub to clean between the toes and to massage the arches. He moves up her legs, sliding the washcloth behind her knees and over her thighs. He rubs her arms and her stomach and the shoulder-blade hollows of her back. He uses the buoyancy of the water to lift her, slipping the washcloth over her bottom and through her legs. He washes her breasts and sees the nipples tighten. He takes the Tupperware cup he keeps on the bathtub ledge and pours clean water over Paige's hair, tilting her head back as the dark-red strands grow sleek and black.

Nicholas wrings out the washcloth and hangs it up to dry. The water is still running in the tub, the level rising. As Paige starts to move, water splashes onto his shirt and in his lap. She reaches forward and makes a low, throaty sound, stretching her hand toward Max's rubber duck. Her fingers close over the yellow head, the orange bill. "Oh, God," she says, turning to Nicholas. "Oh, my God."

It happens very quickly—Paige lurches out of the tub and Nicholas rises up to meet her. She wraps her arms around his neck and clutches at the fabric of his shirt until it pulls over his head. All the time he is kissing her forehead, her cheeks, her neck. His fingertips circle her breasts as her hands struggle to unbuckle and unzip. When they are both naked, Nicholas leans over Paige on the white tile and gently brushes her lips. To his surprise, she locks her fingers into his hair, kissing him greedily and refusing to free him.

It has been so long since he felt his wife next to him, holding him, surrounding him. He recognizes every smell and every texture of her body; he knows the points where their skin will meet and become slick. In the past he has thought mostly of his own body—the heavy pressure building between his legs and the moment he knows to let go and the catch of his heart in his throat when he comes—but now he only wants to make Paige happy. The thought runs through his mind over and over; it is the least he can do. It has been so long.

Nicholas can gauge by Paige's breathing what she feels. He pauses and whispers against Paige's neck. "Will this hurt?"

She looks up at him, and Nicholas tries to read her expression, but all he can see is the absence of fear, of regret. "Yes," she says. "More than you know."

They come together with the fury of a storm, clawing and scratching and sobbing. They are pressed so close they can barely move, just rocking back and forth. Nicholas feels Paige's tears against his shoulder. He holds her as she trembles and closes softly around him; he cries out to her when he loses control. He makes love with a violence bred of passion, as if the act that creates life might also be used to ward away death.

≈≈≈

They fall into a deep sleep on the bed, on top of the comforter. Nicholas curls his body around Paige as though that might protect her from tomorrow. Even in his sleep he reaches for her, filling his hand with the curve of her breast, crossing her abdomen with his arm. In the middle of the night he wakes up, to find Paige staring at him. He wishes there were words to say the things he wants to say.

Instead he pulls her against him and begins to touch her again, much more slowly. In the back of his mind he thinks he should not be doing this, but he cannot stop himself. If he can take her away for a little while, if she can take *him* away, what's the harm? In his profession, he never stops fighting against impossible odds, but he learned a long time ago that not all outcomes can be controlled. He tells himself this is the reason he's trying so hard now not to become involved, not to let himself love. He can fight till he drops, yet somewhere in the back of his mind he understands the margins of his power.

Nicholas closes his eyes as Paige runs her tongue along the line of his throat and spreads her small hands across his chest. For a quick moment he lets himself believe that she belongs to him every bit as much as he belongs to her. Paige kisses the corner of his mouth. It is not about possession and limits. It is about giving everything until there's nothing left to give, and then searching and scraping until you find a little bit more.

Nicholas rolls over so that he and Paige are facing each other on their sides. They stare at each other for a long time, running their hands over familiar skin and whispering things that do not matter. They come together two more times that night, and Nicholas tallies their lovemaking silently. The first time is for forgiving. The second time is for forgetting. And the third time is for beginning all over again.

chapter 44
Paige

I wake up in my own bed, in Nicholas's arms, and I have absolutely no idea how I got there. *Maybe,* I think to myself, *this has all been a bad dream.* For a moment I am almost convinced that if I walk down the hall I will find Max curled in his crib, but then I remember the hospital and last night, and I cover my head with the pillow, hoping to block out the light of day.

Nicholas stirs beside me. The white sheets contrast with his black hair, making him look immortal. As his eyes open, I have a fleeting memory of the night before, Nicholas's hands moving over my body like a running line of fire. I startle and pull the sheet up to cover myself. Nicholas rolls onto his back and closes his eyes.

"This probably shouldn't have happened," I whisper.

"Probably not," Nicholas says tensely. He rubs his hand across his jaw. "I called the hospital at five," he says. "Max was still sleeping soundly, and his vitals were good. The prognosis is excellent. He'll be fine."

He'll be fine. I want to trust Nicholas more than anything, but I will not believe him until I see Max and he lifts his arms and calls for me. "Can we see him today?" I ask.

Nicholas nods. "At ten o'clock," he says, and then he rolls out of bed to step into paisley boxer shorts. "Do you want to use this bathroom?" he says quietly, and without waiting for an answer, he pads down the hall to the smaller one.

I stare at myself in the mirror. I am shocked by the shadows above my cheeks and the red cast of my eyes. I look around for my toothbrush, but of course it isn't there; Nicholas would have thrown it out months ago. I borrow his, but I can barely brush my teeth because my hands are shaking. The toothbrush clatters into the bowl of the sink and leaves a violent blue mark of Crest. I wonder how I ever became so incompetent.

Then I remember that stupid list of accomplishments I made the day I ran away from home. What had I said? Back then I could change a diaper, I could measure formula, I could sing my son to sleep. And now what can I do? I rummage in the drawers beneath the sink and find my old makeup bag, tucked into a corner behind Nicholas's unused electric razor. I pull out a blue eyeliner and throw the cap into the toilet. *1.,* I write on the mirror, *I can canter and jump and gallop a horse.* I tap the pencil to my chin. *2. I can tell myself I am not my mother.* I run out of space on the mirror, so I continue on the white Corian counters. *I can draw away my pain. I can seduce my own husband. I can—* I stop here and think that this is not the list I should be making. I pick up a green eye pencil and start writing where I left off, angrily listing the things I cannot do: *I cannot forget. I cannot make the same mistake twice. I cannot live this way. I cannot take the blame for everything. I cannot give up.*

With my words covering the stark bathroom in flowered curlicues of green and blue, I become inspired. I take the pale-lime shampoo from the bathtub and smear it over the tiled walls; I draw pink lipstick hearts and orange Caladryl scrolls on the tank of the toilet. Nicholas comes in sometime after I am finishing a line of blue toothpaste waves and diving aloe vera dolphins. I flinch, expecting him to start yelling, but he just smiles. "I guess you're done with the sham-poo," he says.

Nicholas doesn't take the time to eat breakfast, which is fine with me, even though it is only eight o'clock. We may not be able to see Max right away, but I will feel better knowing I am closer to my child. We get into the car, and I notice Max's car seat pushed to the side; I wonder how it got that way. I wait for Nicholas to back out of the driveway, but he sits perfectly still, with his foot on the brake and his hand on the clutch. He looks down at the steering wheel as if it is something fascinating he has never seen before. "Paige," he says, "I'm sorry about last night."

I shiver involuntarily. What did I expect him to say?

"I didn't mean to—to do that," Nicholas continues. "It's just that you were in such bad shape, and I thought—hell, I don't know what I was thinking." He looks up at me, resolved. "It won't happen again," he says.

"No," I say quietly. "I suppose it won't."

I look up and down the thin stretch of street that I once imagined I'd be living on for most of my life. I don't see actual objects, like trees and cars and fox terriers. Instead I see eddies of color, an im-pressionist painting. Green and lemon and mauve and peach: the edges of the world as I know it run muddy together. "I was wrong about you," Nicholas is saying. "Whatever happens, Max belongs with you."

Whatever happens. I turn my face up to him. "And what about you?" I say.

Nicholas looks at me. "I don't know," he says. "I honestly don't know."

I nod, as though this is an answer I can accept, and turn away to look out my window as Nicholas backs out of the driveway. It is going to be a cold, crisp fall day, but memories of the night before are everywhere: eggshells scattered through the streets, shaving cream on residential windows, toilet paper festooned through the trees. I wonder how long it will take to come clean.

At the hospital, Nicholas asks about Max and is told that he's been moved to pediatrics. "That's a good start," he murmurs, although he is not really speaking to me. He walks to a yellow elevator bank, and I follow close behind. The doors open, smelling of antiseptic and fresh linen, and we step inside.

An image comes to me quickly: I am in that Cambridge graveyard with Max, who is about three. He runs between the headstones and peeks from behind the monuments. It is my day off from classes; finally, I'm getting my bachelor's degree. Simmons College, not Harvard—and that doesn't matter. I am sitting while Max runs his fingers over the old grave markers, fascinated by the chips and gulleys of aging stone. "Max," I call, and he comes over, sliding to his knees and getting grass stains on his overalls. I motion to the pad I've been drawing on, and we lay it across the flat marker of a revolutionary soldier. "You pick," I say. I offer him an array of crayons. He takes the melon and the forest green and the violet; I choose the orange-yellow and the mulberry. He puts the green crayon in his hand and starts to color in the image of a pony I've done for him, a Shetland he'll ride that summer at my mother's. I cover his chubby hand with mine and guide his fingers gently over lines I have drawn for him. I feel my own blood running beneath his flushed skin.

The doors of the elevator hiss open, but Nicholas stands frozen. I wait for him to take charge, but nothing happens. I turn my head to look at him—he's never like this. Nicholas, coolheaded and unflappable, is scared to face what's coming. Two nurses pass. They peer into the elevator and whisper to each other. I can imagine what they are saying about me and about Nicholas, and it doesn't affect me at all. Another mark for my accomplishment list: I can stand on my own in a world that is falling apart. I can stand so well, I realize, that I can support someone else. "Nicholas?" I whisper, and I can tell by the flicker of his eyes that he has forgotten I am there but he's relieved to see me just the same. "It's going to be fine," I tell him, and I smile for what seems like the first time in months.

The jaws of the elevator start to close again, but I brace them with my strength. "It's only going to get easier," I say with confidence, and I reach across the distance to squeeze Nicholas's hand. He squeezes mine right back. We step off the elevator together and take those first steps down the hall. At Max's door, we stop and see him pink and quiet and breathing. Nicholas and I stand calmly at the threshold. We have all the time in the world to wait for our son to come around.